UNTIL YOU SAY STAY

THE MIDNIGHT MEN

BOOK TWO

NATE WILDER

RIVER AND ASH PUBLISHING

CHAPTER 1

Lark

"Ten bucks says Jack Midnight hooks up with at least one bridesmaid before the night's over," Jayson says, sliding into the seat next to me, a beer in hand and a grin on his face. The chef whites that he usually sports at the Black Lantern have been replaced by a suit that actually fits him pretty well.

I follow his gaze to where Jack Midnight stands with three of his brothers—Theo, Alex, and Dominic, the four of them looking like Dark River royalty in their wedding attire.

Jack's laughing at something Alex said, perfectly at ease in a charcoal suit that fits like it was custom-made. Which it probably was. No tie, top button undone, dark hair looking effortlessly tousled. Like he just rolled out of bed looking like a goddamn movie star, which is deeply unfair to those of us who spent two hours on our hair.

"You're terrible," I tell Jayson, but I'm smiling.

"Just making observations based on historical data," he says, taking a sip of his beer and nodding toward the Midnight brothers. "The guy has a very consistent track record. So what do you say, ten bucks?"

"Hmmm." I set my champagne flute down and lean back in my chair. "That's a sucker's bet and you know it. Jack Midnight at a wedding with an open bar? It's a sure thing. But I guarantee it won't be me. Been there, almost fell for that, and learned my lesson before I could make a complete fool of myself."

Jayson's eyebrows shoot up. "Well, well, well. Lark Reyes, you've been holding out on me. There's a story here I haven't heard."

"Not much to tell, honestly. We flirted at Susan's memorial last year," I say, remembering that night with perfect clarity. "And then I watched him leave with a leggy blonde approximately thirty seconds after I went to the bathroom. Which was a good reminder of why you never fall for a fuckboy's act, no matter how good the act is."

"Smart woman," Jayson says with a nod. "Saves you a lot of trouble in the long run."

"Exactly," I say with a shrug, twirling the stem of my glass between my fingers.

Across the lawn, my best friend Maren is standing near the dessert table with her new husband Calvin, the second oldest Midnight brother. Her dress is this flowing ivory lace that seems to glow in the evening light, making her look like something out of a fairytale. Calvin can't stop looking at her, like he's physically incapable of glancing away for more than three seconds.

"Look at them," I say, nodding toward the couple. "They're in their own little world."

"The honeymoon phase in full effect," Jayson says. "Though with those two, I think it might be permanent."

"Good. If anyone deserves a perfect love story, it's Maren." I watch as Calvin whispers something in her ear that makes her laugh. My heart gives a little squeeze of happiness for her. And maybe something else too. Not jealousy, *never* that with Maren. But as a hopeless romantic with a shitty ex-husband under my belt, maybe just the wish that someday someone would look at me like that. Like I'm their whole world.

The Midnight family property stretches around us, the grand old Victorian house behind us and the Sound glimmering beyond the bluff's edge. Maren and Calvin spent the past year renovating the place, and it shows. The house that was practically falling apart now looks like something from a magazine.

Another burst of laughter cuts through the chatter and I glance over. Becca Chapman, who teaches the yoga class Maren keeps trying to drag me to, has somehow made her way to Jack's side. She's touching his arm and laughing way too hard at whatever he just said.

I get it though. The guy is objectively gorgeous. Even back in high school he was hot, though he was barely ever there. Always off at some racing thing in Europe or wherever. But when he was around? He had this magnetism that made all the guys want to be him or fight him, and all the girls want to date him. Including me, if I'm being honest.

Now, at twenty-six, after one divorce and a whole lot of therapy, I'm definitely smart enough to keep my distance.

Becca laughs again, high and flirty, and Jack leans in with obvious interest. Some things never change in the world of Jack Midnight.

"Someone's having a good time," Jayson comments, following my gaze.

"Apparently."

"Hey, speaking of the youngest Midnight," Jayson says, leaning forward conspiratorially, "did you see that video of him last month? The one with the cocaine and the model?"

I grin. Four years of working together at The Black Lantern bar means that Jayson and I have perfected the art of talking shit while looking professional.

"Oh yeah," I say. "Hard to miss." The video had been everywhere for like two weeks. Short clip, only about thirty seconds, but it was enough. Jack at some glitzy party in Monaco or wherever rich people go to be terrible. Cocaine visible on a glass table, some wild out-of-control scene. Classic tabloid fodder, except this time with Dark River's very own Formula One racing star. Our tiny fishing town's claim to fame beyond the seafood and rainy weather.

"Maren showed me when it first went viral," I continue, watching Jack across the lawn. "Calvin was pretty stressed about it. I think he was worried about Jack's contract situation and the sponsors pulling out or something."

But I don't think anyone was really surprised. Jack had always been the wild one, the partier, the one who pushed every limit. He was the baby of the family who could get away with murder because everyone loved him too much to stay mad, though he'd never been caught with hard drugs, and even I was a little surprised by that. You couldn't see him actually doing anything in the video, but just being there, standing that close to it while it was all happening? Not a good look.

"Can't blame Calvin for worrying," Jayson says. "Sponsors don't typically love it when their drivers get caught partying with illegal substances on camera."

I nod in agreement. But you couldn't tell any of that stress from looking at Jack now. He looks completely relaxed, laughing like nothing in the world could touch him.

"Enough about Jack Midnight," Jayson says. "How's the music going? Any progress with that label?"

Ugh. Not the subject change I was hoping for.

My clutch suddenly feels heavy in my lap. The email from Maya at Tidal Records that I've read approximately forty times since it arrived earlier this week is burning a hole in my phone. She'd reached out after my last video hit 300K views, which was huge for me.

"Oh, you know," I say, forcing my voice to stay light and casual. "I just need to somehow become a social media superstar and a flawless live performer in the next few months. No big deal. I'm also thinking about learning Latin and solving cold fusion in my spare time. Why not take on all the impossible tasks at once?"

"Sounds like you have it all handled," Jayson says. "Very casual, very achievable."

"Oh yeah, I'm the picture of confidence. Just call me Olivia Rodrigo Junior," I say, rolling my eyes. "I'll have it all figured out in no time."

Maya and I had a phone call a few days before the detailed email, and Maya had been enthusiastic about my sound. She'd used words like "fresh" and "authentic" and "marketable," which had made my hands shake with excitement. But then came the requirements list that felt like a bucket of cold water. They need me to quadruple my social media following at the *bare minimum*.

"We need a gimmick for your singing videos," Jayson says thoughtfully. "Something to make them go crazy viral. Everyone at the Lantern could help. Eleanor would probably love to make a cameo, and you know the Romance Raiders would be all over it."

I smile despite the anxiety sitting in my stomach like a rock. "That's not a terrible idea. Get the seventy-something book club ladies in the background of my videos. Very on-brand." I take another sip of champagne. "Then I just have to figure out how to fix my stage fright so I don't throw up during an actual live performance. Small details."

"Easy," Jayson says with a grin. "We'll get you drunk first."

"That's your solution to everything."

"Because it works."

"Very professional," I say dryly.

"Look, I'm just saying, a little liquid courage and you'll be fine."

I laugh, but even now, almost two years after my divorce was finalized, my ex husband Brandon's voice still echoes in my head at the worst moments. *You're embarrassing yourself. The music thing is just a hobby, Lark. It's never going to happen. Stop being unrealistic.* The bastard's words still have power, all these years and thousands of dollars in therapy later.

Laila bounds over, Maren's golden retriever wagging so hard her entire back end moves with her tail. She's wearing a little flower collar that matches the wedding colors.

"Look who it is! Who's the best wedding dog in the entire world?" I lean down to scratch behind her ears and she presses against my legs so enthusiastically she nearly knocks my chair backward.

"Whoa!" Jayson reaches out to steady my chair, laughing. "Incoming!"

"Laila, baby! Careful with the guests!" Maren calls, hurrying over with a laugh. She kneels down in her wedding dress, not caring at all about grass stains or wrinkles, and ruffles Laila's ears. "You're being so good, aren't you? The absolute best girl."

"She's been making the rounds," I tell Maren, grinning. "I'm pretty sure she conned at least three different people into sharing their cocktail shrimp earlier."

"That's my smart girl," Maren says proudly, and Laila's tail thumps harder against the grass. Maren stands up, smoothing her dress. "Okay, Lark, I need to ask you something. A favor."

"Anything," I say immediately. "Name it."

Tonight's not about my career anxieties or my stage fright or the impossible requirements standing between me and my dreams. Tonight is about Maren and Calvin and celebrating the fact that my best friend found someone who loves her the way she deserves.

"So Brett had a bit too much to drink," Maren says, biting her lip in that way that tells me this is going to be good.

"Which one was Brett again?" I ask, mentally running

through the handful of people from Calvin's past as a literary star living in Seattle. It's not a long list, Calvin's more of a quality-over-quantity friend guy.

"Calvin's friend from college," she says, glancing around like she's checking if anyone's listening. Her voice drops lower. "The tall one with the glasses? He was the one who kept hitting on you during the rehearsal dinner."

"Oh yeah, it's coming back to me." I laugh, remembering the guy who found approximately seventeen reasons to come talk to me while I was setting up the bar. Sweet enough.

I'd seen him earlier doing shots with the Romance Raiders, which should have been my first clue something would go wrong. Eleanor and her book club might be in their seventies, but those ladies can drink most people under the table. I've witnessed it personally on multiple occasions.

"Let me guess," I say, leaning against the bar. "Eleanor and her crew got him absolutely obliterated?"

"Specifically Eleanor," Maren confirms, her eyes bright with suppressed laughter. "She challenged him to match her shot for shot. Apparently she's been drinking vodka since 1962 and has the constitution of a Russian sailor. Brett is currently upstairs in the bathroom. Calvin's checking on him, but he definitely cannot MC the rest of the reception."

"That's what he gets for challenging a woman who considers vodka a food group," I say, and Jayson laughs into his beer.

"Right?" Maren giggles. "So will you do it? Take over MC duties for the rest of the night?"

"Of course," I say without hesitation. "You know I love having everyone's attention. It's my natural habitat."

"Thank goodness for that." Maren laughs. "Okay, I should keep making the rounds. The first dance is in ten minutes and I still need to say hi to half these people. You're a lifesaver, Lark. Seriously."

"Go be a bride," I tell her, waving her away. "I've got this handled."

She heads back toward Calvin, Laila bounding alongside her like a fluffy shadow. Calvin's face transforms the second he sees her, going from polite wedding smile to absolutely besotted in half a second. He immediately pulls her close, whispering something in her ear that makes her laugh and swat at his chest.

I glance over at Jack again without meaning to. Becca has lost his attention. He's crouched down now, talking to little Chloe, Theo's six-year-old daughter. She's showing him something on her tablet, pointing at the screen excitedly, and he's giving her his complete focus.

Huh. That's unexpectedly sweet.

"I'll catch you later, Jayson," I say, giving him a little wave. "Duty calls."

"Go make us proud," he replies with a salute. "Remember, Eleanor and the Romance Raiders are counting on you."

I laugh and weave through the crowd toward the makeshift stage area. The night has fully settled in now, string lights glowing overhead and casting everything in a warm, golden haze. The DJ's professional setup is impressive, all polished equipment and carefully placed uplighting that makes the whole reception area look like something out of a magazine.

I'm adjusting my dress and mentally preparing myself for announcing duties when I spot him. Jack Midnight, having left Chloe with Theo, is heading straight for the stage.

Oh, hell no.

The last thing Maren and Calvin need is the wild Midnight brother hijacking their wedding reception with whatever chaos he has planned. I pick up my pace, my heels clicking against the temporary flooring as I angle to cut him off. We reach the base of the steps at the same time, nearly colliding.

"What the hell are you doing here?" I ask, blocking his path with my body.

He looks equally confused, his brows drawing together before his expression shifts to something more playful. "What the hell are *you* doing here?" he asks with no bite, eyes dancing flirtatiously.

Not a chance, buddy.

"Maren asked me to take over for Brett, who is at present puking his guts out after challenging Eleanor to a drinking contest," I explain, planting my hands on my hips in what I hope is my most authoritative stance. "She specifically asked me to handle the announcing."

"Huh." He tilts his head, seeming to consider this. "Well, I don't know anything about that. All I know is Calvin pulled me aside about ten minutes ago and asked if I could MC since Brett was out of commission." He shrugs, all easy confidence. "Figured it was my brotherly duty to step up."

He takes a step closer, and I catch a hint of his cologne. Something expensive and annoyingly distracting.

"So don't you worry about it, Lark." The way he says my name, like we're old friends or something, makes my spine stiffen. "I can take care of this. You should go enjoy the party." He even has the audacity to wink.

"Uh uh. No way." I shake my head firmly. "Maren asked me first, and bride trumps groom. That's wedding law."

"Since when does bride trump groom?" he asks, leaning his forearm against the stage railing like he's settling in for a debate. He looks more amused than annoyed, which is somehow infinitely more irritating. "Last I checked, it was *their* wedding. Equal partnership and all that."

"Since always," I insist, narrowing my eyes and poking him in the chest with my index finger. His chest is surprisingly solid under the suit. Not that I'm noticing. "And besides, the last thing this wedding needs is you giving speeches. I've heard the stories about your toast at Theo's wedding. Something about a stripper and a fire extinguisher? This is a *classy* event, Midnight."

"Lark, you wound me." He places both hands over his heart like I've shot him. "I'm the picture of a gentleman. A paragon of virtue and good behavior."

He looks anything but. Tall and dark and dangerous, with those green eyes that shift between playful and intense in seconds. The definition of trouble wrapped in an expensive suit. The kind of guy who promises motorcycle rides and adventure and heartbreak.

"You're impossible," I say. The situation is too ridiculous. "Okay, here's how this is going to go. We're doing it together, and absolutely no funny business. Got it? No inappropriate jokes, no embarrassing stories about Calvin's college years, or so help me I will knee you right in the balls on that stage in front of everyone."

He laughs, and dimples appear in his cheeks. *Unfair.*

"Fair enough," he says. "I don't want to end up on your bad side. As I recall, you're pretty dangerous in the gym. Those right hooks of yours are legendary at Midnight Fitness."

I snort. Last year when I'd twisted my ankle during boxing class, Jack had been in town training at his brother's gym. He'd helped me out to my car, then insisted on following me to urgent care when I couldn't put weight on it. He'd been so unexpectedly gentle, making stupid jokes the whole way to keep me from freaking out about whether I'd broken it. Not what I'd expected from Dark River's wild child.

A small flutter stirs in my stomach and I mentally squash it like a bug. Nope. Not happening. The man is a walking collection of red flags. A complete fuckboy with a pretty face. That flutter needs to die immediately before it gets any stupid ideas.

I flip my hair back, hoping I look completely unimpressed. "Damn straight. I can drop a man twice my size, and don't forget it." I let out a little sigh. "*Alright,* let's do this, Speed Racer. But remember, I'm watching you."

He grins, that smile that's probably gotten him out of

speeding tickets and into countless beds. "Wouldn't have it any other way." He gestures toward the stage with a slight bow, like some ridiculous parody of chivalry. "After you, m'lady."

I roll my eyes. "You're lucky I need both hands for this dress on stairs or I'd flip you off."

"I'd expect nothing less from you, Reyes," he says, following close behind me up the steps.

We step onto the small stage together. The crowd is still chatting, kids running between tables, the Romance Raiders loudly toasting something that sounds suspiciously like "To Eleanor's liver!"

I tap the mic twice with Jack standing beside me.

"Ladies and gentlemen, if I could have your attention please," I say into the mic, using my best bartender-wrangling-the-rowdy-Saturday-crowd voice. The one that can cut through even the most chaotic nights at the Lantern.

Conversations gradually quiet. Faces turn toward us. Maren and Calvin are near the dessert table, and I watch them both do identical double-takes. They exchange a quick glance and Maren covers her mouth, clearly trying not to laugh. Obviously husband and wife forgot to coordinate their MC replacement strategy.

"We know you're all having an amazing time," Jack says, leaning in to speak into the mic I'm holding. "But we need you to pause the party for just one minute."

"Because it's time for something even better," I add, adjusting my grip on the mic and maintaining what I hope is professional distance. "The moment we've all been waiting for."

"The cake?" someone yells from the back. Eddie from the marina.

"Soon, Eddie!" I call back, laughing. "I know you've been stalking that wedding cake like a predator since you arrived, but you have to wait your turn!"

The crowd laughs. I see Maren pointing at Eddie and

shaking her head fondly. Eddie just grins and gives an unapologetic shrug.

Jack leans in again. "But first, it's time for the first dance of our beautiful bride and groom."

"Or as I like to call them," I can't help adding with a huge grin at Maren, "my favorite couple with my favorite couple name: *Caren*."

Maren's eyes go comically wide and she mouths "NO" at me while simultaneously trying not to laugh. We've had this ongoing joke since they moved in together, and she pretends to hate it but secretly loves it. Calvin's shoulders are shaking with laughter beside her, and he pulls her closer, whispering something in her ear.

Jack gives me a look that clearly says *Really? And you warned ME not to embarrass them?*

He smiles with an *okay-it's-on* look and leans into the mic. "*Caren*?" He draws the word out slowly. "Are we doing couple names now? Did I miss a memo? Was there a meeting?"

"Calvin and Maren. Caren with a C," I explain to the crowd, who are all laughing now. "It's perfect and Maren secretly loves it despite what she tells literally everyone."

"I do NOT!" Maren shouts across the lawn, but she's laughing so hard she's clutching Calvin for support.

"Look at that face," Jack says into the mic, his voice taking on a conspiratorial tone. "That's a woman who *loves* her couple name."

Calvin raises his hand like he's in a classroom. "For the record, I love it!" he shouts, earning himself a playful shove from Maren.

"See?" I say triumphantly. "Calvin's on board. The groom has spoken. Democracy in action."

"We should make this official," Jack suggests, warming to his role. "All in favor of officially adopting 'Caren' as their couple name, raise your hands and say aye!"

The entire crowd erupts, hands shooting up everywhere. Even Calvin's brothers are enthusiastically voting, clearly living for the chaos. Laila starts barking excitedly at all the noise and commotion.

"Traitors!" Maren yells, laughing and trying to shush Laila while giving everyone death glares. "Every single one of you is fired from being my friend!"

"Hey, no interfering with the democratic process, Mrs. Midnight!" I call back. "Now, all opposed?"

Maren raises both hands and one foot, jumping up and down, which just makes everyone laugh harder. She's always been such a good sport. It's one of the million reasons I love her.

"The ayes have it!" Jack declares with the authority of someone announcing race results. "Caren is officially recognized! Let the record show!"

"I'm getting new friends!" Maren shouts, her face flushed with laughter. "All new friends! You're *all* fired!"

"You love us!" I call back, blowing her an exaggerated kiss.

"Highly debatable right now!" she shouts back, but she blows a kiss back, her smile so bright it could light up the entire property.

"Okay, okay," I say, trying to get us back on track while everyone's still chuckling. "Before the bride fires me as maid of honor, let's get these two on the dance floor."

"Caren forever," Jack adds into the mic, which gets another wave of laughter.

We step back from the mic as Calvin leads a still-giggling Maren to the center of the dance floor. The DJ smoothly fades in the opening notes of their song, and the crowd naturally forms a circle around them. The moment shifts from playful chaos to something tender as Calvin takes Maren in his arms, looking at her like she hung every star in the sky.

Maren catches my eye over Calvin's shoulder and mouths "thank you" with so much happiness radiating from her face it makes my throat tight. This is what she deserves. This perfect night, this man who adores her, this entire community showing up to celebrate their love.

I blow her a kiss and she pretends to catch it before melting completely into Calvin's embrace.

"They look good together," Jack says quietly beside me.

"They really do," I agree softly, watching my best friend glow. "They always have."

Jack and I continue our MC duties throughout the night, announcing toasts, keeping the energy up, making sure everything runs smoothly. Theo gives a speech about Calvin that has everyone laughing and crying in equal measure. Alex tells a story about their childhood that involves a tree fort and a very angry raccoon. Dominic's toast is short and sweet, ending with "Welcome to the family, Maren. Sorry about the rest of us."

Jack slides up beside me later by the dessert table where I'm trying to decide between a third slice of cake or maintaining some semblance of dignity.

"Nice work, partner," he says. "We absolutely killed it up there."

"Despite my initial reservations about co-hosting with Dark River's resident troublemaker," I say, finally committing to one of the mini cheesecakes because life is short, "we really did do a good job."

"Resident troublemaker?" He raises an eyebrow, reaching past me for a chocolate-covered strawberry. "I think you have me confused with someone else. Trouble finds *me*. I'm just an innocent victim of circumstance, going about my day when disaster randomly strikes."

"Oh really?" I pop a bite of cheesecake in my mouth. "So that time in high school when you 'borrowed' Principal Walker's car for a test drive and ended up in the lake was just trouble finding you?"

"That car had faulty brakes," he says completely seriously,

biting into the strawberry. "It was a safety hazard. I was doing a public service, really. Just one of many cosmic injustices I've had to overcome. My life is quite tragic when you think about it."

"You poor baby," I say with exaggerated sympathy, patting his arm. "Such hardship. How do you even cope?"

"It's been difficult," he agrees solemnly. "But I persevere."

"Lark!" Maren appears beside us, practically glowing with happiness. Calvin's right behind her, his arm wrapped around her. "You two were amazing! Everyone keeps coming up to me saying how funny you were together! Although Calvin won't stop calling us Caren."

"Hey, what can I say?" Calvin grins, pulling her closer. "I love our couple name. Caren forever. It's got a nice ring to it. Very modern."

"It's ridiculous," Maren says, but she's smiling.

"It's perfect," I correct. "Like I said. I have excellent instincts about these things."

"Debatable," Maren teases. "But I'll allow it for tonight. Now—" She turns to me with a look I recognize. Mischief mixed with determination. "—it's time for you and me to have a proper girl's dance. I've been waiting all night."

"Okay, but first I need to make a very important DJ request," I say, already backing away with a grin. "Don't move."

"I'll be here," Maren says, leaning back into Calvin's embrace. "Take your time."

"Calvin, you better watch out," I say, walking backward and shoving the rest of the mini cheesecake in my mouth, probably not gracefully. "I might steal your wife with my superior dancing skills."

He laughs, his whole face lighting up. "I'd be worried if I hadn't seen your moves at karaoke night last month. I know what I'm dealing with."

"Rude!" I shout back, but I'm laughing.

I whisper my song request to the DJ, complete with dramatic

hand gestures to convey the importance of this moment. He grins and gives me a thumbs up. When I get back to Maren, I hold out my hand like a gentleman caller from a regency romance.

The opening notes of Shania Twain's "Man! I Feel Like A Woman" blast through the speakers.

Maren's eyes light up. "Our song!"

We take over the dance floor immediately, both of us singing along at the top of our lungs like we've done countless times during girls' nights in my apartment. Arms in the air, spinning around, not caring who's watching or judging our moves.

When the song ends we're both breathless and grinning. The DJ immediately flows into another upbeat song and more people flood the dance floor. The party is in full swing now, that perfect sweet spot where everyone's loose and happy and the night feels like it could go on forever.

I grab a water bottle from the edge of the dance floor, pressing the cool plastic against my flushed cheek. Across the crowd, I catch sight of Jack talking to Alex, Theo, and Dominic, all of them laughing at something he said. He glances over and our eyes meet. Heat creeps up my neck before I turn back toward the dance floor where Maren is spinning with Calvin.

I shake my head slightly, smiling at the sight. My best friend is married to the love of her life, surrounded by people who adore them both. And I have my own things to focus on—my music, the label interest, finally figuring out how to get on a stage without my brain short-circuiting.

Everything else is just a distraction.

CHAPTER 2

Jack

The reception is in full swing by the time I finally escape from photo duty. The DJ's playing something upbeat that has half the wedding party on the makeshift dance floor, and the sun is starting to dip lower in the sky.

I grab a beer from the bar and find Calvin and Theo standing near the edge of the dance floor, both of them with drinks in hand, watching the chaos unfold.

"Married," I say, clapping Calvin on the shoulder. "How's it feel?"

"Surreal," Calvin says, grinning. "Good surreal. Like I can't believe I get to be with her forever."

"You're *so* married," I tell him, shaking my head. "It's almost embarrassing to witness."

"Aware of that, thanks." He takes a drink, eyes tracking Maren on the dance floor like she's the only person here before turning back to me. "How's the cabin? You settling in okay?"

Theo glances at me. "You're staying in the cabin?"

"Yep. It's perfect," I say, taking a sip of my beer. "Has everything I need. Bed, shower, coffee maker. The essentials."

"You know the offer still stands, right?" Calvin says. "The main house. I think it's weird for you not to stay inside when you're visiting. We set up your old room as a guest room, got a real bed in there now instead of that ancient thing in the cabin. I mean, it's your childhood house too."

"I'm good where I am," I tell him. The thought of staying in the main house with the newlyweds makes me want to stab myself with a spoon. "Close enough to steal your food when I get desperate, far enough to maintain plausible deniability about hearing any newlywed activities."

Calvin kicks at my shin, but he's laughing. "Hey, jackass, that's my wife you're talking about."

"I have nothing but respect for Maren," I say, dodging his kick and holding my hands up in surrender. "If anything, she's way too good for you. I'm just saying, thin walls, newly married couple, I can do the math."

"You're such a child," Calvin says, but there's no heat in it. "Just because you can't maintain a relationship longer than an Formula One pit stop doesn't mean the rest of us are animals."

"Hey now, that's unfair," I protest, grinning. "Some pit stops are very thorough."

He snorts, shaking his head. "Whatever helps you sleep at night. We'll be in Greece for our honeymoon in a few weeks, so you'll have the place completely to yourself."

"Fantastic. I'll throw the wildest parties. Trash the place. Really make you regret leaving me unsupervised."

"I'm sure you will," Calvin says dryly.

"Uncle Jack!" A small voice yells, and I turn just in time to see Chloe barreling toward me at full speed, still in her flower girl dress.

"What am I, chopped liver?" Calvin calls out as she runs right past him without so much as a glance. "Invisible? A ghost?"

"Hi Uncle Calvin!" she shouts over her shoulder, not slowing down even slightly.

I catch Chloe as she launches herself at me, swinging her up in the air, which makes her giggle.

"How are you always the favorite?" Calvin asks, shaking his head. "I'm the one who actually lives here year-round."

"Natural charm," I tell him, setting Chloe down but she keeps her arms wrapped around my legs.

Theo laughs. "That's what you get, Cal, for being the boring writer uncle. Hard to trump race car driver. Though if it makes you feel any better, Alex put broccoli in her mac and cheese last week at the restaurant, so he's officially dropped to last place."

Calvin grins. "Ah well, at least I'm not the broccoli guy."

"Will you dance with me?" Chloe's bouncing now, pulling on my hand. "Please!"

"Okay, Monster," I say. "Let's show these people how it's done."

She squeals and drags me toward the dance floor. The DJ's playing something fast, and Chloe immediately starts spinning in circles with her arms out, nearly taking out an elderly woman in the process. I grab her hand and spin her properly, and she giggles so hard she almost falls over.

"Do it again! Again!" she shouts, so I spin her again, then dip her dramatically. She shrieks with laughter.

We dance through two more songs before she demands I pick her up and spin her around, which I do until we're both dizzy. When I finally set her down, she makes a monster face at me, complete with clawed hands and a growl that's more cute than scary.

"Perfect monster," I tell her, laughing. "Ten out of ten. Absolutely terrifying."

We head back toward where my brothers are standing. Calvin's gone now, back by Maren's side looking like he can't see anything but her, but Dominic and Theo are there with beers, mid-conversation about something that involves a lot of hand gestures.

"You're actually a pretty good dancer," Theo observes when we approach. "Would have never guessed that."

"Full of surprises," I say, grabbing my beer from where I left it on the table.

"Laila!" Chloe shouts suddenly, spotting the golden retriever across the lawn. She takes off running without so much as a goodbye, pigtails flying behind her.

"Full of *shit*, more like," Dominic says, grinning at me.

I flip him off. "Sarcasm doesn't suit you, Dom."

Theo laughs, nudging Dominic, then looking back at me. "How are you doing being back home anyway? This is like the longest you've been in Dark River in who knows how long."

"It's good," I say. And it is, in some ways. I like being around my brothers, being here for this. But it's weird, too. Dark River has never really been home for me. Not the way it is for them. It's just where my family happens to live. Where I visit between races, between seasons, between lives. I left young, just barely fifteen, heading to Europe to chase my Formula One dreams. Been gone more than I've been here ever since.

Even now I feel that gap between my brothers and me. That distance that never quite closes no matter how many years pass. Mom and Dad were incredible people, truly good humans, but they already had their hands full with four boys when they adopted me at age six. I was the add-on. The one who never quite fit into the existing family dynamics. They loved me, I know that. But I also know I disrupted the balance.

"I give you one week before you start going stir crazy and causing mayhem," Dominic says, taking a sip of his beer.

"Already am going fucking stir crazy," I admit, grinning. "Not much to do around here. But I don't have much choice."

"We're so touched you're gracing us with your presence," Dominic says, his voice dripping with fake sincerity.

"You're welcome," I say, matching his tone. "I know my company is a gift."

Theo laughs, shaking his head. "You two are exhausting."

Chloe and Laila dart past us, nearly knocking Theo over in their chaos. He stumbles back, beer sloshing. "Careful! I—oh and she's gone."

"She's getting big," I say, watching her barrel through the crowd with Laila at her heels. "Last time I was home she was still talking about unicorns. Is she still into unicorns?"

"Oh, unicorns are so last year," Theo says, taking a sip of his beer. "Now it's all race cars and speed machines. Which brings me to something I've been meaning to mention." He narrows his eyes at me. "She's been asking when you're going to teach her to drive a go-kart."

"Really?" I perk up at this. "She's actually interested?"

"God help me, she really is," Theo says, running his hand through his hair. "I shouldn't have let her watch all your races with me these last few years. Now she thinks driving fast is a career option."

"It *is* a career option," I say immediately, nudging him with my elbow. "And a damn good one. Better money than running a restaurant." I'm grinning now, enjoying the horrified look on his face. "Just think about it. Little Chloe Midnight, racing sensation."

Dominic chuckles, shaking his head.

"Don't even joke about this," Theo starts, but he's already smiling because he knows there's no stopping me once I get going. "She already asked for racing posters for her room."

"That's because she'll be my little racing protégé," I say, really getting into it now. "I could have her in a kart by next summer. By the time she's ten, she'll be faster than half the guys on the junior circuit." I'm laying it on thick, watching Theo's expression shift between horror and amusement.

"You're enjoying this *way* too much," Theo says.

"Think about it," I continue, my enthusiasm real now. "First woman Formula One world champion. Chloe Midnight. Has a nice ring to it, right? The sport needs more women anyway, and she's already got natural athleticism. Did you see her running earlier?"

"You mean before she tripped?" Theo asks, pointing to where Chloe is wiping mud off her dress and giggling while Laila licks her face.

"That was just enthusiasm." I wave it off dismissively. "All the greats fell on their face a few times. But she's got the competitive spirit."

"And the complete lack of fear," Theo adds dryly. "Just like her uncle."

Dominic grins. "To be fair, the lack of fear has served him well. The lack of impulse control, however..."

"Impulse control is overrated," I say, waving Dominic off. "That's what keeps things interesting. Chloe's already got that spark. I can see it."

Theo groans but he's grinning now. "Oh no, you're serious about this."

"Completely serious," I confirm. I grab his shoulder, give it a squeeze. "I started at six. Worked out pretty well for me."

"That's exactly what I'm afraid of," Theo says, shaking his head but clearly fighting laughter. "I've spent the last six years keeping her in one piece, and now you want to strap her into a miniature race car." He gestures vaguely at me. "You're going to turn my sweet, innocent daughter into a speed demon who gives me heart attacks every weekend."

"Sounds like good preparation for her teenage years," I say with a wink. "That's the plan. Embrace it now, save yourself the stress later."

"I hate you," he says, but he's definitely smiling.

"I'm the fun uncle." I strike a pose that makes Dominic snort.

"You're the terrifying uncle who's going to teach my kid to drive at a hundred miles an hour," Theo says.

"*Two* hundred," I correct, miming holding a steering wheel and making engine noises. "If she's doing it right."

"I'm going to pretend this conversation never happened," Theo mutters, running a hand over his face. "I'm putting her in ballet. Or chess club. Something safe."

"Good luck with that," I say, taking a drink of my beer. Dominic chuckles, shaking his head at both of us.

My phone buzzes in my pocket. I pull it out, hoping it's something interesting, and immediately wish I hadn't. Luca's name lights up the screen. My old teammate from Formula One, Ferraris' current golden boy.

Luca: *Ciao bello, come stai? Heard through the paddock grapevine that your contract talks still aren't progressing. This is entirely my fucking fault. Please let me help fix this?*

Perfect. Just what I need at my brother's wedding. A reminder that my career is hanging by a thread.

Me: *Thanks but I'm really not worried about it. And I'm home with family right now. Can we do this conversation later?*

Luca: *Sofia still wants to clear everything up publicly. We both feel absolutely terrible about the whole situation.*

Me: *Tell her it's completely fine. Not your fault or hers.*

Luca: *Except it kind of is though? Let us at least make a statement. Clear your name.*

Me: *No way. That just makes everything worse for her. I'm handling it my way.*

Luca: *You're not handling it, fratello. You're ignoring it and hoping it disappears.*

Me: *Strategic patience. There's a difference.*

I turn off notifications entirely and shove the phone back in my pocket. It's been around a month since that video from Monaco went viral. Me supposedly doing lines of cocaine at some party when the reality was I was pulling Luca's little sister

Sofia out of a bad situation before some creeps twice her age could take advantage of an eighteen-year-old who'd had too much to drink. But I can't correct the public story without throwing both of them under the bus, exposing a teenager to tabloid scrutiny and online harassment.

That's the problem with reputations. Eventually they're all people see.

"Everything okay?" Theo asks, glancing over.

"Just Luca checking in," I say, waving it off like it's nothing. "The usual paddock gossip."

"Contract stuff?" Dominic asks, cutting straight to business like he always does. I appreciate that about him. Theo's the one who wants to talk about emotions and check in on my mental state, which is the last thing I want to deal with right now.

"Not really," I say. "The video situation still has everyone spooked. Sponsors are nervous, team's being cautious, everyone's waiting to see if another shoe drops. But it'll blow over eventually. These things always do."

Normally I don't even give a shit about my reputation. Never have. Can't control what people think, so why waste energy trying? But this particular scandal is fucking with my contract negotiations. Not great timing when I'm trying to claw my way back to full-time racing after eighteen months of being stuck as a reserve driver.

"Is Robert still giving you grief?" Theo asks. "Or has he finally relaxed about it?"

"Robert *doesn't* relax. That's not in his programming," I say. Robert Callahan, billionaire, whiskey empire owner, racing enthusiast, and the closest thing I've had to a father figure since Dad died. He's been my primary sponsor since I was twelve years old, believed in me when no one else did, invested millions in my career. His disappointment cuts deeper than any tabloid headline ever could. "He's... concerned. About the optics."

"Optics," Dominic repeats, shaking his head. "What a load of shit."

"Yeah, well. That's the business," I say.

"How's the training going?" Dominic asks. "I saw some practice session clips online last month. You looked fast."

"Going well," I tell him, and it's true. Training is the one thing I can control right now. My fingers automatically tap against my thigh, restless energy with nowhere to go. "Team's had me doing extra simulator time in Maranello. Trying to stay sharp, prove I'm ready whenever they need me."

"When, not if," Theo says firmly. "*When* they need you, Jack. Not if."

I appreciate his confidence even if it feels misplaced most days.

Eighteen months ago I was a Formula One driver for Ferrari. Fast, aggressive, the kind of driver that made other teams nervous and sponsors throw money at me. Then I crashed during a qualifying session in Barcelona. Broken ribs, broken hand, enough internal damage to sideline me for months.

The team replaced me "temporarily" with Davis Barrett while I healed. It didn't help that I got into a bar fight that went viral during recovery.

By the time I was cleared, Davis had settled in. He doesn't crash and is consistent enough, though he never fucking wins and barely scores points. The team had finally had enough of his mediocrity and I was in serious negotiations to get my seat back when that video hit the tabloids. Now everything's come to a screeching halt. Apparently generating messy tabloid fodder matters more than winning races.

"Yeah, well," I say, taking another drink. "We'll see what happens."

I look out at the dance floor, watching people celebrate. That's when I see Lark standing near the edge of the crowd, talking with some guy I don't recognize. Lark's dress is deep blue, fitted in all the right places, showing off curves and legs that make my brain short-circuit for half a second. Her long dark hair is pulled back on one side but falling loose over her shoulder, and she's laughing at something, head thrown back, completely unselfconscious.

She's fucking gorgeous.

"Tsk tsk," Theo says, and I can hear the warning in his voice. "You're playing with fire, Jack. Don't you dare."

"Dare what?" I ask innocently, dragging my attention back to my brothers. "I have no idea what you're talking about."

"He's talking about you eye-fucking Lark from across the lawn," Dominic says bluntly. "And the flirting you were doing while MC'ing earlier."

"I wasn't flirting," I protest. "I was being friendly. There's a difference."

"Sure there is," Theo says, clearly not buying it. "Just watch it, Jack," he continues, tone shifting to something more serious. "Maren would murder you if you hurt her best friend. She's protective of Lark, especially after everything with her ex-husband. I really don't want to have to help bury your body somewhere."

Dominic nods solemnly. "Agreed. It would make family dinners extremely awkward."

"Touched by your concern for my continued existence," I say dryly.

"Hey, anytime," Dominic says with a crooked grin. "That's what older brothers are for."

I glance back over at Lark one more time. She catches me looking and raises her champagne glass in a small cheers. I raise my beer back at her.

"You're fucked," Dominic observes mildly.

"Probably," I admit.

We stand there a while longer, watching people dance. My

phone buzzes, but I ignore it. Probably Robert wanting an update, or my manager Thomas with orders about keeping my head down.

The sooner this video scandal blows over, the sooner I can get back where I actually belong. Behind the wheel of a race car, pushing over 200 miles per hour, competing with the best drivers in the world.

That's the only thing that matters. The only thing that's ever mattered to me.

Everything else is just killing time.

CHAPTER 3

Lark

Tuesday nights at the Black Lantern are usually pretty chill, the kind of easy shift where I can breathe between customers. Tonight's no exception. Just a handful of regulars scattered around the place, nursing beers and chatting quietly. I'm behind the bar rolling silverware into napkins, the repetitive motion almost meditative, while my mind circles back to that email from Maya at Tidal Records for approximately the hundredth time today.

I pull my phone out during a lull, like maybe the words will have magically changed if I stare at them long enough. They haven't. Still the same requirements staring back at me in black and white. Quadruple my social media following. That's what she wants before they'll seriously consider signing me.

I need the numbers, the engagement metrics, the whole packaged influencer experience. Plus there's my own issue with performing live, which I used to love as a kid but somewhere along the way lost completely. Every time I get on stage now I turn into a complete human disaster, freezing up and forgetting lyrics and hearing Brandon's voice in my head telling me I'm not good enough.

It's not even the rejection that stings the most. It's the fact that my actual music isn't what's holding me back from this dream. It's my complete inability to market myself like some shiny product on a shelf. Plus the few times I've attempted performing my own songs in front of people, I've frozen up so badly I couldn't get through a single verse.

Brandon made absolutely sure of that particular damage. Two years post-divorce and he's still living rent-free in my head, criticizing every note before I can even sing it.

The loud crack of pool balls startles me out of my pity party spiral. Jack Midnight's been here for the past hour or so with Mike from our high school and two other guys I vaguely recognize from around town. Probably locals who want to be able to tell people they hung out with a famous Formula One driver, get some reflected glory.

Jack lines up another shot, sinking it without any apparent effort. Based on Mike's increasingly dramatic groaning and head-in-hands despair, Jack's absolutely destroying them.

I'm in the middle of rolling another set of silverware, the fork and knife nestled perfectly in the white napkin, when Jack approaches the bar. His beer glass is empty, and his dark hair is slightly tousled like he's been running his hands through it.

"Let me guess," I say, securing the napkin around the utensils. "Winning?"

"By an embarrassing amount." He slides onto a barstool directly in front of me, setting his empty glass on the polished bar top with a soft clink. His fingers immediately start drumming against the wood in that restless way he always has about him.

"Poor Mike." I place the rolled silverware in the caddy with the others and reach for another set of napkins from the stack. "He's going to complain about this for weeks. Possibly months."

Jack's mouth curves into a half-smile that probably works absolute wonders on racing groupies and models in Monaco. "He's already started making excuses. Something about the lighting in here throwing off his depth perception." He nods with his head toward the pool table where Mike is currently examining the overhead lights like they've personally betrayed him.

"The lighting," I repeat, unable to stop myself from laughing as I fold another napkin with precise corners. "Right. Because that's definitely the problem. Not his complete lack of pool skills."

"That's the story he's going with." Jack taps his fingers again against the bar. "Another beer when you get a chance?"

"Coming right up." I grab a fresh pint glass from the rack overhead and pull the tap, watching the amber liquid fill it steadily. "You know, you could let them win one game. Show some mercy. Be the bigger person."

"Where's the fun in that?" He laughs, accepting the beer and taking a sip. "Besides, it's good for Mike's character. He needs the humbling experience. I'm really helping him out here."

"Such generosity," I say dryly.

He leans forward slightly, those green eyes locking onto mine with an intensity that makes my stomach do this annoying little flip that I immediately try to squash. "You should come play a game. Even the odds a little. Make it more interesting."

"Oh, I bet you'd love that," I say, rolling my eyes. He's good at this, the flirting thing, but you don't bartend for years without getting hit on by absolute experts. Jack Midnight is charming, sure, but he's nothing I haven't handled before.

"I really *would* love that." His smile widens. "Come on. One game."

"And abandon my post?" I gesture toward the bar. "Sarah would murder me." I nod toward my coworker at the other end of the bar who admittedly doesn't look particularly busy at the moment since she's currently deep in conversation with Jayson about something that's making them both laugh.

"Besides," I continue, going back to my silverware rolling, "someone needs to be here serving drinks to your victims when you're done systematically destroying their self-esteem and taking their money."

"So noble of you." He gives me that half-smile again, resting his elbows on the bar and leaning in closer. "Sacrificing yourself for the greater good of drunk men's egos."

"I'm basically a saint," I say, placing another rolled set in the caddy. "A saint who desperately needs rent money, so I'll be staying right here where the tips are."

He takes another sip of beer, watching me steadily over the rim of his glass. "A saint, huh? That's funny, because I seem to recall back in high school you hustling some of the guys on the football team out of their allowance money playing pool at Jason Miller's parties."

I look up at him with a grin now, the memory flooding back instantly. "One of my finer accomplishments. Those guys never saw it coming. Thought I was just some girl who didn't know which end of the pool cue to hold."

"As I recall," Jack says, "you relieved Travis Peterson of two hundred bucks in under ten minutes flat. The guy was absolutely devastated. Pretty sure he cried in his car."

"It was three hundred bucks actually," I correct him, laughing. "And the look on his face when I sank that final eight ball? Absolutely priceless. Best money I ever earned, and I spent it all on concerts and terrible mall food." I shake my head. "I'm shocked you even remember that party. You were barely ever in town for those things. Always off in Europe or wherever racing."

"Are you kidding?" Jack leans forward even more, his eyes bright. "Your pool skills were legendary. The girl who took down half the football team's ego and their wallets in one night? You were famous for like a month." He gestures toward the pool table behind him. "Come on, just one game. I'll even talk Sarah into covering for you." He glances over at my coworker with a look that suggests he knows exactly how effective his charm offensive can be when he deploys it properly.

"Your delusional self-confidence is, as always, deeply entertaining," I say dryly, though I'll admit part of me is tempted. It would be extremely satisfying to wipe that confident smirk right off his perfect face. "But I'm going to stay right here, working like a responsible adult with bills to pay."

He laughs, then slides off the stool with fluid grace. "Fine. But if you change your mind about showing off those legendary skills..."

"Keep dreaming, Midnight," I say cheerfully.

He winks before turning around to head back to his game, and I firmly ignore the way that wink does something stupid to my pulse. Attractive? Obviously, objectively yes. My type? Absolutely not. Total player with a reputation that spans continents. Jack Midnight can direct those dimples and that wink elsewhere. I'm perfectly content enjoying the view from a safe distance.

An hour or so slips by. I've sent Sarah home for the night and I'm currently munching on an order of fries that I talked Jayson into making for me, even though the kitchen was technically closed. The salt and grease are exactly what I need right now.

The door chimes. I glance up casually and my entire body goes rigid. The half-eaten fry freezes halfway to my mouth and I just drop it back into the basket, my appetite vanishing instantly.

Brandon walks in with Kelly. My ex-husband and my former

best friend who chose his side when everything fell apart. *Fuck my actual life.*

I haven't physically seen either of them in almost two years. Brandon moved to Seattle for work right after the divorce was finalized, and I'd managed to successfully avoid them both during his occasional visits back to Dark River. But of course they're both originally from here, so this collision was always inevitable.

Just my spectacular luck that it happens tonight when I'm alone at the bar with absolutely no buffer and no escape route. I would kill to have Maren here right now. She's the best at deflecting Brandon's bullshit.

Kelly's got her arm looped through Brandon's like she's marking territory or proving a point, though her face goes immediately tight with surprise when she spots me behind the bar. Her eyes widen comically, then dart toward the door like she's calculating exactly how fast she could make an escape. She leans in to whisper something to Brandon—probably desperately suggesting they leave—but he's already pulling her toward the bar.

Deep breath. You're not married to him anymore. He literally cannot affect you now. You're a free woman.

I desperately reach for something from my therapy sessions, some piece of wisdom about self-worth or standing in your power. Instead, the only thing that comes to mind is from *The Princess Diaries* when Joe tells Mia that thing about… nobody making you feel inferior without permission? Or consent? Something like that. Pretty sure it's Eleanor Roosevelt originally, but I only know it from a Disney movie I watched while demolishing Ben & Jerry's during the worst of my divorce wallowing.

Great. Just great. My self-help and courage is coming from a teen movie about a girl who finds out she's royalty. Whatever. *Princess Diaries* wisdom, please don't fail me now.

"Lark," Brandon says as they approach, his tone dripping with fake pleasant surprise. "What a surprise seeing you here."

"Brandon." I keep my voice professionally neutral even though my jaw is already clenched tight enough to crack walnuts, possibly diamonds. Then, because I literally cannot avoid acknowledging her existence, "Kelly."

"Hi, Lark," Kelly says quietly, her voice barely above a whisper. She's suddenly absolutely fascinated by her purse, adjusting the strap obsessively, fiddling with the clasp, doing anything possible to avoid making eye contact with me.

"It's been so long, hasn't it?" Brandon continues, settling himself onto a barstool like we're old friends catching up over drinks instead of exes with a spectacularly messy history. Kelly takes the seat directly beside him even though there are plenty of empty tables scattered throughout the bar. "What has it been now, two years?"

"About that." I busy myself with wiping down the already spotless counter, giving my hands something productive to do besides curling into fists or reaching for something to throw.

"Time really does fly when you're living your life," he says, making himself comfortable, elbows claiming space on my bar. This is exactly the kind of power play he loves—showing up in my territory, my workplace, acting like absolutely nothing happened between us, forcing me to perform customer service for him with a smile. "So what can we get here? Still have that decent IPA on tap that you guys used to serve?"

"We have several different IPAs actually." I keep my answers clipped and professional. The less I engage with him, the sooner this nightmare will be over.

"I'll take whichever one you'd recommend then." He gestures vaguely toward the taps. Then he adds without even glancing at Kelly beside him, "And she'll have a pinot grigio."

The casual way he orders for her without asking, without even looking at her, makes my skin absolutely crawl. He used to do that exact same thing to me constantly when we were married. Always ordering for me, deciding what I wanted before I could speak. Back when I'd somehow convinced myself that I actually *liked* dirty martinis just because he kept insisting they were "my drink" and I was too young and unsure to push back. It took months after the divorce to realize I hated them with an absolute passion.

I pour their drinks in deliberate silence, setting them down on the bar with perhaps slightly more force than strictly necessary. The beer foam spills over the rim a bit, creating a small puddle that I don't bother wiping up. Brandon's eye twitches at the mess, at my lack of immediate service, but he doesn't say anything about it. Small victories where I can find them.

I'm desperately hoping they'll drink quickly and leave. Take the hint. But Brandon's never been particularly good at reading a room when he doesn't want to, and he definitely doesn't want to right now.

"So," he says after taking his first sip, leaning back, "I guess I didn't realize you were still working here at the Black Lantern. *Still* here after all these years."

The way he emphasizes the word 'still' makes his meaning crystal clear—that I'm stuck, that I'm going nowhere with my life, that I'm a failure. Like tending bar at a place I love is somehow less valid or important than his corporate construction job with its long hours and its empty promises of advancement.

"Yep, still here." I grab a glass and start polishing it even though it's already clean, focusing intently on making it shine rather than on the overwhelming urge to throw it directly at his smug face. "Steady job, good tips. All the boring adult stuff."

I manage to keep my tone light and casual, like his opinion means absolutely nothing to me. Which it shouldn't.

"Well, good for you then." He takes another drink, and I can see him winding up for something worse, preparing his next attack. "I even heard through the grapevine that you're still doing that music thing of yours. Posting videos online and whatnot."

That music thing. Like I'm a child with a toy piano instead of an adult working seriously toward an actual career.

"That's really... sweet," he continues, and the condescension is dripping from absolutely every word like poison. "Still chasing that dream of yours. Not super realistic at this point in your life, but I do admire the persistence. The refusal to give up despite reality."

What. The. F.

This is classic Brandon, absolutely classic. I spent literal years of my life trying to decipher these kind of mixed messages, constantly wondering if I was crazy for hearing the insult lurking beneath every compliment.

Kelly swirls her wine glass slowly, studying the way the liquid moves like it's the most fascinating thing she's ever witnessed.

"Speaking of life updates," Brandon says, clearly enjoying himself now, "might as well address the elephant in the room here. Kelly and I are together now. Official."

Like I haven't seen their matching pictures on Instagram. Like I don't know they went to Cabo together last Christmas and posted about it extensively. Like I care even remotely about either of them anymore.

"Yeah, I know. Saw it on social media a while back." My customer service voice is failing me spectacularly right now.

Kelly's face tightens noticeably. She takes a long, deliberate sip of wine, still carefully avoiding any eye contact with me whatsoever. If she sinks any lower in her seat, she'll be physically under the bar. Good. She *should* feel uncomfortable. We met in high school and she was one of my closest friends besides Maren, at least until she decided my husband was a better option than our friendship.

"Right, well." Brandon shifts in his seat, putting his hand over Kelly's. "I'm back in town for work now. Got a construction contract that'll run through the summer. Kelly's doing the remote work thing so she can be here with me. So we'll definitely be around Dark River a lot. Probably be seeing each other fairly regularly."

Fantastic. Absolutely fantastic. Just what Dark River needs for the summer—Brandon's massive ego taking up valuable oxygen for months.

"Can't wait." My voice is so dry it could literally dehydrate a cactus, possibly start a small desert.

Brandon either completely misses the sarcasm or deliberately chooses to ignore it. But Kelly catches it—she's immediately back to memorizing every microscopic detail of her wine glass. She's always been fluent in subtext and unspoken communication. It's one of the reasons we were such close friends for so long.

Brandon leans forward, and I recognize that particular look immediately. That's his checkmate expression. The one that says he's been carefully saving his very best shot for last. He's going for blood now. I can feel it coming. I brace myself for whatever's about to hit.

"So what about you, Lark?" he asks, and his tone is so casual it's obviously calculated. "Are you seeing anyone these days? Dating? Or are you still too focused on the whole..." he makes this dismissive gesture with his fingers, like he's physically flicking away something completely insignificant, "aspiring musician thing to make time for a relationship?"

And there it is. There's the knife. The implication that my stupid, unrealistic music dreams are why I'm alone, why I'm undateable. Not because I'm actually enjoying being single for the first time in my life. Not because I've spent almost two years painstakingly rebuilding the self-esteem he systematically dismantled brick by brick during our marriage.

But standing up to Brandon has always felt like trying to argue with quicksand—the more you struggle against it, the deeper you sink.

Fuck. Say something. Anything. Don't let him win this. I'm not that woman anymore, not the one who would shrink herself down to nothing just to keep the peace.

"Actually, yes," I hear myself say before my brain has even remotely signed off on this decision. "I *am* seeing someone."

The words are completely out of my mouth before I can stop them, before I can think. My brain catches up approximately half a second after my mouth makes this absolutely insane decision. *What are you DOING? What the hell are you DOING?*

Brandon's beer pauses halfway to his mouth, frozen in surprise. Kelly looks up from her wine glass for the first time since she sat down, her eyebrows climbing toward her hairline.

"Really?" Brandon's voice is pure skepticism, disbelief dripping from the single word. "Who?"

Panic mode fully activated. Complete system malfunction. ABORT MISSION IMMEDIATELY.

Shit. Who? *Think, Lark.* Make up a name. Any name. Literally any name.

Ryan from high school? No, Brandon's cousin works with him and would know immediately it's a lie. Mike? Currently sulking over his pool game and would definitely contradict me. Tom from the hardware store? He's literally sitting at a table with his wife right this second.

But my mind is completely blank. Every single man I know in this entire town, Brandon knows too. He'll see right through any lie I try to tell. It's not like Dark River is some massive city. Why did I say yes? I should have just told him to mind his own damn business, but no, I had to try to one-up him and now I'm drowning—

"Me, actually."

Wait, *what?*

I spin around so fast I nearly knock over a glass. Jack is walking toward us from the pool table, moving with purpose.

"She's dating *me*," he says.

Before I can even begin to process what's happening, Jack walks confidently behind the bar like he owns the entire place, slipping smoothly around to stand directly beside me. His arm drapes casually over my shoulders, but there's nothing casual about the possessiveness in the gesture. The warmth of his body next to mine sends an electric jolt through my entire system, and I have to actively remind myself how to breathe like a normal human.

"You bothering my girlfriend?" Jack's voice is casual, but there's steel underneath. "Because I'd really hate to have to break your fucking nose again, Brandon."

I've never seen Brandon turn that particular shade of white before. It's impressive how quickly every drop of blood drains from his face.

The high school fight. Oh my god.

Jack was just a freshman when he stood up to Brandon, who was a junior football star at the time. Brandon was being a complete asshole about something or other—nothing unusual there—and Jack had made quick work of it, taken Brandon down almost instantly despite the age difference. They both got suspended, but Brandon's ego never recovered from being humiliated by a freshman in front of half the school.

"Jack Midnight," Brandon finally manages, his voice cracking slightly on the name.

"Brandon." Jack's arm tightens just slightly around my shoulders, the pressure both reassuring and thrilling in a way I don't want to examine. His heart is maintaining a steady rhythm against my side while mine is doing the cha-cha at triple speed. "Didn't expect to see you back in Dark River. Thought you'd moved on."

Brandon's eyes dart frantically between us, trying desperately to process this information, to make it make sense. "You two are... *together?*"

My brain is screaming at me. Say something. Anything. Nod. Blink. Do literally anything except stand here frozen like a deer in headlights. But my mouth won't work. My vocal cords have abandoned me. I'm just standing here, probably looking like I'm having a stroke.

"Yeah." Jack says it so simply, like it's the most obvious thing in the world. Like of course we're together. "Problem with that?"

Right. Right. This is happening. We're doing this. I lean back into Jack slightly, letting my body language sell it, and put my hand over his where it rests on my shoulder. His hand is warm and solid, and fourteen-year-old Lark would be absolutely hyperventilating right now. Though twenty-seven-year-old me honestly isn't faring much better.

"We've been keeping it quiet," I add, trying desperately to sound natural even though my heart is racing so fast I might pass out. "But yeah. We're together."

Kelly's looking between all of us with her mouth hanging open, probably frantically recalculating everything she thought she knew about my life. Dating a Formula One driver definitely trumps dating a construction contractor in her shallow world. Actually, it trumps dating pretty much anyone in anyone's world.

"We should go," Brandon says abruptly, standing so fast his stool scrapes harshly against the floor. The sound cuts through the bar like a record scratch. "This place hasn't gotten any better since I left."

"Probably a good idea," Jack agrees, his voice still carrying that dangerous casual tone. "Oh, and Brandon? Next time you feel like harassing my girlfriend about her career choices or her life?" His voice drops even lower, and I can hear the threat clear as day. "You're going to have a serious problem with me. And trust me, that's really not a problem you want to have."

Brandon's face does this absolutely fascinating journey from shock to anger to something that looks almost like fear. I've never seen him back down from anything or anyone before. And watching it happen is absolutely glorious.

Brandon doesn't respond. He just throws cash on the bar with unnecessary force and storms toward the door like a child having a tantrum. Kelly scrambles to follow, pausing just long enough to shoot me a look that could probably peel paint off walls.

The door swings shut behind them with a decisive thud.

And scene. Someone please cue the credits because this cannot be real life.

My brain is cycling through approximately fifteen different emotions simultaneously, none of which I have time to properly process right now. Shit. I'm still leaning against Jack, my hand still on his, frozen in this position like my body has completely forgotten how to move independently.

"Oh, sorry." I step back quickly, nearly tripping over my own feet in the process. "Thanks for the save. Really. That was… I wanted to show him up so badly that I kind of painted myself into a corner there."

He waves it off easily, looking entirely too pleased with himself. Like a cat who just knocked a very expensive vase off a shelf on purpose and is proud of it. "Don't mention it. Embarrassing Brandon is basically a hobby of mine. I couldn't pass up the opportunity."

"How chivalrous of you." I nod, completely unsure where to direct my nervous energy. My hands are practically vibrating. Damn, I can't wait to tell Maren absolutely everything about this. As the town's number one Brandon hater, she's going to absolutely love this story.

"That guy's been asking for it since high school." His smile turns slightly predatory, reminding me that beneath all the charm and the easy confidence, Jack Midnight has a definite edge to him. An edge that probably serves him well on the racetrack, but makes something flutter low in my stomach when it's directed at me.

"God, yes," I agree. "He really is the absolute worst human." I glance around the bar and spot Mrs. Henderson at her usual corner table, watching us with completely undisguised interest. She's not even pretending to read her book anymore. Just openly staring at Jack and me, probably already mentally composing the text message she'll send to her entire contact list. I stifle a groan. "Shit. Mrs. Henderson saw absolutely everything. This is going to be all over town by tomorrow morning. Possibly by tonight."

"Is that really so bad?" Jack leans casually against the bar, completely unconcerned. Easy for him to say. He doesn't even live here anymore. He'll return to Europe within a month or two.

"Everyone's going to think we're *actually* together," I say, trying to convey the absolute severity of this situation. My reputation in this town has finally recovered from all the divorce drama. And now this.

"And?" He raises his eyebrows, seemingly not understanding the problem.

And you're Jack Midnight, I want to say. Local celebrity turned international race car driver who dates models and actresses and probably actual princesses. Every woman in Dark River is going to want to murder me for apparently snagging the town's most eligible bachelor. Jack Midnight is basically a walking fantasy—dangerous, successful, looks like he stepped directly out of a magazine spread.

"And I'll never hear the end of it," I say instead, wiping my hands on my jeans like I can physically wipe away the anxiety. "When we're obviously not together next week, everyone will want to know exactly what happened. Did he dump me? Was I just another notch on the Jack Midnight bedpost? Did I do something wrong?" The thought of being town gossip again makes me want to relocate to another continent. Maybe Antarctica.

"Wow." He's fighting back a smile now, the corners of his mouth twitching. "Tell me how you really feel. Don't hold back."

"I mean, no offense intended. You're very…" I gesture vaguely at him, at all of him, at the whole overwhelming Jack Midnight experience. The face and the charm and the body and everything else that makes women do incredibly stupid things. Words are failing me, which is deeply inconvenient.

"None taken. Very *what* thought?" He's definitely enjoying this now. His eyes are practically sparkling with amusement, and I have a sudden overwhelming urge to throw a bar rag at him.

"You *know* what you are," I say, refusing to stroke his ego further. Like his ego needs any additional stroking. It's probably already the size of Jupiter. "But your reputation kind of precedes you. The whole player thing. Different woman every week."

"I prefer 'romantically adventurous.'" He says it with such a straight face I almost laugh out loud.

"Sure, let's go with that." I can't help but smile at the absolutely ridiculous phrase. "'Romantically adventurous' sounds like a euphemism someone would use on a dating profile to warn potential matches that they have serious commitment issues."

"It's more elegant than just saying 'afraid of feelings,'" he says with this self-deprecating smile that feels more genuine than his usual confident smirk.

Fair enough. I reach for a clean glass and pull a fresh beer from the tap. "Here." I set it on the bar directly in front of him. "This one's on me. Payment for the Brandon intervention."

"Payment for my excellent boyfriend performance?" He takes a sip, watching me. There's something in his gaze that makes me feel like I'm the only person in the room, which is an extremely dangerous feeling to have around someone like Jack Midnight.

"Something like that." I busy myself clearing away the glasses Brandon and Kelly left behind, needing something to do with my hands.

Mike calls out from the pool table, something about Jack owing him a rematch. His voice carries across the bar.

"You should probably get back before Mike has a complete meltdown," I say, nodding toward where Mike is leaning dramatically on his pool cue like it's the only thing keeping him upright. "I think he secretly loves losing money to you. Glutton for punishment, that one."

"He does look ready to flip the entire table," Jack agrees, picking up his beer. "Better go let him lose another round."

"And hey, thanks again," I say. "Really. That was... you didn't have to do that."

He raises his glass to me in a small salute and heads back to the game, and I turn back to wiping down the bar, trying desperately to process what just happened. Jack Midnight just told my ex-husband we were dating. In front of witnesses. Multiple witnesses. This is going to be absolutely everywhere by morning. It's probably already spreading through town like wildfire. Dark River's rumor mill operates at approximately twice the speed of light.

CHAPTER 4

JACK

I'm still grinning when I get back to the pool table, satisfaction warming my chest from watching Brandon's face drain of color. That fucking asshole.

I never could figure out how Brandon ever landed someone like Lark. Even back in high school she was sharp, funny, magnetic in a way that made everyone want to be around her. And she's always been insanely beautiful, the kind of woman who could get any guy she wanted. How that douchebag ever convinced her to marry *him* is one of the great mysteries of the universe.

Mike's leaning against the table, chalking his cue with the energy of a man who's already lost three games in a row, but is too stubborn to quit. Most of his solids are still scattered on the felt, along with a few of my stripes.

"What was that about?" he asks.

"Nothing important," I say, grabbing my cue and eyeing the table. "Brandon needed a reminder that he's still a piece of shit."

"That was Brandon?" Mike's eyebrows shoot up. "Damn, I thought he moved to Seattle after their divorce."

"Apparently he's back for the summer." My eyes drift back to the bar, where Lark's leaning through the kitchen window, laughing about something with the cook. She's got this animated energy, lighting up the whole space, and I realize I'm staring.

"Lucky us," Mike mutters, startling me out of it.

"Yeah. Lucky us," I say, refocusing on the table. I line up on the eleven ball in the corner pocket.

"He was always such a prick," Mike says, shaking his head. "Remember that time in high school when—"

"When I broke his nose?" I take the shot and the eleven drops clean. "Yeah, I remember. One of my better days, actually."

Mike laughs. "He went down so fast. Everybody thought you were gonna get expelled."

"Worth the suspension," I say, lining up on the thirteen. The memory still makes me smile. Freshman year, Brandon running his mouth about my birth parents being druggies, how I was lucky the Midnights took pity on trash like me. I didn't give a damn about my birth parents—they were abusive addicts who got me taken by the state when I was six. But I'd be damned if I let some entitled asshole use them to try to put me in my place.

So I broke his nose right there in the hallway. The sound of it cracking is still one of my favorite memories.

The thirteen's at a tighter angle than I'd like. I take the shot anyway and it rattles around the pocket before dropping.

I miss my next shot, but Mike immediately scratches, the cue ball dropping into the side pocket. "Shut up," he mutters before I can even say anything. "You're a professional driver with insane hand-eye coordination. This isn't fair."

"Life isn't fair," I say cheerfully, fishing the cue ball out. I've got ball in hand from his scratch, so I place it exactly where I want it for an easy shot on the fifteen. "But I appreciate you donating to my drinking fund anyway."

He rolls his eyes and takes a long pull from his beer. "This is definitely the last time I play pool with you."

"You say that every single time I'm back in town, Mike."

I'm about to take my shot when my phone buzzes in my pocket. I pause, fish it out, and see Thomas's name on the screen. My manager. He's in London right now, which makes it around five in the morning there. So him calling me is either very good news or very bad news, and given how my life's been going lately, I'm betting on bad.

"Give me a second," I tell Mike, setting down my cue and heading for the door. "I gotta take this."

He waves me off, already pulling out his own phone.

I push through the door into the parking lot. The evening air is still warm from the hot day, that dry Pacific Northwest summer heat. "Hey Thomas, what's up?" I answer, trying to sound more casual than I feel.

"Jack. Hope this isn't a bad time." Thomas's voice has that careful quality that means he's about to tell me something I'm not going to like. "Wanted to give you an update on the contract situation. I just got off the phone with Giorgio."

Giorgio Martinelli. My Italian lawyer who's been handling negotiations with Ferrari's legal team for the past two months. If Thomas is calling me at 5 AM his time after talking to Giorgio, this is *definitely* not good news.

"Okay," I say, keeping my voice neutral. "What'd he say?"

"The talks aren't going as smoothly as we'd hoped." There's a pause, papers rustling in the background. "They're highly interested based purely on skill. Your performance numbers are excellent, your race craft is top-tier, and you've proven you can compete at this level."

"But?" I prompt, because there's definitely a *but* coming.

"But your image issues are becoming a problem," Thomas

says bluntly. "The PR team says they were always willing to look past minor stuff. The party reputation, the different women, the general bad boy image. That's almost expected with F1 drivers to some degree. But the fight after your injury, and now the Monaco video? The *cocaine*. The sponsors are nervous, Jack."

Fuck.

I kick a rock in the gravel, watching it skitter across the parking lot. "So what does that mean? Are we dead in the water?"

"No, definitely not dead. They still want you. But we need to do some serious image rehab before they'll finalize the contract." Thomas's voice is firm, the tone he uses when he's in problem-solving mode. "They want to see stability and maturity. They want you keeping your head down, being responsible, not showing up in tabloids and TMZ every other week."

"So what do you want me to do?" I ask, even though I think I already know the answer.

"What you're already doing. Stay in Dark River for the summer, be visible with your family, lean into the wholesome hometown boy thing. We'll fly you out for race weekends and sponsor obligations, then you come right back. No parties, no clubs, no situations that could be misinterpreted." He pauses for emphasis. "Just you at home for family weddings in a cute small town, being a normal responsible adult. That's the image we need to sell right now."

"Got it," I say, running my free hand through my hair. "Whatever it takes to get back in the car."

"I'm serious, Jack. No scandals. No drama. Just you being a normal guy in a normal town doing normal things." Thomas's voice takes on that warning tone. "I know it's boring compared to Monaco and London, but we need this. Can you do that?"

"I said I got it," I reply, sharper than I mean to.

"Good. I'll check in next week after I talk to Giorgio again." He hangs up without saying goodbye, which is very Thomas.

I stand there for a second, phone in hand, staring at the dark parking lot. Then I pocket it and head back inside.

Stay in Dark River. Be visible with family. Wholesome hometown boy.

How the fuck do you fake that when everyone already knows who you are? When your reputation precedes you in every room you walk into?

Mike's still at the pool table when I get back, leaning against it and scrolling through his phone.

"Everything good?" he asks, looking up.

"Fine. Just my manager," I say, picking up my cue.

I sink the fifteen ball easily, then move around to line up my last stripe, the ten ball. My focus is off now though, Thomas's words circling in my head. I take the shot anyway and it drops.

Mike shifts his weight, watching. "So what'd your manager want?"

"Just checking in. Contract stuff."

I've got a straight shot on the eight ball now. Should be simple. But my mind is still stuck on Thomas's call, on the impossible task ahead of me.

The sponsors want stability. They want maturity. They want someone who looks like a safe bet, not a liability. Someone who won't embarrass Ferrari or make their PR team work overtime putting out fires.

I sink the eight ball. Game over.

"Four straight. Damn." Mike pulls out his wallet with a sigh. "I'm buying us another round. Maybe alcohol will improve my game."

"Sounds good," I say, but I'm barely listening.

Wholesome. Stable. Responsible.

Three words that have never fucking described me in my entire life.

CHAPTER 5

Lark

Later, close to closing time, I'm behind the counter on my laptop putting in next week's liquor order. The bar's mostly empty now, just a couple of stragglers nursing their last drinks and chatting quietly. The quiet hum of the refrigerators and soft indie music playing overhead create that peaceful late-night vibe I usually love about closing shifts.

Jack makes his way back to the bar after seeing off the last of his pool buddies. There's a victorious gleam in his eyes that tells me Mike's wallet is significantly lighter than it was at the start of the night.

"Calling it a night?" I ask, saving the inventory spreadsheet before I lose any data.

He nods, sliding his credit card across the bar top. "Time to put Mike out of his misery. The man's been through enough."

I process his tab, pulling up his total. "So what's the final damage report? How much did you take him for?"

"Let's just say Mike's definitely not buying rounds anytime soon." That grin says he doesn't feel even remotely bad about it.

"Though he's already talking about a rematch next week. Guy never learns."

"Glutton for punishment," I say, running his card.

I hand him the receipt and he signs it with a quick scrawl. "So, how long were you and Brandon married anyway?" he asks, his tone casual.

"Several years. Long enough to know better than to ever make that mistake again." I shake my head, the old bitterness rising up before I push it back down. "We've been divorced about two years now, and I've been enjoying every second of freedom away from that particular nightmare."

He smiles. "Good for you. You were always way too good for him. I mean, I think every human on earth would be too good for him, but still, you were always above the rest."

I can't help but laugh. "Wow, Jack Midnight getting sweet and sentimental at a bar."

"And after I heroically rescued you, you're right back to the sarcasm." He *tsks,* tapping his fingers on the bar. "No gratitude whatsoever."

"Hey, I gave you a free beer in exchange for your services. That's payment. I can only be sweet and grateful for so long before it gets exhausting." I toss the rag under the counter. "But fine, to satisfy your wounded ego: thank you again. Very rom-com moment, actually. The whole thing."

"Is it?" He tilts his head.

"Oh yeah. Fake boyfriend swooping in to save the day at the last possible second?" I lean back in my chair, abandoning the vodka inventory for now. "That's like, classic rom-com territory. Straight out of the playbook. And I *love* rom-coms, so I'm always happy to accidentally live one out in real life."

"Well, happy to provide the authentic experience." He does this ridiculous bow that gets a laugh out of me. "But seriously," he says, settling back on his stool, "what was Brandon giving you grief about? Something about your music?"

"Yeah, I know it probably sounds kind of far-fetched," I admit, fidgeting with a pen on the counter. "But I've been seriously working toward being a professional musician. It's been my dream since I was a kid, but I've only really started making a legitimate go of it in the last year or so."

"Hey, it's not any more far-fetched than becoming a Formula One driver," Jack says. "Everyone thought I was absolutely crazy when I started pursuing racing. Kept telling me the odds, how impossible it was, how I should have a backup plan. Fuck anyone who tells you something can't be done just because it's difficult."

Most people either give me these pitying smiles or immediately launch into lectures about backup plans and being realistic. *Have you tried teaching music instead? Maybe focus on songwriting for other people?* It's refreshing to talk to someone who gets what it's like to chase something that seems impossible.

"Thanks." I find myself smiling. "I've been posting videos online and slowly building up my catalog. I got some interest from a label recently. Which is potentially life-changing if it works out."

"That's incredible." He actually sounds interested. "Which label?"

"Tidal Records in LA," I say. "But they want me to quadruple my social media following before they'll seriously consider signing me. Which is a massive problem. Plus I have my own issue where I freeze completely when performing my own stuff."

"Stage fright?"

"The pathological kind." It's embarrassing to admit, but his lack of judgment makes it easier. "I'm usually pretty extroverted, but performing? *Disaster*. Which is ridiculous because I loved performing as a kid, but somewhere along the way I internalized all this criticism and..." Brandon's voice creeps into my mind, and I try to shake it off. "Anyway. Zero stage presence now."

"That's brutal," he says, and I appreciate that he doesn't try to minimize it or offer some cliché advice like 'just imagine everyone naked.'

I smile. "Yeah, well. Now the whole industry's about numbers anyway. Followers, engagement rates, algorithmic bullshit. Sometimes it feels less about music and more about becoming an influencer who happens to sing."

"Tell me about it." His laugh has a bitter edge. "Half my job now is posting workout videos and pretending to love whatever energy drink is paying me. My contract negotiations are stalled because my '*image*' isn't clean enough for sponsors."

"Because of that Monaco video?"

"Yeah. You heard about that?" He looks vaguely uncomfortable, which is new for someone who seems perpetually confident.

"*Everyone* heard about it, Jack. It was trending for weeks." I bite my lip, realizing I probably shouldn't have brought it up.

"'Jack Midnight's Monaco Meltdown' was my personal favorite headline." He tries for a smile but it doesn't quite land. "Total bullshit, but it got clicks."

"Wrong?" I lean forward on my elbows. "I mean, the video looked pretty damning. Not that I'm judging you or anything."

"I *wasn't* doing drugs." He shifts on the barstool. "My old teammate, Luca, called me panicking. His little sister was at this party, completely in over her head with some sketchy older guys. They were feeding her drugs and... well... he was out of the country and asked me to get her out. I wasn't even supposed to be there. I literally showed up, found her, and convinced her to leave."

"Seriously?" My mouth drops open. "So no cocaine? No crazy party?"

"Well, I won't deny that I've been to some crazy parties," he says with a slight grin. "I'm not a saint. But not anytime recently, and definitely not that one. Plus I've *never* done hard drugs. As much as I enjoy a good time, that shit doesn't really work when you need to be in top physical shape for racing. My body is my career, so I can't afford to fuck it up."

"So you really were just there to help someone?" I ask.

"Yeah. The timing and angle of the video made it look bad. Made it look like I was there partying with everyone else when I wasn't."

"Why not say that publicly? Clear your name?" I'm baffled. Who wouldn't want to fix something like this immediately?

"Eh, I don't really give a shit about my reputation anyway." He shrugs, but there's definite tension in his shoulders that contradicts his casual words. "It was already pretty trash to begin with. What's one more scandal on the pile? And Sofia's only eighteen. If I said anything publicly, people would figure out who she was within hours, start harassing her online. It's not worth destroying her life just to save my image."

I blink at him, recalibrating everything I thought I knew about Jack Midnight. The player image, the careless party boy reputation, suddenly doesn't fit. "That's... actually really selfless of you, Jack."

"Don't sound so shocked," he says with a laugh.

"Hey, I'm trying to be a singer, not an actress. I can't hide anything on my face."

"Clearly." That mischievous look is back in his eyes. "The problem is my sponsors aren't nearly as understanding as you. And neither is Ferrari. They're threatening to pull out if I don't clean up my image and..." He trails off and goes quiet, tapping the bar surface. Then his eyes light up. "Holy shit. Wait. That thing you said before about the rom-com save?"

"Yeah?" I'm already suspicious of his look.

"We should do it."

My brain completely short-circuits. I stare at him, mouth open. "I'm sorry, do *what*?"

"Think about it." He's getting animated now, hands moving as he talks. "I'm stuck in Dark River for the next month or so anyway. You need followers for your music career, and you'd get a ton of attention dating me. I need image rehabilitation, so your whole wholesome small-town vibe is perfect. We fake date for a couple months, post some photos, attend a few events, everybody wins."

"Absolutely not." I start laughing because what else do you do when someone suggests something this insane? "That's—no. That's crazy."

"People do this all the time in my world. PR relationships are standard. *And* I've got nine million Instagram followers," he adds, dangling it like bait.

"*Nine* million?" My voice cracks.

"Something like that. Maybe ten million by now. I honestly don't check that often." He says it with a casual wave, like ten million people paying attention to his life is totally normal and not absolutely mind-blowing.

"That's..." I can't even finish the sentence. I should laugh this off. Send him home. Forget this conversation. But those followers...

"Think about it, Lark," he says. "One post from me mentioning your music?"

"Okay, but wouldn't being publicly associated with you be bad for my image?" I try to think logically. "Even if the video isn't true, no one else knows that. The entire world thinks you were doing drugs at a party. That can't be great for me."

"Any publicity is good publicity," he counters immediately.

"Didn't you *just* say that bad publicity is actively ruining your contract negotiations?" I raise an eyebrow.

"Touché." He laughs, not even trying to defend it. "But nobody's going to think less of you for dating me. If anything, it makes you more interesting. *Local girl tames bad boy F1 driver?* People eat that up."

"Tames?" I deadpan. "What am I, a lion tamer?"

"You know what I mean. The narrative changes for both of us. I'm not the party guy anymore, I'm the guy who fell for the talented local musician. You're not just another aspiring artist, you're dating a famous driver."

"So I'm reputation rehab?" I say, trying to look skeptical even though my brain is already frantically calculating how many Instagram followers I could potentially gain from just one post on his account.

"And I'm massive exposure. Fair trade." His eyes are dancing. He knows he's reeling me in.

I think about Brandon's face when Jack's arm went around me. About Maya's email saying they need to see I can bring an audience. About ten million potential fans.

"My sponsors want 'stability and maturity,'" he explains, making air quotes. "A talented girlfriend from my hometown who has actual goals? Doesn't do drugs? You're perfect, nice and wholesome. And you get access to my entire following."

"Oh my god, I'm actually considering this." I press my palms to my cheeks. "This is what rock bottom feels like, isn't it? Standing in an empty bar, seriously contemplating a fake relationship with Jack Midnight purely for Instagram followers. My therapist is going to need her own therapist."

He laughs, loud and genuine, then says, "It's not rock bottom at all, Lark. It's strategic thinking. Like a business merger."

"A *business* merger?" I laugh. "You really know how to sweet-talk a girl, don't you?"

He grins, clearly pleased I haven't completely shut down the idea yet. "Think of the perks. Instagram exposure, Brandon's face whenever he sees us, and you get to hang out with me all summer. Win-win-win situation."

"Your ego is truly something to behold, Midnight."

"It's one of my best features," he replies with a self-satisfied smirk.

I roll my eyes hard. "Okay, but there's a giant hole in your logic. I'm not even that wholesome. I spent more than a few nights in my youth dancing on bar tops during girls' nights out. I literally work at a bar serving alcohol, for crying out loud." I drop my voice to an exaggerated stage whisper. "And last week I said 'fuck' in front of Pastor Miller's seven-year-old daughter during trivia night, and she then went and repeated it word-for-word during Sunday school. I'm basically going straight to hell."

"That's cute, but some dancing and occasional swearing hardly counts as wild behavior," he says with an amused look. "Those are very different kinds of parties than what my sponsors are worried about. Plus this isn't exactly some sketchy dive bar situation. There's a *Connect Four* grid in the corner and you serve mocktails."

I follow his gaze to the stack of board games Maren keeps specifically for family trivia nights. The Black Lantern really is practically a postcard for small-town charm—string lights year-round, locally sourced menu, dogs and kids welcome. Half the town brings their children here for weekend lunch and trivia nights. Dammit, he has a valid point.

"I can't believe I'm negotiating terms." I tap my nails against the bar top anxiously. "If—and I mean IF—we actually did this ridiculous thing, what would we even tell people?"

"The truth, modified." He leans back. "We reconnected at the wedding, sparks flew. The Brandon thing happened, I asked you out. It writes itself."

"Nobody would believe I'd date you," I point out. "I've called you a fuckboy to your face, and behind your back more than once."

His grin widens. "That's exactly what makes it believable. Everyone loves a reformed bad boy story."

"You're not reformed though," I point out dryly.

"They don't know that." He winks, and I hate that it's actually charming.

"How long would we even do this?" I can't believe I'm really asking.

"Two months minimum. Through September." His expression shifts to something more calculated. "My contract stuff should be sorted by then, and that gives you solid exposure."

"And then what happens?" I find myself leaning forward despite my better judgment.

"Mutual, amicable breakup. Distance got too hard with me back in Europe. We tried to make it work but it wasn't meant to be. Still friends, no drama whatsoever."

I chew my lip. "If we did this… I'd have to tell Maren. She's my best friend."

"No way." He shakes his head firmly. "She'd tell Calvin, who'd tell my other brothers. And Alex is a horrible secret keeper. Too many people would know. Too easy for it to get out."

"But she'll know something's off," I say, fidgeting with a coaster. "She can read me like a book."

"Look," he leans forward. "The fewer people who know, the better. Either Maren has to lie to her husband about his own brother, or Calvin finds out and lectures me about responsibility. Neither option is great."

Dammit, he's right. Asking Maren to lie to Calvin isn't fair at all. Putting Maren in that position, making her choose between me and her husband? That's not something I can do to my best friend.

I sigh, already feeling guilty. "Fine. But if she figures it out and gets mad, I'm blaming you entirely."

"Deal. I'll take full responsibility for corrupting you." He places a hand over his heart solemnly.

"Okay, if we're doing this, we need ground rules." I try to think practically. "First rule: no kissing."

"*What?*" he asks, looking at me like I've lost my mind. "I'm not saying we need to make out constantly, but people who are dating generally kiss sometimes."

I cross my arms defensively. "Not necessarily. Some people aren't into PDA at all. For all anyone knows, I'm one of those people."

"Okay, then hand holding at absolute minimum," he counters.

"Obviously," I say, rolling my eyes. "I'm not a prude. Hand holding is fine. And hand on waist is acceptable when we're in public together, I guess. For believability purposes."

"I can work with those parameters." He drums his fingers on the bar, thinking. "You'll need to come to any racing events I have scheduled this summer though. There are a few sponsorship things. Including one in Miami."

I gulp. *Miami*. The only times I've traveled are to visit extended family in Mexico or my parents in Southern California. This is racing world Miami with Jack Midnight. "Okay... sure. And you share me on your social media and mention my music? But naturally, not an obvious promotion?"

"Of course." He flashes that dimpled grin. "Professional and subtle. And we need to be seen around town together regularly too. Coffee shops, restaurants. Full visibility in Dark River."

This is suddenly feeling overwhelming. I'm going to be lying to the entire town. Great. "Alright. And absolutely no drama when we eventually fake break up. I mean it. No messy ending that makes me look like the girl who got dumped by the famous racing driver."

"Scout's honor." He holds up three fingers in what I assume is supposed to be a scout salute.

"Were you even a Scout?" I ask suspiciously.

He shrugs, completely unbothered. "For like three days when I was nine. Got kicked out for hot-wiring the scoutmaster's car and taking it for a joyride around the campground."

I stare at him. "You stole a car when you were nine?"

"Borrowed," he corrects primly. "I brought it back. Even parked it in the exact same spot. But apparently that's 'dangerous' and 'illegal' and 'not appropriate Scout behavior.'" He does air quotes, looking entirely unrepentant.

I burst out laughing. "Oh my god, you've been an absolute menace since birth, haven't you?"

"Pretty much. My brothers have stories that would horrify you." He smirks.

"I'm going to ignore that. OK, most importantly," I say, forcing myself to get serious again, "we both need to remember this is purely a business deal. Nothing more. No getting confused about what's real and what's fake."

"Hey, I'm the one who suggested it," he points out. "If anything, *you* should be the one promising not to fall for *me*."

I roll my eyes. "We're going to fake break up before we even fake start at this rate."

"Nah. We're going to be great at this. Best fake couple Dark River has ever seen." He leans back, completely at ease with this bizarre scenario.

"We're really doing this?" I ask one final time, giving us both one last out.

"We're really doing this." He holds out his hand across the bar. "Shake on it?"

I stare at his outstretched hand for a long moment. This is it. The moment where I either come to my senses or commit to the wildest idea I've ever agreed to.

I reach out and take his hand. His grip is firm and warm and real, and I wonder again what the hell I'm getting myself into.

"Why do I feel like I just made a deal with the devil?" I say, resigned.

"Because you kind of did. But a very helpful devil who's going to make you Instagram famous." He stands up, already pulling out his phone. "Actually, there's a Callahan Spirits event in Seattle next weekend. Black tie, industry people, lots of photographers. Perfect for our public debut."

"*Next* weekend?" My internal panic meter shoots to eleven.

"You're right, that's pretty far away." He frowns, clearly thinking the opposite of what I meant. "We'll need to soft launch way before then. Start the rumors, get people talking." He's already typing something. "Coffee date tomorrow morning? Very public, very visible."

"Um, OK," I manage. "Sure. Late morning though? I'm going on a run early and have errands."

"Perfect. Give me your number. I'll text you the details later tonight."

I recite it and watch him save it in his contacts. My phone buzzes immediately with a text: *Your new fake boyfriend*

"I still can't believe this is happening," I say.

"Believe it." He pauses at the door, turning back with that grin. "I'll text you tomorrow morning about coffee. See you soon." And then he's gone, the door swinging shut behind him.

What the hell have I gotten myself into?

CHAPTER 6

Lark

My alarm goes off at 6:30 AM the next day and I consider throwing my phone across the room. But I promised Maren I'd meet her for our morning run, and I'm trying really hard to stick with this whole "productive morning person" thing.

I drag myself out of bed with all the grace of a zombie in a horror movie, pull on running clothes and try desperately not to think about last night. About the deal I made. About how I'm about to lie directly to my best friend's face. I basically sold my soul for Instagram followers, and am now taking the title as officially the worst friend in the entire history of friendship. *Great.*

The morning air is already warm when I step outside my apartment, July in Washington bringing that summer heat that promises another scorching day ahead. Maren's already at the trail entrance when I arrive, looking like she also just crawled out of bed. Her blonde ponytail is lopsided, though she's wearing the new running shoes I convinced her to buy last month.

"We both actually made it," she says, looking mildly surprised by this achievement. "I nearly talked myself out of it entirely."

"Same," I admit, laughing. "I could have slept for another three hours."

She starts stretching her hamstrings. "How was it closing the bar last night? Jayson said it was *eventful* but when I asked what happened, he said to talk to you."

My stomach tightens. Here we go. "Not too bad, but... Brandon showed up."

"What?" Maren stops mid-stretch, her sleepiness replaced immediately by pure outrage. "Are you serious right now? What did that absolute asshole want?"

"To be an asshole, mostly. His favorite hobby." I focus on stretching my other leg, using the physical movement as an excuse to avoid eye contact. "Came in with Kelly, made absolutely sure I knew they were together now, insulted my music career in that special condescending way he has. The usual Brandon greatest hits."

"That waste of oxygen," Maren fumes, her face flushing with anger on my behalf. "I swear, if I'd been there when he walked in... Kelly actually had the nerve to show up too? Please tell me you threw them both out on their asses."

I smile gratefully at her fierce loyalty. She's always ready to go to war for me at a moment's notice. "I considered it." I bump her shoulder affectionately with mine. "But then something kind of weird happened instead..."

"Weird how?"

My heart's racing and we haven't even started running. "Well, Jack was there. Playing pool."

"Okay..." She glances at me sideways. "And?"

"And, uh, Brandon was being such a condescending dick, asking if I was seeing anyone." I clear my throat. "Implying I'm alone and pathetic because I'm too focused on my 'little music thing' instead of finding another man to validate my existence."

"God, I hate him so much," Maren mutters darkly.

"Me too. So I told him I was seeing someone." I force myself to say it casually. "To shut him up."

"Ooooh. Good for you! Who'd you say?" She grins approvingly as we start jogging.

"That's the thing." I take a deep breath, preparing for the lie. "I didn't have anyone specific to name. My brain completely blanked. But then Jack... He, um, he just came over and told Brandon we were together."

Maren stops jogging so abruptly it's like she hit an invisible brick wall. I'm three full steps past her before I even realize she's not beside me anymore. I turn back to find her staring at me with her mouth hanging open.

"I'm sorry, WHAT?" Her voice rises to a pitch that probably only dogs can hear.

"He just... played along perfectly," I say. "Put his arm around me, told Brandon to stop bothering his girlfriend. It was pretty incredible. Brandon's face went completely white. He practically *ran* out of there."

This part, at least, is completely true, and I can't help the satisfaction in my voice at the memory.

"Jack pretended to be your boyfriend?" Maren's voice goes up another octave. "To Brandon? In front of people?"

"Yeah." I start jogging again because I absolutely cannot look at her while I lie. Movement feels safer somehow, like the truth can't catch me if I keep running fast enough. "And then after Brandon left, we got to talking and he, uh, asked me out for real. So we're going to get coffee."

Maren catches up quickly, grabbing my arm hard enough to slow me down. "Wait, wait, wait. Hold on. Are you telling me you and Jack are together now? Like actually dating?"

The lie sits heavy in my stomach like a rock. "I mean, we're going to try? See where it goes? It's really new." Every single word feels like another shovelful of dirt on the grave of our honest friendship.

"Oh my GOD, Lark!" She squeals. "Jack? JACK MIDNIGHT? Calvin's *brother* Jack?"

"Please don't make a huge deal about it—" I try desperately to sound casual, but my voice comes out strained and weird.

"Don't make a big deal?" She's practically bouncing while running now. "You're dating Calvin's brother! Who is also a Formula One driver!" Her excitement is so genuine that it makes my guilt triple in size instantly. "This is literally the biggest deal! This is huge!"

"It might not be anything serious," I say quickly. "We're just... seeing what happens. Taking it slow."

"Calvin's going to absolutely flip when I tell him. In a good way!" She's gesturing wildly now as she runs. "Oh my god, we can do double dates. This is amazing." She pauses mid-stride, studying my face more carefully. Her expression shifts slightly. "Wait, why do you look like you just accidentally ran over someone's cat? You should be happy."

"I *am* happy. It's just new and weird and I don't want to jinx it by talking about it too much. Jack does have quite the reputation," I point out as we jog along the tree-lined trail. "I don't know if he's ever dated anyone longer than a month. Maybe six weeks tops."

"Yeah, he's definitely not the poster child for commitment," Maren agrees with a laugh. "But I've known him for years now, and underneath all that playboy stuff, I think he's got a good heart." She glances at me, her expression turning more mischievous. "Plus, who says this has to be some serious long-term thing? Maybe a hot, sexy summer fling while he's in town is exactly what you need after Brandon. Some fun without pressure."

"Oh my god, Maren!" I laugh, feeling my cheeks warm.

"What?" She grins, completely unrepentant. "I'm just saying! You two might actually be good together. You're both adventurous, chasing dreams, and both stubborn as hell."

"Maybe. I haven't even had coffee yet. I can't picture anything but caffeine."

"Plus," Maren adds, ignoring me, "if he hurts you, you and I will handle it. Very Dixie Chicks 'Goodbye Earl' style. We've got property with lots of trees. No one would find the body."

I snort-laugh. "*Maren*."

"I'm kidding! Mostly." She grins wickedly. "Though my money's on *you* breaking *his* heart. Jack acts all tough and player-ish, but I've seen him with his family. I suspect that he's actually kind of a softie underneath. Meanwhile you're over here with walls so high they're visible from space."

"I do not have *walls*," I protest.

"Lark, you have *fortified* walls, and a moat. With alligators. And the drawbridge is broken."

"That's called being appropriately cautious after divorce," I say.

"That's called not putting yourself back out there," she says gently. "Which I totally get. Brandon did a number on you. But maybe letting those walls down a little wouldn't be the worst thing? Even if it's just for fun?"

"Maybe," I mutter, hating that she's probably right.

"Look, I'm not saying dive in headfirst. Just... don't shut it down before it starts, you know?" She bumps my shoulder affectionately. "But either way, after how relentlessly you pushed me with Calvin? I'm going to be *soooo* annoying about this."

"Hey, I was completely right about Calvin though," I counter with a grin, grateful for the shift to safer territory. "You probably wouldn't even be married if I hadn't pushed you out of your comfort zone, past all that—" I throw my hand dramatically to my forehead, "'It'll never work! The distance! He's too perfect!'"

She laughs. "Okay, okay, I get it, you smug brat. Yes, it is thanks to you that Calvin and I are now happily married. I owe you my entire life. You're the greatest friend who ever lived."

She gives me an exaggerated bow without breaking her stride, nearly tripping over her own feet in the process.

"Damn right you do," I say, trying to enjoy this moment despite the guilt eating away at my insides. "I'm the matchmaker queen of Dark River. I should charge for my services."

She shakes her head, laughing breathlessly. "Seriously though, I'm really happy for you, Lark. Like thrilled. And Jack is lucky to have caught your eye. He should be counting his lucky stars that you're even giving him the time of day."

She starts running again, practically floating along the trail like gravity has been reduced by half. I follow behind her. The morning sunlight filters through trees, birds singing overhead. Perfect morning for a run with your best friend, except for the massive lie sitting in my chest.

I'm definitely going to hell for this.

An hour after my run with Maren, I'm in my bedroom trying to figure out what to wear. My closet feels woefully inadequate for a coffee date with Jack Midnight, fake or not.

I've already tried on six different outfits. Nothing feels right. Too casual, too formal, too desperate. Coffee with Jack is in forty-five minutes and I'm standing here in my underwear like an idiot, which is completely ridiculous. This isn't even a real date. So why am I stressing about what to wear?

"Because people will be watching," I mutter to myself, tossing aside yet another pair of jeans that suddenly look too casual. "The whole point is to be seen. To look like someone Jack Midnight would actually date."

Do I need to look more glamorous? More sophisticated? More Instagram-worthy? Do Formula One drivers' girlfriends wear sundresses or is that too casual?

My phone buzzes loudly on the dresser, and I see Maren's name light up the screen with a text.

Maren: *Hope it goes wonderful! You deserve only the best. He won't know what hit him!* 🩶🩶🩶

I can't help but smile, even as guilt twinges sharply in my chest. I reply with a bunch of hearts and a blushing emoji, then shove the guilt firmly to the side, forcing myself to focus on the task at hand.

I reach for a cute red sundress I bought last month. The sweetheart neckline and mid-thigh hem show enough skin to be flirty but still leave me looking put-together. Perfect for summer. I slip it on and study myself critically in the full-length mirror.

"This will have to do," I tell my reflection firmly. "It's not like you're trying to impress him for real."

My reflection doesn't look convinced.

I run my fingers through my long black hair. Down seems right for a coffee date, so I add some shine serum Maren got me for my birthday, then use the curling iron to add a few waves. Quick mascara, lip gloss, done.

I grab my purse and keys, take a deep breath. Time to go fake-date Jack Midnight in front of the entire town.

I pull into the parking lot of Perks and immediately spot him.

Jack leans casually against his sleek black motorcycle like he's posing for a magazine spread, one ankle crossed over the other, scrolling through his phone. He's wearing dark jeans and a gray t-shirt that does absolutely nothing to hide the fact that Formula One drivers are, apparently, extremely fit. His dark hair is windblown from the ride, doing that annoyingly perfect thing where it looks messy but somehow better than if he'd tried.

As I park my beat-up Honda in a spot two spaces away, he looks up, spots my car, and immediately puts his phone away in his pocket. The smile that spreads across his face is so convincing that for a second I almost believe he's actually happy to see me.

I step out of my car, suddenly self-conscious in a way I'm absolutely not used to feeling. Jack's eyes track me as I walk toward him.

"You look beautiful," he says, pushing off from his motorcycle.

"Thanks." I smooth down my dress. "You clean up pretty nice yourself."

"This old thing?" He gestures dramatically to his perfectly fitted t-shirt with a grin. "Ready for our big debut?"

"As ready as I'll ever be."

He reaches out and takes my hand, his palm warm against mine. The gesture is casual, natural, but my heart does a little skip that I try to ignore.

The coffee shop is busy, the comfortable murmur of conversations and the hiss of the espresso machine creating familiar background noise. The moment we walk through the door together though, there's a subtle but definite shift in the atmosphere.

A few heads turn our way immediately. Conversations pause mid-sentence, people forgetting what they were saying. It's not full celebrity hysteria—Dark River is too small-town cool for that kind of obvious reaction—but there's definitely an awareness that ripples through the room like a wave. Jack Midnight is here. Jack Midnight is with someone. Jack Midnight is holding someone's hand.

Jack seems completely immune to the attention, his posture relaxed and confident as we make our way across the room toward the counter. Of course he is. He's used to racing in front of hundreds of thousands of people, being photographed wherever he goes, signing autographs for screaming fans at every race.

Behind the register, the barista's eyes widen noticeably as she recognizes him. She's young, maybe college age, with perfectly-winged eyeliner and a nose ring. Her gaze shifts quickly between Jack and me.

"Welcome to Perks," she says, her smile brightening considerably as she focuses primarily on Jack, her voice taking on that slight breathiness people get when they're excited. "What can I get for you today?"

"I'll have a double espresso," Jack says easily, then looks at me with raised eyebrows.

"Iced vanilla latte, please," I say, noting the way her eyes barely flick to me before returning to Jack.

The barista nods. "Anything else? We just took some fresh cinnamon rolls out of the oven a few minutes ago." She says this directly to Jack, a hint of eager hopefulness in her voice, like she's personally hoping he'll be impressed with their pastry selection.

My stomach growls quietly in response. The fresh-baked smell wafting from the pastry case isn't helping my hunger situation.

"Those look amazing," I say, eyeing the warm rolls topped with melted cream cheese icing that's still dripping down the sides.

"Then we'll take two," Jack says, glancing at me before

turning back to the barista with a polite smile. "One for me and one for my girlfriend."

The barista's eager smile falters visibly at the word "girlfriend," her entire expression dimming like someone turned down her brightness setting. "Coming right up," she says, her tone shifting back to purely professional as she turns to prepare our drinks.

As the espresso machine hisses and gurgles loudly, I open my purse and take out my wallet. Jack's eyes immediately drop to my hands, his brows lifting slightly in surprise.

"What are you doing?" he asks.

"Paying for my half," I say matter-of-factly, extracting a ten-dollar bill from my wallet. It seems only fair, even if this is technically a fake date.

"Absolutely not," he looks amused. "I asked *you* to coffee, I'm paying. Plus didn't you tell me last night you were counting your tips to see if you'd make rent?"

"That was an exaggeration," I protest.

He grins, gently pushing my hand back. "Look, Reyes, just let me buy you coffee. Consider it payment for having to pretend to like me in public."

"In that case I should be charging way more," I say, but I'm fighting a smile.

"Probably true," he laughs.

I hesitate. On one hand, I'm perfectly capable of paying for myself. On the other hand, the watch on his wrist probably costs more than I make in a year.

"Fine," I concede, slipping the bill back into my wallet. "But I'm buying next time."

"When you're a famous musician, you can buy me all the coffee you want," he says with a wink.

The barista returns with our drinks, setting them on the counter—his espresso in a small white ceramic cup, my latte in a tall glass. Two massive cinnamon rolls follow, still warm and fragrant enough to make my mouth water.

As we move away from the counter, I can feel several sets of eyes tracking our progress across the room. It's like being under a microscope. We find a spot by the large front window, where the afternoon sun streams in warmly.

Jack settles into the chair across from me, setting our drinks and pastries on the table between us. The sun catches his face at an angle that makes those green eyes of his practically glow like backlit gemstones. It's unfair how some people just win the genetic lottery.

"So," he says, leaning forward slightly, eyes intent and focused on mine. "Tell me about your music. What should I know about your sound? Your style?"

"Singer-songwriter stuff," I say, stirring my latte. The foam swirls in lazy circles while I figure out how to explain. "Pretty intimate lyrics, acoustic foundation. Some songs are just me and a guitar, others have more production layered in. Depends on what the song needs."

"You write it all yourself?" he asks, breaking off a piece of his cinnamon roll.

"Yeah," I nod. "Every word. I write about relationships, but also family dynamics, identity. Whatever story feels worth telling at the time."

"I'd like to hear some of your work," he says, and I feel a flutter of nervousness at the thought of him listening to my music. Of him hearing the vulnerable parts of me. "Where can I find it?"

"YouTube, Spotify, Apple Music," I explain, trying to sound casual even though my heart is beating faster. "I can send you the links if you want."

"Do that," he says, reaching for his espresso. "I should know what my girlfriend's music sounds like, after all."

"What, you mean you haven't already memorized my entire

catalog?" I place my hand over my heart. "And here I thought you were my biggest fan."

"Give me a day or two," he says, amusement dancing in his expression. "I'm a pretty quick study when I'm motivated."

"I'll hold you to that," I warn, surprised by how easily we've fallen into this natural back-and-forth banter. "There might be a quiz. With essay questions."

"I'm not afraid of tests," he counters, leaning back in his chair. "I perform very well under pressure. It's kind of my thing."

The way he says it makes heat rise to my cheeks despite my best efforts. I cover by taking a long sip of my latte, the cold sweetness a welcome distraction.

"What about you?" I ask, setting down my cup and eager to shift the focus away from me. "How do you spend your time when you're not racing or getting into highly publicized scandals?"

He raises an eyebrow at my dig but grins, clearly not offended in the slightest.

"During race season, it's mostly just training, practice runs, endless meetings with the team about strategy and car setup," he says, his fingers drumming the table. "But I tinker with engines when I get actual downtime. I've got a classic car back in Monaco that I've been restoring."

"So you don't get tired of cars and engines?" I ask. "I mean, that's literally your job and also your hobby?"

He gives me an incredulous look, like I've just asked if water is wet or if the sky is blue. "Never. It's pretty much my entire life." The passion in his voice is almost tangible, like I could reach out and touch it. "What about music for you? Do you ever get tired of it?"

"Touché," I concede, smiling. "I guess we both found our thing young and never let go."

"Exactly," he says, and for a moment, we're just looking at

each other across the table, a flash of real understanding passing between us.

I'm the first to break eye contact. "We should probably take a picture," I say, pulling out my phone. "That's the whole point of this, right? Getting seen together? Building the narrative?"

"Right," he agrees, sliding his chair smoothly around to my side of the table without hesitation. "The business arrangement."

He moves in close, his arm coming around my shoulders. The casual touch shouldn't affect me—it's just part of the act, just performance, but I'm suddenly aware of everything. How warm he is, and how solid his arm feels around me.

I snap the photo, capturing us both mid-smile, the morning sun streaming through the window behind us creating a halo effect. When I check the result, I'm startled by how natural we look together, like an actual real couple enjoying a casual coffee date, not two people with an agenda and a contract.

"Perfect," I say, more to myself than to him. "This should definitely get people talking."

"Mission accomplished," he says, moving back to his side of the table.

For the next hour, we talk easily, jumping from topic to topic. He tells me about racing. I share stories about trying to get my music noticed, the frustrating generic rejection emails from record labels. He describes life constantly on the road, and I talk about my writing process and where songs come from. There's an easy rhythm to our conversation that I wasn't expecting.

Occasionally, I notice people glancing our way, whispering behind their hands. It's strange being on display like this, being watched, but I remind myself firmly that's the whole point. This is what we're here for, after all. To look like a couple. To be seen.

"I think our debut is going pretty well," Jack says after a while, his voice low enough that only I can hear him. "Several people have taken photos, and those young women in the corner keep looking over here."

I glance in their direction as subtly as possible, trying not to be obvious about it. Sure enough, a group of what looks like college-aged girls are huddled together, phones occasionally lifting in our general direction. One of them waves enthusiastically when she catches Jack's eye, and he smiles back politely, making the entire table erupt into whispered exclamations and excited squealing.

"You never get tired of that, do you?" I ask, watching the effect his simple acknowledgment has on them. Their entire day probably just got made.

He shrugs, taking a final sip of his espresso. "It's a mixed bag, honestly. The enthusiasm is flattering, sure, but sometimes I can't even stop for gas without someone asking for a selfie."

"Must be strange, being recognized everywhere."

"You get used to it," he says, setting his cup down. "Besides, isn't that what you're signing up for? With the music career, this whole arrangement? Fame, recognition, all of it?"

"I guess," I say, considering it. "Though I'd like to be known for my actual music, not primarily for who I'm dating."

"The way the industry works now, sometimes you need the second thing to get people to notice the first," he says. "But once they're actually listening, your talent will keep them around."

"I hope you're right." The words slip out before I can stop them.

He glances back at me. "I am. If someone like me, who's fucked up as many times as I have, can make it to Formula One, you can definitely become a successful musician. You've always had that thing."

"What thing?"

"That spark. That drive. Even back in high school, you had this intensity about you." He shrugs. "Like you were meant for something bigger than Dark River."

I blink at him, surprised he noticed anything about me back then when we barely crossed paths.

A loud burst of laughter from the teenagers' table draws our attention again.

"We should probably get going," Jack says, checking his watch. "Leave them wanting more, right?"

I nod, mentally batting away the warmth that bloomed at his words.

We stand, and Jack moves toward the door ahead of me. When we reach it, he holds it open, gesturing for me to go first. As I pass him, he places his hand lightly at the small of my back, guiding me through. It's brief but I feel it like a current through my whole body.

Outside, the afternoon sun hits us hard after the air-conditioned comfort of the coffee shop. Jack walks beside me toward my car, his hand dropping back to his side.

"First fake date successfully completed," he says, stopping when we reach my car. "Not bad for a pair of complete amateurs."

"Speak for yourself," I say, fishing my keys from my purse. "I was extremely convincing. Oscar-worthy."

"You were," he agrees, leaning casually against my car. "Though next time, maybe try to look a little more besotted."

"I'll work on my adoring gazes," I promise dryly. "Should I practice in the mirror? Take a class?"

"If it helps," he says, that signature smirk appearing. "Though I find it works best to think of something that actually makes you happy."

"I'll think about my last Spotify royalty check," I deadpan. "I think it was six dollars and eleven cents."

He laughs. "Whatever works. Just sell it like you mean it."

"I should go," I say, motioning toward my car door.

"I'll text you about Seattle," he says. "It's this weekend. Black tie, very fancy, lots of photographers. Think you can handle it?"

"I think I can manage to look like I belong on your arm for one night," I reply, sliding into the driver's seat.

"I know you can," he says.

As I drive away, I check my rearview mirror to see him still standing in the parking lot, watching me go. This is just business, I remind myself firmly, gripping the steering wheel tighter than necessary. Instagram followers and record deals. That's all this is. That's all it can be.

CHAPTER 7

Jack

My motorcycle's engine echoes off the buildings as I pull into the parking lot of Midnight Gym at 7 AM sharp. I can smell salt from the Sound mixing with the trees that border the lot. I cut the engine and swing my leg over the bike, the leather seat still cool from the ride, and grab my gym bag from the storage compartment.

I scan the parking lot, and as much as I'm pretending I'm just taking in my surroundings, I know exactly who I'm looking for. Lark. I've been doing this all week, looking for her everywhere I go. We've been fake dating for almost two weeks now and have gone on a handful of coffee dates, but I'm starting to look forward to seeing her in a way that has nothing to do with the arrangement. Which is really fucking inconvenient.

The morning crowd is already going strong inside—mostly professionals getting their workouts in before heading to office jobs. The woman at the front desk, Sarah something, waves me through with a friendly smile.

The gym really does look good. Dom's done an absolutely

amazing job with the place since taking over after Dad died. What used to be Dad's basic boxing gym is now state-of-the-art —high ceilings, exposed brick, some of Dad's old boxing posters still up, but everything else is upgraded. Top equipment, new flooring, even a physical therapy suite in the back.

I head straight for Dad's old office, now Dom's domain. His door is open and he's sitting at the desk, three computer monitors glowing in front of him, wearing that hyper-focused expression he gets when he's deep in work mode. Always the workaholic, even at seven in the damn morning.

"Morning," I call out, leaning casually in the doorway and rapping my knuckles against the frame.

He looks up, startled like I've pulled him out of deep focus, then checks his watch with exaggerated surprise. "You're on time. Again. I'm shocked at this new version of you lately. Who are you and what did you do with my baby brother?"

"Come on now, I've always taken training seriously," I protest. "I wasn't that bad in my younger years. I showed up. Eventually."

"My memory of your teenage years is a bit different," he says, but he's smiling, that rare Dom smile that softens his usually stern features. "Theo's already here. Pretty sure he's set up in the back corner somewhere with the cable machines."

"You gonna join us today?" I ask, though I already know the answer before the words even leave my mouth.

"Nope. I have a shit ton of administrative work today and a boxing class to teach this afternoon." His eyes are already drifting back to his computer screen, a clear dismissal. Dominic Midnight, absolute master of the brief interaction and quick exit.

I roll my eyes and head through the main floor, nodding at a few people I vaguely recognize from high school. Some of them do visible double-takes when they register who I am. I'm not usually here this early in the morning, and definitely not with this level of consistency.

The past week I've been almost religious about my training schedule, showing up on time, completing every workout Hans sends me. My trainer is both proud and deeply shocked by this development.

Theo's at the cable machine doing lat pulldowns when I find him. His form is perfect, the weights moving smoothly up and down.

"Look who's showing up to morning sessions consistently," he says without breaking his rhythm or even looking at me. "Miracles *do* happen."

"Very funny," I say. "You should tell Dom that one, I think you two are working from the same joke book." I drop my bag against the wall and begin some basic warm-up exercises.

Theo smiles, finishing his set with one final controlled pull. "Dom already give you shit about your punctuality?"

"Oh yeah, first thing. He's efficient about everything, including roasting his youngest brother."

"Well, that's Dom for you." Theo releases the bar and stands, rolling his shoulders. "I'm impressed though, I don't think I've ever seen you stick to any kind of routine this well. Not that we see you much over the years with you always traveling, but still. This is new."

"*Jack 2.0*," I say. "Zero crazy parties, all dedicated responsibility and focus. Since my contract depends entirely on proving I'm not a complete liability, perception is everything right now."

I don't mention that in addition to steady consistent workouts, my fake girlfriend is also helping significantly with this whole perception problem.

"So what sadistic torture did Hans send you today?" Theo grunts, moving to adjust the weight on his machine, adding another heavy plate.

"A mix of HIIT cardio and heavy strength training."

Hans is in Italy but he's checking in constantly. We're tight, been working together since I started in Formula One, but I hate him depending on what workout he sends. Which just makes him send harder ones the next day when I complain.

My phone buzzes loudly in my pocket. I glance at it while continuing to roll my shoulders out, working through the tightness.

Lark: *For the event this weekend I'm planning to drive myself up to Seattle, just a heads up. I can get off early at the bar, but I'll still be running a bit late, so I think it makes more sense for me to just meet you there.*

Me: *Yeah no problem at all. But I can definitely wait for you if you want, I don't mind hanging around.*

Lark: *No it's better this way, I'm guessing you like driving your motorcycle at death-defying speeds.* 😈 *Plus I'd prefer to arrive without looking like I stuck my entire head out of a tornado. Think of what my hair and makeup would look like.*

I almost type that I think she'd look pretty fucking good no matter how messy her hair was, but I think better of it and catch myself. Wrong message to send for a fake relationship. Instead I say:

Me: *Well if you change your mind, I'm always happy to take you. I promise to follow all posted speed limits.* 😇

Lark: *Sure you will. And I'm secretly Dolly Parton.*

I smile down at my phone, then realize Theo's watching me with a knowing look on his face.

"I assume that's Lark?" he asks, setting down his water bottle.

"Uh, yeah, we're going to a thing in Seattle." I tuck my phone away quickly, suddenly very interested in adjusting the weight plates on the nearby bench press. "One of Robert's fancy events."

"So you're really doing this?" he asks, his tone careful.

"Dating Lark. I mean I know it's only been a few dates, but like I said the other day, you're playing with fire here, Jack."

Theo, if only you knew the truth. "Relax, I actually really like Lark," I say, which isn't technically a lie. She's great—funny, talented, smart, no bullshit. "I wouldn't date her if I thought it was going to crash and burn spectacularly."

Nice, another strategic half-truth. Man, this whole fake dating thing isn't nearly as difficult as I thought it would be.

"Good. I'm glad to hear that." Theo turns to face me fully, giving me his complete attention. His tone is light but there's something more serious underneath it. "I'm not trying to tell you what to do with your life—well, maybe I am a little bit—but I'm just watching out for both of you. Lark's great, really great, and I don't want to see either of you get hurt. And I definitely don't want to see you create another complicated mess."

"Listen, we're taking things slow," I say, loading heavy plates onto the barbell for squats. "Getting to know each other properly. It's not like my usual thing at all."

"That's exactly what worries me. You don't do slow, Jack. You don't do relationships that last. You do three weeks of intense fun and then you're gone, off to the next thing."

"That was before." I position myself carefully under the bar, feeling the familiar heavy weight settle across my shoulders and upper back. The tension in my traps is a welcome distraction from this increasingly uncomfortable conversation. "I'm twenty-six now, not twenty-one anymore. Things change. People mature."

"Do they though?" He's smiling slightly as he watches my form with a critical eye. "Because from where I'm standing, you're still fundamentally the same Jack who went through all the women in Dark River before you even turned twenty."

"Now come on, that's a gross exaggeration," I counter. "I never dated Lucy Hardwick."

"Why do I even try with you?" Theo looks up toward the ceiling like he's seeking divine intervention. "You're impossible."

I laugh. "You worry *waaaay* too much, Theo. You've gotta learn to relax a little."

"Impossible with you as my brother."

I move into my next set of squats, really focusing on keeping my core tight and my back perfectly straight. Theo's watching my form with that critical coaching eye, but he doesn't offer any corrections or adjustments, which means I'm executing it correctly.

My phone buzzes again from where I've set it on the nearby bench. I finish my entire set before checking it, not wanting to break my focus.

Lark: *OMG the label just emailed! They said the Instagram post you did a few days ago has them "very excited about trajectory and growth potential." Their exact words not mine* 😂

Me: *Hell yeah! That's amazing! Damn we might actually pull this whole thing off.*

Lark: *Scary thought. But eeek!*

I smile, feeling unexpectedly pleased for her. Lark's a great person and she absolutely deserves this break, this opportunity. She's working her ass off for this dream, and it's about time someone noticed. I'd spent an entire evening earlier this week listening to nearly all her music on Spotify while doing recovery stretches, and she's crazy talented. It's insane that the label hasn't scooped her up already.

"You're grinning at your phone again," Theo observes, adjusting the weight on the cable machine for his next exercise.

"Shut up," I respond automatically with an eye roll, tucking my phone away and refocusing on the workout in front of me.

"Jack Midnight?" A female voice suddenly interrupts our banter.

I turn to see a woman in her mid-twenties, blonde hair pulled back in a high, tight ponytail, wearing perfectly color-coordinated workout gear. She's giving me a very thorough once-over, her smile widening considerably as our eyes meet.

She's attractive. Objectively. The kind of girl I would've definitely talked to a few months ago.

"Oh my god, I thought it was you but I couldn't believe it," she says, twisting a strand of hair around her finger in what's probably supposed to be a flirtatious gesture. "I'm a huge Formula One fan. Like obsessed."

Great. I try to be nice to fans because without them I wouldn't have a career, but being approached while mid-workout isn't exactly ideal timing. Though I'll admit it's still significantly better than that time in an airport bathroom in Germany when some guy asked for an autograph while I was standing at the urinal. That was a new low.

"Thanks, I really appreciate that," I say.

"I just can't believe you're here. I'd heard rumors you were originally from Dark River, but I thought you'd be in Europe right now. I'm Melissa, by the way." Her hand reaches out and touches my arm briefly, the contact very deliberate.

"Nice to meet you, Melissa. Yeah, I'm just here for the summer break. Hopefully I'll be back in Europe competing full-time soon." I take a small but noticeable step backward, creating some physical distance between us.

Her smile falters momentarily at my retreat, but she quickly perks back up. "Well, I was gonna grab a coffee after this workout. Maybe you'd want to join me? I'd absolutely love to hear about what it's like on the circuit, racing at those speeds."

"Thanks for the offer, but I'm in the middle of a training session with my brother." I nod toward Theo, who's watching this entire exchange with barely concealed amusement dancing in his eyes. "And I've got plans later today with my girlfriend."

The old Jack would've said yes. Easy.

"Oh." Her face falls. "Girlfriend. That's… nice for you. Well, if things ever change...' She trails off before walking away, throwing one last hopeful glance over her shoulder.

I turn back to find Theo staring at me, his expression somewhere between shocked and reluctantly impressed.

"Wow, you really are a changed man," he says slowly, crossing his arms over his chest. "No flirting at all. Not even a little bit. The old Jack would have had her number in thirty seconds flat and probably already had plans for drinks."

"You think that lowly of me that I'd cheat on Lark?" I say, a bit offended. Sure, I've had my considerable share of casual relationships over the years, but I've never cheated on anyone. Not once. "Come on, Theo. I'm not that big of an asshole."

"Debatable," Theo says, laughing as he easily dodges the towel I throw directly at his head.

Before I can form a proper comeback, my phone rings loudly. Robert's name flashes on the screen, and my stomach immediately does an unpleasant flip. "I need to take this," I tell Theo quickly.

"Of course you do." He waves me off dismissively, already turning back to his workout routine.

I grab my water bottle and head for the exit, pushing through the door into the parking lot. The morning sun hits my face with warmth as I find a quiet corner away from the steady stream of gym-goers coming and going.

"Robert," I answer. "Good morning."

"Jack." His voice has that particular tone that means serious business. "I saw the latest Instagram post. You and the girl at some coffee shop."

"Lark," I correct immediately, a flicker of annoyance rising sharply at his dismissive tone. "Her name is Lark."

"Right, Lark. The musician." He actually sounds pleased. "Good to see you out in public with someone stable instead of at some party. She looks like she has a clean image, real career goals. This is exactly the kind of thing we need. Keep it up."

Robert Callahan was born into serious money and built it into an empire through shrewd investments, but his true passion has always been motorsports. He tried racing professionally in his twenties but didn't have the reflexes or instincts for it. So he pours all that competitive drive into developing young talent instead. Thank god he found me karting when I was twelve. My family never could have afforded to support a racing career without him.

"We're coming to the event," I tell him, pacing along the edge of the parking lot. "Already confirmed with your assistant."

"Excellent. Make sure she's prepared. This isn't some casual small-town gathering. I know she's just a local girl, but there'll be serious media, major sponsors. You'll need to coach her on how to handle herself."

I bristle immediately. My jaw tightens. "She *knows* how to handle herself. Lark's not some kid who needs coaching."

"Jack, I'm sure she's lovely, but this is a different world than what she's used to. These aren't Dark River people. Make sure she understands—"

"She'll be fine," I cut him off, irritated now. The assumption that she needs training like some kind of show pony pisses me off more than it should.

"Good," he says. "Because I've been working hard to smooth things over after Monaco. This relationship is exactly the narrative change we needed. Stable, mature, committed."

The irony of calling our fake relationship "stable" almost makes me laugh. If only Robert knew this whole thing was cooked up over beers at The Black Lantern by two people who barely knew each other.

"Jack." His tone shifts noticeably, becoming more paternal. It's the voice he's used since I was twelve years old and he first decided to sponsor my racing career, to invest in my future. "I'm proud of you. You're finally taking things seriously. Making smart, mature choices for once."

The guilt twists sharply in my gut like a knife. Robert's been there through absolutely everything—my parents' deaths, the Barcelona crash, every scandal and every success. Lying directly to him feels somehow worse than lying to my brothers. My brothers would eventually get it. They might be pissed, but they'd forgive me. But Robert's forgiveness has always come with conditions, with expectations attached.

"Thanks," I say, my throat suddenly tight and uncomfortable.

"This girl, she's good for you. I can see it already in just these few weeks. You're focused, training properly, staying out of trouble and bad headlines. Don't screw this up, Jack."

"I won't." Another lie, since the whole plan is to eventually stage a "breakup" when I head back to Europe for the season. But that's a problem for my future self to deal with.

"Good. See you and Lark Saturday evening."

I stand there for a long moment, looking down at my phone, the morning sun warming my skin despite the distinct chill settling into my thoughts. Great. More pressure to sell this relationship convincingly. But then again, isn't that exactly what we wanted? For everyone to believe it? The fact that it's working so well should be a good thing, a positive development.

I shove my phone back in my pocket, looking out at the parking lot. The problem is I'm starting to look forward to our fake dates a little too much, and it's beginning to feel like I'm digging myself into a hole I might not be able to climb out of.

CHAPTER 8

Lark

The Callahan Spirits headquarters is in Bellevue, tucked into one of those polished neighborhoods where even the trees look expensive and intentional. It's a modern glass building that somehow manages to be thirty floors tall without being obnoxious about it, all clean lines and subtle logos etched into the glass. Very understated wealth.

I arrive at the designated entrance, where a small fleet of luxury cars is queued up at the valet station. Men in crisp black uniforms efficiently whisk away Bentleys and Mercedes like they're handling ordinary sedans. I hesitate for a moment, suddenly very aware of my Honda with its duct-taped side mirror sitting in this line of vehicles that probably cost more than my entire apartment building.

Should I have arranged for a rideshare instead? Too late now. I'm committed.

As I pull up to the valet stand, a young man in a perfectly tailored uniform opens my door with the same courteous professional smile he probably gave to the Maserati that just pulled away ahead of me.

"Welcome to Callahan Spirits, miss," he says smoothly, handing me a ticket. "The event is on the top floor. The elevators are just inside and to your left."

"Thank you," I reply, trying desperately to act like I do this every single day. I watch as he slides into the driver's seat and carefully drives my car away, probably to some hidden corner of the garage reserved for vehicles that don't quite qualify as luxury.

I smooth down my dress with slightly damp palms. It's black, floor-length with a slit up the left side that shows leg when I walk. The neckline dips low enough to show off some cleavage, which was the whole point when I bought it last year, and the fabric is some kind of silky material that moves well.

But I'm about to walk into a room full of people who probably think Prada is casual Friday wear. At least I splurged on the good mascara tonight, my eyeliner cooperated, and the red lipstick I'm wearing makes me feel like I can fake confidence for an evening.

Okay. Deep breaths. This is fine. *You're fine. Everything is fine.*

Though I'll admit the fake dating performances we've been doing over the past two weeks at the coffee shop and around Dark River have felt a hell of a lot easier than this mega-fancy corporate event in Seattle with actual stakes. Two hours, I tell myself firmly. Make it through two hours of smiling and small talk and then find a polite excuse to leave. Jack can't possibly expect me to stay this entire night.

I follow the discreet signage through the gleaming lobby to a private elevator bank, where a woman with an iPad is checking guests against a list. She's wearing a professional headset and her posture screams efficiency and organization.

When I give my name, her expression brightens immediately. "Ms. Reyes, welcome. Mr. Midnight mentioned you'd be arriving separately. Please, this way."

I'm escorted into an elevator that looks more luxurious than most hotel rooms I've stayed in—polished brass accents catching the light, a backlit panel of what appears to be actual marble.

I pull out my phone as the elevator glides upward.

Me: *I'm here, in the elevator, heading up.*

Jack: *Great, making my way to you now.*

Thank god. The idea of walking into this event without Jack as a buffer, having to navigate this world alone, isn't remotely my idea of a good time. I check my reflection one more time in those flattering mirrors. I'd straightened my hair so it falls sleek down my back, but I spot a slightly wavy strand that I'd missed. Great. No help for that now.

The elevator opens directly into a stunning atrium that makes me forget to breathe for a second. The ceiling soars at least twenty feet high, glass and polished steel, with the evening sky visible. The space is already filled with people in formal wear—women in elegant dresses and men in fancy suits. Waitstaff in crisp black and white circulate smoothly with silver trays of champagne flutes and delicate hors d'oeuvres that look more like tiny art installations than actual food.

On one side of the massive room, a gleaming Formula One race car is displayed on a slowly rotating platform, dramatic lighting highlighting every aggressive curve of its aerodynamic design. The car looks like it's ready to launch off the platform at any second.

Nearby, an impressive motorcycle sits on its own illuminated display, chrome and leather, and a third platform showcases what looks like maybe a rally car covered in sponsor decals, all three vehicles bearing the Callahan Spirits logo prominently. A small crowd is gathered around them, taking photos and pointing at various features, their animated conversation carrying across the space.

I hover uncertainly near the elevator, trying to look like I'm intentionally standing alone rather than completely out of my depth. These people look like they stepped directly out of a Vogue editorial, with perfect hair and casual wealth and confidence. I can practically smell the old money in the room, mixing with expensive perfume and privilege and power.

I feel suddenly, acutely out of place. This isn't just stepping into a different social circle; it's stepping onto an entirely different planet. These people live in a completely different universe than I do, with different rules and expectations and—

Then I see him.

Jack is making his way through the crowd, navigating the sea of designer wear with the ease of someone who absolutely belongs here. His eyes lock with mine, his whole face lights up.

He looks absolutely incredible in a perfectly tailored charcoal suit that fits him like it was made specifically for his body. Because it probably was. No tie, just an open collar that somehow makes the formal outfit look effortlessly cool rather than underdressed. More than a few heads turn as he passes by.

I'm suddenly aware of exactly how many people are watching him, and by extension will be watching me. The girlfriend. The small-town bartender playing dress-up in the big city. What was I thinking agreeing to this?

But as Jack approaches, his smile widening with what looks like genuine pleasure at seeing me, some of that anxiety starts to recede like a tide going out. There's something reassuring about having him as an anchor in this sea of strangers and wealth.

"Hey," he says when he reaches me, immediately leaning in to kiss my cheek. His lips are warm against my skin, and his cologne—expensive and woodsy with hints of citrus—is making my head spin. Then he stays close, his mouth near my ear. "You look incredible."

The way he says it, low and rough, sends heat straight through me.

"Thanks." I fidget with my clutch, trying to ignore how my whole body just lit up from his proximity. Damn, he looks good in that suit. *Like, make-me-want-to-do-stupid-things good.* "You clean up pretty well yourself."

"This old thing?" he jokes, just as he had on our date at the coffee shop, running a hand along the sleeve of his suit with a grin. "Had it lying around in my closet."

"I'm sure you did," I reply dryly, grateful for his attempt to ease my nerves even while I'm fighting the urge to run my hands over his chest. "So this is your world, huh?"

Jack laughs, his hand settling on the small of my back. "Well this is the sponsor side of things. The corporate side is a whole different game. Wait till you see an actual race day. Energy drinks instead of champagne, deafening engines, less pretension."

"I'll stick with the champagne tonight," I say.

"Ready to mingle? Robert's been asking where you are."

I take his offered arm, the hard muscle under the suit not helping my situation. "As ready as I'll ever be. Who exactly is here tonight? I need to mentally prepare for the types of conversations I'm about to fake my way through."

"A mix of people," he begins guiding me further into the room, his hand warm against my arm. "Racing industry people, Callahan executives, local Seattle business elite, some media. The usual corporate event crowd."

"Just follow my lead," he continues. "And remember, you belong here as much as anyone else in this room."

I give him a skeptical look. "I'm pretty sure that's false. My car is literally held together with duct tape, Jack."

"You're my girlfriend," he says, lowering his voice. "That means you have a place here." He squeezes my arm. "Besides, half these people are pretending to belong too. That's the secret, everyone's faking it to some degree."

"Well, at least I'm in good company for faking things," I murmur, and he laughs, drawing glances our way. I shouldn't enjoy making him laugh this much. It's becoming a problem.

A waiter passes and Jack smoothly snags two champagne flutes, handing me one. "Anyway, brace yourself. Robert will want to meet you, and he's..."

"What?" I take a larger sip than appropriate. "Scary? Judgmental? A vampire who feeds on unsuccessful souls?"

"Direct," Jack says, mouth twitching. "He doesn't waste words. Just remember he's been intimidating people since before we were born. It's his hobby. Possibly his superpower."

"So reassuring." I take another fortifying sip, the bubbles tickling my nose.

We stop to chat with several people, a racing team manager who asks detailed technical questions, a sleek marketing executive who compliments my dress, a journalist Jack seems to know well who asks a few questions about our relationship.

"Jack! There you are." A silver-haired man in an impeccable navy suit appears in front of us suddenly, cocktail in hand. His posture screams authority and power, shoulders back, chin up, and his eyes, sharp and assessing, immediately move from Jack to me with the focus of someone who misses nothing. "And this must be Lark."

I straighten instinctively under his scrutiny, my spine going rigid. This must be Robert Callahan himself, the man who's been sponsoring Jack since he was a child.

Jack's hand presses slightly firmer against my back, a silent reassurance that grounds me. "Robert, this is Lark Reyes. Lark, Robert Callahan."

I extend my hand, pleased to find it steady. "It's a pleasure to meet you, Mr. Callahan. This is quite an impressive event."

Robert's handshake is firm, the handshake of someone with absolutely nothing to prove because everyone already knows his power. "The pleasure is mine, Ms. Reyes. So, Jack mentioned you're a musician?"

"I am," I say, meeting his gaze directly and refusing to look away first.

"Interesting." He sips his drink, studying me. "Difficult industry. Competitive."

"So is racing," I counter, and his mouth twitches. Almost a smile.

"What kind of music?" he asks.

"Singer-songwriter, mostly indie pop with some acoustic influences. I've been building a following online over the past year. Streaming platforms mainly."

"She's got real talent," Jack says, and the real pride in his voice catches me off guard. "Great melodies, smart lyrics. You know, that song of yours, 'Autumn Echoes,' should be getting way more attention than it does." He gives me a gentle nudge with his elbow.

I blink at him. He listened to "Autumn Echoes"? Something warm spreads through my chest. It's one of my favorite songs I've ever written. Deeply personal, but barely anyone listens to it. It's nowhere near my most popular tracks. He must have actually dug through everything, not just skimmed the top songs like I assumed he would for our fake dating backstory.

Robert nods slowly, his expression giving away absolutely nothing. "Music industry's a tough one. Unforgiving. What's your distribution strategy?" He asks the question like a businessman evaluating a prospective investment, with cold calculation.

"Currently on all the major streaming platforms," I answer, slightly thrown by the business angle but trying to keep up. "But I'm also in talks with Tidal Records right now."

"Tidal, yes I know of them," he says with a brief nod, almost to himself like he's filing the information away. "Medium-sized outfit, but they do have some decent artists on their roster." He says it like he's weighing his assessment internally, as if he's running complex calculations in his head about my potential ROI.

Before I can determine if he approves of this potential business decision or thinks I'm making a mistake, his sharp gaze shifts to Jack.

"Jack, Alessandro Vitale from Ferrari is here," Robert says, his tone all business. "He oversees partner strategy and factory backing. He asked to speak with you specifically. If you're serious about getting that seat back, he's someone you want on your side."

"Of course," Jack says smoothly, his voice taking on a more professional tone. "I'll make sure to find him."

"Good. And make sure you see Lucía Álvarez from Santander before she leaves." Robert's already scanning the room, predatory eyes searching for his next target. Then he glances back at me. "Pleasure meeting you, Ms. Reyes. If you've got even half this one's natural talent," he gestures to Jack with his cocktail, "you'll go far. Hopefully with less of the attitude problem."

"She has twice my talent, not half," Jack says quickly. "And I've been nothing but a perfect gentleman tonight."

"Yes, for all of twenty minutes," Robert says dryly, checking his watch. "Let's see if you can maintain it." And with that, he's gone, moving through the crowd like a shark through water.

I exhale hard, taking a substantial gulp of champagne. "That was…"

"Robert," Jack finishes, amused. "He doesn't waste words."

"Is he always that terrifying? I feel like I just got interrogated by the FBI."

"Pretty much. But he liked you. I could tell."

"How?" I turn to stare at him. "His face didn't move once. He has less expression than a marble statue."

"He asked follow-up questions about your music," Jack

explains. "Trust me, that's a very good sign with Robert. If he wasn't interested, the conversation would have been ten seconds max."

Jack guides me deeper into the party, his hand a constant presence at my back. He introduces me to a blur of executives, racing team members, and business associates. Everyone seems to know him, respect him, want a piece of his time and attention.

The next hour passes in a blur of conversations and Cristal. I talk to a Ferrari engineer about aerodynamics I don't fully understand, a Callahan executive who asks surprisingly smart questions about streaming algorithms, and a food blogger who wants restaurant recommendations in Dark River. The champagne flows freely, and Jack keeps me close, his hand finding my back or arm whenever we move between groups. Each touch sends little sparks through me that I'm trying very hard to ignore.

At one point, we pause near the display vehicles, and I take a moment to really look at them up close. They're absolutely stunning, with sleek, aggressive curves and gleaming surfaces that seem designed purely for speed and nothing else.

"Is this one of the cars you've actually driven in races?" I ask, admiring the Formula One machine in front of us.

"No, this is just a show car for events like this," he explains, his eyes lighting up. "The real race cars are all back in the factory in Maranello. But it's built to look exactly the same, same paint scheme, same sponsor decals."

"It's still incredibly impressive," I say, reaching out to touch the carbon fiber body before pulling my hand back. "Am I allowed to touch it?"

"Go ahead," he encourages. "It's here for people to see."

I run my fingers lightly over the smooth surface. "It feels expensive."

"There's a ton of work that goes into building them," he says, gesturing towards different parts of the car. "The teams start designing each car over a year before it even hits the track. We test everything extensively in wind tunnels and computer simulations, constantly tweaking tiny details, trying to find even a fraction of a second advantage over the competition."

"You really miss it, don't you?" I ask, noticing how his entire demeanor changes when he talks about racing. How alive he becomes.

"Yeah," he admits, looking at the gleaming car with unmistakable longing in his eyes. "Racing's always been the one thing that made complete sense to me. Everything else gets complicated, but racing is pure. I think I go a bit stir-crazy without it."

"I can imagine," I say softly. "I get the same way about music sometimes. When I go too long without playing or writing, I feel like I'm missing a fundamental part of myself. Like a limb."

"Exactly," Jack says.

A photographer approaches, interrupting our moment. "Jack, could we get a few shots of you with the vehicles for the press package? Your girlfriend too, of course."

"Sure," Jack says easily, his public persona sliding back into place. "Lark, you up for a few photos?"

"Lead the way," I smile, slipping back into our roles.

The photographer positions us carefully by the vehicle, Jack standing slightly behind me with his arm around my waist. I try to look natural and comfortable, like I'm used to being photographed at fancy corporate events with my race car driver boyfriend.

"Beautiful," the photographer says, snapping several shots. "Very natural together."

The party continues into the evening, and I'm surprised I'm enjoying myself. Most of the Callahan whiskey crew and racing sponsors are passionate about their work. Their enthusiasm is infectious—I'm drawn into conversations about engine designs and whisky aging that I never thought could be interesting. By the time Jack suggests leaving, I'm not as eager to escape as expected.

In the elevator, Jack shrugs out of his suit jacket with relief, draping it over his arm and rolling up his sleeves. I watch his forearms as he works the cuffs, then force myself to look away.

"You were amazing tonight," he says, leaning against the mirrored wall.

"Years of bartending—I can talk to anyone about anything," I reply, adjusting my dress strap that's been digging in all night. "Honestly, it was more interesting than expected. You might turn me into an F1 fan."

His eyes light up, a smile spreading across his face. "Perfect. Secret mission accomplished. By next race, you'll be debating tire strategy."

"Let's not get carried away," I laugh, bumping his shoulder. "I have approximately a million things to learn first."

The elevator doors open, and we step out into the marble-floored lobby. We head toward the valet stand, where Jack gives them both our tickets. While we wait I take in the Seattle skyline visible across Lake Washington, lit up against the darkening sky like a postcard. I'm so rarely away from Dark River apart from some concerts in Seattle over the years, but it's fun to be somewhere different, somewhere alive with energy and possibility.

Jack glances at me. His eyes scan our surroundings briefly to make sure no one's in earshot before continuing quietly. "Thanks for coming tonight. I think this whole thing is going to work out great for both of us."

I smile, leaning against one of the decorative marble pillars. "I think so, too."

The valet pulls up with my Honda, and Jack walks me to the driver's side, his eyes immediately going to the duct tape holding my side mirror together.

"Okay, you absolutely have to let me fix this for you," he says, tapping the mirror gently with one finger. "This is offensive to cars everywhere."

"Hey, it's been holding up just fine with my expert tape job," I say defensively, unlocking the door. "Though I'm never one to turn down a free service, so if you're offering to put those mechanic skills to actual use, feel free to take a crack at it."

Jack smiles, shaking his head slightly. "I'll stop by your apartment sometime this week. Just text me when you're free and I'll bring my tools. It'll take twenty minutes, tops."

"Sounds good," I laugh, opening the door. "Goodnight, Jack."

"Goodnight, Lark," he replies.

As I drive home through the quiet streets, the lights of Seattle twinkling in my rearview mirror, I find myself smiling. The night was absolutely nothing like I expected. Less awkward, more enjoyable, and Jack… well, Jack was surprisingly good company.

Maybe this fake relationship won't be as complicated as I thought. Maybe it will even be fun.

CHAPTER 9

Jack

Pacific Raceways outside Seattle is already busy with activity when I arrive at seven in the morning. Ferrari has the track booked for the entire day to test their 488 Challenge Evo cars that they use for their high-end Corse Clienti program.

There's a full crew here, engineers with laptops, mechanics with tool carts, data guys hovering over screens, plus someone from marketing with an expensive camera who keeps asking me to "look contemplative" while staring at tires. The morning air smells like racing—rubber, fuel, hot metal. The smell that means I'm home. Everything else fades to background noise.

Giovanni, the Ferrari tech they sent along for this test, is already plugging his laptop into the car's diagnostic systems when I arrive. He's one of those guys who loves data and gets visibly excited about tire temperature variations.

"Morning, Jack," Giovanni says without looking up from his screen. "We'll start with the baseline setup, then make incremental adjustments based on your feedback. Standard protocol."

"Sounds good," I say, heading toward the garage area to get into my race suit. The familiar pre-drive routine settles over me.

I hear Lark's distinctive Honda engine pulling into the parking area while I'm zipping up my suit. We'd planned this earlier in the week, figured it would be excellent Instagram content to have her at a track day, show the supportive girlfriend angle to the sponsors. But hearing her car approach makes me unexpectedly happy, this warm feeling in my chest that has nothing to do with social media strategy. Like the day just got significantly better.

"Give me five minutes," I tell Giovanni, already walking toward the parking area.

"Take your time," he replies, completely absorbed in his system checks. "I need at least ten minutes to finish the diagnostic calibration anyway."

I head out to the parking area, where Lark's getting out of her car. She's wearing dark jeans that fit her perfectly, a burgundy sweater that makes her skin glow, and her long black hair is pulled back in a ponytail that shows off her neck. Sunglasses pushed up on her head, camera bag over one shoulder, large thermos of coffee in hand.

She looks fucking gorgeous.

"Morning," I say, unable to keep the smile off my face. "You found it okay."

"GPS is a wonderful modern invention," she says, smiling back. "Plus you were right, the track is visible from the highway. Kind of hard to miss."

"Thanks for coming out here," I say, and I mean it more than the casual words suggest. "I know this is probably not the most exciting way to spend a Tuesday morning. Watching cars go in circles."

"Are you kidding? I get to see behind the scenes of your actual job," she says, looking around at all the equipment and people, curiosity lighting up her face. "This is fascinating. Plus, Instagram content." She holds up her phone with a wry smile.

"Right," I say, feeling that strange twinge in my chest again. "The content."

Giovanni waves from the garage bay.

"I should get going," I tell her reluctantly. "There's a covered viewing area up on that hill, or you can hang out in the garage. They're all friendly if you have questions."

"Go do your thing," she says, shooing me away with her free hand. "I'll explore and try not to touch anything expensive."

The first hour is methodical, technical work. Ten careful laps, come in, give detailed feedback to Giovanni about understeer in the low-speed corners. They make minute adjustments to the suspension geometry, I go back out and test again. I love this part of the job—the problem-solving, the collaborative process, the tiny adjustments that make huge differences. This is where racing becomes as much science as instinct, where engineering meets art.

Between my second and third session, I spot Lark chatting animatedly with Lorenzo, the lead engineer. Lorenzo is famously taciturn, barely speaks to anyone, so seeing him engaged in what appears to be an enthusiastic conversation is surprising. He's using his hands to gesture at something on his monitor while Lark nods along, asking questions.

"Your girlfriend's made friends," Giovanni observes, following my gaze with an amused expression.

"She has that effect on people," I say, watching her. She fits anywhere. With anyone.

We run three more intensive sessions over the next two hours, getting the car more dialed in each time. The understeer is completely gone, the balance feels perfect. Between runs, I keep finding myself looking for Lark. She's moved around the facility, talking to different people, taking photos with her camera.

"We're done with the technical runs," Giovanni announces after my final session, closing his laptop with satisfaction. "Really good data today. The team will be pleased with these results."

I pull off my helmet, running a hand through my hair. "Can I take Lark out for a few laps?" I ask, the idea forming as I say it. "Show her what we've been working on all morning?"

Giovanni considers for a moment, glancing over to where Lark is reviewing photos on her camera screen. "Insurance covers it as long as she signs the waiver. Just be reasonable out there."

"Always," I say, already heading toward her with a spare helmet in hand.

"Want to go for a ride?" I ask as I approach. "See what it feels like from inside?"

She looks up from her camera, eyes bright. "In the car? Like, while you're driving it fast?"

"Three laps. I promise I'll be gentle." I grin. "*Mostly* gentle."

"Define gentle," she says suspiciously, but she's already standing, setting her camera carefully aside on a workbench.

"Gently terrifying," I admit.

"Well, when you put it that way," she laughs, taking the helmet from my hands. "Let's do it."

Giovanni appears with a clipboard and Lark scrawls her signature without even reading it. I help her with the helmet, adjusting the straps, my fingers brushing her jaw. Her skin's so soft I have to resist running my thumb across her cheek. I slide into my seat and she's gripping the door handle before I've even started the engine.

"Relax," I tell her, settling in and beginning my pre-drive checks. "I'm very good at this."

"What about Barcelona?" she asks, referencing my crash.

I laugh. "Oh come on, that was in the rain with some idiot

taking me out. Today is a completely clear track with just us. No idiots allowed."

"If you say so," she says, but her grip on the door handle doesn't loosen even slightly. "Just remember if I die here, I'm haunting you forever. And I will be an extremely annoying ghost."

"I'll be sure to keep that in mind," I say, firing up the engine.

I keep the first lap reasonable—fast enough to be exciting, but not so fast that she never wants to get in a car with me again. Through the first real corner her hand shoots out to grab my arm as the g-forces push her hard into the seat.

"Oh my god!" she shouts over the engine noise. "This is insane!"

By the second lap she's relaxed enough to enjoy it, her head turning to watch the track fly by. So on the third lap I really go for it, climbing past 150 miles per hour on the main straight and drifting through the corners with more aggression than Giovanni would probably approve of.

"JACK!" she screams, but she's laughing too, and the sound makes something warm settle in my chest.

When we pull back into the garage, she fumbles with the harness and yanks off her helmet. Her hair is everywhere, her face flushed, eyes bright with adrenaline.

"That was the most terrifying fun thing I've ever experienced!" she says, still breathless.

"So not too scary?" I ask.

"Oh, *incredibly* scary," she admits, trying to fix her hair. "But also... I kind of want to do it again."

"Anytime," I say, and I mean it.

We take photos after that for Instagram—some by the car, some in the cockpit with Lark sitting in the driver's seat. When she suggests including the crew, they crowd in enthusiastically. It's supposed to be for the narrative we're building, but I keep catching myself just watching her interact with everyone, the way she makes people smile without even trying.

"Food?" I ask once we've wrapped up. "There's a good place nearby that does amazing burgers."

"Yes," she says immediately, emphatically. "Adrenaline makes me absolutely starving."

We walk out to the parking area and I gesture toward my bike. "We can take the motorcycle if you want."

She looks at it, then back at me. "I've had enough excitement for one day. Let's take my car."

"Sure," I say, then pause. "Uh, mind if I drive?"

"You just spent four hours driving at ridiculous speeds," she points out, eyebrows raised. "Aren't you sick of it by now?"

"I never get sick of driving," I say. "Plus I'm terrible at being a passenger."

She stops walking and looks at me, a slow smile spreading across her face. "Wait, are you *scared* of being a passenger?"

"Not scared," I say, feeling my face heat slightly. "I just strongly prefer being in control of the car."

She chuckles. "Jack Midnight, who drives two hundred miles per hour for a living, can't handle being a passenger?" She's absolutely delighted by this discovery, eyes sparkling with amusement. "This is amazing. You have a completely normal person fear! You're human!"

"It's not a fear—"

"It's *totally* a fear!" she interrupts, laughing, and I can't help but grin at the sound. She has the best laugh, genuine and unrestrained and infectious.

"Okay fine, it's a fear," I admit. "But when I'm in Formula One, I'm racing with nineteen of the best drivers in the world in cars built with millions of dollars of safety tech. Out on regular roads? Anyone who managed to pass a driving test is out there texting, eating, doing who knows what. So... not being in control is basically my personal nightmare."

"Yeah, yeah, that makes sense." She laughs. "Lucky for you I hate driving anyway, so this works out perfectly."

"Good," I say with relief, catching the keys she tosses me. "Though I can't believe you hate driving."

"It's true!" she says cheerfully as we get in the car. "If I could teleport everywhere, I absolutely would. Lucky for you though, I love being a passenger. So congratulations, you're now officially my chauffeur."

"Happy to be of service, ma'am," I say, adjusting the seat and mirrors while she buckles in.

"Just drive, Jeeves," she says with a grin, and I'm laughing as I start the car.

As I navigate through the winding roads that lead away from the track, Lark fiddles with the radio dial until she finds a station playing something indie-folk that I don't recognize. She hums along quietly, seeming perfectly content and completely relaxed.

"So that's really what you do," she says after a few minutes of comfortable silence. "Day in and day out."

"More or less," I say. "Though Formula One is a whole different level. Way faster, more intense, more technically complex. But this part of the job is fun too. Testing, giving feedback, problem-solving."

"I can't even imagine. What a cool job."

I glance over at her, feeling oddly pleased that she enjoyed it. I'd been showing off for her all morning like I couldn't help myself, wanting her to be impressed, wanting to steal all her attention and keep it. Which is dangerous, a voice in the back of my head warns. This is how people get confused, how fake becomes real, how someone gets hurt.

We pull into the restaurant parking lot and I push those thoughts aside.

The restaurant is one of those elevated gastropubs Seattle

does so well, and we slide into a booth near the back. The waitress brings menus and water with a friendly smile.

"Ooooh, they have mac and cheese with Beecher's cheese!" Lark's eyes widen as she scans the menu. "That's my weakness."

"Get it," I tell her. "Their burger's incredible too, I'm getting that."

"Done," she says, closing her menu. "And I'm stealing bites."

We order, and after the waitress leaves, Lark starts playing with her straw wrapper, folding it into smaller squares. "Can I ask you something?" she says, looking up at me.

"Shoot," I say, leaning back.

"How did you really get into racing?" She looks up. "I mean, you've told me the basic story about going to a track once and falling in love and all that stuff with Robert sponsoring you. But I don't know, I guess I just wanted to hear more."

I consider deflecting with the usual polished lines I give reporters and sponsors. But something about Lark makes me want to give her the real answer. Maybe it's because she's shared her own shit with Brandon, her own struggles. Or maybe it's just *her*.

"I was a pretty angry kid," I start, staring at my water glass. "Had serious issues. My brothers were all adopted younger, but I was six when I arrived at the Midnights and just furious at the world. Not at them specifically, though I took it out on them plenty. My birth family was..." I trail off. "They weren't good people. Drugs, neglect, some physical abuse. The state finally stepped in."

She nods, her expression softening, but not with pity.

"So even with my adoptive parents being incredibly patient—my mom Susan especially tried so hard with me—I was a terror." My throat tightens thinking about her. She never gave up on me, even when I gave her every reason to. "When I saw that first karting race, I fell in love immediately. Then behind the wheel, it was like something I could finally control. When everything felt chaotic, in a car it's just me and the machine."

Lark nods. "Having that one space where you're completely in charge. Where skill matters, not your history."

"Exactly. Plus it gave me somewhere productive for all that energy. Kept me from worse trouble. My parents were saints to put up with me." I take a drink. "The racing became where I put all of it. The anger, the fear, the need to prove I was worth keeping."

Our food arrives, her mac and cheese bubbling golden, my burger looking perfect.

I watch her take a bite of the mac and cheese, closing her eyes briefly in pure appreciation. "So since we're opening up here," I say, "how did you actually get into music? Anything beyond the loved-theater-when-you-were-in-school story?"

She sets down her fork, considering her answer. "My mom taught piano and guitar when I was little. She taught lessons out of our house for years. I was a lonely kid, so music and songwriting just always felt so safe and like my way to connect with people."

"You're definitely good at connecting," I say. "I've been listening to your stuff pretty much non-stop this week."

She rolls her eyes. "Flatterer."

"No," I insist, leaning forward. "Listen, Lark, and hear me. *Really* hear me. You're the real deal. This fake dating thing is helping you get followers, sure, but you would have made it without me. You've got that special thing—talent, magnetism, honesty, and ability. You're the whole package."

She looks down at her food. "Thanks. That means a lot. Most people think it's better as a hobby, apart from Maren and Calvin. They're my cheerleaders."

"I had plenty of people telling me racing was a pipe dream," I say. "Even after Robert started sponsoring me, coaches said hardly anyone makes it to Formula One. That I should focus on NASCAR or IndyCar instead."

"What did you do?" she asks, taking a bite of her mac and cheese.

"Used it as fuel. Every time someone said I couldn't do it, I trained harder. Though it helps when you have someone like Robert who believes in you and writes checks to prove it." I take a bite of my burger.

"Yeah," she says, "money always seems to be the deciding factor." She pushes her mac and cheese around the plate. "Maybe this Tidal thing will work out. Though my mom's still asking when I'm getting a job with benefits. They're good people. Supportive. They just don't think music is realistic."

"My parents had similar concerns. They always wanted to make sure I had a backup plan," I say. "Do you talk to yours much?"

"Yeah, they're in Southern California now. They're from there originally and moved back to help with my mom's parents." She twirls her fork in the mac and cheese. "We Face-Time every Sunday."

"That's nice, to stay close like that."

"They're great, just practical. They worked hard for stability, so me chasing music at twenty-six doesn't compute." She smiles. "Mom cried when I told her about the label interest. Happy tears mixed with relief that maybe it's not just an expensive hobby."

"Makes sense they'd want security for you," I say, dragging another fry through ketchup.

"Yah, I understand it. Especially since my mom's parents came here from Mexico with nothing. Built everything from scratch. So the idea that I'm choosing uncertainty when I could have a steady job?" She shakes her head.

I watch her for a moment, the afternoon light catching her hair. "Can I ask you something?"

"Seems fair since you've been pretty open. Go for it."

"What happened with performing?" I ask. "You said you loved it as a kid, then it all changed?"

She shrugs. "Before Brandon, I loved it. I still had pretty bad nerves, but I could push through. And when we first got together, he *acted* kinda supportive."

"What changed?"

"Started with subtle comments. How I was being 'unrealistic,' needed to 'think about the future.' Then it escalated. My voice was too shaky. My lyrics too personal. My stage presence was awkward."

I clench a fist under the table. How the fuck did Brandon even get Lark? She's so far out of his league it's laughable. And then he spent their entire marriage making her feel small? "Sounds like he was deliberately trying to tear you down."

"Exactly," she says, meeting my eyes. "And the worst part is, it worked. I started second-guessing everything about myself. By the end of our marriage, I'd almost stopped playing music altogether. Just worked at the bar and came home."

"What a complete asshole," I say, not bothering to hide my anger.

She takes a sip of water. "The night I finally decided to leave, we had this massive fight because I'd told him I wanted to record some of my songs professionally. Nothing fancy, just book time at a small studio in Seattle."

"What happened?" I ask, though I have a sinking feeling I know.

"He laughed. Said, 'Lark, be serious. You're a bartender who likes to sing. Let's not pretend it's more than that.'" The hurt's still raw in her voice. "Something broke inside me. I realized I'd spent years with someone who fundamentally didn't believe in me."

"I'm glad you left him," I say, resisting the strong urge to reach across the table and take her hand. No cameras here though, it wouldn't be appropriate for our arrangement. "He was dead fucking wrong about all of it."

"I hope so," she says. "But even now, almost two years later, I still hear his voice sometimes when I'm about to perform. I still feel myself freezing up. I'm mad at myself for letting him get to me still, for letting him have that power over me."

"Emotional shit sticks around," I say. "It just means you're human and he was an effective manipulator."

"I guess," she says, picking up her fork again. "The fake dating thing is helping though, weirdly enough. Seeing my follower count go up, getting that excited email from the label… it's like proof that he was wrong. Though I guess we'll really find out at the open mic in a few days." She fiddles with her fork.

This time I can't fight the impulse and I do reach across and take her hand. She looks up in surprise. "You're going to do great. I mean it. You have real talent, Lark. And if it doesn't go exactly how you want, I'll personally kick anyone's ass who makes you feel like shit about it."

She smiles, studying me for a long moment. "You know, you're not what I expected, Jack."

"Is that good or bad?" I ask.

"Still deciding," she says with a teasing smile. "I'll let you know when I figure it out."

The conversation switches to lighter topics, with her eventually quizzing me on which wild online stories about me were real versus completely fabricated.

"Okay," she says, leaning forward conspiratorially. "The Monaco afterparty incident with the champagne fountain? The one where you supposedly rode a motorcycle through the hotel lobby at three AM?"

"It was a Vespa, not a motorcycle," I say with a grin. "But the champagne fountain? Unfortunately true. Though the damage wasn't nearly as expensive as reported. And I did pay for absolutely everything."

"I knew it!" She points her fork at me triumphantly. "What about the fistfight with that Ferrari driver? The Italian one with the perfect hair?"

"Marcelli? Completely false." I take a sip of water. "We argued loudly after he cut me off in qualifying, but no actual punches were thrown. The media loves a good rivalry though. Makes for way better headlines and clicks."

"Disappointing," she says. "Okay, what about the thing with the married Swedish model and the yacht? The tabloids were all over that one for weeks."

I shake my head emphatically. "Completely fabricated from start to finish. I've never even been to Sweden. Never met the woman in my entire life. I think they just photoshopped two separate pictures together and hoped no one would check."

"Really? Honest?" she says, wiping away a tear from laughing. "But the pictures looked so convincing!"

I place my hand over my heart solemnly. "I swear on my Formula One car, and that's how serious I am about this. It was such a ridiculous rumor. I was in the UK for a race that weekend, then flew straight to Barcelona for testing. My alibi was broadcast on international television with timestamps."

Lark is still laughing. "The stuff they make up about you is absolutely wild. Being your fake girlfriend is very educational," she says, dabbing at her eyes. "I'm learning so much about the jet-setting lifestyle."

"Don't worry, I'll make sure to include you in my next fabricated scandal," I promise. "Maybe we can stage a dramatic public argument in the middle of Pike Place Market for maximum attention."

"Ooh, I could throw a fish at you," she suggests eagerly, her eyes lighting up. "That would definitely make TMZ."

"See? You're a complete natural at this fame thing already."

After lunch I drive us back to the track, though every part of me wants to keep this day going, to stay in this bubble we've created. The parking area is mostly empty now, just a few crew members loading the last of the equipment into trucks.

My motorcycle sits waiting in the late afternoon sun, exactly where I left it. I pull up next to it and we both get out. I pass her keys back and she takes them, leaning against her Honda. Neither of us seems ready to end this. Or maybe that's just wishful thinking on my part.

"Thanks for coming today," I finally say, breaking the silence. "The Instagram stuff obviously, but also just… being there."

"Thanks for the terrifying ride," she says with that smile that crinkles the corners of her eyes. "And lunch. I had a really good time, Jack."

"Thanks for listening," I say, hoping she understands I mean the real stuff, the family history and vulnerability I rarely share with anyone.

She gets in her car and rolls the window down. "I'll text you details about the open mic?"

"I'll be there," I promise without hesitation. "Front row. Cheering embarrassingly loud."

"Good," she says, a flicker of vulnerability crossing her face. "I'll need a friendly face in the crowd."

She starts the car, gives me one last smile, and drives away.

Then I'm alone in the empty lot with my bike and this feeling I don't know what to do with. My dates with Lark are feeling less fake each time, and it's getting harder to convince myself that I'm not falling for her.

Then again, Lark deserves better than me. Someone stable, someone who stays in one place, someone whose relationship history isn't three weeks of fun before moving on to the next thing.

I watch until her Honda disappears around the corner, the sound of the engine fading into the distance.

What the hell have I gotten myself into?

CHAPTER 10

Lark

The Blue Room is already packed when we arrive, and it's only ten o'clock. The venue is a forty minute drive from Dark River and used to be something industrial—a warehouse or maybe a factory—but now it's one of those places where indie bands play and people who think they might be the next big thing test out their material.

The walls are painted black, covered in layers of concert posters and graffiti that's been shellacked over so many times it looks like art. The stage isn't huge, but it's legitimate, with real lighting rigs and a sound system that can handle live music without turning everything into feedback.

I lean against the back wall of the venue, guitar at my feet, trying to keep my breathing steady. My palms are already sweating. I haven't performed live much in the last year—just a few small open mic nights at local spots and the stage fright has been overwhelming. And this venue is ten times the size of those. Tonight feels like jumping off a cliff and hoping the parachute works.

"This place is cool," Jack says, returning from the bar. He passes me my drink, a cucumber-lime mocktail that had looked refreshing, and watches as the current performer works the crowd. "Even better than I expected. I can't believe that after I've moved away, Dark River gets an awesome underground scene nearby."

Jack's surveying the venue with interest. He seems completely at ease in this unfamiliar environment, which I both envy and find reassuring.

"Friday nights here are usually good," I tell him, grateful for the distraction from my impending doom. I take a sip of the drink, the tartness cutting through my anxiety for a moment. "It's a pretty supportive crowd too. Thank *god*, because I need only supportive comments tonight. All compliments, all the time. No criticism allowed within a ten-foot radius of me."

"Deal. In that case, in addition to being endlessly talented, you also look great tonight. Friend to friend, I mean." He raises his bottle in a mini-toast.

I feel a flutter of pleasure warming my chest at his compliment. I'd told him to just come for my set, no point sitting through a whole lineup of other performers. We could grab photos after for Instagram, assuming I didn't completely bomb. But he'd insisted on driving me here and staying the whole time.

Now, I'm grateful for his presence. Maren would've been here if she could—she'd even offered to cut her honeymoon short when I mentioned the show, which was *so* her it made me want to cry. But I'd told her absolutely not and to enjoy her trip. Having Jack here helps more than I expected.

The guy on stage finishes his set to enthusiastic applause. He's followed by a girl with a voice like smoke and honey, the crowd immediately falling silent as she begins. I watch them lean in, completely captivated. She's effortlessly confident, moving across the stage like she owns it, her voice filling every corner of the venue without any apparent strain. My stomach tightens. This is the kind of performer labels want. Polished, professional, completely at ease in front of an audience.

"She's *sooo* good," I say, feeling my confidence shrink with every perfectly delivered verse. "Maybe I should just leave now. Preserve what's left of my dignity."

"There's always going to be other talented people," Jack says, his tone gentle. "Doesn't mean you're not one of them."

Next up is a guy with just an acoustic guitar who covers Johnny Cash, then comes a woman who does spoken word poetry over electronic beats she creates live on some kind of loop machine. It's mesmerizing and weird and the crowd loves it.

With each performer, my anxiety climbs. They're all so good, so unique, so confident. Brandon's voice starts creeping in: *You're not good enough for this to be anything more than a hobby.*

"You're next," the stage manager says, appearing beside me with a clipboard.

My stomach drops, landing somewhere around my shoes. I grab my guitar case, hands shaking now. Jack catches my arm gently and gives it a squeeze.

"Hey," he says. "You belong up there. I know you do."

His voice is so sure that it loosens the knot in my chest. I take a full breath for the first time in an hour and force a small smile. "Thanks," I manage.

"I'll be right here," he promises. "Now go show them what you've got."

The walk to the stage feels both endless and way too short. The stage lights are brighter than expected, turning the audience into a mass of shadows and shapes at first. I can hear them though, conversations continuing, drinks being ordered, that low hum of a crowd that's not quite paying attention yet.

I position my stool and adjust the mic stand, my fingers feeling clumsy. When I glance up to scan the crowd, I spot Jack near the front, leaning against a pillar with his eyes fixed on me.

"Hi," I say into the mic, cringing at how small my voice sounds. I clear my throat. "I'm Lark Reyes. Thanks for having me."

A few polite claps, a couple of encouraging whoops. I start to strum the opening chords of my first song, a mid-tempo piece about leaving home. My fingers are on autopilot, muscle memory taking over as I focus on keeping my breathing steady.

The first verse comes out a bit shaky, my voice not quite finding its center. I stare at a point on the back wall, too nervous to make eye contact with anyone. But as I reach the chorus, the melody becomes familiar terrain, and I can feel myself settling into it.

By the second verse, my fingers find the chord changes without thinking. My voice steadies, even though my heart is still racing. When I reach the bridge, I force myself to look up from my guitar and find Jack's gaze. He gives me a small, encouraging nod. Don't think about the crowd. Don't think about how many people are watching. Just focus on the next line.

I take a deep breath and let my voice soar into the higher register, hitting the notes I sometimes shy away from. They land cleanly. My hands are sweating on the guitar neck and part of my brain is screaming that I'm about to forget the words, but somehow I keep going. Somehow it's working.

When the song ends there's a beat of silence, then applause. Decent, maybe *more* than decent. I feel a tentative smile, though my pulse is still hammering.

"Thank you," I say into the mic, gripping it a little too hard to keep my hand from shaking. "This next one is called 'Paper Hearts.'"

Just two more songs. I can do two more songs. The worst is over, right?

I'm adjusting my guitar strap, trying to breathe through the adrenaline, when I see him.

Brandon's standing near the bar, arms crossed and scowling. Kelly's next to him, looking deeply uncomfortable. But Brandon's watching me with that familiar expression, the one that says he's waiting for me to fail, expecting it, maybe even counting on it.

How did he even know about this? A distant part of my brain remembers—Kelly is Elle Smith's granddaughter. I chatted with her during a Black Lantern shift last week, and mentioned the open mic. Fuck.

My fingers completely botch the next chord change, turning what should be a smooth transition into an ugly, jarring mess. I stumble on the lyrics. I try to recover, push through, but I've completely lost it now. The crowd's attention evaporates.

From the stage I can see Brandon's smirk, that satisfied expression that says he's getting exactly what he came for. By the final song, I'm just going through the motions. There's no feeling in it, no connection. Even Jack's steady presence at the front can't salvage this. He's still watching, still focused, but I can't meet his eyes.

"Thanks," I say when it's finally, mercifully over. The applause is perfunctory, already dying before I'm off stage. Someone actually says "*at last*" as I walk past, though maybe that was about their drink order. Maybe.

I don't wait around backstage. Don't stay to support the other performers like you're supposed to, like everyone else has been doing. I grab my guitar and head straight for the exit, needing space, needing to be anywhere but here.

The cool night air hits my burning face as I push through the door.

Jack catches up with me in the parking lot before I make it to my car. "Lark, wait," he calls, his footsteps quick on the pavement behind me. His hand touches my arm gently. "Hey, slow down for a second."

I stop abruptly, turning to face him. "What?" The word

comes out sharper than I intend, but I can't help it. My throat is tight, my chest aching with humiliation.

His eyebrows draw together, concern written all over his face. "Are you okay?"

"I'm fine," I lie, my voice cracking on the last word. "Can we just go?"

"Lark—"

I swallow hard against the lump in my throat. "Can we just not talk about it right now?"

He studies me for a long moment, and I can see him weighing whether to push or give me space. Finally, he nods. "Yeah, of course."

He takes my guitar case and walks with me to the car—Calvin's, which Jack's using while Calvin and Maren are on their honeymoon. We drive in silence for the first twenty minutes. Jack doesn't try to make me talk, and I'm grateful for that at least. He just drives, one hand on the wheel, occasionally glancing over at me like he's making sure I'm still breathing.

"I'm sorry," I finally say, breaking the silence. My voice sounds small in the darkness of the car. "I didn't mean to snap at you back there."

"Don't apologize," he says immediately. "You don't have to be okay right now."

I take a shaky breath. "I really thought I could do it. For a minute there, it actually felt good. Like I was really doing it, you know? And then..." The tears threaten again. "I choked. I completely fell apart up there."

Jack is quiet for a moment, his jaw working. Then he says, "That's not what I saw. I saw someone with real talent own that stage for the first half of that set. The way you connected with the crowd, the way you moved, your voice. That thing that makes people unable to look away. I couldn't take my eyes off you. Neither could anyone else in that room."

I turn to look at him, surprised by the intensity in his voice.

"So what if it didn't go perfectly," he continues. "It was your first time back on a big stage in years. These things take time."

My throat tightens. "It doesn't feel like that. It feels like I proved I can't do this."

"No," he says firmly. "You proved you can get up there. The rest is just practice." He pauses, glancing at me. "We can talk through what you were feeling. I don't know if that would help, but maybe analyzing it would give you something to work with next time."

I tense slightly at the suggestion. I could tell him about Brandon being there, but the shame of it stops the words in my throat. Two years after the divorce, and he still has that kind of power over me? After all my big talk about trying to move on. The humiliation is too much.

"I don't really know what it was," I lie, staring out at the darkness beyond my window. "Just general stage fright, I guess. It just... hit me all at once."

He nods slowly, like he can sense there's more I'm not saying, but won't push. "Whatever happened up there doesn't change the fact that you're the real deal. You just need to trust that."

A tear finally escapes down my cheek. "You know, for a fake boyfriend, you're not half bad at the comfort thing."

"I'm full of surprises," he says, and his hand finds mine in the darkness, squeezing. "And I mean what I said. You have something special, Lark. Don't let one rough night make you forget that."

His thumb strokes across my knuckles. I want to believe him. I want to believe that tonight wasn't proof of failure, that I really do have whatever he thinks he saw.

"You know," he says, "my first professional race was a *complete* disaster."

I turn to look at him. "Really?"

"Really. I qualified well, started in fourth position, and then proceeded to make every rookie mistake possible. Spun out, almost took out another driver on the restart, and finished dead last." He taps his fingers on the steering wheel. "The F1 press had a field day with it. There was this one headline—'Midnight's Career Over Before It Begins.'"

"What did you do?" I ask, wiping my nose with the back of my hand.

"I went back to the hotel, got spectacularly drunk, and swore I'd never race again," he admits with a self-deprecating laugh. "Then I woke up the next morning, threw up, and realized that if I quit after one bad day, I'd never know if I could have made it."

I smile, picturing young Jack on his own in Europe, thousands of miles from home, terrified but too stubborn to give up. "So you kept going."

"So I kept going," he confirms, nodding as we pass under a streetlight that momentarily illuminates his face. "And the next race was better. Not great, but better. And the one after that was better still. And then I bombed again, and then I bounced back. That's how these things go. Ups and downs, good performances and disasters. Nobody's consistent all the time."

I turn to look at him, studying his profile. "How do you do that? Just decide something and make it happen?"

"Years of practice," he says with a small smile. "And a healthy dose of delusion. It's basically my superpower."

That makes me laugh, breaking through some of the tension I've been carrying since I walked off that stage.

"Thanks for coming with me tonight," I say after a moment. "Even though it was a disaster."

"It wasn't a disaster," he insists. "And I wouldn't have missed it. That's what fake boyfriends are for, right? Showing up for the important stuff?"

The words settle warm in my chest. Because it doesn't feel fake, him being here. The way he's looking at me, the comfort of his hand still holding mine, none of it feels fake. But that's territory I can't let myself think about right now.

We drive in comfortable silence, and by the time we reach Dark River, the tightness in my chest has eased. Part of me doesn't want this to end. I want to ask him to come up, to keep talking, to let his presence chase away the lingering shame of tonight. But that's a terrible idea for about a dozen reasons, so I swallow the impulse down.

Jack walks me to my door, guitar case in hand. He sets it down gently against the wall and looks at me for a long moment, like he's trying to decide whether to say something. Finally, he just pulls me into a hug. It's warm and solid and I let myself sink into it for a few seconds before pulling back.

"Get some rest," he says. "Tonight doesn't define anything."

I nod, not trusting my voice. He waits until I'm inside with the door locked before I hear his footsteps heading back down the stairs.

Once inside my apartment, I lean against the door, letting out a long breath. The night plays on a loop in my head. The good start, seeing Brandon, the collapse.

The embarrassment is bad enough, but what really twists the knife is how easily Brandon can still throw me off. Two years of divorce, months of therapy sessions, boxing classes with Dominic, countless hours building my life back piece by piece, and that man can still get in my head with nothing but his presence.

Maybe I would have bombed even if he hadn't showed up. The stage fright was real before I saw him. But seeing his face in the crowd, that familiar smirk, it was like all those years of him making me feel small came rushing back. Him systematically dismantling my confidence one comment at a time until some part of me started to believe it.

I know intellectually it's not true. Therapy taught me that. But sometimes it feels like his words took root somewhere deep in my bones, and no amount of rational thought can dig them out completely.

I push off the door and head to my bedroom, setting my guitar in the corner. Tomorrow I'll think about next steps. Tonight, I just need to sleep and try to forget.

CHAPTER 11

JACK

The Black Lantern is dead for a Monday night. Just three regulars huddled at the far end of the bar arguing loudly about the upcoming football season and me at the other end, watching Lark check her phone every thirty seconds like it might spontaneously combust in her hands.

She's been on edge since Friday's performance, her usual confident attitude replaced by this nervous energy that has her constantly fidgeting with everything—her phone, the bar towels, the edge of her apron. Her black hair is pulled back in a bun, a few strands escaping to frame her face, and she's beautiful in a way that makes it physically hard to look anywhere else.

"You've got to stop looking at that thing, it's unhealthy," I say, reaching out and tapping my finger against her phone screen to get her attention. "Take it from someone who has entire Reddit threads dedicated to analyzing his facial expressions during post-race interviews. Trust me, you don't want to go down that rabbit hole."

"I can't stop checking," she says. "It's become a compulsion at this point. I keep expecting someone to have posted a video with a title like 'Local Woman Forgets How to Sing, Traumatizes Audience.' Or 'Musician's Career Dies On Stage, Witnesses Still in Therapy.'"

I laugh, shaking my head. "You really do have an incredibly creative mind, I'll give you that. But trust me, nobody filmed it. We never posted about it on social media beforehand, per your very specific request—"

"*Thank god* I had the foresight to not draw attention to it until I knew if it would work out or not," she interrupts, putting her phone down on the bar only to pick it right back up.

I roll my eyes. "Yes, yes, you're very wise. The point is no one filmed it, so at some point you've got to stop torturing yourself with imaginary scenarios."

"No, I'm actually a masochist," she says. "I enjoy the pain of reliving my humiliating failures over and over in vivid detail. It's my hobby."

"In that case there are much more effective methods." I grin, raising my eyebrows. "Repeatedly checking your phone for nonexistent videos seems like an amateur approach to self-torture. Since no one filmed it, you're not even getting your money's worth."

"It's actually *more* depressing when you put it that way," she says, but she's starting to smile. "I wasn't even interesting enough to mock online. I couldn't even fail spectacularly enough to go viral."

"I thought you were very interesting," I say, leaning my elbows on the bar, closing the distance between us slightly. The familiar scent of her perfume—something with vanilla and spice—mingles with the scents of the bar. "The voice crack? Fascinating artistic choice. Very avant-garde."

"Jerk," she laughs, swatting me on the arm.

I try to ignore the small surge of pleasure I get from making her laugh like this. Three days since the performance, and this is the first real laugh I've gotten out of her. It's ridiculous how good it feels to see that smile again, to know I put it there.

"Thanks for trying to make me feel better," she says.

"Is it working?" I ask, raising an eyebrow and taking another deliberately slow sip of my beer, watching her over the rim of the glass.

"Maybe," she admits, finally putting her phone face-down on the bar and actually leaving it there. "At least the label didn't see it. That's something."

"There's that positive attitude I know and love," I say with a smirk.

"Hey Midnight!" Mike calls from the pool table, his voice carrying across the mostly empty bar. "You said 'one quick beer' fifteen minutes ago. You playing or what?"

Lark's eyes dance with amusement as she looks at me. "You know he's right. You did promise him a rematch."

"I didn't realize you were so eager to get rid of me," I say, leaning slightly closer over the bar, dropping my voice lower.

"Oh, I'm not," she says with a smirk that does things to me. "But I can't have it on my conscience that Jack Midnight doesn't honor his sacred pool commitments. Plus you've successfully distracted me from my own spiral, happy?"

"Very," I say, sliding off the barstool. "Don't check your phone while I'm gone."

"No promises," she calls after me.

I head back to the pool table where Mike's already racking the balls, a shit-eating grin on his face like he genuinely thinks he's got a chance in hell of winning this time. I grab my cue, line up my shot, but my eyes keep drifting back to the bar. To *her*.

This was supposed to be simple. A straightforward deal. A business arrangement with clear boundaries. I help her get Instagram followers and music industry attention, she helps me look stable and responsible for my racing contract and sponsors. No complications. Just two people helping each other out for mutual benefit.

But nothing with Lark feels simple anymore. I can't stop thinking about her. Every time I'm near her, I want to be closer. Every time I leave, I'm counting the hours until I see her again.

Thursday evening I pull up to Lark's apartment building on my bike. I've been looking forward to this all day, way more than I should be for what's technically a fake date. Just another performance, though this time for my family. I'm just shutting off the engine when Lark comes out the front door of her building.

Holy. Fucking. Shit.

She's wearing this deep burgundy skirt that hugs her hips perfectly and shows off legs that go on for miles, paired with a silky cream-colored top that dips just low enough to make my mouth go completely dry. Her dark hair is loose in soft waves, and she looks like every fantasy I've ever had, walking toward me with that little half-smile that drives me absolutely crazy.

"You're on time," she says, sounding surprised as she approaches. "I figured I'd have at least five minutes to panic about what I'm wearing and change three more times."

"You look..." I trail off, momentarily unable to find words that won't get me slapped or make this weird. Amazing? Gorgeous? Fuck-me stunning? "Perfect."

She rolls her eyes but I catch the flush spreading across her cheeks. "Thanks. I figured I should make an actual effort for the whole family dinner thing."

Her eyes drop to my bike and she grimaces slightly. "Though I definitely didn't plan this outfit with motorcycle riding in mind."

"We could always take your car if you want," I say.

"No, no, I actually like the bike," she sighs, eyeing it. "I just didn't think through the logistics of a skirt this short and your motorcycle. Poor planning on my part, but we'll make it work."

"You know," I say, "no one at dinner will believe you're with me when you look like that."

"Please," she scoffs, taking the spare helmet I offer her. "You could wear a literal trash bag and still look like..." She stops abruptly, her eyes widening.

"Like what?" I press, grinning now because I can't help myself.

"Like someone who thinks entirely too highly of himself," she finishes quickly, but the flush on her cheeks deepens.

I laugh, swinging my leg back over the bike and settling into the seat. "Come on, let's head out."

She glances down at her skirt, then back at the bike with hesitation written all over her face. Then she does a little maneuver, hiking the skirt up just enough to swing her leg over the seat while maintaining some semblance of modesty.

Her thighs press warm against mine, her arms sliding around my waist, and I have to take a deep breath before starting the engine. It's going to be a long ride trying to focus on the road with her pressed against me like this.

"Hold on tight," I tell her, my voice coming out rougher than intended, and I feel her arms tighten around me immediately. I feel myself stiffening in my jeans. Christ, this was a terrible idea.

The ride to Theo's house is pure torture. Every turn, every stop has her shifting against me, her body warm and soft pressed against my back. Her thighs squeeze around mine on each corner I take, and all I can think about is pulling over somewhere dark and private, spreading those legs even wider, and burying my face between her thighs until she's screaming my name.

By the time we pull up to Theo's house, I'm counting backward from a hundred and trying to think about anything other than how wet I could make her with just my mouth.

Theo's place sits on a gentle slope overlooking the water, a renovated craftsman with a wraparound porch that he's proud of. The yard is absolutely immaculate—Theo's pride and joy—with a winding stone path leading to the front door.

"This is beautiful," Lark says as we walk up the path, and I realize this is her first time seeing Theo's place in person.

"He's spent the last five years getting it exactly how he wants it," I explain. "He's obsessive about it."

The door swings open before we even reach the porch steps, and Theo stands there in dark jeans and a button-down shirt, dish towel thrown casually over his shoulder.

"There you are!" He pulls me into a quick, brotherly hug before turning his attention to Lark. "And Lark, so glad you could finally make it for dinner. You know, you're the first girl Jack's ever been serious enough about to bring home to meet the family."

I watch the guilt flash across Lark's face before she hides it with a bright smile. Another sharp reminder that this whole thing is fake, something I seem to be having increasing trouble remembering lately.

"Thanks for having me," Lark says warmly, her natural charm kicking in. "Your home is absolutely gorgeous from what I can see so far."

"Wait until you see the view from the back deck," Theo says enthusiastically, stepping aside to let us in. "Come on in, everyone's already here."

"Is that Lark?" Maren's voice calls from somewhere in the living room, and then she's peeking around the corner. "Oh my god, you're here!"

She rushes over immediately, pulling Lark into a tight hug.

"Look at you!" Maren says, holding Lark at arm's length. "That outfit is stunning. Seriously, you look like the star you are."

"Thanks," Lark says, smiling. "And look at you! You're absolutely glowing. Tell me everything about the honeymoon. I want to see all the pictures."

"I have like three hundred to show you," Maren grins. "Greece was incredible."

Calvin appears from the kitchen. "Hey, you two made it," he says warmly, pulling me into a quick hug and clapping me on the back before turning to Lark. "Good to see you, Lark."

"You too," Lark says with a smile. "So you loved Greece?"

"It was life-altering," Calvin says. "Absolutely incredible. Best two weeks of my life." He nods toward Maren. "Mostly because of her."

"I'm so happy for you guys," Lark says.

We follow them through the house, and I watch Lark take it all in with obvious appreciation. Theo's place really is something special—open and airy with huge windows that look out over the Sound. It's the kind of home that feels lived-in and comfortable despite being beautifully decorated. Very Theo.

Dominic and Alex are in the middle of some heated debate by the windows overlooking the water.

"Hey, look what the cat dragged in," Alex says, breaking away from Dominic to clap me on the shoulder. "About damn time you showed up. We've only hung out twice since you've been home, which is a crime against brotherhood. I can't *believe* you're spending more time at the gym with Dom than with me."

"That's on you," I laugh, giving Alex a light shove. "You're too busy being a psycho perfectionist chef to spend time fucking around Dark River with your baby brother."

"Artist, I prefer the term artist," Alex corrects dramatically. "Cooking is my canvas. Food is my medium."

"Your canvas is pretentious as hell," I reply, punching his arm lightly, making him laugh.

Dominic comes over, giving me one of his characteristically firm handshakes that could probably crush steel. "Jack. Good to see you. Lark's been kicking serious ass at the gym lately, by the way. Her form on the heavy bag is really good."

"So I hear," I say, glancing over at Lark, who's now talking animatedly with Maren about something on her phone, both of them laughing.

"Uncle Jack!"

I turn just in time to see Chloe racing toward me at full speed, markers and paper clutched in her little hands. I catch her easily as she launches herself at me, swinging her up onto my hip.

"Hey, monster," I say, tapping her nose gently. "What are you drawing?"

"A race car," she says proudly, shoving the paper directly toward my face. "It's for you! See the flames? It's super fast. The fastest car ever."

"My favorite kind of car!" I examine the blue scribble with orange flames shooting out the back with complete seriousness, like I'm studying technical blueprints. "You know, monster, you're so good at art, you might have to be both a Formula One driver *and* an artist. You're just too talented for one career."

She nods seriously. "Yes, it's very stressful to be so good at too many things."

I throw my head back laughing, caught completely off guard by her deadpan delivery. "That's a tough cross to bear, kiddo."

Chloe wiggles to be put down and returns immediately to her artwork, tongue sticking out in concentration. Lark returns from what must have been a quick tour of the house with Maren and our eyes meet across the room. Something electric passes between us that makes my breath catch.

"Dinner's almost ready," Theo announces. "Everyone to the table."

The dining room is a large, solid table Theo built himself, positioned perfectly to capture the stunning view of the Sound through floor-to-ceiling windows.

"This is beautiful," Lark says, taking it all in. "You guys really know how to do family dinner right."

"Alex is the culinary mastermind," Calvin says, pulling out Maren's chair. "Theo the front of the house genius. The rest of us just show up and eat whatever they put in front of us."

"That's not true," Dominic protests. "I brought wine."

"Buying a box on the way over doesn't count as contributing," Calvin teases.

"It's the thought that counts," Dominic insists, and everyone laughs.

Theo and Alex bring out platters of food—arugula salad with roasted beets and creamy goat cheese, perfectly cooked halibut with some kind of herb crust, and roasted root vegetables that remind me that fall is on its way. Alex insists we open his special wine instead of drinking "Dominic's corner store selection" with his carefully prepared halibut.

As soon as the first piece of fish is served, Theo's gray-and-white cat, Nala, makes her entrance like she owns the place, tail high, circling the table with slow, deliberate steps. She pauses at each chair, taking stock of the guests, the laughter, but mostly the scent of halibut drifting through the air. When she reaches the spot closest to the platter, she glances up at it—just once—then looks away as if she couldn't care less. Theo always said she acts like a queen above mortal things, and now I see why.

As Nala settles onto the couch, dinner flows easily, conversation bouncing around the table—stories about the honeymoon, Chloe's upcoming first day of school, Dominic's plans to expand the gym, Alex's new restaurant menu. Lark fits in seamlessly, laughing at inside jokes, asking questions, charming every person at the table without even trying.

After dinner, we move out to the back deck. The sun has set, but the sky still holds a faint glow, turning everything a soft, hazy blue. String lights crisscross overhead, creating a warm, intimate atmosphere. From here, the view of the Sound is impressive, but I know there's an even better spot.

"Want to see something cool?" I ask Lark as the others settle into comfortable conversation around the deck.

She nods, and I gesture toward a winding stone path that leads down toward the water's edge, disappearing into the trees that line the property. "Theo built a gazebo down by the water. It's got the best view."

"Lead the way," she says, stepping away from the railing.

We head down the path, out of sight from the deck above. The stepping stones wind through Theo's immaculate landscaping, each one lit by small solar lights guiding our way down the gentle slope toward the shoreline. The sounds of conversation fade gradually behind us, replaced by the gentle lapping of water against the shore and the distant hum of boat engines on the Sound.

The gazebo sits at the edge of the property, through the trees, giving way to the natural rocky shoreline.

"Wow," Lark breathes, stepping inside the gazebo and moving to the railing. "This view..."

"Yeah, Theo built this thing a few years back," I say, joining her at the rail, close enough to smell her perfume. "After his divorce, actually. I think he needed something else to focus on after his marriage fell apart."

We stand there quietly, both looking out at the water. She shifts slightly closer and suddenly I'm hyperaware of everything. The minimal space between us. The soft curve of her lips that I haven't been able to stop thinking about.

Before I can think better of it, before I can stop myself, I reach out and touch her face, brushing a strand of hair behind her ear. But instead of pulling back like I should, my hand lingers, tracing the line of her jaw slowly, feeling her pulse quicken under my touch.

She looks up at me, those big brown eyes dark with something that makes my cock stir behind my zipper. I should stop. I should step back. This isn't part of our deal, our arrangement.

Instead, I slide my hand to the nape of her neck, feeling the silky strands of her hair between my fingers as I grip her firmly. She doesn't pull away. She leans into my touch, swaying toward me like gravity's pulling her in, like she can't help herself any more than I can.

"Jack..." she whispers, and my name on her lips is like a spark catching dry tinder.

I pull her closer, my other hand finding her waist, and her hands immediately fist in my shirt. I dip my head, drawn to her by something I can't fight anymore and don't want to. Our lips are so close I can feel her warm breath, can smell that perfume she wears that's been driving me insane all night. I want to pin her against this railing and hike that skirt up around her waist, fake relationship be damned.

My grip tightens in her hair, tilting her head back just enough to make her gasp. Her lips part, inviting me in, and I'm a heartbeat away from claiming her mouth with mine. I can see her pupils dilate, feel the way her body arches toward me, desperate for contact. Desperate for *me*.

"Uncle Jack! Lark! Daddy says it's dessert time!"

Chloe's voice shatters the moment completely. We spring apart so fast that Lark stumbles backward and I have to grab her arm to steady her. My heart's pounding like I just finished a race, and Lark's breathing fast, her cheeks flushed.

"Coming!" Lark calls back, but her voice cracks slightly. She clears her throat, tries again. "Be right there!"

We stand there as Chloe's footsteps retreat back up the path, the sound of her shoes on stone fading. Neither of us says anything about what just almost happened. We both just start walking back to the house with at least three feet of careful distance between us.

Dessert is Alex's chocolate mousse, which is one of my favorites, but I barely taste it. Lark and I are trying so hard to act normal that we're borderline being weird about it. We contribute to conversation when directly spoken to, laugh at Chloe's silly jokes, but that almost-kiss sits between us like a third person at the table that only we can see.

Finally, people start leaving. Dom has an early client at the gym tomorrow morning. Maren and Calvin need to get home to let their dog Laila out. Everyone's hugging goodbye, making plans for next week, and then it's just Lark and me walking to where I parked the bike.

The night air has cooled considerably, the crickets chirping loudly in Theo's perfectly manicured lawn. Lark hugs her arms around herself as we walk down the driveway. Neither of us mentions what happened at the gazebo.

She climbs on the bike behind me, settling onto the seat with a careful distance that doesn't last once the engine roars to life. Her arms slide around my waist, tentative at first, then tightening as we pull away from the curb. Every inch of her pressed against my back feels like fire.

As we wind through the roads back into Dark River, her thighs bracket mine, her chest against my back, hands splayed across my stomach. I try desperately to focus on the road, on the cool night air whipping past, on anything but the woman holding onto me.

She's been through enough already. That asshole ex-husband of hers did a real number on her confidence, made her second-guess her music, her talent, herself. The last thing she needs is me complicating her life when she's finally getting her shot at her dreams.

And what could I offer her anyway? I'm just passing through

Dark River temporarily, waiting to get back to Europe. Back to racing full time after fucking up my own contract. I've never stayed anywhere long, with anyone. She deserves better than a guy who ruins everything he touches, who can't maintain a relationship longer than it takes to change a tire.

When I pull up to her building, the yellow security light casting harsh shadows across the parking lot, she climbs off the bike, smoothing her skirt. I kill the engine, and the silence feels heavy between us. She pulls off the helmet, shaking out her hair, and hands it back to me.

"Thanks for bringing me to dinner. Your family is great. Really great." She shifts her weight, eyes darting around, looking everywhere but directly at me.

"Thanks for coming," I say.

She bites her lip, and I hold my breath, not sure if I want her to bring up what happened or not. Part of me hopes she will, just to clear the air and acknowledge it. A bigger part hopes she won't, because I don't trust myself to do the right thing if we actually talk about it.

"So, uh, goodnight. I'll talk to you later," she says instead, clearly deciding to pretend nothing happened.

"Goodnight," I say, feeling both relieved and disappointed. Then she's gone, disappearing inside before I can say something stupid that I can't take back.

I sit on the bike for another long minute, engine off, trying to get my body under control. The almost-kiss keeps replaying on loop in my head. Her lips parting. My hand in her hair. How close we came to crossing a line we can't uncross.

I drive home too fast, taking the corners aggressively, trying to burn off this energy coursing through me. The wind whips at my face, but it does nothing to cool the heat under my skin. The arrangement was supposed to be simple but nothing about this feels simple anymore.

September can't come fast enough. Or maybe it's coming *too* fast. I don't know. All I know is I'm fucked. Because whatever this is—it sure as hell isn't fake anymore.

CHAPTER 12

LARK

My guitar rests across my lap, phone propped precariously against a stack of books on the living room floor. I'm cross-legged, trying to record the bridge section for a song I wrote last night when sleep was impossible. My fingers find the chord progression again, and I'm about to hit record when my phone buzzes loudly. The notification covers half my makeshift recording setup.

Jack: *Need to go over Miami stuff. Can I stop by?*

We've seen each other exactly twice since the almost-kiss at Theo's gazebo three days ago—once at the gym, and once at the coffee shop for a very public lunch—and both times we pretended absolutely nothing happened. Which is the right move. The smart, mature move. Even if I keep replaying that moment on an endless loop, when he leaned down and I went up on my toes and we were so close I could feel his breath warm on my lips.

God knows I wanted desperately to kiss him, and much more than that. Every time I think about it, which is approximately every four minutes like clockwork, my heart does this ridiculous racing thing that makes me feel like a teenager with her first crush instead of a grown woman who should absolutely know better.

Me: *Sure. When?*

Jack: *20 mins?*

I look around my apartment with fresh horror. Half-empty coffee cups on every available surface forming a timeline of my caffeine addiction, and clothes scattered everywhere, including the bra hanging off the back of a chair from when I'd flung it off last night after getting home from work.

Me: *See you then!*

I spend the next fifteen minutes frantically shoving things into closets and drawers in what I call my "oh shit someone's coming over" dance—a frenzied ritual of grabbing armfuls of random stuff and shoving them anywhere they might possibly fit. Why couldn't I be one of those naturally tidy people who never have to panic clean?

I kick a pile of sheet music under the couch, toss three days' worth of empty coffee cups into the sink with a clatter, and nearly dislocate my shoulder trying to force my closet door shut against the avalanche of clothes and random junk threatening to spill out like a dam breaking. The hinges make an ominous creaking sound, like they're plotting revenge.

I then make a desperate dash to the bathroom mirror, where I'm confronted with the harsh reality of what happens when you wash your hair before bed, sleep on it wet, throw it in a bun all day, and then release it from captivity right before an attractive man shows up at your door. It's a disturbing cross between 80s hair band volume and "just stuck my finger in an electrical socket" texture. I attempt to tame it with wet fingers, which only makes certain sections go flat while others reach new ambitious heights of rebellion.

"Traitor," I mutter at my reflection, digging frantically

through bathroom drawers for a hair tie, lip balm, anything that might make me look less like I've been living in a cave for the past week.

I'm debating whether to change out of my ratty old University of Washington sweatshirt when I hear his motorcycle pull up outside. Through the window, I watch him take off his helmet, and it's completely unfair how good he looks. Some people are just the universe's favorites, blessed with genetic coding that makes them look like they stepped out of a magazine spread even after a motorcycle ride. He's carrying something—a bottle of wine, it looks like.

My stomach does that flutter thing again. Harder this time. *Shit.* I definitely should have changed into a cuter outfit.

I open the door before he can knock. "Hey," I say, aiming for casual but it comes out sounding vaguely creepy and weirdly deep like I'm auditioning for a horror movie.

He hesitates slightly, his smile faltering for just a second before returning. "Hey," he says, holding up the wine bottle. "Figured we should plan this Miami thing out properly instead of winging it. And planning requires wine. It's just science."

"Oh, well if it's science," I say, stepping aside to let him in. His dimples are making me feel dangerously light-headed in a way that cannot possibly lead anywhere good. Jack Midnight has a reputation for a reason, and men like him don't suddenly change their entire approach to relationships.

I can't let myself do what I desperately want to do. No, absolutely not. Keep it together, Reyes.

"Were you working on something?" he asks, noticing my guitar and the makeshift recording setup immediately. His eyes linger on the notebook I've hastily closed, curiosity evident in the slight tilt of his head. "I can come back tomorrow if this is a bad time—"

"No, it's fine," I say quickly. "I was just messing around. Nothing important."

"Your music's *not* nothing important," he says in a matter-of-fact way that makes my cheeks flush.

"Well, uh, Miami planning," I say, changing the subject before I say something embarrassing. "That's why you're here, right?"

"Right," he says. "Miami."

I get wine glasses from the cabinet while he opens the bottle. He brought a nice Oregon Pinot Noir, and we settle on my couch with his phone pulled up to the weekend schedule.

"Friday there's a big sponsor event. Miami does this motorsports festival every year. GT racing, demos, the whole thing. It's not Formula One, but all the teams send people for sponsor obligations and PR. Some of my old teammates will be there, plus drivers from other teams. Pretty major event for corporate networking. Press will be everywhere. Plenty of opportunities for photos."

"Sounds good," I say as I take a sip of wine. "What else?"

"Friday night there's also a big gala event hosted by a real estate developer named Bernard Montgomery. Black tie, lots of press, sponsors, team executives." He scrolls through his phone. "Saturday's more casual, a bunch of press interviews and sponsor obligations throughout the morning. You don't have to come to those if you don't want to. Could just be me doing the boring corporate stuff."

"No, I want to come," I say immediately. "This stuff is pretty interesting to me. Seeing how all of it works behind the scenes."

And it is fascinating. Jack is so passionate about racing that it's infectious. I've even been watching a few of his old races on YouTube and they're thrilling. Though I'd convinced myself that was just research, part of being a convincing fake girlfriend. Nothing more.

He looks up from his phone, something warm in his expression. "Yeah?"

"Yeah. Plus more photo ops, right? That's kind of the whole

point." I take another sip of wine. "And honestly, watching you do press interviews sounds entertaining. I want to see your media-trained face in action."

"Oh, you'll love it. I have this whole repertoire," he says, his expression shifting through different variations of the same polite smile. "Confident but humble. Grateful for the opportunity. Excited about the future. I can do all of them while saying absolutely nothing of substance."

I'm laughing now, and Jack's watching me with an intensity that makes my skin warm all over. "What?" I ask.

"Nothing," he says, but his smile softens. "You just... you have a great laugh."

I take another sip of wine to have something to do with my hands, which suddenly feel awkward and too big for my body. When did compliments from Jack start hitting me so differently than from anyone else? It's like his words bypass all my normal defenses and land somewhere deeper, more vulnerable.

"So what were you working on?" he asks, nodding toward my guitar, his eyes brightening with interest. "When I interrupted?"

"Just a new song," I say, trying to sound casual even though my pulse picks up. "It's not ready yet. Still figuring out the bridge. It's called 'Magnolia Street.' It's about growing up and my mom teaching me piano."

"Can I hear it?" he asks.

Oh no. "It's really rough," I warn, taking a big sip of wine for courage.

"Let's hear it," he says, leaning back into the couch cushions, making himself comfortable. He looks good here, in my cluttered apartment with its secondhand furniture and mismatched throw pillows. *Too* good. Like he belongs. It does dangerous things to my imagination, making me picture other nights like this, him bringing wine after work, talking for hours, staying until morning.

I pick up my guitar, take a deep breath, and start playing. The opening chords are gentle, nostalgic, pulling me back to childhood. I keep my eyes fixed on my fingers moving across the frets, not daring to look up, because I can feel Jack watching me. The weight of his gaze is a physical sensation against my skin, raising goosebumps along my arms.

The song builds as it goes, the melody swelling, and by the time I reach the final chorus, I've forgotten to be nervous. I'm just singing, letting the music flow through me the way it's supposed to, the way it feels when everything clicks.

When I finish, there's a moment of silence that stretches between us like a living thing. I finally look up at Jack, and the expression on his face steals my breath. He's completely still, lips slightly parted, eyes dark and intent.

"That was beautiful," he says. The timbre of it sends a shiver down my spine that has nothing to do with the air conditioning. "Really beautiful, Lark."

"Thanks," I say, suddenly shy under the intensity of his gaze. "It's still a work in progress."

"It's perfect as it is," he says, and the sincerity in his voice makes me believe him.

We look at each other for a moment too long, and I feel that same pull from the gazebo. That magnetic thing that keeps drawing me to him despite all the reasons I should stay away.

I set the guitar down carefully against the arm of the couch. "Do you want a glass of water? I never offered," I say, making a desperate dash for the kitchen before he can even answer, needing space and air and approximately seventeen ice cubes down my shirt.

My phone dings in my pocket, and I pull it out to silence it. An email notification stares back at me. The sender name makes my heart stop completely.

Maya Stone, Tidal Records.

Oh my god.

My hands start shaking as I tap it open, my eyes skimming so fast I have to go back and reread to make sure I'm not having some kind of stress-induced hallucination brought on by wine and sexual frustration.

Lark,

I wanted to reach out following up on our call last week. We've been extremely impressed with your growing online presence. You really have created substantial buzz in exactly the demographics we're targeting. The team here is very excited about the potential of working together.

We're hosting a label party soon in Seattle at The Vine—mostly industry people, some press, very casual atmosphere. We'd love for you to attend if you're available, and please feel free to bring Jack if you're comfortable. It would be a great opportunity for you to meet some of our team in a relaxed setting. Details attached.

Best, Maya

"OH MY GOD!" The scream bursts out of me before I can stop it. This is happening. The fake boyfriend plan is *actually* working. I'm going to a label party. A LABEL PARTY. With industry people and press and everything I've been dreaming about since I was twelve years old writing terrible songs in my bedroom about boys who didn't know I existed.

Suddenly Jack bursts into my tiny kitchen, eyes wild and scanning for immediate threats. "What?! Are you okay? What happened?"

"Tidal Records!" I'm waving my phone around like a flag of victory. "They emailed! They said they're impressed with my social media and they want me at their label party in Seattle with industry people and press and this is *actually* happening!"

Without thinking—because thinking has clearly abandoned me entirely—I launch myself at him, throwing my arms around his neck with enough force that he stumbles back a step.

His arms come around me immediately, catching me easily and lifting me straight off the ground. Which should probably be alarming but mostly just makes me acutely aware of how strong he is. How solid. How good he smells.

"This is real!" I'm practically squealing into his shoulder, clutching him tight enough that I'm probably cutting off his air supply.

"That's incredible!" He's laughing, and I can feel the vibration of it through his chest where I'm currently plastered against him like plastic wrap.

His firm chest. His very broad, very solid, very warm chest that smells like leather and wood and citrus. And I'm pressed against all of him, my feet dangling off the ground, his hands warm and strong where they're holding me up. One hand spread across my back, the other gripping my waist, and I can feel every finger through my thin shirt.

It's at this spectacularly inconvenient moment that my brain decides to supply me with an extremely detailed image of him walking me backwards until we slam against the counter, his mouth on my neck, those hands sliding up under my shirt, grazing my nipples before dropping down past my belly button, hooking beneath the edge of my panties—

ABORT. ABORT MISSION IMMEDIATELY.

I drop back down to the ground so fast I nearly twist my ankle, practically leaping away from him like he's suddenly radioactive. My face is on fire. Like I-just-had-an-extremely-pornographic-thought-about-my-fake-boyfriend fire.

"Sorry!" The word comes out too loud, too frantic. "Got excited. About the email. The news." I'm gesturing wildly at nothing. "You know how it is."

"Don't apologize," he says, grinning. "It's exciting. What exactly did they say?"

I shove my phone into his hand, desperate for literally any distraction from the fact that I just had a very detailed fantasy about him in the middle of celebrating my career breakthrough. "Here. Read it yourself. I'm too scattered to explain properly."

He reads it, his face breaking into a wide smile. "Lark, this is huge. Getting invited to a label party this early? That's a really good sign."

"I know!" The excitement is bubbling up again, temporarily overriding my mortification at my complete loss of self-control. "And it's so soon, which means they're serious about this, right?"

"Definitely," he says, handing my phone back. "You should go. We both should."

"You can make it?" I ask, surprised by how much I want him there.

"Of course," he says easily. "That's what fake boyfriends are for."

We spend the next couple hours talking about everything. The label party, what I should expect, how to navigate industry conversations. Jack tells me stories about racing events, about dealing with press and sponsors, giving me advice that's actually helpful. I talk about my music, about the songs I've been writing, about what I hope happens with Tidal. We finish the wine, order pizza, and laugh until my sides hurt. It's comfortable in a way that scares me. Easy. Like we've been doing this for years instead of weeks.

"Well, sorry to keep you so long," he says eventually, standing up and stretching. "I should go. I have an early gym session with Theo and Alex tomorrow."

"You haven't been keeping me," I say. "It was nice having someone to talk to about all this."

I walk him to the door, that strange tension from the gazebo returning as we navigate the small space of my entryway.

"Congratulations again," he says at the door, his hand on the knob. "You deserve this, Lark. All of it."

"Thanks," I say softly. "For everything."

He looks like he wants to say something else, his mouth opening slightly, but then he just smiles. "I'll text you tomorrow."

"Sounds good," I manage.

Then he's gone.

I close the door and lean against it, letting out a long breath. The fake relationship was supposed to be simple, but there's nothing simple about the way my heart races when Jack looks at me. Nothing easy about how right he feels in my space, how much I wanted him to stay, how hard it's getting to remember that none of this is real.

This is dangerous territory. I need to remember what I'm actually after here—my career. My music. Not a relationship that'll inevitably crash and burn when reality sets in and he remembers he dates models and actresses, not bartenders from small towns who write sad songs.

Even if that bartender really, really wants to climb him like a tree.

The next morning I wake up gasping, my thighs clenched together and my heart racing. The dream is still vivid. Jack and I were on stage at some venue, and we were lying on some fancy velvet couch, with him fucking me while I sang to the crowd.

Where the hell did that come from?

I press my palms against my face, feeling the heat radiating off my cheeks. I've had maybe three sex dreams in my entire adult life, and none of them involved public performance venues or anyone I actually know. Definitely none that felt that mortifyingly good.

I drag myself out of bed, gulping down water like it might somehow wash away the lingering heat between my legs. This *has* to stop. I cannot be having dreams like that about him. That's a recipe for disaster, for blurred lines, for getting my heart broken. I mean, he doesn't even live on this continent, for crying out loud.

My workout clothes are already laid out on the dresser from the night before, a habit I developed years ago to make early mornings easier. I need to burn off this energy, and Dominic's 8 AM boxing class is exactly what I need right now.

But Midnight Gym means the possibility of Jack, and I'm not sure I can handle seeing him right now. Not when my body is still thrumming with desire. The idea of running into him while I'm already this wound up seems like asking for trouble.

I pull into the parking lot, scanning for Jack's motorcycle. No sleek black bike in sight. I feel an odd mix of relief and disappointment as I grab my gym bag and head inside, annoyed at myself for both reactions.

Midnight Gym is already busy with the morning crowd, the air filled with the familiar sounds of weights clanking and treadmills whirring. I wave to the girl at the front desk, then make my way across the main floor, a massive open space with weight racks along one wall and cardio equipment on the other.

Dominic's already in the boxing area at the far end, wrapping fresh tape around one of the heavy bags. He's always here early, probably arrives before dawn for his own training. I wouldn't be surprised if he actually lived in some hidden room in the gym.

I start warming up, stretching out my shoulders, loosening my wrists, wrapping my hands carefully. The ritual soothes me, focusing my scattered thoughts. Other regulars filter in, greeting each other with nods or brief conversations.

Ted with his perpetually untied shoelaces that Dominic always calls him out for. Karen who could probably knock out a heavyweight with her right hook and never stops talking about her grandkids.

And then there's Pink Gloves. I knew her name once, two

years ago, but now we're firmly in that awkward "too late to ask without looking like a jerk" territory. I secretly suspect Dominic's forgotten her name too, since he never says it during class.

"Morning, everyone," Dominic calls out at exactly 8 AM, his voice cutting through the chatter. He never starts late, never ends early. "Partner up for warm-up drills."

Pink Gloves immediately makes her way over to me with a smile.

"Hey, Lark!" she says brightly as we tap gloves in greeting. "It's been forever! How have you been?"

"Good, really good," I say, smiling back as we fall into the familiar rhythm of jabs and blocks. My mind is desperately trying to recall if her name starts with an A or a J. Amy? Julie? Nothing's coming. "How about you?"

"Oh, you know, same old," she replies, throwing a jab that I block easily. "So, you and Jack, huh? I saw your pictures on Instagram. When were you going to tell us you're dating Dark River's biggest heartthrob? I mean, what a score."

Even here I can't escape him. The very place I came to clear my head. I focus on my footwork, maintaining proper stance.

"It's, uh, still pretty new," I say, trying to sound casual even though my face is heating up.

"Well, you two look amazing together," she continues enthusiastically, her eyes practically sparkling with gossip excitement. "I've followed him since his rookie season. I mean, those eyes! That jawline! You're seriously the luckiest girl right now."

"Hey!" Dominic's voice cuts through her celebrity gossip session like a knife, sharp and annoyed. "This is boxing, not social hour. Focus on your form!"

Thank goodness for Dominic's no-nonsense approach. Saved by the perpetually gruff gym owner. We eventually move to the heavy bags, and Dominic calls out combinations. The rhythm of the workout takes over, and I lose myself in it. Sweat drips down my back, my arms burn with exertion, but I keep pushing.

With each hit against the bag, I work through the confusion in my head. Punch: Jack's face when he nearly kissed me. Jab: The way he looked at me when I played for him. Cross: How he held me when I got the label email. Hook: The fact that none of it is real.

"Good form, Lark," Dominic says, holding the bag steady as I throw a particularly vicious combination, his approval rare enough to mean something. "Channel that energy."

If only you knew where this energy was coming from.

By the end of class, I'm drenched in sweat, my muscles pleasantly exhausted and my thoughts of Jack pushed to a distant, manageable hum. This is why I come here, why I keep coming back. To find that place where my body takes over and my mind quiets down, where everything becomes simple for just a little while.

"Good work today," Dominic says as I gather my things.

Coming from him, it's high praise. He's not one for empty compliments.

"Thanks, Dominic. Great class as always," I say, grabbing my water bottle and gym towel, still catching my breath. "I'll see you next time."

He nods, already turning his attention to setting up for the next class.

After a shower and quick breakfast, I head home to change before making my way to The Black Lantern. The morning sun shines bright, Dark River's small downtown coming alive with activity as I drive through.

It's still a few hours before we open, but I told Maren I'd help her with some inventory work. The familiar smells of wood polish and beer greet me as I unlock the door. I drop my bag behind the bar, flipping on lights as I call out, "Hello?"

"In the storage room!" Maren calls back.

I find her counting bottles of tequila, clipboard in hand, blonde hair pulled back in a bun. Her face lights up when she sees me, breaking into a wide smile.

"Hey! Well well well if it isn't my little star!" she says with a grin, setting down her clipboard to give me a quick hug, her excitement palpable.

I'd texted her ridiculously late last night to tell her about the email and Seattle label party, but she'd been up writing anyway so we'd had a full-on freak-out session via text. "I know, right? I can hardly believe it!"

Jayson pokes his head around the corner, arms full of boxes from a delivery. His curly hair is already covered by his favorite bandana, ready for a day in the kitchen.

"Morning, Lark. I hear congratulations are in order about the music thing?" he asks warmly.

"Yeah," I smile, still not quite believing it myself. "Thanks, Jayson. It's pretty exciting."

"Listen, you gotta thank us in your Grammy speech, alright?" he says with a wink. "The Black Lantern, where it all began."

"Don't worry," I laugh. "You, Maren, and my parents are first on the list."

"Perfect," he says, disappearing back to the kitchen, whistling some tune.

"I still can't believe you're going to a fancy label party!" Maren says, bouncing a little with excitement as she counts vodka bottles. "And then Miami? This is all just so insane."

"I know," I say, and I can't help the smile that spreads across my face despite all the Jack-related confusion. "I've barely ever been out of Dark River. I can't wait. I always wanted to travel, and now it's all happening so fast. I just hope it all goes how I want it to."

"You'll do great," she says confidently. "You always do. You're so good with people and a natural in situations like that. Besides, think of it as prep for all the press you're going to get when you're a famous singer."

I laugh, helping her stack the counted bottles back on the shelf. "God, you really do have all the faith, don't you?"

"It's easy when your best friend's a superstar," she says, nudging me with her shoulder playfully. "And I'm so happy for you and Jack, by the way. It was really fun at dinner the other night."

The guilt hits me like a physical weight pressing down on my chest. I've been lying to my best friend for weeks. The one person who's always been there for me, who knows all my secrets except this one. I promised Jack I wouldn't tell anyone, but every time Maren gets that excited look in her eyes when she talks about us as a couple, I feel worse.

"Yeah," I say, my voice tight. "It was a good night."

Maren pauses mid-count and gives me a look, her best friend radar clearly pinging. "Okay, what's that face for?"

"What face? There's no face," I say, busying myself organizing the tequila bottles by size.

"That's your 'I'm hiding something' face," she says matter-of-factly, setting down her clipboard. "I've known you for years, Lark. Spill it."

"It's nothing."

"Is everything okay with you and Jack? Did you guys have a fight?" Her concern is genuine, which makes me feel even worse.

"No, nothing like that." I take a deep breath, the words catching in my throat. I can't do this anymore. I can't keep lying to Maren. "It's just… I haven't been completely honest with you."

She sets down her clipboard slowly, turning to face me fully. "About what?"

This is such a bad idea. I promised Jack I wouldn't say anything. What if it ruins everything? But this is Maren. "About me and Jack," I finally say, forcing myself to look her in the eye, my heart pounding. "We're not... actually dating."

She blinks, confusion crossing her face. "What are you talking about? I've seen you together."

"I know, I know. We're together, but not like that. It's..." I swallow hard. "Remember when I told you about how Jack pretended to be my boyfriend that night Brandon came into the bar? And then I said he asked me out for real after?"

Maren nods slowly.

"Well, he didn't. Ask me out for real, I mean," I say. "We did get to talking after the whole Brandon thing that night. And he proposed an... arrangement for mutual benefit."

"Mutual benefit," Maren repeats, her face unreadable. "Meaning...?"

"He needed image rehab for his racing career, that whole scandal thing in Monaco. And I needed a boost in social media following before the label would even consider moving forward with me. So we made a deal." The words tumble out faster and faster, like I can't stop them now that I've started. "Three months of pretending to date, and then a clean break in September when he goes back to Europe."

Maren's mouth drops open like I've just dropped the biggest scandal bomb of the century.

"You're telling me," she says slowly, her voice rising with disbelief, "that you and Jack have been FAKE DATING this ENTIRE TIME?"

I wince, glancing toward the kitchen nervously. "Could you maybe say that a little louder? I don't think they heard you in Seattle."

"Are you serious right now?" Her voice is hushed but intense, her eyes wide. "Like actually serious? This isn't some weird joke?"

"I'm completely serious," I say, twisting my hands nervously. "I make him look stable and wholesome, dating someone nice and hardworking, like a cute hometown story. And his followers have been going crazy, which has been making my music spread like wildfire on social media."

"Holy shit," Maren breathes, eyes wide.

"I wanted to tell you, but I promised Jack I'd keep it quiet. It was part of our agreement. He didn't want to risk his brothers knowing and it getting out, and normally I would have said fuck it I'll do as I want, but I knew asking you to lie to Calvin would be so selfish. So…" I trail off.

Maren stares at me for another long moment, and then bursts out laughing.

"Oh my god," she wheezes, clutching the shelf for support, her whole body shaking with laughter. "This is, this is the most ridiculous thing I've ever heard!"

"Maren!" I hiss, eyes darting toward the kitchen like Jayson might materialize any second.

"I'm sorry, I'm sorry," she gasps, trying to catch her breath, wiping tears from her eyes. "This is just so unhinged. I literally would have never guessed that this is what you were going to say."

Her laughter is infectious, and despite my anxiety, I find myself smiling too. "I know. I still can't believe we're pulling it off."

"Wait, wait, wait," Maren says, her laughter subsiding into giggles, her expression delighted. "So when you two were all cozy at dinner, making eyes at each other across the table…"

"All for show," I confirm, though something twists uncomfortably in my stomach at the memory.

Maren shakes her head in disbelief, still grinning. "I can't believe this. I was completely convinced."

"So… you're not mad that I lied to you?" I ask tentatively, relief flooding through me.

"Not at all," she says, picking up her clipboard again, her tone reassuring. "I get it. I'm only peeved I haven't been able to talk through all of this with you. Especially the part where it's completely obvious that you have a crush on him. That's SO not fake."

My cheeks flush hot. "It's not like that. I told you we're *acting*."

Maren's eyes narrow. "Bullshit. You aren't that good of an actress."

"We have good chemistry!" I protest weakly, knowing how unconvincing I sound. "That's what makes it believable!"

"So," she says, folding her arms and giving me a knowing look, "you spend all this time with Jack, pretending to be his girlfriend, looking at him with those big doe eyes, and you haven't developed any feelings at all?"

"Fine!" I throw my hands up, the admission bursting out. "I might have a tiny little crush on him. But it's nothing serious. Just a small, completely manageable attraction because, you know, the man is unfairly gorgeous. But that's it. Tiny!"

Maren squeals so loudly that I'm sure Jayson can hear her in the kitchen.

"*I knew it*!" She slaps her hands together, practically vibrating with excitement. "I fucking knew it! The way you look at him…"

"It's just physical," I insist, trying to sound convincing even though I'm failing miserably. "Nothing I can't handle. The arrangement ends in September, he goes back to Europe, and that's that."

"Mmhmm," she says. Her skepticism couldn't be more obvious. "Nothing's happened? Not at all? You're telling me two hot young people are pretending to date with crazy chemistry and you've managed to keep your hands off each other?"

My face burns even hotter. "Nothing happened."

"*Lark*, like I said, bad actress," she says smugly.

"OK… that night at dinner, when we disappeared to the gazebo, we were talking and… we might have almost kissed," I admit reluctantly, the words coming. "Before Chloe interrupted us. But we didn't! It's been totally, well mostly, back to normal since."

Maren practically dances in place, her glee unmistakable. "This is exactly how it happens! First comes the fake dating, then the real feelings, then the real kissing, then—"

"It was a momentary lapse in judgment," I say, cutting her off before she can finish that thought. "It won't happen again."

"Sure, sure," Maren says, leaning forward. "So what happens in Miami when you share a hotel room?"

Jack and I had already planned for this. Everyone knows we're arriving together so we can't get separate rooms without it looking suspicious. "We have a plan," I say, trying to sound confident. "We're getting a bigger room with two beds and sleeping way way far apart. Nothing is going to happen."

"A weekend of pretending to be madly in love while fighting your very real attraction," Maren sighs dramatically, her tone making it clear she thinks I'm delusional. "Oh, you are *so* getting some."

"It's not like that," I protest, but it sounds weak even to my own ears.

"Uh huh, tell that to your face," Maren grins, clearly enjoying this way too much. "You better keep me updated on everything. And don't worry, I won't tell Calvin. I'll let Jack handle that conversation whenever he's ready. Calvin's pretty focused on work right now anyway, so I don't think he'd live for the drama the way I am."

"Thank you," I laugh, squeezing her hand. "And Mare? I'm so glad you know. I hated lying to you."

"Aw, I know you did," Maren says, her expression softening before she points at me with mock sternness. "But damn right you should feel bad. From now on, you tell me *everything*. No more secrets between us."

"Deal," I say as she pulls me in for a quick hug.

"Good." She pulls back, eyes sparkling. "Because this is way more entertaining than even the best reality TV."

I laugh, rolling my eyes. "Well, I'm glad my love life can provide quality entertainment."

She picks up her clipboard again. "I expect a full debrief after Miami."

CHAPTER 13

JACK

The fifty-pound bag of mulch hits the ground with a satisfying thud. Calvin's at the community college teaching his summer writing workshop, so Maren recruited me for garden duty with the promise of lunch. Which really just means I would have helped anyway, but now I get food too. Plus, Maren makes these sandwiches with some kind of fancy aioli that's basically crack in condiment form.

"Thank god you were free," she says, kneeling by her raised beds with a trowel, blonde hair already escaping from her ponytail. "I was too impatient to wait for Calvin to get home from work, and these beds need to be prepped before the rain comes tomorrow."

"Happy to help," I say, hefting another fifty-pound bag like it weighs nothing. Training six days a week has its advantages. "Besides, you had me at 'food.' I'm easy that way."

Maren laughs, shaking her head. "The way to a man's heart, apparently. Even Formula One drivers aren't immune to good sandwiches."

We work in a comfortable rhythm for a while. Maren's one of those people who doesn't need to fill every silence with conversation, which I appreciate. She hums while she works, occasionally muttering creative threats at weeds that dare to exist in her carefully planned garden beds.

"So," she says after a while, sitting back on her heels and wiping her forehead with her arm, which just smears more dirt across her face. "You excited to get back to Miami and get out of Dark River for a bit?" She gives me a look, and I've interacted with Maren enough over the years to know she always has this way of seeing through people's bullshit.

I smile, setting down another bag. "Do I seem that miserable here?"

She laughs, brushing dirt off her knees. "Not when you're with Lark."

"Yeah well, she makes Dark River bearable," I say. Not a lie. "And it's not that I hate it here, I guess I just loved my life before all this and, I dunno, it's..." I trail off, not sure how to explain the restlessness that's been eating at me.

"Not home?" She looks up, her eyes too perceptive, seeing more than I want to show.

"Yeah, exactly. Not like it is to Calvin now, or Theo or Dominic. Even Alex to some extent. They've all found their place here, put down roots. I'm just passing through, killing time."

"I get that," Maren says, digging up another stubborn weed with focused determination. "Hopefully you'll get the contract stuff sorted soon and get back to where you belong."

"Thanks, I like the being-around-family part," I say, moving another bag of mulch into position. "Just Dark River itself isn't quite right for me anymore, or maybe never was. Not that Miami is home either, but at least it's back in my world. Back in racing."

"I'm happy for you," Maren says. "And for Lark, too, with

Miami coming up. She's always wanted to travel more. And I know she's still thinking about the open mic night and being so nervous about future performances, so a bit of travel and distraction is great to take her mind off it."

"You know her performance was incredible," I say. "Her songs and her voice are something special. She has that thing, that presence that you can't teach. It was just at the end I think her nerves came through."

She attacks a particularly stubborn weed with renewed vigor. "Ugh, tell me about it. God, when she told me what happened I wanted to go and key his car that night!"

A cold feeling settles in my stomach, realization creeping over me like ice water. "Whose car?" I ask carefully.

Maren pauses mid-weed-pull and looks up at me, panic crossing her face. "Uh, what?"

"Whose car?" My voice is deceptively calm even though everything inside me just went still and dangerous.

"Shit. I thought she had told you already." She drops her trowel, looking distressed. "If you don't know then she probably didn't want anyone else to. Fuck."

"Brandon was there?" I ask, voice level. "At her performance?" My jaw clenches. "And that's what threw her off?"

"I mean, yes. But I think it was more that it brought back all that stage fright she's had before." Maren's words come faster now, apologetic. "She gets nervous when Brandon is there or not, but I think she thought maybe she could push through it this time, and then he showed up and sat right in front and just... yeah. But you can't do anything, okay? Ugh, I can't believe I said that."

My hand tightens on the bag of mulch I'm holding. Fucking Brandon. At Lark's performance. The first time she'd gotten up on a big stage in years, and that asshole showed up.

"It's alright, really. I'm not going to do anything stupid." I force myself to sound casual, like the information isn't making my blood boil. "I just fucking hate that guy."

She snorts, going back to her weeding. "Well, there's something we can definitely agree on."

We go back to working in silence for a few minutes, me hauling mulch with more force than necessary, her meticulously arranging her garden beds. I try to keep my movements measured, my expression neutral, but inside I'm already planning. That's the last fucking time he messes with her.

"Jack," Maren says, watching me too closely, "promise me you're not going to do anything stupid about Brandon. He's a scumbag, but he's not worth getting into trouble over."

I nod, trying to hide the rage building inside me like a pressure cooker. "Yeah," I manage, my voice carefully controlled. "Don't worry about it. I'm not going to do anything."

"You better not be lying to me, Jack," she says, pointing her trowel at me like a weapon. "I know that look."

"Don't worry, Maren. Scout's honor." The lie slips out easily. Too easily.

We finish up the gardening work with conversation about her and Calvin's plans for the rest of the landscaping, about the Miami event, about anything but Brandon. Maren keeps shooting me worried glances, but I'm careful to keep my expression neutral, my movements measured and controlled. Inside, I'm already calculating. I've seen Brandon's truck at a construction site in town where he's been working on the new retail development. I know exactly where to find him.

"Thanks for your help," Maren says as I'm packing up to leave, wiping her dirty hands on her jeans. "You sure you don't want to stay for lunch? Those aioli sandwiches I promised?"

"Rain check," I say, wiping my hands on my jeans. "Just remembered I've got some errands to run."

I'm on my bike and halfway to the construction site before I even really think about what I'm doing. The rage that's been simmering since Maren's revelation is now a full boil.

Maybe Lark's not really my girlfriend, but that doesn't change the fact that she deserves better than having her piece of shit ex-husband showing up to mess with her head. Lark can fight her own battles, but some people only understand one kind of language.

And I've always been fluent in making sure bullies understand exactly where they stand.

The construction site is easy to find. New retail development, supposed to bring jobs to Dark River or whatever bullshit the town council said to get it approved.

I park across the street and check the time. 11:47 AM.

When noon hits, workers start streaming out toward their trucks, hard hats in hand, ready for their lunch break. Brandon's easy to spot even in the crowd. Still has that same walk—shoulders back, chin up, strutting like he owns the place.

I get out of my car, but before I can approach him he stops beside a kid who can't be more than seventeen, new to the crew, judging by the clean boots and wide eyes. Brandon's barking at him, voice sharp enough to cut through the air. "What'd I tell you about dragging your feet? You screw up one more measurement and you're done, you hear me?"

The kid mutters an apology, cheeks red, and Brandon waves him off like he's garbage.

That's when I cross the street. "We need to talk," I say.

Brandon turns, already pissed, eyes glassy and mean—like maybe he started his lunch break early with something stronger than soda. "What the hell do *you* want?" he growls, stepping in close. Then he shoves me in the chest hard enough to make it clear he's looking for a fight.

I don't give him another chance.

The punch lands clean. Right on his jaw, exactly where I aimed. His head snaps to the side and he stumbles backward, crashing against his truck with a metallic thud. Blood immediately starts pouring from his split lip, running down his chin.

"What the fuck!" he sputters, hand flying to his face. His fingers come away covered in blood and his eyes go wide. "Jesus Christ, Midnight!"

My knuckles throb, already starting to swell. Completely fucking worth it.

"We need to have a conversation," I say, closing the distance between us before he can recover. I'm taller than him by a few inches, and I use every bit of that height now, stepping into his space until he has to tilt his head back to look at me. He's pressed against his truck, nowhere to go. "About you showing up to Lark's performance."

His eyes widen. "It's a public venue," he says, blood dripping from his lip. He wipes at it with the back of his hand, smearing red across his skin. "I can go wherever the hell I want. It's a free country."

"You can go lots of places," I agree, my voice deadly calm. I plant my hand on the truck beside his head, caging him in. "The grocery store. The hardware store. That shitty sports bar you like. But Lark's performances?" I lean in closer and I see his Adam's apple bob as he swallows. "Those are off limits."

"You can't tell me—"

"I can tell you whatever the fuck I want, you little shit," I interrupt, and my voice drops even lower. "You're done showing up to watch her perform. You're done showing up at the Black Lantern. You're done with whatever pathetic little game you're playing."

"You don't know shit about our marriage," he says, but his voice is weaker now. Blood keeps dripping from his lip, leaving dark spots on his work shirt.

"I know you showing up at her performance was deliberate," I bark. "I know you sat right in front where she couldn't miss you. And I know you're done pulling that shit."

His jaw tightens but he doesn't respond.

"Here's what's going to happen," I say, leaning in even closer. "You're going to stay the fuck away from her. You see her in public? You turn around and go the other direction. You hear she's performing somewhere? You stay home."

He stands there smoldering, then wipes blood from his lip and holds up his fingers as if showing it off. "I could sue you, Midnight."

I actually laugh at that. "Go ahead. Press charges. I've got lawyers who'll bury you in paperwork for fun." I lean in closer, dropping my voice. "And you'll have to explain to everyone why it happened. Tell this whole town you showed up at Lark's performance to intimidate her. See how that plays out for you."

His face goes pale. More blood drips from his lip onto his shirt.

"This town loves her, Brandon," I continue quietly. "It *tolerates* you."

His jaw works like he wants to say something, wants to have the last word, but self-preservation finally kicks in. "Fine," he mutters, fumbling for his keys with shaking hands. "Whatever."

"You've been a piece of shit since high school," I say quietly, my eyes locked on his. "So understand me when I say this." I lean in even closer. "If I hear you've been anywhere near her, if you so much as breathe in her direction, I will make what just happened look like a fucking warm-up. I will put you in the hospital. Do you understand me?"

Fear flashes across his face, real and undeniable now. His face flushes red, anger and humiliation mixing together. But he doesn't say anything. Just wipes more blood from his chin and reaches for his truck door.

I step back, finally giving him space. He fumbles with the

handle, gets the door open, and practically throws himself inside. Slams the door hard enough to make the whole truck shake. Blood smears across his steering wheel as he starts the engine.

He peels out of the parking lot, tires squealing, spraying gravel. A few other construction workers are watching now, probably since I threw the first punch. One of them catches my eye and quickly looks away. No one's going to say shit.

I stand there for a minute, letting the adrenaline drain out. My hand throbs. The knuckles are already swelling, skin split across two of them. There's a little of Brandon's blood on my hand too. I wipe it off on my jeans.

I head back to my bike, flexing my fingers. The pain is sharp but satisfying. Lark deserves to perform without looking out into the audience and seeing his face. She deserves to chase her dreams without him showing up to remind her of every insecurity he spent years building.

The label party is at this place in Seattle called The Vine. Exposed brick walls, Edison bulbs hanging from industrial ceilings, the kind of bar that knows what they're doing with their cocktails.

Lark's been buzzing with energy all day. On the drive over, she talked nonstop, jumping from topic to topic—whether her outfit worked, which producers might be there, random observations about Seattle architecture. Her excitement is contagious, and I found myself smiling the whole drive, just listening to her.

Now, standing outside the entrance, she takes a deep breath and shoots me a grin. "Okay, I'm ready," she says, squaring her shoulders. "Or at least I'm pretending really hard that I'm ready, which is basically the same thing. Fake it till you make it, right?"

"Exactly. That's all any of us are doing." I put my arm around her as we walk inside. "You've got this."

She's wearing dark jeans and a black blazer that makes her look polished and confident, and I'm having trouble not staring. The blazer fits perfectly, showing off her curves, and when she moves the fabric shifts in ways that make me want to peel it off her. I shove the thought away. Not helpful.

The place is already packed, music playing low enough for conversation but loud enough to create energy. The crowd's a mix of industry types in expensive casual wear and artists trying to look like they're not trying too hard. Dim lighting, exposed ductwork overhead, bottles backlit behind the bar casting colored shadows across faces. Before we can even get our bearings, a woman starts making her way toward us through the crowd, waving.

"Lark? Jack?" She's younger than I expected, maybe early thirties, with that polished LA look—statement jewelry, perfectly styled hair. "I'm Maya. So glad you both could make it."

"Oh hello! So lovely to meet you in person," Lark says, and I can feel the slight tension in her back under my hand even though her smile is perfect and warm.

"You as well." Maya's handshake is firm. She turns to me with an appraising look. "And you must be Jack? I've heard so much about you. Great to meet you."

"You as well," I say, shaking her hand.

She returns her gaze to Lark, her expression shifting to pure business excitement. "I was just talking to our A&R team about you. We've been following your numbers since our call last week and they just keep climbing. Really impressive growth. Your streaming numbers are up almost forty percent this month alone, so we're so glad you were able to make it tonight."

Lark's smile widens. "Thank you so much! I've been working really hard on content consistency and engagement."

"It shows," Maya says. "The algorithm loves consistency, and your fans are incredibly engaged. That's what we look for, not just numbers, but *real* connection." She gestures for us to follow her deeper into the bar. "There are people who've been asking to meet you."

She leads us through the crowd toward a group gathered near the windows overlooking the street. The space opens up here, floor-to-ceiling glass reflecting the city lights back at us. I notice Lark's hand fidgeting slightly with her clutch, the only tell that she's nervous underneath all the confidence she's projecting.

"Everyone, this is Lark Reyes," Maya announces to the group with enthusiasm. "The artist I was telling you about. Lark, this is Harrison, one of our senior A&R executives."

Harrison is maybe mid-forties with salt-and-pepper hair. He extends his hand. "Lark, really great to finally meet you. We've been impressed with what we've been seeing."

"Thank you," Lark says, shaking his hand firmly.

"Of course," Harrison says, leaning in slightly like he's sharing something important. "Seems like you've got some loyal fans developing, and they're actively sharing your content. That's gold in this industry."

"I've been really intentional about engagement," Lark says, and I can hear her confidence building. "Responding to comments, sharing behind-the-scenes process stuff."

"That's exactly what we like to see," Harrison says, nodding. "Artists who understand the business side of things." He pauses, studying her with interest. "So tell me, what's your songwriting process like? Your lyrics have this narrative quality that's really compelling. Very story-driven."

And just like that, Lark's off. The nervousness fades completely as she talks about her music, her hands moving expressively as she explains how she builds songs from small observations or overheard conversations. She's funny too, making self-deprecating jokes about her writing process that have Harrison and the others laughing.

I watch her work the room, and something twists in my chest. She's magnetic without even trying. Smart, funny, talented as hell. Every person she talks to leans in, interested in what she's saying.

"I have about three hundred voice memos on my phone that are just me humming melodies at random times," she says with a grin. "My neighbors probably think I'm losing it. Just this woman wandering around her apartment singing the same three notes over and over trying to figure out if they work together."

"That's the creative process though," Harrison laughs, clearly charmed. And who wouldn't be. She's incredible. "Some of our biggest artists have the same habit. The voice memos, the random middle-of-the-night recording sessions. It's all part of it."

Maya introduces her to more people over the next half hour. A producer named Sam who immediately starts asking technical questions about her vocal range and recording experience. Another artist on the label, a guy named Devon Kane who Lark clearly recognizes and tries not to fangirl over. Each conversation, I watch her get more comfortable, more herself.

I hang back mostly, letting her do her thing. This is her moment, not mine, and she doesn't need me hovering. But I can't help watching her. Can't help feeling proud of her. I'm not her actual boyfriend. I'm just here to boost her image, make her look good for the label.

Except it doesn't feel fake when I watch her light up talking about music. It doesn't feel like a business arrangement when I realize I'd rather be here watching her shine than anywhere else.

Fuck. I'm in trouble.

After about forty-five minutes of networking, Lark finds me

near the bar. Some producer had pulled her away earlier with an enthusiastic wave and a "I promise I'll give her back!" and a wink.

"Hey there, thought I'd lost you to the industry vultures," I say as she makes her way over.

"You nearly did," she says, leaning against the bar beside me with a small sigh of relief. "I managed to break away but I *desperately* need a five-minute break where I'm not trying to be impressive. Plus my face literally hurts from smiling so much. I need a cocktail to give me the courage to go back out there."

I laugh, signaling the bartender. "What would you like? I'm at your service."

She considers this, tapping her fingers thoughtfully on the bar. "Ugh, what to pick. Something that tastes good but won't make me embarrass myself. I still have to be charming and articulate for at least another hour and I can't do that if I'm making weird faces at my drink or slurring my words."

"So no tequila shots then?" I tease. "Or should I order you a Long Island iced tea? I remember a certain story about a high school party…"

"Absolutely not," she says, shooting me a withering look that could probably kill plants before breaking into a grin. "I learned that lesson the hard way and I'm never revisiting it. I should have never told you that. That night is *banned* from all future discussions."

I hold up my hands in surrender, laughing. "Message received. Long Island iced teas are off the table forever. How about a French 75?"

"Ooh, that sounds good actually," she says, her face lighting up. "I made that for someone a few days ago, but it's been ages since I've had one myself."

I order her drink and another beer for myself. When the bartender slides the elegant champagne flute across to her, she takes a careful sip and makes an appreciative sound.

"Okay, this is dangerous," she announces. "I forgot how good these are."

"That's how they get you," I say, amused.

She takes another small sip, then turns to survey the room before looking back at me. "This is insane though, right? Thanks for being here, by the way. Moral support and all that. Really helps to have someone to ground me when I start overthinking everything. And to have arm candy that makes me look good."

I laugh at that. "Happy to provide aesthetic enhancement to your professional reputation."

"Thank god for that." She takes another sip, her eyes scanning the room before landing back on me. "Speaking of music, Sam was telling me he used to work with Joni Mitchell back in the day. I mean, can you believe that? I just about died. I wanted to ask a million questions but I didn't want to seem like a total fangirl."

"Wow. Joni's a legend," I say, taking a sip of my beer. "One of the best songwriters of all time."

She glances over, eyebrows raised. "I'm surprised you've even listened to her. She doesn't really scream race car driver."

"Always such a lack of faith, Lark," I say. "I spend half my life alone in cars and hotel rooms with a pair of headphones. I've listened to her album *Blue* a hundred times."

She laughs. "Okay, now you have to tell me your favorite song from that album. This is a test and there are wrong answers."

"Well, the title track is objectively perfect," I say without hesitation. "Fight me on that."

"I'm not going to fight you when you're correct," she laughs, looking genuinely delighted. "Though I think *A Case of You* is a close second."

"That's a solid choice," I concede.

"Still can't believe you're a Joni fan. We *need* to compare playlists! I don't know how we haven't done that yet."

"Done," I laugh, taking another sip of my beer. "We have a long flight to Miami tomorrow. I'll show you mine if you'll show me yours."

"Not a bad way to spend a flight," she declares. "Though I know some of your taste is questionable since you told me you liked that Neon Wolf album the other night."

"I am going to change your mind about that album." I say, shaking my head. "It's good and you're just being stubborn."

"Not a chance, though I am excited to see what else you're hiding in there. Maybe some guilty pleasure pop?" She's teasing now, her eyes dancing with amusement. "Or like, European techno to get pumped up before races? Heavy bass drops and no lyrics?"

"I do like European techno," I admit. "If we're ever in Europe together I'll take you to this club in Berlin. *Berghain*. It's legendary. Twelve-hour DJ sets, complete sensory overload."

"Yeah? I think I'd actually like that." She laughs, leaning her hip against the bar. "I haven't been dancing in years but I *love* it. So we can stay out until sunrise if the music's good."

"Deal. And trust me, the music's always good."

We stand there for a moment, just looking at each other, and a warmth settles deep in my chest. This easy back-and-forth, discovering we like the same things. Like we just found another piece that fits together.

Maya appears at Lark's elbow suddenly, breaking the moment. "Lark, there's someone I really want you to meet. Harrison's boss just arrived and he's only in Seattle for tonight. He's been asking about you specifically."

"Oh, I'd love to meet him," Lark says, shooting me a quick wink before returning to Maya. "Lead the way."

She gives me one more smile over her shoulder as Maya guides her back into the crowd, and I watch her go. She's magnetic without even trying. And I'm completely fucked because I can't stop thinking about how much I want this to be real.

We stay another hour. Lark works the room like she was born for it, collecting business cards and making connections. Every time I catch her eye across the room, she's smiling. This is what she's been working toward for years, and watching it happen feels like being part of something bigger than our arrangement.

Finally, around eight, we make our excuses because of our morning flight and head out to the parking lot. The night air is cooler now, a relief after the warmth of the crowded bar. In her car, I drive while she tells me all the details of conversations I missed when she got pulled away.

"I mean, three people gave me their actual business cards with their direct phone numbers," she says, practically bouncing in her seat. "Not assistants, their actual numbers. And Maya said she'll be in touch next week, that the team has a lot to discuss. That's huge!"

"You killed it in there," I tell her, merging onto the highway that'll take us back to Dark River. "Everyone in that room wanted to work with you. You could see it."

"I still can't believe it," she says, pulling the business cards out of her clutch to look at them again like they might disappear. "That this is really happening."

"It's happening because you're talented as hell and you've worked for it."

"And because you've been helping with the Instagram thing," she adds, looking over at me with gratitude clear in her expression. "Don't pretend that didn't matter. Maya mentioned our engagement rates multiple times tonight."

"Your music got you in that room," I say firmly. "The Instagram stuff opened the door, but your talent is what made them pay attention."

We're quiet for a few miles after that, comfortable silence with just the highway noise and the radio playing low. The city lights fade behind us as we head north, replaced by darker stretches of road lined with Douglas firs.

"Hey, I wanted to ask you something," she says, shifting in her seat to look at me.

"Shoot," I say, glancing over briefly before returning my eyes to the road.

"So Maren called me earlier," she says slowly.

I already know where this is heading, and it was bound to come out sooner or later.

"She was telling me that she felt terrible about accidentally mentioning something to you. About Brandon being at my performance. And she said after she told you, you suddenly had very urgent errands to run."

"I did have errands," I say, glancing over with a half smile.

"Jack." She rolls her eyes. "What did you do?"

"I had a conversation with Brandon," I admit, drumming my fingers on the steering wheel. "And I explained that he should find other entertainment options on Friday nights. Ones that don't involve watching you perform. Or visiting you at The Black Lantern. Basically nowhere near you."

She's quiet for a long moment. "Did you punch him?"

"Once," I confirm. "But he started it. And I didn't hit him hard enough to do any real damage. And I could have."

"Not that I think he doesn't deserve it, because he absolutely does. But why risk getting in trouble over someone like him? That could get out and mess up your reputation even more. It's too risky with everything you've worked for."

"I don't really care about that," I say. And it's the truth, at least when it comes to Lark. "When Maren told me he showed up at your performance, I just couldn't let that slide. And I know you don't need me fighting your battles for you. You're tough as hell. But you deserve to have someone in your corner who'll tell him to fuck off when he crosses a line. And Brandon's not particularly good at taking hints."

Her hand finds my arm, warm even through my jacket, and squeezes gently.

"Thank you," she says softly. "I think he gets off on trying to ruin things for me. And he had it coming. Though I *still* think you shouldn't have done it. It's risky for your career."

"Come on, you don't think I'd let some dickhead mess with you just to protect my image?" I look over at her with a grin. "I've got enough money and lawyers to handle whatever Brandon wants to throw at me."

She swats at me, laughing. "Just don't let it go to your head, action hero. I can take care of myself. This doesn't make you my knight in shining armor or whatever."

"I know," I say. "I've seen you at Dom's gym. You're legitimately terrifying. Those boxing lessons have turned you into a weapon."

She smiles at that, flexing her arm dramatically. "Damn right I am. Dom says my right hook could drop someone."

"I believe it," I say, glancing at her flexed bicep, which actually is really impressive. "Remind me never to piss you off."

We drive in silence for a while, the miles disappearing beneath us. By the time we pull up to her apartment, I park in a visitor spot next to where I left my bike earlier. I walk her to her door, moving slower than necessary, not wanting the night to end quite yet.

"So… Miami tomorrow," she says, unlocking her door but not opening it yet. She turns back, leaning against it and looking up at me.

"Yep. Eight AM pickup," I confirm, shoving my hands in my pockets because if I don't, I might reach for her and fuck up whatever this fragile thing between us is.

She looks up at me. "Thanks for tonight. For coming with me, for being there. For… everything."

"Anytime," I say, and I mean it more than she probably realizes.

She steps closer and rises up on her toes, pressing a kiss to my cheek. Her lips are warm and soft and it takes everything in me not to close the distance, to turn my head and capture her mouth with mine. She pulls back, only slightly, looking at me with those brown eyes that I've thought about every night for weeks.

Then her mouth is on mine.

My hands move to her waist before I can even fully process what's happening and I'm kissing her back. She tastes like champagne and something sweeter, and every fantasy I've had about this moment disappears because nothing compares to the reality of her lips on mine. Her hand comes up to rest against my chest and I pull her closer, needing more of this, more of her, more of everything.

The kiss deepens and for a few perfect seconds there's nothing else. Just her.

She breaks away suddenly, stepping back. Her cheeks are flushed and she's breathing hard.

"Uh," she says, her voice unsteady. "Thank you. I just wanted to say thank you. For the Brandon thing. I wanted to thank you… for that. I… goodnight!"

Before I can respond, she's turning away, pushing open her door.

"Lark—"

The door closes. The message is pretty clear. Instant regret.

I stand there in the hallway staring at her closed door, my heart hammering against my ribs, the ghost of her kiss burning like a brand on my lips.

CHAPTER 14

LARK

The plane touches down in Miami with a jolt that makes my stomach swoop unpleasantly. Flying isn't my favorite thing in the world, never has been. Though the complimentary champagne in first class helped. As did keeping my eyes glued to the in-flight entertainment system for six straight hours, watching three movies back-to-back like my life depended on it.

Anything to avoid talking to Jack. Anything to avoid having to acknowledge what happened last night. Because every time I look at him, all I can think about is kissing him in my hallway. And then running away like a complete idiot.

I don't know what came over me. It's like I finally couldn't fight it anymore, like every moment we'd spent together over the past month just built up until I kissed him before remembering all the reasons why making a move on him is a terrible idea.

He lives in Europe. Insane job that keeps him gone half the year. Serial dater who's allergic to commitment. I'm already in too deep as it is and a broken heart is practically guaranteed.

Plus I have my own shit to focus on—my music, my career, building something that's mine instead of falling for someone who'll be onto their next conquest before I can blink.

But the kiss keeps replaying in my mind anyway because, damn, the man can *kiss*. But now the movies are over and we're on the ground and I need to fill the silence with something. Anything.

"You know, flying like this is going to ruin me for all future travel," I tell Jack, stretching my legs in the actually-human-sized legroom. "Going back to coach after this will be like going from a spa day to medieval torture."

Good. Casual airplane conversation. Nothing awkward about that.

Jack grins as he unbuckles his seatbelt. "Just one of many advantages of fake dating a racing driver. Free drinks and actual legroom at 30,000 feet."

Right. Fake. A good reminder that I definitely need right now. I clear my throat.

"Bold of you to assume I didn't fake date you specifically for the airline perks," I say, raising an eyebrow. "But honestly, if I'd known these were the benefits, I would've started fake dating celebrities years ago. I've been doing this all wrong."

He's been completely normal all morning. Greeting me at the airport like nothing happened, making easy conversation during boarding, offering me the window seat without any weird tension. Meanwhile I've been avoiding eye contact for six hours straight.

The flight attendant wishes us a pleasant visit as we deplane into the terminal. Jack pulls a baseball cap low over his eyes and slips on sunglasses, but it doesn't do much to hide him. Three separate airport employees do double-takes as we walk past, and a group of teenagers whispers excitedly, phones already out and recording. He acknowledges them with a friendly nod but keeps moving, his hand lightly guiding me through the crowded terminal.

"Does this happen everywhere you go?" I whisper as we navigate toward baggage claim, weaving through clusters of travelers.

"Pretty much," he says with a shrug, like it's no big deal. "You get used to it."

I'm not sure I would ever get used to strangers taking my photo while I'm just trying to walk through an airport, but Jack handles it all with ease. He stops to sign a couple autographs for kids who approach, crouching down to their level and asking their names, and then we're back on our way.

"Ready for your introduction to Miami summer?" Jack asks as we approach the exit doors.

"How bad can it be? I visit my parents in Southern California pretty regularly," I reply with a confident shrug. "I can handle a little heat."

The answer hits me the moment we step outside. This is nothing—NOTHING—like California. It's like walking face-first into a hot, wet blanket that immediately wraps itself around you and refuses to let go. I swear I can feel the humidity immediately making my hair start to expand to twice its normal size, each strand rebelling against my careful styling, and sweat beading at my hairline within seconds.

"Oh my god," I say, "Okay I take it back. I take it all back, this is insane."

Jack laughs, looking completely unfazed. "Welcome to Miami."

"It's been ten seconds and I already feel like I'm drowning in it." I fan myself uselessly with my hand as we make our way through the pickup area. "I should have packed scuba gear. Or gills."

We walk along the sidewalk for a few minutes and I try not to whine like a complete baby, but after a six-hour flight from

Seattle and me having made the catastrophically stupid decision to wear a cardigan, the heat is making me regret every life choice that led to this moment. I fear I have about three more minutes before I turn into the Wicked Witch of the West, melting in a puddle of bad decisions and misplaced confidence.

"Uh, how much further is it?" I ask, feeling my makeup actively sliding off my face with each step.

Jack looks down at me and laughs, his eyes crinkling. "Just right down there. I can see Carlos. You alright over there?"

"Oh I'm good," I wave it off as though I'm not dissolving into a human puddle. "Just getting my Miami glow on."

A middle-aged man with brown skin and distinguished salt and pepper hair greets us with a "Midnight" sign next to a sleek black car.

"Mr. Midnight," he says with a nod of recognition and a smile. "Welcome back to Miami."

"Thanks, Carlos," Jack says, shaking the man's hand warmly. "Good to see you again. This is Lark."

"Ms. Reyes," Carlos says, his eyes kind. "*Bienvenida a Miami*. First visit to our city?"

"*Sí, primera vez*," I reply with a smile. "*Y estoy muy emocionada*."

Carlos looks pleased as he opens the car door for us. "*Ah, habla español! Excelente*. You will love Miami, I think. The city has a lot to offer."

As we slide into the blissfully air-conditioned back seat, I take a deep breath of the cool air like it's liquid gold and settle into the luxurious leather. The seats are butter-soft, the interior smelling like that indefinable new car scent mixed with something subtly expensive. Carlos closes the door and circles around to the driver's seat.

"I didn't realize how much I'd miss air conditioning in the few minutes we were outside," I say, leaning back against the seat and letting the cool air wash over me. I glance over at Jack and narrow my eyes suspiciously. "Why aren't you sweating? Are you even human?"

Jack smirks. "Racing suits in summer. Try sitting in a fire-proof oven with the cockpit pushing a hundred and thirty degrees around you."

I laugh and roll my eyes. "Oh great, so you're basically heat-proof. Meanwhile I'll be the puddle following you around all weekend."

I watch Miami pass by outside the window, mesmerized. Palm trees line wide boulevards, their fronds swaying in a breeze I can't feel through the glass. The sun is setting, casting everything in pinks and oranges, lighting up the glass skyscrapers like they're on fire. It's so different from Dark River's evergreens and grey skies, so vibrant and alive.

"So, is this how you always travel?" I ask, gesturing around the luxury car. "The first class tickets, fancy car service, everything?"

"Pretty much, yeah. Not when I was younger and a rookie, but the more famous you get, the more perks come with it," Jack says, watching the city roll by. "My manager, Thomas, handles all the logistics for events like this."

I nod, taking in the colorful storefronts and outdoor cafes we pass. "It's definitely a step up from my usual travel experience. Though I did once splurge on TSA PreCheck, so I'm basically a VIP too."

Jack smiles. "Well, get ready for the full treatment this weekend. Tomorrow is the event on the track, then a fancy gala in the evening. That's the black tie one I told you about, very high-end. Caviar, champagne fountains, the works."

"Looking forward to it," I say, mouth watering at the thought of fancy appetizers. Despite the fake nature of our relationship and the mortifying kiss still looming over me, I can't help but be excited about experiencing his world for a weekend. It's like getting a backstage pass to a life I've only seen in magazines and

Instagram posts. His world, not mine. "Though I will try not to get too used to it. Going back to my regular life after all this luxury might be a shock to my system."

"Nah, this is just practice for your future tour," Jack says, nudging my shoulder with his. "You'll have people carrying your guitar and bringing you green M&Ms or whatever your rider demands."

"From your lips to the universe's ears," I reply, hoping desperately that he's right. "So what's the plan again for tonight? You mentioned you have to meet your manager?"

"Yeah, Thomas wants to go over some contract stuff tonight," Jack says, checking his watch. "But that's just me. You've got the evening free to enjoy the hotel or explore Miami if you want. The hotel has a pool on the rooftop. Probably the best view in Miami."

"Oh, I am definitely hitting that pool," I say, already picturing myself lounging with a fruity drink and zero responsibilities. "Who knows when I'll get a chance to use a rooftop infinity pool again? I'm milking this weekend for all it's worth."

Jack laughs. "That's the spirit."

The hotel comes into view as we round a corner, and I gasp. It's absolutely spectacular, a tower of white stone and glass soaring up from the beachfront like some kind of modern palace. Flags flutter from the entrance, and a fountain shoots crystal clear water in elegant arcs out front.

"The Azura," Jack says. "One of the best in Miami."

The car pulls up to a circular driveway paved with gleaming marble. A row of palm trees stands at attention along the entrance, and uniformed staff greet arriving guests with the kind of professionalism that must come from years of catering to the ultra-wealthy.

A valet in a crisp navy uniform opens our door before the car fully stops. "Welcome to the Azura, sir, madam," he says.

Jack thanks Carlos and tips him generously before we step

out. I take a moment to absorb the grandeur of the place. The massive fountain with water that dances in patterns, the subtle fragrance of jasmine in the air, the sense of exclusivity that hangs over everything like expensive perfume. This is the kind of place where celebrities and billionaires come to escape.

As we walk through the soaring glass doors, the blast of cool air is a welcome relief from the Miami heat. The lobby stretches out before us, modern design with marble floors, tasteful art installations, and a ceiling that seems impossibly high. A massive chandelier of cascading crystal catches the light, sending prisms dancing across the walls.

"Wow," I murmur to Jack, trying not to gawk too obviously. "This place is incredible."

"Wait till you see the pool," he says with a smile.

At the reception desk, a sleek expanse of what looks like polished onyx, a woman in an impeccably tailored suit greets us. Her silver hair is styled in a perfect chignon. "Mr. Midnight," she says with warmth, "welcome back to the Azura. So good to see you again."

"Thank you, Claudia," Jack says, leaning against the counter casually. "It's good to be back."

"And Ms. Reyes," she turns to me with a welcoming smile, "welcome. We're delighted to have you joining us for your first visit." Her fingers move across the keyboard, perfectly manicured nails catching the light. "Let me get you checked in."

I smile, still taking in the opulence around me. In my head, I run through our plan once more. We couldn't get separate rooms without looking suspicious, so Jack arranged a suite with a separate living room. Jack would take the pull-out couch and I'd get the bedroom. All very practical, appropriate.

The receptionist looks at her screen again, her expression brightening. "Oh! I see there's been a change to your reservation."

Jack raises an eyebrow. "Is there?"

"Yes, your manager called this morning. He requested our Oceanfront Romance Suite for your first trip together as a couple." She smiles professionally. "It's been arranged as a complimentary upgrade for you both."

Jack shoots a quick glance at me, and I try to hide my panic, instead plastering on a smile that I hope looks pleased rather than alarmed.

"How thoughtful," he says smoothly.

"Very generous," I add, matching his calm tone while wondering what exactly a *Romance Suite* entails.

"The suite is our *most* romantic," the receptionist continues enthusiastically. "Thirty-fifth floor, ocean views, private hot tub on the balcony. We've included champagne and chocolate-covered strawberries."

Just what I need right now. Romance suite. Hot tub. Champagne. With the guy I'm actively trying not to think about kissing. Perfect.

"Wonderful," Jack says, accepting the key cards she hands over. "Thank you."

A bellhop in a tailored uniform appears with our luggage on a gleaming brass cart. "I'll bring these right up for you, Mr. Midnight," he says with a polite nod.

We follow the bellhop to the elevator, a glass capsule that offers panoramic views of Miami as it rises. The city stretches out below us, a colorful tapestry of buildings, waterways, and greenery, all shimmering in the setting sun.

"The view is spectacular," the bellhop says, noticing my awestruck expression as I press my face against the glass. "Wait until you see it from your suite. Best in the hotel."

The elevator opens onto the thirty-fifth floor and we follow the bellhop down a hallway lined with plush carpet that muffles our footsteps. The corridor is minimalist and elegant—soft lighting, tasteful artwork, and a sense of hushed exclusivity.

He stops at a set of double doors at the end of the hall,

swipes the key card, and opens them with a flourish. I step inside and my jaw goes slack.

The suite is stunning, modern luxury with floor-to-ceiling windows that showcase an endless stretch of turquoise ocean. Everything is crisp whites, soft blues, and natural wood tones, creating an atmosphere of sophisticated calm.

"Oh my god," I breathe, frozen in the doorway.

In the center of the room sits a giant heart-shaped bed. Not figuratively heart-shaped, but *literally* shaped like a Valentine's Day heart, with crisp sheets and rose petals scattered across it in an artful pattern. It's so ridiculous that I feel my cheeks flush immediately.

A bottle of champagne chills in an ice bucket beside fancy chocolate-covered strawberries arranged on a silver platter. The bathroom visible through an open door is a temple to luxury, all marble and glass, with a tub that could fit a small swim team and a shower with more jets than a rocket ship.

The bellhop arranges our bags, then gives us a tour of the amenities with obvious pride. He demonstrates the hot tub controls, then moves to a discreet panel on the wall.

"And this is our ambient lighting system," he says, flipping a switch that subtly changes the room's lighting. "Ten different settings for various moods and occasions, from 'Ocean Sunset' to 'Midnight Glow.'" He cycles through a few options, each one creating a different ambiance in the room.

I catch Jack's eye as the bellhop enthusiastically shows us how to activate the "Romantic Evening" setting, which bathes the room in a soft, rosy glow. Jack's expression remains neutral, but I can see the hint of amusement in his eyes. Meanwhile, I'm fighting the urge to crawl under that ridiculous bed and hide forever. This entire room is basically screaming "SEX! WE ARE HAVING SEX HERE!" in neon letters, and I've never been more mortified in my life.

"The champagne is complimentary, of course," the bellhop continues, gesturing to the ice bucket.

I nod and smile as though this is all perfectly normal and not making me want to spontaneously combust. When the bellhop finally leaves with Jack's tip, we both stand in the middle of the room, staring at the bed that seems to dominate the otherwise tasteful space.

"So, uh..." I gesture at the ridiculous bed as if words have completely failed me, which they temporarily have. "This is..."

"It's...different," Jack says, looking as uncomfortable as I've ever seen him.

I scan the room desperately for a couch, a daybed, anything else that might serve as a second sleeping option. Nothing. Just the giant heart-shaped bed and a couple of plush chairs that aren't nearly big enough to sleep on unless you're a contortionist or a very small child.

"I can sleep on the floor," Jack offers, following my gaze. "I've crashed in worse places."

"We'll cross that bridge when we come to it," I say, not wanting to deal with the sleeping arrangements just yet. I glance back at the heart-shaped monstrosity and for a split second, my traitorous brain conjures an image of Jack and me tangled up in those sheets together. I feel my face heat up and quickly look away. "Let's just enjoy the view for now. And the free champagne. We might as well get something out of this awkward situation."

I head for the balcony, needing some fresh air and about five minutes where I'm not thinking about last night. The sliding glass door opens silently, and I step out into the warm Miami evening. The view momentarily makes me forget about our sleeping situation and the kiss and all the other complications I've created for myself.

The ocean stretches endlessly before me, beaches below dotted with colorful umbrellas and tiny figures enjoying the last hours of sunlight. The setting sun turns everything golden, the water sparkling like it's filled with diamonds.

Jack joins me, leaning against the railing. "Not bad, huh?"

"Wow," I breathe, feeling the breeze lift my hair. "I think this is one of the most incredible views I've ever seen."

He nods, looking out at the horizon. "Yeah, it's pretty amazing. I always love staying at this hotel. Though this isn't usually my room." He looks over at me with a hint of a smirk.

I laugh. "You mean you don't usually book the giant heart bedroom for your race weekends?"

"God no," Jack says with an exaggerated shudder. "I have a reputation to uphold. Can you imagine what the other drivers would say?"

I smile at him and look back out at the water. "You know I've never seen the Atlantic before. I wanted to travel when I was younger. But my dad and mom, we weren't poor, but we could only afford a trip every year or two, and we always used it to visit my grandparents in SoCal. Or my extended family in Mexico. This is… this is so cool."

He smiles at me, his expression softening. "Well, I'm glad your first view of it is a good one."

We stand in silence for a moment, taking in the panorama before us. A gentle breeze carries the scent of salt and something tropical—jasmine, maybe, or frangipani from the gardens below.

Jack checks his watch. "I should probably head out soon to meet Thomas. The restaurant's downstairs."

"Go," I wave him off. "I wasn't kidding about that pool. I plan to be horizontal with something fruity and alcoholic within the hour."

"Sounds like a solid plan," he laughs. "I'll try not to be too late."

"Take your time," I tell him. "Seriously. I've got a date with that giant bathtub after the pool. I might just turn into a prune and never come out."

Jack grabs his phone and wallet, heading for the door. "If I find you dissolved into soap bubbles when I get back, I'll be sure to tell a heroic story about how you died."

"My legacy is in your hands," I say solemnly, then break into a grin. "Now go, before your manager thinks you've stood him up."

Once he's gone, I flop back on the ridiculous heart-shaped bed, staring up at the ceiling. This weekend is going to be... interesting. Sharing a bed with Jack Midnight. Pretending to be a couple in front of his entire racing world.

No problem at all. What could possibly go wrong?

After Jack leaves, I take advantage of having the suite to myself. A long, hot shower washes away the travel grime and Miami humidity, and I dig through my suitcase for my favorite bikini—a deep cobalt blue that looks fantastic against my light brown skin if I do say so myself. I love the way I feel in it—confident, sexy, and unapologetic. I bought it after the divorce in a fit of rebellion against Brandon's constant criticism of how I dressed. "Too revealing," he'd say. "You're trying too hard." Fuck that.

I slip it on, turning to check myself out in the bathroom mirror. Not bad, Reyes. Not bad at all. The top shows just enough cleavage, and the bottoms showcase the results of all those squats at Dominic's gym. I throw on a light cover-up dress for the walk to the elevator, grab my phone and room key, and head up to the rooftop pool.

The rooftop is what can only be described as paradise. The infinity pool stretches toward the horizon, its edge seeming to melt into the ocean beyond. Now that the sun has set, the entire space is transformed into a luxurious nighttime oasis. Soft lighting glows from beneath the water, casting everything in a dreamy blue hue. Around the pool, cabanas draped in white fabric, and sleek lounge chairs are arranged for optimal sunset viewing. Miami's skyline twinkles around us, a vertical constellation of lights against the darkening sky.

A few other guests lounge around, but it's not too crowded. I find a perfect spot near the edge of the pool, drop my things on a plush lounge chair, shed my cover-up, and slip into the water. It's the perfect temperature—refreshing in the still-hot night air. I float on my back for a while, staring up at the stars, letting the water carry away the day's stress.

After enough floating to turn my fingertips pruney, I climb out and settle into my lounge chair. A server in a crisp white uniform appears beside me with a warm smile.

"Good evening, miss. Can I get you something to drink?" he asks.

"Something tropical with rum, please," I say, returning his smile. "Bartender's choice. I trust your expertise."

"I love an adventurous spirit," he says with a wink. "I'll be right back."

He returns minutes later with a gorgeous sunset-colored cocktail in a crystal glass, garnished with fresh fruit and a perfect twist of orange peel. It looks like liquid art.

"A house specialty rum cocktail with local passion fruit, mango, and a hint of ginger," he explains. "We call it the Miami Sunset."

"It's beautiful, thank you," I say, accepting the drink. I take a sip and nearly moan. The rum hits first, warm and potent, followed by the perfect sweet-tart balance of the fruit. When I get back home I'm going to pester Maren to add this to the menu at The Black Lantern.

I position my drink with the twinkling Miami skyline in the background and snap a photo for Maren. She made me promise to send "excessive updates" about every detail of the trip. "Visual evidence or it didn't happen," were her exact words before I left. This view should definitely qualify.

My phone buzzes within a minute with her response:

Maren: *Holy shit, are you in heaven?? That view!*

Me: *It's incredible. Like stupid incredible. I may never come home.*

Maren: *So how are things going after THE KISS? Still pretending it meant nothing?* 😏

I roll my eyes. She's been relentless since I called her approximately five seconds after it happened to tell her everything. She sees right through my denials about any real feelings, which is annoying because I've been working really hard on lying to myself about how I feel about Jack.

Me: *It was nothing, just a moment of insanity* 😂 *But there's been a slight complication. His manager upgraded us to the "Romance Suite." Complete with heart-shaped bed.*

Maren: *NO WAY. This is TOO perfect! The universe is literally throwing you two together.* 🔥

Me: *The universe is trying to make things supremely awkward, that's what.* 🙄

Maren: *Denial isn't just a river in Egypt, babe. So you're sharing the heart bed, right? Please tell me you're not making him sleep on the floor after all your lectures to me about making a move back when I was lovesick over Calvin.*

Me: *That was different and you know it. And we haven't figured it out yet. I'm at the pool actively avoiding the whole situation. With my fun cocktail.* 🍹

Maren: *Chicken. You literally pushed me into Calvin's arms and now you're running away from your own heart-shaped destiny?* 🤨

Me: *I hate you sometimes.* 💕

Maren: *No you don't. Now go get your man and text me all the dirty details.* 🐓

Me: *He's not MY anything. And there will be no dirty details. I'll send you purely professional updates about the racing events, thank you very much.*

Maren: *Sure you will. Enjoy your night in the sex suite* 🌝

I put my phone down with a laugh and take another long sip of my drink. I settle back into my lounge chair, letting the Miami night envelop me. The rum is warming my veins, the ocean breeze is perfect, and for a moment I let myself just enjoy being here, without overthinking the sleeping arrangements waiting for me back in the room.

As my stomach starts to rumble, I signal the server and order dinner—the grilled mahi-mahi with mango salsa that another guest was having. When it arrives, it's a work of art, the fish perfectly seared and the salsa vibrant with colors that pop even in the evening light. It's one of the most delicious things I've ever tasted.

I'm savoring the last few bites, watching the city lights reflect on the water, when a familiar voice breaks into my thoughts.

"Found you."

I look up to find Jack standing beside my lounge chair, and my breath catches in my throat. He's changed into dark slacks and a crisp white button-down with the sleeves rolled to the elbows, exposing tanned forearms. His expensive watch catches the pool lights, and his hair is slightly damp, like he's just showered. He looks like he stepped straight out of a men's fashion magazine, the kind that makes you stop flipping pages and stare.

"I went back to the room after meeting with Thomas," he says, sitting on the lounge chair next to mine. "When you weren't there, I figured you'd be up here."

His eyes drop to my bikini for just a second before snapping back to my face, but that brief glance is enough to send a flush of heat through me that has nothing to do with the Miami temperature. I suddenly become hyper-aware of exactly how much skin I'm showing and how the fabric clings to all my curves. Part of me, a part I should definitely ignore, feels a little thrill at his quick look. I resist the urge to arch my back slightly, just to see if his eyes would dart down again.

Crap. Maybe that drink was stronger than I thought.

"I thought you'd be longer," I say, reaching for my glass anyway and taking another sip to hide whatever my face might be doing. "How was the meeting?"

"Thomas had to run," he says, signaling a server. "Some issue with one of his other clients."

The server approaches, and Jack orders a beer. I notice the way the female server's eyes linger on him, taking in the rolled sleeves and the way his shirt fits across his shoulders. I can't blame her, honestly. The man looks good enough to eat.

"How was the pool?" he asks, looking around the rooftop oasis.

"Amazing," I say, gesturing to the view. "This whole place is unreal. I feel like I accidentally stumbled into someone else's life."

He smiles. "Wait till you see the track tomorrow. It's a whole other level of surreal." His eyes light up with excitement. "Well, for me at least it's the best part of Miami. Nothing beats the smell of racing fuel and the sound of engines."

We chat about the schedule for tomorrow as we finish our drinks—track tour in the morning, driver meet-and-greet at noon, then back to the hotel to change for the gala. Jack explains each event with obvious passion for the racing elements and tolerance for the sponsor obligations.

Eventually, I stifle a yawn, the long day and travel catching up with me. The cocktail isn't helping my sudden wave of tiredness.

"We should probably head back," Jack says, noticing. "Tomorrow starts early. And you look about five minutes from falling asleep in that chair."

I nod and gather my things, very aware that heading back means facing the heart-shaped bed situation. We ride the elevator down a few floors, neither speaking, and there's a tension that wasn't there before, an awareness of what's waiting for us.

Back in the suite, the heart-shaped bed looms large, impossible to ignore. I grab my pajamas and retreat to the bathroom to change and go through my skincare routine, taking longer than strictly necessary. When I finally emerge in sleep shorts and a t-shirt from Dolly Parton's *Plain & Simple* tour, Jack has changed into sweatpants and a tanktop and is arranging a makeshift bed on the floor with extra pillows and blankets.

"You really don't have to sleep on the floor," I say, feeling guilty as I watch him try to create a comfortable sleeping spot on the plush-but-definitely-not-meant-for-sleeping carpet.

"It's fine," he insists, fluffing a pillow. "I've slept in worse places."

I climb into the heart-shaped bed, which is extremely comfortable despite its shape, and try to settle in. But after ten minutes, I can't take it anymore.

"This is stupid," I say, sitting up. "This bed is huge. Just get up here. We're adults. We can share a bed without it being weird."

Jack hesitates, clearly weighing his options.

"Seriously," I add. "I promise not to steal all the covers. Or push you out of the heart. I'll even build a pillow wall to protect your virtue if it makes you feel better."

He laughs at that, finally relenting. "Well, when you put it that way. But only because this floor is harder than it looks. And I'm holding you to that cover-stealing promise."

The bed dips as he climbs in on the other side, keeping respectful space between us.

Totally normal. Just two adults sharing a giant heart-shaped bed. We're joking about it, which means we're handling this maturely. Nothing awkward about two fake-dating people maintaining appropriate space in a bed literally designed for the opposite.

Jack shifts slightly, turning to face me. The moonlight streaming through the balcony doors washes over him, highlighting the sharp angle of his jaw, the curve of his lips, the intensity in his eyes. My mouth goes dry.

"Goodnight, Lark," he says, his voice lower than before.

"Goodnight," I manage to reply, quickly turning to face the wall before he can see what must be written all over my face. My heart is pounding so loudly I'm sure he can hear it.

Every cell in my body is aware of him—the rhythm of his breathing, the lingering scent of his cologne, the heat radiating from him. If I moved just a few inches back, I'd be against him. The thought sends a shiver down my spine. I could finish what I started last night in my hallway. The kiss flashes through my mind unbidden—the way he pulled me closer, the heat of his mouth on mine. How *incredible* it felt before I came to my senses and ran.

I squeeze my eyes shut and try desperately to think about anything else. The schedule for tomorrow. New song lyrics. The sponsors I'll meet. Anything.

But all I can think about is Jack. Jack Midnight is in bed with me, just inches away. Jack, with his quick smile and quicker wit. Jack, who looks at me sometimes like he can see right through me. Jack, who I absolutely should not be thinking about in the way I definitely am right now.

This is going to be a very long night.

CHAPTER 15

JACK

I wake up gradually, awareness seeping in slowly before I open my eyes. The bed is impossibly soft beneath me, sheets of expensive Egyptian cotton against my skin. For a moment, I can't remember where I am, and then it all comes flooding back. Miami. The Azura. The ridiculous heart-shaped bed.

Lark.

She's still asleep beside me, facing me now. Her black hair fans across the white pillow like spilled ink, one hand tucked under her cheek, her breathing deep and even. Peaceful.

The early morning light filtering through the balcony doors casts a golden glow across her skin. My gaze traces the curve of her shoulder, the delicate line of her collarbone, the fullness of her lips. She's beautiful in a way that makes my chest tighten and my cock hard.

I should get up. I should look away. Instead, I lie there, memorizing her. The way her eyelashes fan against her cheeks. The small freckle near the corner of her mouth that I've thought about kissing every single time I've seen it. The rise and fall of her chest with each breath.

I slip out of bed as carefully as possible, trying not to disturb her, but the movement makes the mattress shift. She stirs slightly, murmurs something incomprehensible, then settles back into sleep. I grab my phone from the nightstand and head for the bathroom, stepping into the shower and letting the water run hot over me.

Under the spray, I try to focus on the day ahead instead of Lark. Anything but thinking about the *very* long list of dirty things I'd like to do to the barely clothed woman in my bed. The woman who kissed me, then bolted.

I need to get my head fucking straight. Focus on what actually matters this weekend.

The Miami Motor Speedway is hosting their annual International Motorsport Festival this weekend, a massive celebration with everything from GT racing to drift competitions, vintage exhibitions, and manufacturer showcases. Formula One isn't racing here, but most teams send representatives, and as a Ferrari driver—albeit currently a reserve driver—with a huge following, I'm contractually obligated to be here.

My manager Thomas sees it as the perfect opportunity to continue my "image rehabilitation" campaign, and he's right. With Ferrari executives, sponsors, and racing journalists from around the world all in one place, it's my chance to remind everyone why they should put me back in a race seat instead of keeping me in this reserve driver limbo hell.

Since Barcelona, I've been stuck watching from the sidelines while Davis drives my car. He can barely crack the top ten when my old teammate Luca is fighting for podiums in the identical car. But Davis doesn't throw parties that end up on TMZ or get caught on video with questionable substances. And apparently that matters more to the team than actual racing results.

Or it used to. Ferrari is starting to get restless with his performance. Which is why this weekend matters so much. It's another chance to show them I've matured, that I'm worth the risk again.

I towel off roughly and wrap it low around my waist. When I come out, Lark's awake, sitting on the edge of the bed scrolling on her phone. Her hair falls in soft waves around her shoulders, slightly mussed, and when she looks up, that smile hits me right in the chest like a physical blow.

"Morning," she says, her voice still rough with sleep in a way that makes me think about other ways to make her voice sound like that. "Shower free?"

I clear my throat, shoving down thoughts that definitely aren't helping the situation.

"Yep, all yours," I reply, grabbing a shirt from my bag and trying not to stare at the way her sleep shorts ride up her thighs. "Sleep okay?"

"Yeah, actually. You?" She meets my eyes for a moment before glancing away, a slight flush on her cheeks.

"Great," I say, but it's a total fucking lie. I barely slept with her next to me, her scent surrounding me, her warmth just inches away, her everything making it impossible to think about anything else. Most of the night had been a war between my brain and my cock, fighting the urge to roll over, pull her underneath me, and bury my face between her thighs until she forgot every man who came before, especially fucking Brandon. Show her exactly what I thought about that kiss.

But she disappeared back into her apartment. Ran away from me. And it's probably for the best. She's way too good for me anyway. As much as I want her, I want more than anything not to hurt her, not to fuck this up like I've fucked up so many other things.

We dance around each other getting ready, her in the bathroom, me in the bedroom, careful not to invade each other's space too much. The whole morning routine feels like a carefully choreographed dance designed to avoid addressing whatever's building between us.

An hour later, we're in the car heading to the track. Miami International Speedway is packed despite not being a Grand Prix weekend. The parking attendant recognizes me immediately, waves us through to the VIP section with an enthusiastic thumbs up.

Even though there's no Formula One race this weekend, the place is buzzing with activity. A GT race series is running, but the paddock area is full of Formula One displays, sponsor booths, and team personnel. It's a corporate showcase disguised as a racing event, designed to keep sponsors happy and engaged between actual Grand Prix weekends.

The familiar smell of fuel and burning rubber hits me as we walk through the gates, and something settles in my chest. This is my world. This is where I belong, where everything makes sense. For all the corporate bullshit that comes with it, nothing beats this—the energy of a racetrack, the machines, the competition. I've missed it more than I want to admit.

"This is incredible!" Lark says, turning in a slow circle as we walk through the paddock. Her eyes are wide, taking everything in, the sleek cars on display, the team hospitality areas, the organized chaos of it all.

"Wait till you see the actual racing," I tell her, putting my arm around her. Even this casual touch sends heat through me that I have to ignore. "Nothing like hearing all the engines fire up at once."

"I can't even imagine," she says, practically buzzing with excitement that makes me want to show her everything.

I spot Thomas waiting by the entrance of the Ferrari hospitality suite, phone in one hand, expensive coffee in the other, looking as stressed as always. He sees us and walks over immediately.

"Right on time," he says, checking his watch before extending his hand to Lark. "Thomas Reeves. Jack's manager. And you must be Lark."

"Nice to meet you," Lark says, shaking his hand with a warm smile.

Thomas gives me a quick once-over, professional as always, assessing. "Schedule's tight today. We have the media pen in fifteen, then the meet and greet, and then Autosport wants an interview."

"Morning to you too," I say, clapping him on the shoulder. "Good to see you, Thomas. How are you? I'm fine, thanks for asking."

Thomas rolls his eyes but his mouth twitches with a suppressed smile. We've been working together since I was sixteen, when I first signed with a junior racing team. He knows my shit by now.

"Yeah yeah yeah," he says, "Look, I've got to run, but keep up the good behavior today—lots of eyes watching. And nice to meet you, Lark."

"We'll give them a show," I assure him, placing my hand around Lark again.

Jessica, Thomas's assistant, appears with a tablet and a stack of badges dangling from lanyards. "Your credentials," she says, handing them over. "I've arranged for Lark to have full access to all areas."

"Thanks, Jess," I say, slipping the lanyard over my neck.

The paddock area is buzzing with activity—sponsor displays being set up, media crews filming interviews with drivers and team principals, and GT teams prepping their cars. Lark and I make our way through it all, stopping frequently to introduce her to people I've known for years. Everyone wants to meet her, curious about the woman who's been all over my Instagram lately.

"Jack!"

I turn at the familiar voice and see Luca Rossi cutting through the crowd, sunglasses perched on his dark hair and his trademark grin already in place. My teammate at Ferrari before I was bumped to reserve driver. We've been friends and fierce rivals since we were twelve years old, pushing each other to be better on every track from karting to Formula One.

"Luca!" I say, breaking into a smile. He pulls me into a quick back-slapping hug that's more collision than embrace.

"I didn't expect to see you here," I say, stepping back. "I thought you'd managed to get out of this corporate circus."

Luca shrugs, sliding his sunglasses back over his eyes against the bright Miami sun. "Last minute call from PR. They said the event needed someone with actual personality, so naturally they called me. Figured I'd save everyone from the boredom of just having you here."

"Still an asshole, I see," I say, but I'm smiling. This is how it's always been between us—constant competition wrapped in friendship.

I turn to Lark, who's watching our exchange with obvious amusement dancing in her eyes.

"Luca, this is Lark. Lark, this is Luca Rossi. Only driver on the grid who occasionally gives me real competition."

"Occasionally?" Luca laughs, shaking Lark's hand with both of his. "I'm leading you in points this season, *amico*."

"I don't have *any* points," I shoot back. "But only because they won't let me drive."

"Details, details," Luca says, turning on the full Italian charm for Lark. "A pleasure to meet you, truly. You're even more beautiful in person than in Jack's posts, which I didn't think was possible."

"The pleasure's mine," Lark says, clearly amused by his shameless flirting. "I've heard a lot about you from Jack."

"All terrible things, I'm sure," Luca laughs. "I apologize in advance for anything this one has told you about me. Most of it is lies designed to make himself look better."

"Actually, he speaks very highly of you," Lark says, and I can see the mischief in her eyes. She leans forward and drops her voice to a dramatic whisper. "Though he did mention you cheat at poker and owe him money from last season."

Luca throws his head back and laughs, a full belly laugh that makes people around us turn to look. "Only because he can't accept losing gracefully! And I don't owe him money, we have a disagreement about whether that last hand counted."

"It counted," I say firmly.

"We'll never agree," Luca says, waving his hand dismissively before looking between us with open curiosity. "So how did you two meet? Jack never tells me anything anymore."

"We grew up in the same town," I say, sticking to our rehearsed story. "Reconnected recently since I've been home for the summer."

"Ah, childhood sweethearts reunited," Luca says. "This is like a movie, no? Very sweet. Smart move, Jack. You finally got something right in your life. First good decision you've made all year."

"See, that's what I keep telling him," Lark says, and I laugh. "Someone needs to keep his ego in check. It's a full-time job but somebody has to do it."

Luca looks at her with delight. "You and I are going to be very good friends, Lark. Finally someone who understands how insufferable he can be." He runs a hand through his dark hair, then his expression turns more serious as he looks back at me. "So, I must know, how are the contract talks actually going? Any real progress with the team? The paddock rumors are flying around like crazy, but you know how reliable those are."

I shrug, trying to appear casual. "Getting there slowly. Thomas is optimistic about the meetings this week. Today should help. Show my face, remind everyone I clean up well and know how to play the corporate game without causing international incidents."

"Davis was P14 in the last race," Luca adds with a pointed look, lowering his voice slightly. "Team's not happy about his performance. There's talk in the garage."

"Their mistake putting him in my seat," I say, tapping my Ferrari lanyard against my leg. A nervous habit I can't seem to break.

"Non è giusto," he says, switching to Italian. *"Meriti di essere là fuori."*

It's not fair. You deserve to be out there.

I respond in the same language, having picked it up from years in Europe, driving for an Italian team. *"Non ti contraddirò su questo. Ma devo ancora convincerli che la mia reputazione è nel passato."*

I won't argue with you on that. But I still have to convince them my reputation is in the past.

Lark gives me a surprised look, her eyebrows raising. "You speak Italian?" she asks.

"Just enough to tell this guy to fuck off," I reply with a grin. "And order beer. Most of the people working at Ferrari are Italian, plus spending most of my time with this guy..."

"He's modest," Luca interrupts. "He actually speaks it very well. *Parla come un italiano quando è ubriaco."*

Lark shrugs at Luca, and I translate for her. "He said I speak like an Italian when I'm drunk."

Lark looks at me, snorting. "Well, well, you're full of surprises today. What else are you hiding? Can you juggle? Do magic tricks?"

I try not to look too pleased with her reaction. "I like to keep people on their toes. Maintain an air of mystery."

"Next time you're drunk I'll have to test this theory," Lark says, her eyes sparkling with amusement.

"Do you speak Italian? Dear God, I should be careful what I say around you," Luca says with a laugh.

"No, no, but I speak Spanish and it helps me understand quite a bit of it," Lark says, her eyes dancing between us. "Don't worry, I heard nothing too incriminating. Your secrets are safe."

"Oh, now I know not only are you too beautiful for him but too smart as well. Careful Jack, half the paddock will try and steal her away," Luca says with a wink, and I feel a swell of pride as if she really is my girlfriend, as if this whole thing could be real for more than just a moment.

Before I can formulate a response, Thomas appears at my elbow like a ghost materializing from nowhere. "Jack, *Autosport* is ready for the interview. They're set up in the media tent."

"Duty calls," I tell Luca with a resigned sigh. "Save me a beer for later? I'm going to need it after this."

"Always, *amico*," he promises, then turns to Lark with that charming smile. "It was lovely to meet you."

"You too," Lark says warmly.

The rest of the morning is a blur of handshakes, sponsor meetings, and carefully rehearsed answers to the same questions. Yes, I'm focused on getting back in a race seat. No, the incident in Monaco wasn't what it appeared to be. Yes, I'm more mature now, more dedicated. No, I won't comment on Davis's recent performances (even though we all know he's underperforming).

Through it all, Lark stays by my side, handling it like she was born for this world. She's smart, engaging, makes people laugh with her quick wit. I find myself watching her when I should be focusing on the sponsors.

By early afternoon, we've done our mandatory rounds and watched the GT race from the Ferrari suite. Lark's enthusiasm was infectious throughout the race, her eyes bright with excitement. During the final lap battle, she sprang to her feet when the Ferrari GT executed a perfect hairpin overtake, her drink splashing over her fingers as she let loose a cheer so unfiltered, so joyful, that I couldn't help but grin like an idiot watching her instead of the race.

Something twisted in my chest watching her. This urge to keep her in my world longer than our September expiration date, to steal her away to more races, more cities, more of everything.

Back at the hotel, we have a couple of hours before the evening gala. We share the bathroom getting ready, but once I'm dressed in my tux, she shoos me out with a "I need space for all this," gesturing to her array of makeup and hair products spread across the marble counter like a small pharmacy.

"How much space could you possibly need?" I ask, eyeing the arsenal.

"More than you can comprehend," she says, physically pushing me toward the door. "Go. Drink something. Watch TV. Just be anywhere but here."

"Bossy," I say, but I'm grinning as she shuts the door in my face.

I pour myself a whiskey from the minibar and wait in the living area of our suite, scrolling through messages from Thomas about the day's meetings. The bathroom door's been closed for almost an hour when I finally hear it open. I look up.

Holy fuck.

Lark stands there in a deep blue dress that clings to every curve before flowing to the floor. The front is elegant but shows just enough cleavage to make my heart race. She grins, spinning slightly, and I see the back is almost entirely bare, a smooth expanse of her skin from her shoulders to just above the curve of her ass. Her black hair is pinned up with a few strands falling loose, framing her face like art, exposing the elegant line of her neck.

I grip my glass a little tighter. My brain short-circuits with the vivid thought of walking across the room, picking her up and carrying her out to the balcony to fuck her right there against the railing, hotel neighbors and passing boats be damned.

"Jack?" Her voice snaps me back to reality. "Is it too much?"

"No," I manage, my voice thick. I clear my throat, trying to get blood back to my brain instead of other regions. "You uh… you look incredible."

A flush spreads across her cheeks. "You don't look half bad either," she says. "Very James Bond."

"We should go," I say, standing and offering her my hand. If we don't leave now, I'm going to do something stupid.

The glass elevator descends, giving us a view of Miami at night—city lights stretching into the distance, the water beyond reflecting the moon like scattered diamonds. The lobby is still crowded despite the hour, and more than a few appreciative glances follow Lark as we cross the marble floor toward the exit.

The heat hits us immediately as we step outside. Miami's night air is still warm and heavy even after sunset. A valet in a black vest is already waiting at the curb with a low, impossibly sleek Ferrari in glossy black, engine idling like it is alive. He steps forward the second he sees me, offering the key fob with both hands.

"Mr. Midnight," he says. "Your car is ready."

Lark blinks. "*Your* car?"

"Loaner from the team for the weekend," I tell her, trying not to sound smug. "All my cars are in Monaco right now, so Ferrari set me up with this while we're in Miami."

Her eyes move over the car, taking in the badge and the

carbon fiber. It's so low to the ground it barely looks street legal. I open the passenger door for her and offer my hand so she doesn't catch her dress on the door sill. She lets out a laugh.

"You are actually serious," she says. "I'm getting into a Ferrari to go to a gala in Miami. This is full James Bond."

"Please," I say. "Bond *wishes* he had this car."

She laughs, sliding into the leather seat. "I cannot believe this is real."

I walk around to the driver's side and drop in. The cabin smells like leather and heat, and the engine note settles into my chest the way it always does. I ease us out from the hotel portico and onto the street.

Miami at night opens up in front of us. The streets are wide and lit with neon—blues and pinks reflecting off the wet pavement from an earlier rain. Palm trees line the boulevard, their fronds catching the colored light. I downshift and the engine snarls, the sound filling the cabin.

"So, remind me who's hosting this shindig?" Lark asks.

"Bernard Montgomery," I tell her. "Real estate developer who loves to remind everyone he raced in amateur series for two seasons twenty years ago."

"Ah, one of those," she says with a smile. "Like that guy at the bar who played high school football and still wears his letterman jacket at thirty-five."

"Exactly like that, but with a fifty-million-dollar mansion mansion," I laugh.

The car pulls through massive iron gates into a circular driveway lined with palm trees wrapped in tiny white lights. The mansion itself is sprawling Mediterranean-style, with fountains flanking the entrance.

The valet opens the door, and I offer my hand as Lark steps out. She takes it, squeezing lightly as she stands, her eyes widening as she takes in the full scale of the place.

"Wow," she says, looking up at the mansion. "You forget

places like this actually exist until you're standing in front of one. It's like a movie set."

"The guy has a Picasso in the bathroom," I say. "The *bathroom*."

"Of course he does." She rolls her eyes, but there's amusement in her voice. "Because where else would you put it?"

We climb the steps and the entryway opens to a massive foyer with marble floors and a crystal chandelier that probably weighs more than my bike. Staff in black and white uniforms circulate with trays of champagne and tiny, artistic food. A string quartet plays in the corner, barely audible over the hum of conversation.

"Jack Midnight!" Bernard Montgomery booms, approaching us with the enthusiasm of a game show host. He claps me on the shoulder hard enough that I have to brace myself. "The man himself! Good to see you, my boy!"

"Bernard," I say, shaking his hand firmly. "Thanks for having us. This is my girlfriend, Lark Reyes."

Bernard turns his attention to Lark, taking her hand in both of his. He leans in slightly too close, enveloping us in a cloud of cologne so strong it could strip paint. I catch Lark's slight wince before she composes her expression into a perfect smile.

"Enchanted, my dear. Absolutely enchanted. The famous musician! I've heard all about your talent."

"All good things, I hope," Lark says with a warm smile, subtly extracting her hand from his grip.

Bernard laughs loudly. "You know, I used to sing a bit myself. Back in my racing days. Had quite the voice, they said." He puffs up slightly. "Maybe we should do a duet later! I'll have someone bring out the karaoke machine."

"That's very generous," Lark says smoothly, "but I wouldn't want to overshadow the other guests."

I bite back a laugh. She's good.

"Charming," he says. "Well, enjoy yourselves. The east

terrace has the better champagne, just between us." He winks and moves on to his next victims.

"Karaoke machine?" I murmur as we move away. "At a black-tie gala?"

"He's definitely singing Sinatra's *My Way* at some point tonight," Lark predicts. "I'm calling it now."

We grab champagne from a passing server and make our way through the crowd. The mansion is packed with racing executives, Miami socialites, people who look important but I have no idea who they are. Everyone wants to stop and chat. We smile, nod, make small talk about the Formula One season and Lark's music. After twenty minutes of this, I steer us toward the terrace doors, needing air.

The terrace is less crowded, opening onto a view of the water. String lights are draped overhead, and the ocean breeze cuts through the Miami heat. A few other guests stand in small clusters, but it's quieter out here. Calmer.

Lark takes a sip of her champagne and leans against the railing. "Okay, Bernard was annoying, but this champagne is incredible."

"One of the perks of this life," I say, taking a sip of my own. "The champagne almost makes up for having to talk to Bernard."

She laughs. "I think my sinuses are permanently damaged from his cologne."

"You handled him perfectly," I tell her, bumping her shoulder lightly with mine. I spot Luca across the balcony, and he catches my eye, excusing himself from a conversation to make his way over.

"There you are," he says, kissing Lark on both cheeks European-style before clapping me on the shoulder. "I was beginning to think you'd found something better to do than grace us with your presence."

"We considered it," I reply, "but we didn't want to deprive you of our company."

Luca turns to Lark with a warm smile. "That dress is stunning on you. Though you could make a potato sack look like *haute couture*."

"You're incorrigible," she laughs. "Does that Italian charm work on everyone?"

"On most people," Luca says with a wink. "Jack's just sick of hearing it after all these years."

"He's been using the same lines since we were fifteen," I add, taking another sip of champagne. "You should hear his pickup lines in Italian. Even worse."

We talk for a while, Luca regaling Lark with embarrassing stories from our karting days. How I once crashed because I was so focused on beating him I forgot about the actual racing line. How he threw his helmet at me after I "accidentally" bumped him wide in the final corner.

"He's always been like this," Luca says, gesturing to me with his champagne. "Competitive about everything. Even who could eat the most pizza after a race."

"Who won?" Lark asks.

"I did," we both say at the same time, then glare at each other.

As she laughs, an older woman in diamonds that could probably pay off a small country's debt approaches us, all air kisses and calling everyone "darling." She immediately monopolizes Lark, asking about her music, her Instagram aesthetic, her skincare routine, whether she does Pilates.

Lark handles it gracefully at first, nodding and smiling. But after about five minutes, I catch her eye. There's a slight panic there. *Help me.*

"Sorry to interrupt," I say smoothly, sliding my hand to Lark's lower back. "But I need to steal my girlfriend away for a minute."

"Oh, of course, of course," the woman says, waving us off. "Lovely to meet you, dear!"

As soon as we're out of earshot, Lark exhales. "Thank you. She was telling me about her juice cleanse and I was about to fake a medical emergency."

"I could tell," I say, grinning. "You had the look."

"What look?"

"The 'get me out of here before I say something I'll regret' look."

We make the rounds after that, moving through the crowd more deliberately. I introduce her to more drivers, some of whom she recognizes from watching races. Team principals who ask polite questions about her music.

And I keep noticing the way men look at her. The appreciative glances that linger too long. The handshakes that hold on just a beat past professional. The way they lean in slightly too close when they talk to her, invading her space with the excuse of hearing better over the crowd. My hand stays on her back almost constantly. A reminder to everyone here that she's with me.

"Ready to get out of here?" I ask Lark later, finding her by the dessert table where she's contemplating a tray of tiny chocolate sculptures with intense focus.

"God, yes. These shoes are basically torture devices. Beautiful, expensive torture devices that I regret nothing about wearing," she says, popping a truffle into her mouth.

I laugh, texting the valet service to bring the car around. "The price of beauty is steep."

"And yet men get away with flat shoes and still look incredible," she says, eyeing my perfectly normal dress shoes with mock resentment. "The injustice."

"One of life's great unfair advantages," I say with a grin. "Along with pockets that actually fit things."

"Yes, that too!" she exclaims, pointing a second truffle at me.

"What even is the point of fake pockets? Just cruel fashion trickery."

We say our goodbyes to Bernard and make the rounds one last time. The night air hits us as we step through the mansion's massive doors, warm and heavy with the scent of the ocean.

The Ferrari is waiting, engine already running. I hold her door, watch her slide into the seat, that dress riding up slightly on her thigh. Good God. I close the door before I can think about it too long.

I slide into the driver's seat and pull out of the circular drive. The engine purrs as we ease onto the main road, Miami's nightlife glowing around us. Clubs with lines around the block, restaurants with outdoor seating packed with people, the energy of the city humming even at this hour.

Lark leans her head back against the seat, eyes half-closed. She looks tired but content, a small smile on her lips.

At the hotel, the elevator carries us to our floor. Lark steps out first when the doors open, heels clicking against marble. Inside the suite, she kicks off her shoes immediately, groaning with relief as she stretches her toes.

"I know I already complained, but man, they're killers," she says, holding one shoe up and examining it with a mixture of admiration and betrayal. "Though I still love them. Beauty and pain, the ultimate toxic relationship."

I can't help but smile as I loosen my tie. "You handled tonight like a pro. Everyone loved you."

"Even the woman in the red dress who kept calling me 'Jack's little musician friend'?" Lark asks, reaching behind her neck to massage a sore spot.

"Especially her. I saw her asking for your Instagram before

she left," I say, tossing my tie over the back of a chair. "She probably wants her daughter to take lessons or something."

Lark snorts, reaching up to pull pins from her hair one by one. Each pin releases another strand, her hair falling in waves around her shoulders. My fingers itch to touch it, to bury my hands in it, to feel if it's as soft as it looks.

"Probably wants to make sure I'm good enough for racing royalty Jack Midnight."

"You're way too good for me, Lark," I say, the words coming out before I can stop them.

She looks up, something flickering across her face that I can't quite read. The moment hangs between us, charged with all the things we aren't saying. The suite suddenly feels too small, the distance between us both too much and not enough.

"We should probably get some sleep," I say, running a hand through my hair. "Big day tomorrow."

She looks at me for a long moment. "Right, of course."

We move around each other carefully, taking turns in the bathroom, maintaining that careful distance. But when I come out she's standing at the window in her sleep shorts and t-shirt, looking out at the Miami skyline. I could cross the room. Turn her around, finally do what I've been wanting to do for weeks.

Instead I get into bed.

The fake dating plan is working perfectly. Too perfectly, maybe. Everyone's bought the story—sponsors, teams, fans. My image rehab is right on track. Her music is getting attention. Everything going according to plan.

Except for one thing. I'm falling for her.

Have been for fucking weeks now, well before the kiss. But this can't go anywhere. The plan has an expiration date—September—for a reason. By then, if things keep going like today, I'll be back in a race car, back to flying around the world, living out of hotel rooms between races.

I fuck things up. I always do. Can't stay in one place. Can't commit to one person. I get restless, then reckless, then I bolt. It's what I've done with every relationship I've ever had. Racing is the only constant, and even that I managed to jeopardize.

And Lark deserves better than that. She's finally building something real with her music after Brandon spent years making her feel small. She's got label interest, a growing platform, actual momentum. The last thing she needs is me fucking it up because I can't keep my hands to myself.

Because I'll only end up hurting her. And that's the one thing I can't do.

CHAPTER 16

Lark

The media staging area buzzes with activity, cameras trained on Jack while I hang back in the wings where the PR team told me to wait. Miami humidity has turned my hair into something that belongs in a before photo for anti-frizz products. Jack rented a motorcycle here after getting sick of being chauffeured everywhere, and while the wind on the ride over was refreshing, the helmet definitely didn't do my styling any favors, but at least I'm not on camera.

It's our last full day in Miami, and the International Motorsport Festival is still in full swing around us. Press everywhere, their equipment creating a maze of cables and light stands that I'm trying not to trip over. Fans cluster behind barriers with phones held high, hoping for glimpses of their favorite drivers. Team personnel rush between obligations with clipboards and headsets.

I shift my weight from one foot to the other, feeling the sticky Miami heat press against my skin. My jeans are practically glued to my legs at this point, and I'm already fantasizing about the breeze we'll get on the ride back to the hotel.

Jack catches my eye mid-answer to some question about his training regimen and throws me a quick wink. The interviewer notices, follows his gaze to me with interest, and Jack smoothly pivots to answering a question about his "incredibly supportive girlfriend" without missing a beat.

I smile on cue, playing my part like I've been doing all weekend.

Except it doesn't feel like playing anymore. That's the problem.

I've been watching him all morning, hell all weekend really, and this is where he belongs. Completely in his element. He's confident without being arrogant, handling questions about his comeback with the kind of grace that only comes from years of practice and media training. This isn't the party boy from the tabloids or the reckless kid who made headlines for all the wrong reasons.

This is a professional. A fighter. Someone who's clawed his way to the top of one of the most competitive sports in the world and is now fighting like hell to reclaim what he lost.

The dedication is obvious in every answer he gives, every composed smile, every careful word choice. And it's attractive. Really attractive.

It's pretty fucking hot, if I'm being completely honest with myself.

Which I'm trying very hard not to be. Not out loud, anyway. Not even in my own head if I can help it.

But the truth is sitting heavy in my chest: part of me doesn't want to go home tomorrow. This trip has been amazing. Exhausting, yes, but also exciting in a way I haven't felt in years. Maybe ever. I get it now, why he loves this world so much. The speed, the constant adrenaline rush. The way everything moves so fast you don't have time to overthink or second-guess yourself.

But it's not really the world, it's him. The way he makes everything feel like an adventure, and the way he looks at me like I'm the most interesting person in the room even when we're surrounded by celebrities and racing legends. The way I feel when I'm with him—adventurous and vibrant and like someone who doesn't have to shrink herself down.

"And that's a wrap!" the interviewer says cheerfully, his voice cutting through my thoughts. "Thank you so much for your time, Jack. Best of luck with the contract negotiations. We're all rooting for you."

"Thanks, mate. Really appreciate it," Jack says, shaking his hand with that million-dollar smile still perfectly in place. Then he turns to me, and his expression changes immediately, softens in a way that makes my stomach flip. Like he can finally drop the performance now that the cameras are off. "Ready to get out of here?"

"Sure," I tell him, trying not to sound as affected as I feel by the way he's looking at me. "Where to next? Please tell me somewhere with air conditioning."

"We're free the rest of the day," he says, reaching for my hand like it's the most natural thing in the world. "How about lunch? I'm starving and I know a place that's not too far."

"Sounds perfect," I say, and my stomach chooses that exact moment to growl loudly enough that he definitely hears it.

He grins, clearly amused. "Guess you're hungry too."

"Traitor," I mutter at my stomach, and he laughs.

We start walking through the crowd, Jack's hand still holding mine. A few people stop him for autographs and photos, and he's gracious about it, signing hats and posing for selfies while I stand off to the side trying not to photobomb anyone.

It's kind of sweet, actually, watching how patient he is with the fans. A little kid in a Ferrari shirt asks for a high five, and Jack crouches down to the kid's level, giving him his full attention and making him feel like the most important person in the world for those few seconds.

He's really good at this part. Better than I expected.

But then more people start to notice him. The crowd grows, pressing closer with that excited energy that borders on aggressive. Suddenly there are at least forty people surrounding us, all calling his name, waving Ferrari merchandise, holding out phones to capture the moment.

"Jack! Jack, over here!"

"Can I get a picture? Please?"

"Is that really Lark Reyes? From Instagram?"

"Jack, sign my hat!"

Security personnel start moving toward us, trying to create some breathing room, but the crowd keeps swelling. Not just fans anymore, now I can see paparazzi too, pushing through the crowd with a predatory energy. The energy shifts completely, becomes aggressive and invasive. Security is trying to push through to us, but they're caught in the crush of people. This is different from the controlled events we've been attending all weekend. This is chaos. Actual chaos.

Jack looks down at me, and his hand tightens protectively around mine. Then he's leaning close enough that I can hear him over the noise, his breath warm against my ear. "You trust me?"

"What?" I manage, my voice coming out higher than normal.

"Do you trust me?" he asks again, pulling back just enough to look me in the eye, and there's something wild there.

"Yes," I say without thinking, even though I have no idea what he's planning.

His grin is wicked, the kind that should come with a warning label. "Then run."

"What?"

But he's already moving, pulling me through the crowd with him. We dodge around a cluster of surprised fans, weave between two security guards who look completely confused about what's happening, and then we're sprinting through the paddock area like we're in some kind of action movie chase scene.

My sneakers slap against the hot pavement, and I'm laughing. I can't help it. The absurdity of running away from paparazzi in broad daylight, Jack's hand tight and sure around mine, the way people are literally diving out of our way with shocked expressions. It's insane. It's completely ridiculous.

It's the most fun I've had in years.

"This is crazy!" I shout, stumbling slightly over my own feet, and Jack's grip on my hand keeps me upright and moving.

"I know!" he shouts back, and he's grinning like an absolute lunatic, his eyes bright with adrenaline. "Keep up, Reyes!"

We cut through a narrow gap between two team trailers, and I can hear the paparazzi behind us, shouting, cameras still clicking away, but we're faster. Jack knows exactly where he's going, leading me through the maze of the paddock.

We burst out into the parking area, and there's his motorcycle, black and chrome in the Miami sun like it's been waiting for us.

"Jack!" someone shouts from behind us, way closer than I expected.

"Put it on!" he says urgently, tossing me a helmet.

I jam the helmet on, fumbling with the strap because my hands are shaking from adrenaline and breathless laughter. Jack swings his leg over the bike with ease, and I climb on behind him, wrapping my arms around his waist.

I can feel his heart pounding through his shirt. Or maybe that's mine. Maybe it's both of us, hearts racing together.

"Hold tight," he says over his shoulder, his voice rough with excitement, and then the engine roars to life with that gorgeous, throaty sound.

We peel out of the parking spot with a squeal of tires, and I hold on tighter as he accelerates hard. The wind whips past us, hot and fast, and I can hear him laugh, feel it vibrate through his entire body, and I'm laughing too.

The world blurs into speed and sound and pure sensation. Jack weaves through Miami streets with the kind of speed that should probably terrify me but instead makes me feel completely, utterly alive.

Buildings fly past in streaks of color, palm trees bend in our wake, glimpses of glittering water appear between structures. The sun is hot on my bare arms, the wind pulls at my clothes and hair, and I can feel him shift and move as he leans into turns with perfect control.

I glance back once and see a car trying to follow us. Paparazzi, determined. But Jack spots them in his mirrors. He takes a sudden sharp right down a side street, then a quick left, then another right, weaving through traffic until I lose track of where we are completely.

We're flying down quieter residential streets now, cutting through neighborhoods with tree-lined sidewalks, until finally he pulls onto a road that runs along the water. The engine noise drops from a roar to a purr as he slows, then stops at a small overlook. Just a strip of concrete with a low wall and a view of the bay stretching out blue and glittering under the afternoon sun.

He kills the engine.

My heart is still pounding, adrenaline singing through my veins like electricity, and I start laughing. I can't help it. The sound bubbles up from somewhere deep in my chest, uncontrollable and genuine.

"That was insane," I say, pulling off my helmet. "Absolutely insane. We just ran away from paparazzi like we robbed a bank."

"Welcome to my world," Jack says, taking off his own helmet and running a hand through his hair. When he turns to look at me over his shoulder, he's still grinning. That devastating smile that makes my pulse kick up another notch. He swings off the bike.

"Come on," he says, offering me his hand. "I want to show you around. I've found some great spots over the years that aren't on the tourist maps."

I take his hand, letting him help me off the bike, and my legs are still shaky. From the adrenaline rush, obviously. Not from being pressed against him for the last fifteen minutes. Definitely not that.

"Lead the way, Midnight," I tell him, and his smile gets even wider.

The rest of the day unfolds like a dream I don't want to wake up from.

Jack takes me to his favorite spots—the places he's discovered over the years racing in Miami. A tiny Cuban restaurant tucked into a neighborhood where all the signs are in Spanish and the woman behind the counter greets him like family.

The ropa vieja is the best I've ever had, falling apart on my fork, and the tostones are perfect. We eat until we're stuffed, and Jack tells me about finding this place his first year with Ferrari, nineteen and alone and wandering through Miami. Nineteen-year-old Jack, alone in a strange city, finding these little pockets of warmth and holding onto them.

Outside, the heat hits us again after the air-conditioned restaurant. Jack checks his phone, then grins at me with that look that means he's got something planned. "Okay, next stop. But we need the bike for this one."

We walk back to where he parked the motorcycle, and I climb on behind him, already getting used to the way we fit together. He takes us through Miami streets I don't recognize, past neighborhoods that shift from commercial to residential and back again, until finally the buildings start to open up and everything is covered in color.

We end up in Wynwood, and it's overwhelming in the best way. Every surface covered in art. Massive murals span entire buildings, vibrant colors that seem to pulse in the afternoon sun. Abstract patterns blend into photorealistic portraits. Political statements sit next to whimsical creatures. It's chaotic and beautiful and somehow cohesive.

"This is intense," I say, stopping in front of a piece that covers an entire warehouse. A woman's face in shades of blue and purple, her eyes somehow following you no matter where you stand.

"I know. I love this place," Jack says, coming to stand beside me. "Every time I come back, there's something new. Some pieces get painted over, new ones go up. The whole place evolves. Here, I'll show you my favorite, if it's still around."

He takes my hand and pulls me through the streets, weaving between tourists and locals until we stop in front of a massive mural. It's a landscape—mountains and sky and water—done in colors that shouldn't work together but somehow do. Deep purples bleeding into oranges, blues that fade to pink. It's breathtaking, and it triggers something in me. Some kind of nostalgia I can't quite place, like a memory of a place I've never been.

"It's beautiful," I say quietly.

Jack looks at it like he's greeting an old friend. "This one's been here for three years. Most don't last that long."

We wander through more streets, Jack pointing out pieces he recognizes and ones he's never seen before. A memorial for a local activist, her face surrounded by butterflies. A celebration of Cuban culture, bright and joyful. A massive collaborative piece that somehow works despite having at least a dozen different styles competing for attention.

Eventually the buildings thin out and I catch glimpses of water between them. Jack takes my hand again, pulling me toward the beach. Not the famous South Beach with its Art Deco buildings and crowds of tourists. This is quieter—South Pointe Park, he tells me. Families spread out with coolers and beach blankets. Teenagers play volleyball. Surfers bob beyond the break, waiting patiently for waves.

Jack buys us mango *paletas* from a cart, and we find a spot on the seawall to sit. The concrete is warm beneath me, and I dangle my legs over the side, watching the water.

The *paleta* is perfect. Sweet and tart and cold, already melting faster than I can keep up with. Juice runs down my fingers despite my best efforts.

"So this is the good stuff?" I ask, licking mango off my wrist. "Your secret Miami?"

"Part of it," he confirms, watching a family nearby trying to keep their beach umbrella from blowing away. "The festival and sponsor events are necessary. Nothing beats race day for me, obviously. But I love getting any off time I can to just... exist. Explore the city. Not that I get a ton of time off when I'm racing, but over the years I've managed to find these spots."

"Thank you for showing me all these places," I say. "I loved today."

We sit in silence for a while. The waves roll in with a rhythmic sound that's almost hypnotic. Children shriek with laughter as they chase each other at the water's edge. The sound of someone's speaker playing reggaeton mixes with the cry of gulls overhead.

Down the boardwalk, a street musician has set up with a guitar and a small amp. He's good—playing something jazzy and complex that drifts over the sound of the waves. A few people have stopped to listen, dropping bills into his open case.

Jack and I both turn to watch him. He's older, maybe in his sixties, with weathered hands that move over the strings with ease. There's something mesmerizing about watching someone who's truly skilled at their craft, even in a setting as casual as this.

"I hope I get to come back here one day," I say, the words slipping out before I can think about them.

He looks at me. "You will. You're probably going to stop here on tour at some point."

I laugh, but it comes out more uncertain than I intended. "Well, fingers crossed the LA meeting goes well. And I can magically overcome my stage fright. I'm just avoiding thinking about that, honestly."

He's quiet for a moment, watching the musician pack up his guitar and count his tips. "No, you will. You've got it, Lark. That magnetic thing. I saw it in our videos, and when you performed at the open mic. I know you look at that night as a failure, but I wish you could see it how I saw it. You faced your fears. You went up there and you were incredible. Yeah, maybe it was your first time in years so it didn't go exactly how you wanted, but you had it. That magic." He turns to me, his green eyes intense and serious. "I'm not just saying this as your fake boyfriend. I hope you know that."

My throat feels tight. The sincerity in his voice, the way he's looking at me like he actually believes every word—it breaks something loose in my chest.

"That means a lot," I say. "Coming from you."

He smiles and reaches over, taking my hand and giving it a squeeze. His palm is warm against mine, and I don't pull away.

We sit like that for a moment, watching the water, his hand in mine. Then he looks back at where the musician was, something thoughtful crossing his face.

"You know, I have an idea for one last stop," he says. "Unless you're too tired?"

I grin. "Not tired at all."

"Perfect." He stands, pulling me up with him. "Because this next place is my favorite. And I think you're really going to like it."

CHAPTER 17

Lark

The venue is in the heart of Little Havana, and I can hear the music from a full block away. Live horns and percussion cut through the humid night air, the kind of music that demands attention, that pulls you toward it whether you want to go or not.

As we get closer on the motorcycle, I see people spilling out onto the sidewalk, drinks in hand, some of them dancing right there on the pavement like the party can't be contained by walls. The whole street feels alive, electric. Jack parks the bike and I pull off my helmet, immediately hit by the energy of it all. The bass is so loud I can feel it vibrating through my chest, through my bones, through my entire body.

"What is this?" I ask, trying to take it all in. The lights, the people, the music pouring out the doors.

"La Casa de la Música," Jack says, pulling off his own helmet. "You said you liked dancing, right? Back when we joked about going to a club in Berlin together?"

I blink at him, surprised. "I *do* love dancing. Though I'm not great at it, and I haven't gone out in forever." I tilt my head, studying his face. "I'm surprised you remembered that. It was such an offhanded comment. I didn't think you'd pay attention to it."

"I always pay attention when you talk," he says, and his expression makes me forget how to breathe properly for a second.

I swallow and turn to take in the building. It's covered in colorful murals. Bright tropical flowers, dancing figures, abstract swirls of color that seem to move in the glow of the string lights crisscrossing overhead. Jack takes my hand and pulls me through the crowd toward the entrance. My palms are already a little sweaty, but whether it's from the Miami heat or what he just said, I can't tell.

Inside, the space opens up bigger than I expected. Exposed red brick walls, a proper bar along one side packed with people ordering drinks and shouting to be heard, small tables scattered throughout where groups lean in close to talk over the music. And at the center of it all, a stage where a full band is mid-set. Guitar, bass, drums, congas, bongos, horns that shine under the stage lights, and a woman singing with a voice that raises goosebumps on my arms despite the oppressive heat.

The dance floor in front of the stage is packed. Hips moving, feet flying through complicated patterns, partners spinning and dipping like they've been doing this their whole lives. It's mesmerizing and slightly intimidating.

The air is thick with humidity and rum and sweat and perfume all mixed together into something intoxicating, something that makes me want to move closer to Jack, that makes my inhibitions feel like they're already dissolving.

"I love this," I say, and I have to raise my voice to be heard over the music, over the crowd, over everything.

Jack's grin widens, his eyes bright with excitement and something else I can't quite name. "Just wait. It gets better."

I don't know how it could possibly get better than this, but I believe him.

Jack keeps his hand on the small of my back as we navigate through the crowd toward the bar. Bodies press close on all sides, and I catch fragments of conversations in Spanish and English, laughter, someone shouting something that gets drowned out by the horns hitting a particularly loud crescendo. The energy is intoxicating. I can feel the music in my chest, my whole body wanting to move.

We squeeze into a gap at the bar, and Jack leans down close so I can hear him. His breath is warm against my ear, sending a shiver down my spine. "What do you want to drink?"

"What are you getting?" I ask, practically shouting back.

"Old Fashioned. They make them strong here."

"I'll do the same," I say. It's a whiskey kind of night.

He catches the bartender's attention, holding up two fingers. "Two Old Fashioneds!"

The bartender nods, a guy in his fifties with salt-and-pepper hair and forearms like he's been slinging drinks for decades, and gets to work with the confidence of someone who could do this in his sleep, despite the chaos around him. The bar is absolute madness, but there's a rhythm to it. Everyone swaying slightly to the music while they wait, nobody in a real rush because the night is still young and full of possibility and why hurry when everything is this good?

Jack pays when the drinks arrive, waving off my attempt to contribute, and I take a sip. The whiskey hits immediately, burning a path down my throat and settling warm and pleasant in my stomach. It's strong and smooth and perfectly balanced, and it makes me feel bold in a way I haven't felt in years. Like I could do anything. Be anyone. Take risks.

"Good?" Jack asks, watching my face closely.

"Really good," I confirm, taking another sip and feeling the warmth spread through my chest like liquid courage. "You weren't kidding about strong."

His eyes haven't left my face, and the look in them makes my pulse kick up several notches. There's something in his expression I haven't seen before. Something darker. Hungrier.

The song ends to thunderous applause and cheers, and the band launches immediately into something new. Faster, more upbeat, the kind of rhythm that makes it physically impossible to stand still. Around us, people are already moving, heading back to the dance floor or dancing right where they're standing at the bar.

Jack's nodding his head to the beat, and I realize I'm doing the same thing without thinking about it. My hips are already moving slightly, my body responding to the music before my brain even processes it. The whiskey is making everything feel more intense, more alive.

"You want to dance?" he asks, and there's something in his voice that makes the question feel like more than just an invitation to the dance floor.

I look toward all those people who clearly know what they're doing, and feel a flutter of nervousness in my stomach. But then the woman on stage hits this incredible high note, and the crowd goes wild, and the whiskey is warm in my veins. *Fuck it.*

"Yeah," I say. "Let's dance."

Jack's grin is immediate and devastating. He downs the rest of his Old Fashioned in one long swallow that shouldn't be as attractive as it is, and I do the same, feeling the burn all the way down, feeling it settle in my stomach like fire.Then he takes my hand and pulls me toward the dance floor.

We weave through bodies, squeezing past a couple executing some impossibly complicated spin that nearly takes out my shoulder. The dance floor is even more packed than it looked from the bar, everyone pressed close together, moving as one mass of rhythm and heat and pure joy.

Jack finds us a spot near the middle and turns to face me, his hands already reaching for me. "Fair warning, I'm not great at this."

"That makes two of us," I say, though I'm fully prepared to embarrass myself.

He reaches for my hand, placing his other hand on my waist with confidence that contradicts his words, and when the band shifts into the next song, he starts to move. I immediately realize he's lying through his teeth. He knows exactly what he's doing. He's confident, leading me through steps with the kind of ease that only comes from practice and natural rhythm.

"You're a liar," I accuse, laughing as he spins me out and pulls me back in smoothly. "You said you weren't great at this."

"I said I'm not great, not that I'm terrible," he says as he leads me through another turn that makes my head spin pleasantly. "And I like keeping you on your toes, remember? I had a girlfriend briefly when I was twenty who was obsessed with salsa dancing. So we went out a lot and I picked up a few things."

"Thank her for me later," I say, and I can hear the breathlessness in my own voice, and can feel my heart racing. A guy who can actually dance is ridiculously, unfairly attractive. And when that guy is Jack Midnight, with his hands on my waist and those green eyes locked on mine like I'm the only person in this entire packed room, and his body moving against mine with perfect rhythm? I'm in *way* over my head. Drowning and not even trying to surface.

We keep moving, and gradually I start to relax into it. Stop thinking so hard about where my feet should go and just feel the music instead. The percussion vibrates through the floorboards, and the horns cut through everything, bright and joyful and demanding.

Jack spins me again, and this time I don't stumble or hesitate.

When he pulls me back in, I have to tilt my head all the way back to look up at him. He's so tall, and solid, and warm, and the way he's holding me makes me feel both completely safe and utterly reckless at the same time.

"You're actually really good at this yourself," he says, his voice warm with approval that makes pride bloom in my chest.

"That's only because you're a good lead," I point out breathlessly, my words coming fast.

Around us, the other dancers are in their own worlds. An older couple moving with the kind of synchronization that only comes from years together. A group of friends laughing as they try to coordinate some complicated move. A woman dancing solo with such pure joy on her face it makes me smile just watching her.

The song builds, tempo picking up, and Jack matches it perfectly. His hands tighten on my waist as he leads me through faster steps, more spins, and I'm laughing, breathless, feeling more alive than I have in years.

"Having fun?" Jack asks, his mouth close to my ear so I can actually hear him over the music and the crowd.

"So much fun," I admit. When was the last time I felt like this? Completely present, completely in my body, completely free? I honestly can't remember.

Jack's hand stays firm on my back, guiding me through turns and steps with confidence, and I stop overthinking and just follow his lead, letting the music take over. For once I'm not in my head about performing or being perfect. I'm just dancing. Just having fun.

We dance through two more songs, then three. My hair is starting to stick to the back of my neck with sweat, my heart is racing, and I can't stop smiling.

The fourth song starts with a shift in mood. Still upbeat but with a sensual undercurrent that changes everything. Around us, dancers pull their partners closer, movements becoming more intimate.

Jack hesitates for just a second, his eyes meeting mine like he's asking permission. Then he draws me in. Closer. *Much closer.* Our bodies are pressed together now, moving together as one, and I can feel the heat radiating off him through his shirt. His hand slides from my waist to my back, fingers splaying wide and possessive, and I have to look up to meet his eyes.

The space between us has shrunk to almost nothing, and every single point where we touch feels electric, charged. His hand on my back burning through my shirt. My hand in his, our fingers intertwined. The way our hips move together with the music, synchronized without any conscious effort. The solid strength of him as he leads me through the steps, so sure and confident and completely in control.

This stopped being fake somewhere between the beach and here. Who am I kidding? It was never really fake at all. Not for me. Maybe not for him either, judging by the way he's looking at me right now.

The song shifts, tempo slowing but the rhythm getting deeper, more sensual. Around us, couples press together, lost in the music and each other. His hand tightens on my back. My fingers curl into his shirt. We're not really dancing anymore, just swaying together, bodies pressed flush, and the tension between us is so thick I can barely breathe through it.

"Lark..." he says, and my name is a warning and a question and a plea all at once.

I tilt my face up, and we're so close now I can feel his breath on my lips. "Jack."

His gaze drops to my mouth and stays there, intense and focused. His hand slides up to cradle the back of my neck, fingers threading into my hair at the base of my skull, and the warmth of his palm against my skin, the slight pressure of his fingers, sends shivers down my spine despite the oppressive heat, despite how much I'm sweating.

My heart is hammering so hard I'm sure he can feel it, sure everyone can hear it over the music.

"Tell me to stop," he says, his voice barely audible over the music, over the blood rushing in my ears.

"No," I say, and my voice comes out steadier than I feel. I'm done pretending I don't want this. Done lying to myself.

"Lark—"

"No," I repeat, more firmly this time, and rise up on my toes, closing the last bit of distance between us.

The second my lips touch his, he responds instantly, pulling me against him with enough force that I gasp into his mouth. He tastes like whiskey, and when he bites my lower lip I moan, opening my mouth for him, inviting him in, giving him everything.

His tongue sweeps into my mouth and everything else disappears completely. The music becomes distant white noise. The crowd vanishes into nothing. The heat and the lights and the fact that we're in public surrounded by hundreds of people all fade away into irrelevance until there's only Jack's mouth on mine, his hands on my body, the way he kisses me.

One of his hands tangles in my hair, gripping it tight. The other hand splays against my lower back, hauling me flush against him, and oh God, I can feel every hard plane of his body pressed against me, and can feel exactly how much he wants this too.

I press closer, my hands sliding up his chest to curl around his neck, and he makes this low sound in his throat that goes straight through me. His hand pulls me impossibly closer, making me gasp, and he takes advantage, deepening the kiss until I'm dizzy with it.

I press in hard, eliminating even the suggestion of space between us, my hands sliding up his chest to curl around his neck. He groans into my mouth, the sound vibrating through both of us, and his grip on me tightens. Claiming.

And God, I want him to. I want him to claim me, to mark me, to make me his in every way possible. I want him so badly that I can barely think straight, barely remember why I ever thought this was a bad idea, barely care about consequences.

We break apart because we have to, because we need air, both of us panting, and stare at each other for a long moment. Around us the club is alive—people dancing, drinking, shouting to be heard over the band, living their lives completely unaware that mine just shifted on its axis. The music is so loud my ears will probably ring tomorrow, but right now I can barely hear it over the sound of my own heartbeat.

"Fuck," Jack whispers against my lips, his forehead pressed to mine.

His eyes are dark, and I can see him thinking, can see him trying to make a decision, trying to figure out what to do next. His gaze flicks away from mine, scanning the room frantically, looking for something. An exit. A solution. Anywhere we can go that's not here in front of all these people.

I follow his line of sight and see what he's spotted. Past the bar, down a narrow hallway barely visible through the crowd, several doors.

His eyes snap back to mine. A question.

I don't hesitate. I nod.

Yes. Right now. Please.

He takes my hand and pulls me through the crowd, past the bar, toward the back of the venue. We weave between tables and dancers, moving fast, urgent. Jack leads me down the narrow hallway past the bathrooms, past a door marked "Private," to another unmarked door at the very end. He tries the handle. It turns, and he pulls me inside.

Storage room. Liquor boxes stacked against walls, old concert posters peeling at the edges, and a desk pushed against the opposite wall covered in papers and supplies. A single bare bulb casts everything in dim, warm light.

The music from the main room is still so loud it vibrates through the floor, through the walls, through my chest. Voices and laughter bleeding through like we're not really separate from the crowd at all, like we could be discovered at any second. None of that stops the desire coursing through me.

The second the door clicks shut, we're on each other. His mouth crashes into mine and I'm already fumbling behind him for the door handle, trying to find a lock.

There isn't one.

"Fuck, there's no lock," he growls against my mouth, having reached the same realization.

"Then I guess you better hurry up," I say, looking directly into his eyes, and who even am I right now? This bold version of myself who says things like that? Who doesn't care about locks or privacy or consequences?

He grins. "Oh, so you're not gonna bolt after this one?"

"You're a real smug—"

He cuts me off, pulling me in and kissing me until I'm dizzy with it, before he pulls back, hands framing my face, large and warm, and I have to tilt my head back to look at him. "I don't have a condom," he says, breathing hard. "I didn't exactly plan for this to happen tonight."

My stomach flips. "I have an IUD. And I've been tested." I'm practically panting. Jack has lit a fire in me that I thought was extinguished forever, and I now feel like I might burn up from the inside out.

His thumbs brush my cheekbones gently. "I'm clean too. Team health screenings every few months as part of our contracts. Last one was June, no one since way before then." His eyes search mine, serious despite the desire written all over his face.

"I want this," I say firmly.

"Are you sure? We talked about boundaries and an expiration date. Once we do this, I can't go back to pretending." His voice is strained, like it's taking everything in him to even speak instead of just taking what we both clearly want. "This has been killing me."

The relief that floods through me is almost as strong as my desire. I haven't been alone in this. I know if we cross this line it will probably blow up eventually. That he'll move on, go back to Monaco and his racing world. And I'll be in Dark River focusing on my music. But in this moment I don't care. I only want him.

"Good, because it's been killing me too," I say, pulling him closer. "So if you don't start fucking me I'll—"

He kisses me before I can finish the threat, cutting off my words with his mouth, swallowing whatever I was going to say. And then his hands are working on my shirt, pulling it over my head and tossing it somewhere behind me, and I don't care where it lands because his mouth is on my neck, on my collarbone, trailing kisses down my skin that make me shiver and arch into him.

He pulls back just long enough to yank his own shirt over his head in one smooth motion. *Holy shit.* He's all hard muscle and tan skin and definition that looks like it was carved by an artist. My hands move to his chest, exploring the planes and ridges, the warmth of his skin, the way his muscles flex under my touch, and he sucks in a breath when I trace the V that disappears into his pants.

His hand catches my jaw, tilting my face up to his, and he pulls me against him, kissing me so hard I see stars, so thoroughly I forget my own name. He backs me up until we hit the door with a solid thud that rattles it in the frame, that probably echoes into the hallway if anyone's out there to hear it.

Footsteps pass by outside. Voices. Someone laughs. The music pounds through the walls, bass shaking the floor under our feet.

I don't care. Let them hear.

His hands find the clasp of my bra and it's gone in seconds, joining our shirts somewhere on the floor. Then his mouth is on my breasts and I gasp, the sound loud even over the music still pounding through the walls. My hands fly to his hair, holding him there, and he makes this satisfied sound like my desperation is exactly what he wants.

He makes quick work of my jeans and underwear, pushing them down my hips in one smooth motion. The fabric pools at my feet. I step out of them awkwardly, almost tripping because my legs are already shaky, and kick everything aside.

For a split second I feel exposed standing here completely naked while he's still partially clothed. But Jack's looking at me like I'm the most incredible thing he's ever seen. His gaze travels slowly down my body, taking his time, and everywhere his eyes touch feels like a physical caress. My skin heats under his inspection, flushing from my chest up to my cheeks.

"You're so fucking beautiful," he says, his voice coming out rough and reverent at the same time. "Every part of you, Lark."

Before I can respond, he presses against me and he's everywhere. Like nothing else exists in the universe except this moment, except us. I can feel every hard inch of him through his jeans and the friction makes me gasp, makes me roll my hips against him desperately seeking more contact.

"You have no idea what you do to me," he says against my ear, his breath hot on my skin, his voice wrecked. "How crazy you make me. How much I've wanted this."

Oh my God. The way he says it makes my knees actually weak.

I reach for his jeans with frantic hands, fumbling with the button. Button popped. Zipper dragged down. He shoves his jeans and boxer briefs down and then—

Oh.

His cock is huge. Bigger than any man I've ever been with, and part of me is wondering how that's going to fit. I can see pre-cum glistening at the tip, evidence of how much he wants this, wants me.

Before I can wonder much longer about the logistics, he's grabbing me and pressing me back against the door, capturing my mouth with his and kissing me so hard and desperately that I moan into his mouth without caring who might hear.

Then he's lifting me, his hands gripping my ass like I weigh nothing. He carries me across the room toward where I vaguely remember seeing that desk, and when we reach it he sets me on the edge and sweeps his arm across the surface. Papers and pens and supplies scatter to the floor with a loud clatter that makes me laugh breathlessly.

His mouth finds my breast again and I lean back on my hands. Some small corner of my mind remembers there's no lock on the door, that if someone came in right now they would see both of us, me spread out on this desk like an offering while Jack Midnight devours me whole.

And I don't care.

Any bit of shyness I had has transformed completely into exhilaration. It's like the fear I get before performing, but the thrill is too fucking good to stop, too intoxicating to resist.

His mouth moves lower, kissing down my stomach, my hip bones, teeth grazing skin, and lower still until he steps back slightly to look at me, fully naked and spread before him. His hands run up my thighs slowly, deliberately, pushing them apart wider, opening me up to his gaze.

"Fuck, Lark," he breathes, staring with such raw intensity it makes me shiver, makes me feel seen and wanted in a way I've never experienced before. "Look at this perfect pussy. Already so wet for me."

I'm panting, chest heaving, but I can't even find it in me to be embarrassed. He looks up at me, lips hovering just above where

I desperately need him, eyes questioning and hungry, looking at me like a predator through those dark lashes.

And I like it. I like the way he's looking at me. I like feeling wanted and desired and powerful all at once.

"Lark, are you sure?" he asks, giving me one more out. "I need to hear you say it."

"Yes, please, yes I want this so much," I sound whiny and desperate and I don't even care. I'm panting, wriggling closer to him on the desk.

He grins like the devil himself. "First I want you to beg for it."

He punctuates this by slowly kissing my pussy, sending shivers and waves of pleasure through me but not giving me what I really need, teasing. I've never had a man talk to me like this before, but my body responds instantly.

"Please," I gasp. "Jack please, I'm begging you. I need your mouth on me." Fuck. I've never been so turned on in my entire life.

"As you wish." His mouth is on me properly and I cry out. The sensation of his lips and tongue on me makes my whole body arch. I can't think, can't breathe, can only feel. My hands fly to his hair, gripping tight, and a broken sound escapes my throat that I don't even recognize as my own.

"Fuck yes," he growls. "I've been dying to taste this pussy. Been thinking about it all goddamn night."

He licks me, slow and deliberate, and I whimper. My thighs start to shake. I can hear how aroused I am, the sound embarrassingly loud even over the music pounding through the walls.

"God you're so fucking wet," he says, and I can hear the satisfaction clear in his voice. "All for me?"

Heat floods my face even as pleasure floods everywhere else. Part of me wants to hide from how obvious my need is, how desperately my body is responding to him. "Yes," I manage to gasp out. "All for you."

He slides one finger inside me, then two, and I gasp at the stretch and the fullness. The music pounds through the walls relentlessly, people talking and laughing on the other side, but I don't even care. Maybe I even like the thrill of it.

"More," I beg, my hands gripping his shoulders. "Jack, please."

He adds a third finger and I groan at the stretch, at how full I feel.

"Oh God, right there, don't stop, please don't stop—" I moan.

His mouth works me with dedication, alternating between fast and slow, building me up. I can barely hold on. He devours me like he's starving. My vision goes blurry and part of me feels boneless, untethered. No man has ever done this to me like this before. Not with this intensity, this dedication to my pleasure.

I call out loudly and embarrassment washes over me automatically, a trained response I can't quite shake. Instinctively I clap my hand over my mouth to muffle the sound, to contain myself, to be quieter, to be less.

Jack stops immediately. His fingers still inside me, and he pulls back to look at me, concern replacing the hunger in his eyes. "Hey," he says, his free hand catching my wrist and pulling my hand away from my mouth with gentle firmness. "Don't you dare."

"It's just…" I gasp, shame flooding hot through me despite the pleasure still humming through my body. "I'm being so loud, it's too much and—"

"So fucking what?" He stares at me, and then something almost feral takes over his expression. "I want them to hear you. I want everyone in this entire building to know exactly how good I'm making you feel."

My throat feels tight. "Jack…"

He strokes my cheekbone tenderly with one hand, his thumb brushing my skin like I'm something precious, while his other hand thrusts hard inside me, curling upward, fingers working me relentlessly.

"You're not too much," he says, and his voice is so certain, so absolutely sure, it makes my chest ache. Like he can see straight through me to all the places Brandon carved out, all the spaces where I learned to make myself smaller. "You're *never* too much. Not for me."

His hand moves to cup my jaw, holding me in place, forcing me to keep eye contact as he moves inside me. I'm panting, struggling to catch my breath, and his eyes are locked on mine, watching every reaction, every gasp. The gentleness of his grip on my face while he's so rough with the rest of me—it's too much. I whimper, trembling. I arch off the desk with a broken moan, my whole body trembling.

I bite my lip hard, trying to hold back, and then his fingers hit that spot and my eyes roll back at the immediate rush of pleasure, more intense than anything I've ever felt. I cry out, the sound loud and unrestrained and uninhibited, and the satisfaction that flashes across his face is almost as intoxicating as what his fingers are doing.

"That's it," he growls, and there's approval in his voice, pride even. "Don't you dare hold back. I want every sound, every moan. I want to know exactly what I'm doing to you." His eyes hold mine, dark and hungry and focused on me.

The intensity in his eyes, the raw desire, the way he's looking at me like my pleasure is the most important thing in the entire world, like making me feel good is his only goal—it breaks something open in my chest that's been locked down tight for years. Breaks through every wall I built, every lesson I learned about making myself smaller, quieter, less.

"Tell me you won't hide from me," he commands, his fingers moving faster now, more deliberately, and I can feel myself getting closer, tension coiling tighter. "Tell me you'll give me everything."

"I won't hide from you," I gasp out, meaning it more than I've ever meant anything. "I'll give you everything. I promise."

"That's it, Lark." There's approval in his voice, pride even. "Just like that. You're perfect. Every sound you make. Every moan. Every gasp." His eyes hold mine, dark and hungry and completely focused on me. "So you're not going to hold back anymore. You understand me?"

"Yes, Jack, yes," I manage.

"Say it," he commands, his fingers moving faster now, more deliberately, and I can feel myself getting closer, tension coiling tighter. "Say you won't hide from me. Say you'll let me hear everything."

"I won't hide from you," I gasp out, meaning it more than I've meant anything. "I'll let you hear everything. I promise."

"Good girl," he says with deep satisfaction, and something about that praise, about being told I'm good for being myself, for being loud, for taking up space—it does something to me that I don't have words for.

He puts his mouth back on me and this time when I cry out, I don't try to muffle it. I let the sound escape freely, let it fill the small room, let it probably drift down the hallway to where people are getting drinks and dancing and living their normal lives. The music pounds through the walls, the bass matching my racing heart, and I don't care. I don't care who hears. I don't care if someone walks in.

"That's my girl," he says, his breath hot against me. My body reacts instantly, tightening around his fingers, my hips lifting toward his mouth without thinking.

He lifts his eyes just enough to find mine, to check in, to make sure I'm okay. "You like when I call you that."

It's not a question, but I answer anyway. I swallow hard, face flushing deeper. "Yes."

"Fuck yes, you do," he says, voice rough. "My girl."

Heat floods through me. *His.*

He works me with his mouth and fingers, building me up slowly this time, deliberately drawing it out. My thighs are shaking, my breathing ragged, sweat gathering at my temples and the small of my back. Every time I get close, when that tension coils so tight I can taste the release, when I'm right there on the edge, he pulls back.

Changes the rhythm. Slows down. Makes me start the climb all over again until I'm a desperate, writhing mess on the desk, until I'm begging shamelessly, until I've lost all sense of pride or dignity or anything except need.

"Jack," I gasp desperately, my whole body trembling, my hands tightening in his hair hard enough that it must hurt but he doesn't stop, doesn't complain. "Oh God, right there, don't stop, please—"

"Please what?" He pulls back slightly, and I could cry from the loss, from the frustration.

"Please let me come," I beg shamelessly, and I'm not even embarrassed anymore, not even self-conscious, just desperate. "I can't take anymore, I need—I need—"

"That's what I wanted to hear," he says with satisfaction, like my complete surrender is exactly what he was waiting for. His fingers move rougher now, more demanding, his mouth working me relentlessly without mercy, and his eyes lock on my face, watching every reaction, cataloging every expression. "That's it, baby. So perfect. Come for me."

The orgasm hits hard and sudden, crashing over me like a tidal wave that pulls me under. I scream his name, just like he told me to.

"JAAAACK!"

I call it out loud and broken and desperate, my head flinging back so hard it thuds against the wall behind me but I don't care, don't even feel it. My whole body convulses, clenching around his fingers so tight he groans against me, the vibration adding to the sensation. The orgasm seems to last forever, wave after wave rolling through me, each one more intense than the last, until I'm gasping and trembling and completely oversensitive, until I can't tell where one wave ends and another begins.

Jack works me through it, his fingers and mouth not stopping, drawing out every last aftershock until I'm gasping and trembling and trying to push him away because it's almost too much, almost too intense. Almost too everything.

"Perfect," he says finally, pulling back, and then he's bringing his fingers to his mouth, maintaining eye contact with me the whole time, watching my reaction as he tastes me.

The sight makes heat flood through me all over again even though I just came so hard I can barely think straight, can barely remember my own name. "Oh my God."

"You taste incredible," he says, his voice full of a need that matches my own.

Then his mouth is back on me with soft kisses and I'm so sensitive I try to squirm away, try to escape the overwhelming sensation, but his hands grip my thighs, holding me in place with gentle firmness. "Not till I say you're done."

He kisses my pussy, reverently, like he's worshipping me, drawing out the aftershocks until I'm whimpering and trembling all over again, until I'm not sure if I'm trying to get away or press closer.

Finally, he stands up between my legs, and the sight of him makes my breath catch all over again.

He's huge. Like, genuinely huge. And I haven't done this in two years and even then it was never with someone who looked like him, who made me feel like this, who looked at me like I'm everything he's ever wanted.

Nerves flutter in my stomach, reality crashing back in for just a second. Can I do this? Can I take him? What if I can't? What if—

But I push the doubts down. I want this. I want him. I want to know what it feels like to be with someone who sees me, really sees me, and wants me anyway. Someone who thinks I'm perfect exactly as I am.

"You okay?" he asks, reading my expression like he always does, always so attentive, always checking in.

"Yeah." I swallow hard, forcing honesty. "Just... you're really big."

His mouth curves into a smile that's half pride, half concern, and all affection. "We'll go slow. I'll take care of you."

"I don't want slow," I say, and it's true. I'm nervous but I'm also desperate, aching, needing him inside me with an urgency that overrides everything else. "I want you. Now. So do something about it."

His eyes darken with promise. "With pleasure."

CHAPTER 18

JACK

I wrap my hands around her thighs and spread them wider, positioning myself between her legs. Her skin is flushed all the way down her chest, her nipples are hard, and she's biting that bottom lip in a way that makes me want to bite it too.

She's fucking gorgeous. Completely naked on this desk, looking up at me with those wide brown eyes that are half nervous, half desperate. Her hair is a mess from my hands, tangled and wild around her face. Her lips are swollen from my mouth, red and full.

I've wanted this for weeks. I wanted to see her like this, spread out and ready for me. And in this moment, every inch of her belongs to me.

I grip myself, already slick with precum, and line up at the entrance of her pussy, and just the heat of her against me makes my jaw clench so hard. Her wetness coating my tip, dripping down, and my whole body shudders with the effort of not just slamming forward.

"Look at you," I murmur, running my hands up her inner

thighs slowly, feeling the softness of her skin, the way she trembles under my touch. "So wet for me. So ready. You want my cock, don't you?"

"Yes," she breathes. "God, yes. Please."

"Then you're going to be a good girl and do exactly what I tell you." I grip her thighs harder, spreading her even wider. "Can you do that for me?"

"Yes," she gasps. "Anything. I'll do anything."

"That's what I like to hear." I slide one finger through her wetness, gathering it, feeling how soaked she is. "Now lean back. I want you to watch while I fill you up. I want to see your face when you take every inch of my cock."

She nods, still biting her lip, and I push in slowly. Just the tip. The sensation makes every muscle in my body tense and I have to force myself not to slam in, not to take her the way every instinct is screaming at me to.

"Oh God," she gasps, her back lifting slightly off the desk. One hand shoots out to grip my forearm, nails digging in hard enough to leave marks, and I fucking love it.

I grit my teeth and go slow, watching her face closely. Her mouth opens and her eyes go wide.

"Fuck," she whispers, looking up at me with those huge eyes, completely spread open for me on this desk, vulnerable and trusting and so fucking beautiful. "You're really—God, you're so big. I don't know if—"

The words send a bolt of pride and possession straight through me. "You can take it," I tell her firmly, pushing deeper, watching her eyes flutter. "I know you can. Your body's made for this. Made for me." I push in another slow inch. "Feel how wet you are? How you're opening up for me? Your pussy wants my cock, Lark. It's pulling me in."

She moans at my words, and I feel her clench around me, trying to pull me deeper.

"That's it," I groan. "Just like that. Open up for me."

"Yes," she moans. Her tongue meets mine, desperate and needy. She's kissing me back like she's drowning and I'm air. When I pull back, her lips are swollen and wet, and she's panting harder.

Her chest rises and falls rapidly, her breasts brushing against my chest with each breath. I push in another inch, slowly, giving her body time to adjust. She's so hot around me, so slick and tight, and the feeling is overwhelming.

"Please," she gasps. "Please don't stop. I need more."

"More?" I push in another inch, slowly, giving her body time to adjust even though it's killing me. "You sure you can handle more?"

"Yes! God, yes, please—"

"Greedy girl," I murmur, but I'm smiling. She's so hot around me, the feeling is overwhelming, almost too much. "You want all of me?"

"Yes," she moans. "I want to feel all of you. Want to be completely full."

"Then take it," I say, and push in deeper. "Take my cock. Show me how much you want it."

She gasps, her whole body shuddering, and I can feel her trying to relax, trying to open up for me. "It's so much. You're so much—"

"You're doing so fucking good," I tell her, my voice ragged with praise, with desire. "Look at how well you're taking me. Look at how your pussy is stretching around my cock. So perfect. Made for this. Made for me."

The praise makes her clench around me and I have to stop moving completely and breathe through it. "Fuck, don't do that or I'm not going to last."

"Don't do what?" she asks, and she's looking at me like she knows exactly what she's doing to me. Then she does it again. Deliberately. Testing me. Teasing me. The little smirk on her face is the sexiest thing I've ever seen.

"You're going to pay for that," I growl, and thrust in the rest of the way in one motion.

"Yes!" she cries out, loud and unrestrained, her back arching so hard she lifts off the desk completely. I stay buried as deep as I can go, letting her feel every inch of me, letting her body adjust to being completely full. I lean down and kiss her, hard and possessive, tasting the salt of sweat on her lips.

When I pull back I say, "You look perfect like this. Spread out on this desk with my cock buried inside you. Fucking perfect."

"Fuck, yes," she gasps. "Like that. Please, just like that and—"

I lean down and capture one nipple in my mouth, sucking hard, and she cries out, her hands flying to my hair, holding me there. I bite down gently and she moans, lifting up and pushing her breast further into my mouth. I move to the other one, giving it the same attention, marking her, claiming her, making sure tomorrow when she looks in the mirror she'll see evidence of me everywhere.

Her tits bounce with every thrust and I can't look away. Can't stop watching the way her body moves, the way she takes everything I give her, the way her face shows every bit of pleasure she's feeling.

I establish a rhythm, and she's making these sounds that are driving me insane. Little gasps and moans that tell me exactly how good this feels for her. The desk is shaking with every thrust, the legs scraping against the concrete floor. More supplies slide off and crash to the ground. The music is still pounding through the walls, bass vibrating through the desk, through both of us.

"You like this?" I ask, pulling back. "Like being fucked on this desk where anyone could walk in?"

"Yes!" she gasps. "God, yes. Harder."

"Good. Because you look fucking incredible like this. Taking my cock so well. Being such a good girl for me."

I give her exactly what she wants, pounding into her without mercy, without holding back. She screams and the sound echoes off the concrete walls and I know everyone can hear what we're doing, can hear her getting fucked, can hear her falling apart. I should care but I don't. Let them hear.

"That's it," I growl, watching her face, memorizing every expression. "Take it. You can handle it."

"Yes, Jack," she gasps. "I can take everything you give me."

"Fuck, Lark," I groan, and the sound comes from deep in my chest, primal and raw. The feeling of her wrapped around me is overwhelming. Hot and tight and absolutely perfect. Like her body was made specifically for mine, like we fit together in a way that shouldn't be possible but is. "You feel incredible. So fucking good. Better than anything I've ever felt."

I can feel her starting to tighten around me, can see all the signs that she's getting close. Her breathing goes ragged and uneven, her moans get higher and more desperate. Her whole body starts to tense, coiling tight like a spring.

"You going to come for me?" I ask, my voice strained.

"Yes," she gasps, her eyes locked on mine. "So close—"

I reach between us, finding her clit with my thumb, and rub hard circles over it. She screams my name, the sound loud enough that I'm certain everyone in this entire building can hear it.

"That's my girl," I growl, watching her face. "Come for me. Let me feel it."

She does, her whole body seizing up, going completely rigid for a second before she starts shaking. I can feel her clenching around me, pulsing and gripping me so tight I can barely move.

"Fuck," I groan, feeling my own release building fast and inevitable, pressure coiling at the base of my spine, my rhythm starting to falter. "Lark, I'm going to—"

"Inside," she gasps immediately, still trembling beneath me, still coming. "Come inside me. I need to feel it."

"Lark, I—"

"Please, Jack, fill me up—"

I thrust deep one more time and come harder than I ever have in my entire life, seeing actual white behind my eyes, my whole body locking up with the intensity of it. I can feel myself pulsing inside her, emptying everything I have, and I can feel her still gripping me, milking every last drop, her body taking everything I give her.

"Fuck," I groan against her neck. "Fuck, Lark—"

For a long moment I just stay there, buried inside her, both of us breathing hard. My heart is racing so fast it feels like it might burst out of my chest. The music is still loud, but it feels distant now, irrelevant compared to what just happened, compared to this.

I kiss her, soft and sweet this time, tender, pouring everything I can't say into it. She kisses me back with what feels like everything she has. When I pull back, I rest my forehead against hers, neither of us speaking, just breathing together.

"You okay?" I ask quietly, my hand coming up to cup her face, thumb stroking her cheek.

"Yeah," she breathes, her eyes soft and a little dazed. "So okay. More than okay."

"I wasn't too rough?" I search her face.

"No. God, no. You were perfect." She smiles up at me. "That was perfect."

I kiss her forehead, then her temple, trailing soft kisses down the side of her face to her jaw. She shivers under my attention, her fingers threading through my hair, holding me close.

"That was incredible," she murmurs, her voice still breathless.

"Yeah," I agree against her skin, kissing back up to her mouth, taking my time. "It really was. You're really beautiful, you know that?"

"You're not so bad yourself."

She's smiling when I kiss her again. I pull out slowly, carefully, watching her face. She winces slightly and cum immediately starts leaking out of her and I can't help but watch it, something primal and possessive surging through me at the sight.

"Like what you see?" she asks, and there's mischief in her voice now, playfulness returning.

I look up at her face. She's biting her lip, eyes sparkling with trouble. "Very much."

She reaches down between her legs, her fingers sliding through the mess we made, gathering my cum on her fingertips. Then she brings her hand up slowly, deliberately, holding my gaze the entire time. Her fingers glisten in the dim light and she brings them to her mouth, licking them clean while maintaining eye contact.

"You're unreal," I breathe, my cock twitching hard at the sight.

But she's not done. She hops off the desk, a little wobbly, and drops to her knees in front of me. Before I can process what's happening, her tongue drags up the length of my cock, licking away the evidence, tasting everything.

"Fuck, Lark," I groan, my hand flying to her hair. I'm already getting hard again, which should be impossible. My body shouldn't be capable of this. But apparently where she's concerned, normal rules don't apply.

She looks up at me through her lashes, her mouth wrapped around the head of my cock for just a moment, before she pulls back with a satisfied smile. "What? Just cleaning up."

I groan. "You're going to kill me."

"Maybe," she says, pressing a soft kiss to the tip of my cock. "But what a way to go."

She takes me into her mouth again, deeper this time, all the way to the back of her throat, and I feel her swallow around me.

My hand tightens in her hair and she moans, the vibration going straight through me.

"Fuck," I groan. "Lark, if you keep doing that—"

She pulls back, looking up at me with dark eyes. "What? This?" And she does it again, taking me deep.

I pull her up and she gasps. "Hotel. Right now. Because I'm going to fuck you properly in a bed where I can take my time with you."

She grins, looking absolutely pleased with herself, satisfied like a cat. "Yes, sir."

I wake up to sunlight streaming through the open balcony door and Lark sprawled half on top of me, one leg thrown over mine, her hair everywhere. The sheets are tangled around us, half on the bed, half on the floor. There's a pillow by the door to the balcony. Another one near the bathroom. Evidence of last night is scattered throughout the room like a map of everywhere we touched.

We'd barely made it out of the hotel elevator before starting again, the night turning into one long blur of her skin against mine, her sounds in my ear, the way she said my name over and over.

The bed first, where I'd buried myself between her thighs and made her come on my tongue twice before she begged me to fuck her.

Then the shower around midnight where she dropped to her knees on the tile and took my cock in her mouth, looking up at me with those dark eyes. And then the balcony at three in the morning, bending her over the railing, one hand clamped over her mouth while I fucked her from behind, both of us knowing damn well everyone could probably hear her muffled screams against my palm.

Fuck. My body responds to the memory immediately, my dick stirring even though I have no idea how that's possible. I'm completely spent. Every muscle in my body is sore, wrung out, exhausted. But apparently my cock didn't get that memo.

I look down at her sleeping on my chest, her face relaxed and peaceful. She's so fucking beautiful it makes my chest ache. Dark lashes against her cheeks and wild hair spread across my skin.

She's mine now. Actually mine. Not fake, not for show, not for the cameras. Mine. The thought makes something warm and satisfied settle in my chest. I get to wake up like this. I get to have her in my bed, in my life, in everything. And fuck if that doesn't feel incredible.

She makes this soft sound and stirs against me, her body shifting. Then her eyes flutter open slowly, adjusting to the light. When she sees me already awake and watching her, a sleepy grin spreads across her face. She's devastatingly beautiful.

I can't help myself. I stroke her cheek with my thumb, feeling the softness of her skin, then let my fingers slide into her hair. The strands are still tangled from my hands being in them all night.

"Morning," she mumbles, her voice husky and slightly rough in the most delicious way. From taking me so deep in the shower. From the way she begged me not to stop when I was between her legs. From screaming my name on the balcony.

"Morning." I smile, unable to resist stroking her face again, tracing the line of her jaw like I'm trying to memorize it, like I'm trying to burn this moment into my memory. My thumb brushes across her bottom lip, and I remember biting it last night.

Her grin widens, eyes sparking with heat and mischief even in her sleepy state. "Happy memories?"

I laugh, the sound rumbling through my chest, and brush my thumb across her lip again. "Very happy memories."

She flushes pink, biting that lip. "I can't believe we did all of that."

"Which part?" I tease. "The storage room? The shower? The balcony where everyone could hear you?"

"All of it," she says, but she's smiling. "Every single part."

She lifts her head and looks around the room, taking in the absolute destruction. Clothes everywhere, scattered like we couldn't get them off fast enough. Which we couldn't. Sheets askew and half falling off the bed. The open balcony door with the curtains blowing in the breeze, letting in the salt air and the sound of waves. Her eyes widen and she starts laughing.

"Oh, damn," she says, looking back at me. "We absolutely destroyed this room."

I grin, tucking her hair behind her ear. "We did a pretty thorough job."

She sits up slightly, and the sheet falls away from her chest. Her breasts are completely exposed in the morning light, full and soft and it takes everything in me not to pull her back down and start all over again, but at the same time I've got nothing left. She took everything I had and more.

She points at the balcony, her face flushing. "You're never going to be allowed to return to this hotel. People definitely heard us."

I laugh. "Worth every second. You don't have any regrets, do you?"

"No," she admits, turning back to me with a smile. "Not one."

"Good. Because I don't either." My fingers trail down her neck. "Though I had no idea you were such an exhibitionist. I mean, you were the one who wanted the balcony."

"I'm not usually!" she protests, but she's laughing, throwing her head back like she can't quite believe what we just did. "I'm really not. I've never done anything like that before. Never even thought about it. You must have brought it out in me."

"Did I?" I pull her back down against me.

"Yes," she says, snuggling closer. I can feel her pressed against me everywhere. "I've never felt like that before," she continues softly, her breath warm against my skin. "That wild. That…" She pauses, searching for the word. "Safe. Which is crazy because we were literally on a balcony where anyone could see, but I felt safe with you."

Something inside me cracks at her words.

"Good," I say quietly, my hand stroking down her spine. "That's exactly how you should feel. Always."

For a long moment we just lie there in the sunlight, her body warm and soft against mine, the sound of the ocean filtering in through the open door. My fingers trace slow patterns on her back, over her hip.

Then she shifts, sitting up. The sheet falls away and she sits cross-legged facing me, completely naked in the morning light. My brain short-circuits for a second because fuck, she's beautiful. The sunlight catches on her skin, and I have to force myself to focus on what she's about to say.

"So," she says, her voice going quiet. "I mean… are we, should we—"

"I want to be with you," I tell her, sitting up to face her properly. My hand reaches out to cup her jaw, thumb brushing her cheek. "For real. No fake dating anymore. I think I've been struggling with it being fake since the beginning."

She lets out a breath, her shoulders relaxing. "OK good. Because I think I have too. I kept trying to convince myself it was just the arrangement, just playing a role, but…" She trails off, shaking her head. "It stopped feeling fake pretty quickly."

"Yeah," I agree, relieved. "It did." I half expected her to say this was a mistake.

"But how do we make this work?" Her brow furrows. "You're

going back to Monaco in September. I'm focusing on my music. Long distance is really hard, Jack. Your schedule is insane."

"We'll figure it out," I tell her, pulling her closer. "I'll fly back whenever I can. Between races, during breaks. Fly you out to races when your schedule allows. We'll make it work because I'm not walking away from this."

"Jack," she says slowly. "I feel like I need to say this. I know you don't really... I mean, you don't date seriously. Which is fine, that's your life. But I don't know if you should change everything for me just because we slept together. I don't want you to feel obligated or—"

"Lark." I cut her off gently. "I know I haven't dated seriously before. I know my reputation. But this isn't about obligation or changing who I am. This is about you. You're different. You make me want things I didn't think I wanted."

She bites her lip. "And your life? I mean, listen, I like a good time, but I'm very serious about my career. And I know you were only at that Monaco party for Sofia, but other things like that... the lifestyle, the constant travel, the insane parties. That's not really my world. I'm pretty focused and grounded, and I know you are too about racing. I don't mean to say that you're not serious, it's just with your history I think—"

"I know," I interrupt. "And I won't deny I've had some wild times. But a good portion of those were when I was younger, more reckless. And I've never been more serious about my career than I am now, especially after feeling what it's like to have it slip away." I cup her face, making sure she's looking at me. "And you... you're something I never saw coming. I think I've completely fallen for you."

The words come out before I can overthink them.

Her eyes widen, and then her face breaks into a devious smile. "You *bastard*," she says. "You snuck up on me. I've fallen for you too."

I pull her down for a kiss, deep and thorough, pouring

everything I feel into it. When we break apart, we're both breathing hard.

"So we'll figure it out," I say, my forehead against hers. "Long distance, the schedules, all of it. I don't know exactly how yet, but I know I want this. I want you."

"I want this too," she says softly. She pulls back slightly to look at me. "But that means we have to be completely honest with each other, alright? To make this work. I mean, we started by fake dating, so we need a real foundation now. No more pretending, no more playing roles. Just us, being real."

"Deal," I say immediately. "Complete honesty. No bullshit."

"Good." She kisses me again, softer this time. When she pulls back, she's smiling. "So we're really doing this? You and me?"

My hands slide up her back, pulling her closer. "You have no idea how badly I've wanted you to be mine. Actually mine, not just for show."

She pulls back to look at me, and her smile is radiant. "Then I'm yours. And you're mine."

"Damn right you are," I tell her, and kiss her again. She kisses me back with everything she has, her arms wrapping around my neck, and it feels like coming home.

I've spent years running from anything that mattered, anything that could hurt me. But with her, I want to stop running. We'll figure out the distance, the schedules, all the logistics that seem impossible right now. Because this, what we have right here, is worth fighting for.

She's worth fighting for.

CHAPTER 19

LARK

The morning light creeps across my bedroom ceiling in slow golden strips, and I can't stop smiling.

My comforter is pulled up to my chin even though it's definitely not cold. More like I'm trying to hold onto the warmth of last night, the feeling of Jack's arms around me, his weight pressing me into the mattress. The ceiling fan above me clicks with every rotation, a rhythmic sound that normally lulls me to sleep but right now just reminds me that I'm alone in this bed when I'd much rather be tangled up with him.

We got back to Dark River late last night, but Jack had to turn around and go back to Seattle this morning. He has an early meeting with Robert about contract stuff, then a full day of sponsor obligations and media appearances before he can finally drive back tonight. Which means I'm here, in my apartment, alone, and already missing him bad.

I turn over and bury my face in my pillow, groaning. One night together and now I'm completely ruined for anyone else. Completely gone for Jack Midnight in a way that should probably terrify me but instead just makes me grin into my pillow like a maniac.

The physical part was mind-blowing. Like, I-didn't-know-my-body-could-do-that levels of incredible. Six orgasms. Six. But it was everything else too. The way it felt to be with him. Safe and free, like I could just be myself without constantly editing.

And now we're actually together. My phone buzzes on my nightstand and I grab it immediately.

Maren: *Incoming with caffeine. You up?*

I grin, typing back quickly.

Me: *Yes I'm up and oh my god you are not going to believe the updates I have for you*

Maren: *!!!!!!*

Maren: *Screaming. I am racing there right now*

Me: *Good because the tea is piping hot*

Maren: *Be there in 5 minutes!*

I laugh, tossing my phone aside and snuggling back into the pillows. Five minutes later I hear my front door open and close, then Maren's quick footsteps practically running down the hallway.

"Lark!" she calls out, breathless.

"In here!" I call back, already grinning.

She bursts through my bedroom door holding two to-go cups from *Bean There*, one of our favorite coffee shops, wearing black leggings and an oversized cream sweater, her blonde hair in a ponytail. She has this huge grin on her face, cheeks flushed.

I laugh. "Did you actually *run* here?"

"Of course! You teased gossip like dangling a carrot and I am starving for details," she says, slightly out of breath. "And for some reason everyone is home today and parked in your apartment complex so I had a hell of a time finding a spot." She climbs onto the bed immediately, settling cross-legged facing me. "Okay, you're grinning like a lunatic. Start talking right now."

I accept the latte she hands me, wrapping both hands around the warm cup. The vanilla smell hits me and I take a sip. "So, Miami was incredible."

"Yes, yes, I figured that much by the cryptic texting." She waves her hand impatiently, leaning forward. "But come on now, don't hold back! Details. All of them. What happened?"

I take another sip of coffee, my face already heating up. "Jack and I slept together."

Maren squeals so loud I'm pretty sure my upstairs neighbor heard, her hand flying to her mouth. "I *knew* it! After that hallway kiss, I knew there was no way you two weren't going to end up together. The tension was going to combust!"

"You were right," I admit, laughing. "We couldn't even wait for the heart-shaped bed. I mean, we did eventually use the heart-shaped bed, but first we had sex in a storage closet at this club."

"Wait, WHAT?" Maren's eyes go huge. "Back up. Storage closet? Lark, who *are* you?"

"I know!" I'm laughing now, half embarrassed and half still kind of amazed I did it. "I don't know what came over me. We were at *La Casa de la Música*, this club in Little Havana, which was incredible by the way, but more on that later, and so we were dancing. But not just like casual dancing. It was intense."

Maren is grinning, completely invested. "Like how intense are we talking?"

"Like *Dirty Dancing* intense," I tell her, feeling my face get even hotter. "You know that scene where Baby first dances with Johnny and it's all this tension and heat and you can just feel it building between them? Or later when they're practicing and you know they're about to kiss?"

"Yes! Sexy lift scene energy!" Maren looks delighted.

"Exactly that energy," I confirm. "So we were dancing and it was so hot, Mare. And he can dance."

She lights up, eyes going wide with excitement. "Really? I *love* when a guy can actually dance!" She's practically bouncing now. "When Calvin and I danced at the wedding I think I literally swooned."

"Yes, exactly! So rare for a man to be a good dancer," I say, grinning. "And I would have never danced but he could *move*."

"My god!" She says, taking a sip of her coffee. "So come on, how did it happen? Give me the play-by-play."

"It just was building up all day, hell for weeks really. And then the club was so incredible, so much ambiance. And the dancing turned from like fun and free to slow and sultry. And then suddenly we're kissing and I can't think straight and the next thing I know we're in this storage room with mops and cleaning supplies and no lock on the door."

"And people were right outside?" Maren asks, her voice rising with excitement.

"Literally right outside," I say. "Dancing and drinking and having no idea what we were doing in there. And I've never done anything like that in my entire life. Never even thought about it. But with Jack it was like if I didn't have him right that second I was going to lose my mind."

"This is the best story I've ever heard," Maren says, practically bouncing now. "Okay so storage room sex, which is already wild. Then what happened?"

"Then we went back to the hotel," I continue, my grin widening. "And we basically didn't leave the room until we had to pack for the airport. We ordered room service and stayed in bed and just... kept going."

"How many times are we talking?" Maren asks, leaning in conspiratorially.

"Six orgasms in one night," I tell her, and watch her jaw drop.

"Six? In one night?"

"Yep. Six." I confirm, making a little popping sound on the 'p' for emphasis. "I mean I know you're used to crazy good sex now, but I'm pretty sure my vagina had cobwebs before last night. Like actual cobwebs."

She laughs, blushing and nearly choking on her coffee.

"And you know my entire sexual history before this was just depressingly bad," I continue. "Brandon of course was criminally selfish in bed. Like should-be-investigated-by-authorities levels of selfish."

Maren snorts into her coffee. "He really was the worst in every possible way."

"Agreed. And even the guys before him." I shake my head. "They couldn't have found my clit if I'd given them a map, a flashlight, and written instructions. Remember those few dates I went on after the divorce? Those men didn't even know what foreplay was. One guy literally went from 'hey, we should do this again sometime' to trying to get my pants off with zero buildup."

"I remember that." Maren looks appropriately horrified. "Bob something."

"Bob something," I agree. "Total loser behavior. So I decided I was done with terrible sex. If a man didn't know what he was doing, he wasn't getting anywhere near me. I'm not going to train someone. But with Jack it was just… effortless. Revolutionary."

"That's how it should be," Maren says, smiling.

"I know! But I'd never experienced it before. Not like that." I take another sip of coffee. "And Mare, it wasn't just the physical stuff, though that was incredible. We talked for hours. About everything. His childhood and the adoption and his relationship with his brothers. My music and what I want for my future. It felt so natural, like I could tell him anything."

"That sounds perfect," Maren says softly. "So what's happening now? Are you guys together? Like actually together?"

"Yes!" The word bursts out of me, too loud and too excited, but I don't care. "We talked about it and we both want this. We're going to figure out the long distance situation and just make it work."

"Lark!" Maren grabs my hands, squeezing them. "This is amazing! I'm so happy for you!"

"I know!" I'm laughing now. "Jack Midnight is my actual boyfriend."

We sit there for a moment, both grinning like idiots, and I feel this bubble of energy building in my chest. "Okay, I have way too much energy to burn off right now. Gym before work?"

"Deal!" Maren's already standing, pulling me up with her. "Let's go. I want to hear more Miami stories while we're on the elliptical."

I laugh, following her to grab my workout clothes. Tonight feels impossibly far away, but at least I have Maren and endorphins to keep me busy until Jack gets back to Dark River. Until I can see him again and kiss him and remember that this is real now, not just some perfect weekend I dreamed up.

The Black Lantern is slowing down after a busy dinner rush, mercifully easing into that comfortable lull between chaos and closing time. A few regulars are playing Settlers of Catan in the corner with occasional shouts of "I need wheat!" and "Stop blocking my longest road!" Some folks up from Seattle are huddled at a table going over hiking maps while nursing IPAs. And me behind the bar doing the closing side work I should've started an hour ago.

I'm rolling silverware, but my mind wanders between thoughts of my music and Jack, each fighting for equal attention. He should be back in a few hours and coming straight to my apartment after. I'm practically vibrating with excitement, that restless energy that comes from wanting something so badly, time feels like it's moving through molasses. I have a new song I want to work on before he gets here, so the second I wrap up this shift I'm heading straight home to my guitar.

My phone buzzes on the bar top and I glance at it absently, expecting another Instagram notification or maybe my mom asking if I've eaten anything besides bar food this week. Instead, Maya Stone's name stares back at me from an email notification.

My hands freeze mid-roll, the fork clattering against the bar with a sharp metallic sound that makes me wince. I set down the half-finished bundle and wipe my suddenly sweaty palms on my jeans before picking up my phone with shaking fingers.

"You good over there?" Maren asks from where she's restocking beer in the cooler, her voice muffled by the heavy door.

"Yeah, just..." I tap the notification, watching the email app load with agonizing slowness. *Come on, come on.* "Maya from Tidal just emailed me."

The cooler door swings shut with a solid thud and Maren's head whips around so fast I'm surprised she doesn't give herself whiplash.

I open the email, my eyes skimming so fast over the words that I have to go back and reread the whole thing twice. This can't be real. This is not actually happening.

Lark,

Following up on our last talk. We've been tracking your streaming numbers and social media momentum and have been very impressed.

I know this is short notice, but we'd love to fly you out to LA to meet with our team next weekend. It gives us a chance to sit down in person and discuss your sound and vision more in depth. After getting to chat with you at the label party, we've decided we have serious interest in moving forward. Would love to discuss in person what that would look like, and potentially get you in a recording studio to do some demos after the meeting if we decide we're a good fit.

We have connections to a producer in Seattle that would be perfect for getting some initial recordings done. Full transparency: we're looking at several artists right now, but there's real interest in what you're building. This trip would help us figure out if we're the right partners to help you break through.

My assistant will reach out with travel details. Let me know if you can make it work.

Best, Maya

I read it again because surely I'm misreading something. The words can't possibly say what I think they say. LA. Studio time.

Maren appears behind me trying to read over my shoulder, practically climbing onto my back. "What does it say? Tell me!"

"They want me to fly to LA," I manage, my voice coming out high and squeaky. "For a meeting to discuss moving forward. And possibly record some demos!" The words tumble out in a rush, barely coherent.

"Lark!" Maren's squeal is so loud the Catan players look over with annoyed expressions. She grabs my shoulders and shakes me, bouncing on her toes. "This is huge! This is everything!"

"I know!" I laugh, the sound coming out slightly hysterical, and I nearly drop my phone, fumbling to keep hold of it. "I can't believe this is real!"

"It *is* real!" Maren pulls back but she's still grinning like a maniac, her eyes shining. "You're going to LA!"

"It's absolutely terrifying, but I'm going to shove that down deep and deal with it later." I rub my face with both hands, trying to breathe normally.

I wish Jack was here right now. I want to tell him, want to see his reaction, want him to pick me up and spin me around. But he'll be back tonight and I can tell him everything then.

The kitchen door swings open and Jayson pokes his head

through, looking between us with raised eyebrows. "Did someone just say LA?"

"Yes!" Maren announces, turning toward him with the enthusiasm of someone sharing news about their own success. "Meetings with the label people!"

I can't suppress the ear-to-ear smile that's making my face hurt.

"Holy shit!" Jayson's whole face lights up and he pushes through the door fully, wiping his hands on his apron. "That's incredible! When do you go?"

"Next week," I say, still trying to process it myself. "This is crazy. Fancy LA meetings with actual record executives who want to talk about my music."

"You're going to crush it," Maren says firmly, gripping my shoulders. "This is what you've been working toward."

The Blue Room disaster is still fresh in my mind, stage fright the ever-looming monster waiting to sabotage me at the worst possible moment. I've been practicing at home, doing the visualization thing my therapist suggested ages ago. Playing through entire sets in my living room like there's an actual audience there.

"You're talented as hell, Lark," Jayson adds enthusiastically. "It's about time everyone else figured that out."

"Thanks, you guys." I laugh, feeling tears prick my eyes. Happy tears this time. "Stop, you're gonna make me cry."

A loud timer dings from the kitchen, the sound cutting through our celebration.

Jayson's face changes immediately. "Oh shit, the flatbreads. I completely forgot." He's already backing toward the kitchen. "Gotta check those before they burn. But Lark, this is amazing! We're celebrating later!"

He disappears into the kitchen as a customer approaches the bar, an older guy I recognize as a regular who always orders the same wheat beer.

"I got this," Maren says immediately, squeezing my arm. "You go reply to Maya and say yes to everything. Go!"

She's already moving toward the guy with her best customer service smile, and I sink onto a stool at the end of the bar. My phone feels heavy in my hands, Maya's email still glowing on the screen.

I can't believe this is real. This is my shot. The one I've been working toward for years, through the bad marriage and the worse divorce and all the self-doubt Brandon planted in my head that I'm still trying to weed out.

LA meetings with a real record label. People who believe in my music enough to fly me out there. I'm terrified. But I'm also more excited than I've been in years.

And I'm not going to let fear hold me back anymore.

CHAPTER 20

Jack

The meeting with Robert ran late, then the media obligations dragged on forever. Smile for the camera, answer the same questions about my "maturity" and "focus" for the hundredth time, pretend I give a shit about anything other than getting back to Dark River.

Getting back to her.

By the time I'm finally in my car heading out of Seattle, it's nearly 8 PM, and I'm wired. The highway stretches out in front of me, taillights bleeding red in the dusk, and I push the speed limit more than I should. I can't help it. My foot wants the accelerator down, wants to close the distance between here and Lark's apartment as fast as physics will allow.

When I finally arrive I punch in the code she gave me and push the door open. The apartment is quiet except for music drifting down the hallway from her bedroom. Soft guitar chords and her voice weaving through them, and I stop in the entryway just listening for a second.

I close the door quietly and follow the music down the hallway. Her voice draws me forward, this ethereal quality that gets under my skin. It's delicate but powerful at the same time, the kind of sound that wraps around you and doesn't let go.

I stop in her bedroom doorway and just watch her. She's sitting cross-legged on her bed, guitar cradled in her lap, hair piled on top of her head in a bun with pieces falling down to frame her face. She's wearing a grey sweater that's slipping off one shoulder and black leggings, and she's so focused on what she's playing that she hasn't noticed me yet.

I lean against the doorframe, unable to stop the smile spreading across my face. This is what I've been missing all day. Not just her, but this. Seeing her do what she loves, completely in her element, that little furrow between her eyebrows when she's concentrating.

"That sounds amazing," I say.

She jumps about a foot in the air, her head snapping up. The guitar makes a discordant twang as her fingers slip.

"Jack!" Her face lights up even brighter than before, shock melting into a wide smile, and she's already setting the guitar aside carefully, scrambling off the bed with zero grace. "You're back! I didn't hear you come in!"

"I didn't want to interrupt," I tell her, crossing the room and catching her as she throws herself at me, my arms wrapping around her waist automatically. I lift her slightly, and fuck, she feels perfect pressed against me. "You were in the zone."

"I've been working on this song all afternoon," she says, her arms wrapping around my neck, and then she's kissing me and I forget about everything else.

She tastes like something sweet, probably that strawberry chapstick she's always wearing, and I can't get enough of her. I kiss her deeper, my hands sliding under her sweatshirt to touch bare skin, and she makes this little sound that drives me absolutely crazy.

"Missed you," she mumbles against my mouth when we finally break apart for air, both of us breathing hard.

"Missed you too," I tell her, my hands still on her waist, thumbs brushing circles on her hipbones. "So fucking much. Today was torture."

"Tell me about it," she says, pulling back just enough to look at me, and her eyes are sparkling with happiness and heat. "I didn't expect you to get back from Seattle so fast. Feels like you just texted that you were leaving Robert's."

"Yeah well, I drive fast," I say as I lean in to kiss her again because I can't help myself. "It's kind of my thing."

She rolls her eyes, laughing against my mouth. "How did it go with Robert?"

"Good. Contract talk is still ongoing but he seems optimistic." I brush my fingers along her jaw, loving how she leans into my touch. "Ferrari's been making noises about wanting me back in the sim more often, which Thomas thinks is a good sign."

She grins, her hands sliding down to rest on my chest. "I'm so happy for you." She pauses, biting her lip in that way that tells me she's excited about something. "Speaking of good news, I got an email this afternoon from the label!"

The way her whole face lights up when she's happy—I could watch that forever. "Yeah? What'd they say?"

She pulls back completely, practically bouncing now as she grabs her phone from the nightstand. "Okay so basically Maya said they're super impressed with the Instagram growth and they want me to come to LA!"

"Lark, that's incredible!" I pull her back against me, lifting her off her feet for a second. Her laugh is bright and unrestrained, and I want to bottle that sound. Want to hear it every day for the rest of my life. The thought should scare me but it doesn't.

"I know!" she says when I set her down, her hands gripping

my arms. "They want to talk about my sound, my vision, where I see my career going. It's all happening next weekend."

"That's huge," I say. "You're going to kill it."

"I'm terrified," she admits, but she's still grinning. "But also so excited I could throw up. Maybe both at the same time."

"They'd be insane not to sign you," I tell her firmly, my hands on her shoulders so she has to look at me. "Your songs, your voice—you're the whole package, Lark."

"You have to say that, you're sleeping with me," she teases.

"I'd say it even if I wasn't," I counter.

She laughs. "It's next weekend. Are you free to come? I mean, if you don't have Formula One commitments or anything. I know the timing might not work with your schedule."

"I'll be there," I say without hesitation. I'd cancel whatever I had to cancel. "Wouldn't miss it for the world."

Her smile could light up the entire fucking city. "Really?"

"Really," I confirm, pulling her close again. "I want to be there. Plus I could use a few days in LA anyway. We can make a trip out of it."

"Thank god," she breathes, melting against me. "I've been dying to tell you all day. I wanted to tell you in person but I've been going crazy keeping it to myself."

Warmth spreads through my chest hearing that she was thinking about me, that I'm the person she wanted to share this with first. That I get to be the one here for these moments.

"I'm glad you waited," I tell her, pressing a kiss to her temple. "This deserves celebrating in person."

"You know," she says as a wicked smile spreads across her face, the one that makes me want to do *very* bad things to her. "I was thinking about you even *before* that email came through."

"Oh yeah?" I slide my hands down to her hips, pulling her flush against me, feeling the heat of her through our clothes. My pulse kicks up. "What were you thinking about?"

"I think," she says slowly, deliberately, rising up on her toes so her mouth is barely an inch from mine, her breath warm against my lips, "it's better if I actually show you."

"I don't know," I murmur, my hands tightening on her hips. "You're pretty good with words. Songwriter and all."

"Jack, if you don't shut up and kiss me right now—"

I kiss her hard, cutting off whatever threat she was about to make, and everything else disappears. Her mouth opens under mine immediately and I deepen the kiss, tasting her, claiming her. My hands slide down to grip her ass, pulling her hard against me so she can feel exactly what she does to me, and she gasps into my mouth.

"Get to the bed," I manage to get out against her lips, already walking her backwards. "Now."

She doesn't need to be told twice. Her hands are pulling at my shirt, tugging it up as we stumble across the room. The backs of her knees hit the mattress and we fall onto the bed together, me above her, her underneath me with her hair spread out on the pillow. Fuck, she's gorgeous.

I pull my shirt over my head and toss it somewhere behind me. Her hands immediately wrap around my neck.

"Hi," she says, grinning up at me.

"Hi yourself." I lean down and kiss her again while the tips of my fingers brush over her cheekbones. Her skin is so soft I could touch her forever.

Her hands slide to my jeans, working at my belt. I lean back just enough to shove my jeans and boxers off, then reach for the hem of her tank top. She lifts her arms and I pull it off, revealing she's not wearing anything underneath.

"Fuck," I breathe.

I lean down and take one nipple in my mouth. She makes this intoxicating sound, half surprise, half pleasure, and her hips roll up against mine.

I kiss down between her breasts, taking my time to taste every inch of her skin. Kissing her feels addictive. I hook my fingers in the waistband, pulling it inch by inch down her thighs, past her knees, off completely along with her underwear. She's completely bare now, laid out in front of me like a feast.

I can see how wet her pussy is already, glistening and ready for me, and my mouth waters.

"Lark," I murmur, pressing a kiss to her clit. She moans and her whole body responds. "You're already so wet."

"I told you," she gasps out, her hips rolling up to seek more pressure. "I've been thinking about this all day."

I slide one finger through her folds slowly, and circle her clit once, twice. She makes this desperate sound and her thighs shake.

"More," she breathes. "Jack, please."

I slide one finger inside her and she's so tight and hot and wet that my dick throbs painfully. Her inner walls clench around me immediately, gripping my finger. I work her slowly, in and out with deliberate strokes, and curl my finger to hit that spot inside her.

"God, yes," she moans, and her head falls back against the pillow while her hands fist the sheets beside her.

I add another finger, stretching her, working her with steady strokes while my thumb finds her clit to circle and press. She's getting wetter by the second, her arousal coating my fingers, and her hips are rocking up to ride my hand.

"Jack, please," she pants, her voice strained.

"Please what?" I ask, curling my fingers to hit that spot again.

"Use your mouth too," she gasps. "Please, I need your mouth."

I grin and keep working her, maintaining that steady rhythm. "What was that? Couldn't quite hear you."

"Jack!" She's panting now. "Please. I need... I need your mouth on me. Please."

"Maybe I just like hearing you beg," I say, and I curl my fingers again, stroke that spot, and she moans.

"You're such an asshole," she gasps.

"Well," I say. "Since you asked so nicely."

I lean in and press my mouth to her clit, sucking hard.

"Oh god." Her hands immediately go to my hair, fingers tangling, holding me there like she's afraid I'll stop.

Not a fucking chance. I lick her with long, firm strokes from her entrance up to her clit, tasting every inch of her. She's so fucking wet, so sweet on my tongue, and I could do this for hours, just taste her and make her fall apart with my mouth.

I take my time. She tastes incredible and the sounds she's making are driving me absolutely insane. When I add my fingers back, curling them just right, she makes this high, desperate sound that tells me she's close.

"Jack, I'm—" She can't even finish the sentence, her whole body tensing.

"I know," I murmur against her. "Let go. I've got you."

She comes apart with my name on her lips, her ass rising off the bed, her thighs clamping around my head. I work her through it, drawing it out as long as I can, until she's pushing at my shoulders, oversensitive and shaking.

I kiss back up her body, taking my time, until I'm hovering over her again. She's flushed all over, her hair a mess, breathing hard, looking thoroughly wrecked.

"Holy shit," she says between breaths, and her voice is completely hoarse.

I look down at her. "Good?"

"Shut up." She pulls me down for a kiss that's deep and messy, her tongue sliding against mine. When she pulls back there's heat in her eyes. "Your turn."

She pushes at my shoulder and I roll onto my back, letting her take control. She straddles my thighs for a moment, her hands running over my chest, then she's kissing down my body, her mouth hot against my skin, making me groan.

Then she slides off the bed and settles on her knees between my legs on the floor.

The sight of her like that makes my breath catch. Dark hair messy and wild, completely naked and on her knees for me. "Lark..."

"Shhhh." She wraps her hand around me and just holds me for a moment. The heat of her palm against my skin makes me groan. She strokes once, twice, up and down. Her thumb swipes over the head and spreads the bead of precum on the tip of my cock.

Then she leans down and licks me from base to tip in one long stroke.

"Fuck, Lark," I groan. She does it again, licking and tasting me, her tongue swirling around the head. I fist my hands in the sheets to keep from grabbing her hair and forcing her deeper.

Then she takes me in her mouth and sinks down in one smooth motion.

Every coherent thought evaporates. The heat, the wetness, the suction are almost too much.

"Fuck," I breathe, watching her because I can't look away.

She takes me deeper until I feel myself hit the back of her throat, looking at me with those dark eyes. I thrust into her mouth and she moans in response.

"You like that?" I ask, thrusting again.

"Mmmm," she hums around me, and the vibration nearly undoes me.

"Touch yourself, Lark. I want to see you touch yourself while you're sucking my cock."

Her eyes go wide and she pulls back, gasping, saliva connecting her lips to my dick. Her hand never stops working me. A grin spreads across her face and her free hand slides down between her thighs. Then she takes me back so deep I nearly lose it right there.

The pleasure builds too fast. Heat spreads through my body

and my balls draw up tight. She starts moaning against me while her hand moves faster between her legs. My whole body tenses. If she keeps this up for another thirty seconds I'm going to come down her throat.

"Alright, that's enough." I reach for her but she pulls back on her own, releasing me with a wet pop.

"Not yet," she says. Before I can process what's happening, she's pushing at my shoulders. "Lie back."

"Lark—"

"I said lie back, Jack." The command in her voice shoots straight through me.

I do as she says, watching as she straddles my hips. The sight of her above me, flushed and confident, makes my cock twitch.

She notices and smiles. "Like what you see?"

"You have no idea."

She reaches between us, positioning me at her entrance. Then she sinks down in one smooth motion, taking me deep. We both groan at the sensation.

"Fuck," I breathe, my hands finding her hips. "You feel incredible."

She braces her hands on my chest and starts to move. Slow at first, finding her rhythm, rolling her hips in a way that has us both gasping. I let her set the pace, watching her take what she needs.

"That's it," I encourage, running my hands up her sides. "Take what you want."

She picks up speed, confidence growing with each movement. When she leans back slightly, changing the angle, we both moan. Her breasts bounce with each movement and I reach up to cup them, thumbing her nipples.

"God, Jack," she gasps, riding me harder now. The sight of her using my body for her pleasure is the hottest thing I've ever seen.

I can feel myself getting close, the heat building at the base of my spine. My grip on her hips tightens. "Lark, I'm gonna—"

"Not yet," she says, and suddenly she's lifting off me.

I make a sound of protest, but she's already moving down my body with purpose.

"What are you—"

She doesn't let me finish the question. "I want to taste us," she says, and then her mouth is on my cock again. She takes me deep, one hand working what she can't fit in her mouth, the other cupping my balls.

"Fuck, Lark, I'm—" The warning is all I can manage.

She doesn't pull back. Instead, she takes me deeper, hollowing her cheeks and humming around me. Her eyes meet mine, dark and determined, and that's what undoes me.

I come hard, groaning her name as pleasure crashes through me. She takes everything, swallowing around me as I pulse in her mouth. Her hand keeps stroking, drawing out every last drop until I'm shaking, until I black out momentarily.

Finally, she releases me and crawls back up my body. I pull her into my side instinctively, both of us breathing hard. She curls into me without hesitation, her head on my chest right over my still-racing heart. One leg thrown over mine, her arm draped across my stomach.

I'm still floating somewhere outside my body, absolutely destroyed in the best possible way. That was… fuck, there aren't even words.

She lifts her head and looks at me. There's something soft and open in her expression, vulnerable in a way that makes me want to shield her from everything bad in the world. "I'm really glad you're here," she says.

"Me too," I tell her, and I mean it more than I've meant anything in a long time. I brush her hair back from her face gently and tuck the dark strands behind her ear. "Wouldn't want to be anywhere else."

Because being here with her feels right in a way nothing else in my life ever has.

CHAPTER 21

LARK

The plane touches down at LAX with a jolt, and I look out the window at the California sun beating down on the tarmac like it's personally angry at everyone. Los Angeles. I'm *actually* in Los Angeles because a record label flew me out.

The thought keeps circling back, equal parts thrilling and terrifying.

"You're quiet," Jack says beside me, and I realize I've been staring out the window without actually seeing anything for the past few minutes, just watching the ground crew move around in their bright orange vests.

"Just processing," I say, finally tearing my gaze away from the tarmac to look at him. "This still feels surreal. Like I'm going to wake up any second."

"It's real." He squeezes my hand, his thumb rubbing slow circles on my palm in that way that somehow always calms me down. "And you're going to be incredible."

"We'll see about that," I say, raising an eyebrow. "Big fancy label meetings with people who actually know what they're doing. It's new to me."

"You know what you're doing," he says firmly. "They reached out to *you*, remember? They want you."

"True," I admit, feeling some of the tension in my shoulders ease slightly. "That's a good point."

"Plus you've got me as your cheerleader," he adds with his trademark cocky grin. "My presence alone guarantees success."

"Oh, is *that* how it works?" I laugh despite my nerves. "Your ego is showing, Midnight."

"Confidence, not ego," he corrects, still grinning. "There's a difference. And I have complete faith in you, which you should too."

The plane finally reaches the gate and everyone immediately stands up even though we're clearly not going anywhere for another five minutes. Jack doesn't move from his seat, so neither do I, and I'm grateful for the extra minute to just sit here and breathe.

"Ready?" Jack asks when people finally start moving down the aisle.

"As I'll ever be," I say, taking one more deep breath.

He grabs our bags from the overhead compartment with easy strength and we file down the aisle with everyone else, shuffling slowly toward the exit.

LAX is exactly how I remember it from childhood—massive, overwhelming, full of people who all seem to know exactly where they're going. My parents were both born in Southern California, and we used to come down every couple of years to visit family. Dad's aunt in Pasadena who had approximately ten cats and opinions about everything. My grandparents in Orange County whose entire extended family would somehow materialize for Sunday dinners that turned into hours of talking and laughing while I fell asleep on the couch.

But even back then, driving past all the billboards and seeing the Hollywood sign in the distance, I remember hoping someday I'd come back here for music. To play at actual venues like the Troubadour or the Roxy, to meet with labels, to make something of the songs I was writing in my bedroom. It seemed impossible then, a fantasy that belonged to other people, not to a ten-year-old from Dark River who was still figuring out basic guitar chords.

And now I'm here. Because Tidal Records thinks I might be worth investing in.

We collect our bags from the carousel—mine is bright turquoise and impossible to miss, which was the entire point when I bought it—and head outside into the Southern California heat. It hits me immediately, that dry warmth that's so different from Miami, so different from the damp Pacific Northwest air I'm used to.

The sky is this perfect cloudless blue that feels aggressively cheerful, like it's personally invested in my success here. Palm trees everywhere, that hazy sunshine that makes everything look slightly filtered.

There's a black SUV waiting with a driver holding a sign that says "Reyes," which still feels completely surreal. Like I'm in a movie about someone else's life.

"Ms. Reyes?" the driver confirms.

"That's me," I say, trying to sound like someone who has drivers waiting for them all the time and not like someone whose usual transportation involves a fifteen-year-old Honda Civic with a broken air conditioner.

He loads our bags and we're on the freeway heading toward West Hollywood, and I'm watching the city slide past the windows like a highlight reel of everything that makes LA simultaneously fascinating and overwhelming.

Billboards advertising movies I haven't seen, albums I haven't heard. Endless lanes of traffic even though it's early afternoon. Palm trees lining every street like they're required by city ordinance.

"Oh, look that's Pink's," I say, pointing at the iconic hot dog stand as we pass. "My aunt on my dad's side refused to take us because she said it was 'tourist trap nonsense,' but I really wanted to go because I loved the name. So one time my mom snuck us there."

"Rebels," Jack says, grinning at me.

"Right? We felt so dangerous." I laugh, remembering it. "Eating chili dogs in a parking lot like criminals. I think she hated them, but I loved it. I got chili all over my shirt and we had to stop at a gas station to clean me up before we went back. Pretty sure my aunt knew but never said anything."

"Your family sounds fun," he says.

"They're chaotic. Maybe you'll see them at Christmas." The words are out before I fully process them, and then my brain catches up. Christmas. With my family. That's months away and also a very couple-y thing to say and maybe too soon to be casually throwing out there like it's a given.

But Jack just squeezes my hand. "I'd love that."

He's not freaked out. He's not backpedaling or making a joke to deflect.

"Fair warning though," I say, trying to sound normal and not like I'm already imagining him at my family's table, "my *abuela* will try to feed you until you can't move."

He laughs, and I love that sound. "Even better. I'm extremely motivated by food."

We keep talking as the car weaves through traffic, and I can't stop pointing at things out the window. The taco place my dad still talks about. The corner where we got hopelessly lost trying to find the beach. That weird statue I thought was haunted when I was seven.

Jack listens to all of it, grinning, asking questions, telling me about the time he got mobbed at an In-N-Out and had to be escorted out by security without even getting his burger. Somewhere between the stories and the familiar streets passing by, the knot in my chest loosens.

When we pull up to the hotel, the driver gets our bags and I take a deep breath. West Hollywood. I'm in West Hollywood for meetings with a record label. It's a gorgeous boutique place called The Redbury that looks like someone with an unlimited budget and very strong opinions about design brought their Pinterest board to life.

It's the kind of place where you instinctively lower your voice when you walk in because it feels too nice for normal conversation volume. Check-in is smooth because Tidal already handled everything. The front desk person is friendly in that way that makes you feel both welcome and acutely aware that you're probably not their usual clientele.

Then we're heading up to our room, and I'm trying not to visibly gawk at how nice everything is. The elevator has mirrors and mood lighting. The hallway has actual art on the walls, not just generic hotel prints.

Jack opens the door to our room and I stop in my tracks.

There's floor-to-ceiling windows overlooking the city, and the room looks like it belongs in an interior design magazine. There's a bottle of champagne on ice with a handwritten note from Maya: *Looking forward to our meeting tomorrow.*

"Holy shit," I breathe, walking over to the windows. The view is insane. You can see all the way to the Hollywood sign from here, those big white letters perched up in the hills like they're surveying their kingdom. The city sprawls out below us, buildings and palm trees and hazy sunshine that makes everything look like a movie set.

"This is what they give artists they're interested in?" I ask, turning to look at Jack who's set down our bags and is watching me with an amused expression. "Like, is this standard?"

"They're courting you," he says, walking over to wrap his

arms around my waist from behind. His chin rests on my shoulder and we both look out at the view. "Showing you what life could look like if you sign with them. The nice hotels, the good treatment, all of it."

"It's working," I admit, leaning back against him. "I'm very courted. Extremely courted. If they showed me a walk-in closet right now I'd probably sign anything they put in front of me."

"Don't sign anything without reading it first," he says, and I can hear the smile in his voice. "That's how they get you. Fancy suites and promises of walk-in closets."

"Too late," I laugh. "I've already been seduced by the thread count on these sheets."

He turns me around to face him, his hands still on my waist. "How are you doing? Real answer, not a jokey deflection."

I consider giving him a joke anyway because it's easier, but he's looking at me with those green eyes that always seem to see more than I want them to, and I find myself being honest instead. "I'm nervous. The label party was one thing, casual, low pressure. But this is the real pitch meeting. What if I say the wrong thing? What if they decide I'm not what they're looking for after all?"

"They already know what you're capable of. They've heard your music, they met you in Seattle, and they liked you enough to fly you out here." He tucks a strand of hair behind my ear. "Tomorrow is just about seeing if you're a good fit with each other. And if they can't see how great you are, then they're idiots and not worth your time."

"Okay," I say, taking a deep breath. "You're right. I can do this. It's just a meeting."

"Just a meeting," he agrees, pulling me closer. "Now let's go explore LA."

I smile despite the nerves still fluttering around. "Okay. Let's go see LA."

The waiting area outside the conference room has uncomfortable-looking modern furniture and walls covered in platinum records. Framed magazine covers featuring artists I've never heard of. Which is doing absolutely nothing for my confidence right now.

Somewhere downstairs in the lobby, Jack is waiting for me. I'd told him this morning he didn't need to come, that he should stay at the hotel and relax by the pool or explore or literally do anything besides sit in a lobby for however long this meeting takes. But he'd insisted. Said he wanted to be there the second I got out.

I was secretly thrilled when he said that. Relieved, even. Because as much as I tried to sound like I had this handled, I definitely want him there the second I walk out of this room.

Yesterday was perfect. We spent the afternoon exploring LA after we arrived, and it reminded me of traveling with him in Miami. How easy it felt, how natural. Like we've been doing this for years. But today the pressure is back, sitting on my shoulders like something physical and heavy, making it hard to breathe properly.

Maya appears from around the corner, looking effortlessly put-together in that LA way, wearing expensive jeans and a sharp blazer.

"Lark, good to see you," she says with a quick handshake. "How was your flight? Hotel working out okay?"

"The flight was good, and the hotel is amazing. Thank you again for arranging everything," I say, trying to project confidence I absolutely don't feel.

"Of course, we're glad to hear that. We're ready for you when you are." She gestures toward a hallway. "Everyone's looking forward to talking with you."

The building itself is exactly what you'd expect from a

successful label. Glass conference rooms where people are having important-looking meetings. Music playing faintly somewhere. People moving around with that purposeful creative energy that makes me feel both excited and completely out of my depth.

I follow her down the hall, past more platinum records and framed photos of artists at award shows. I take a deep breath, trying to be discreet about it. This is like stage fright except instead of forgetting lyrics I might accidentally agree to sign away my soul. Is there such a thing as *meeting-fright*?

Maya opens a door to a conference room where two people are already waiting around a long table. They look up when I enter, smiling in that friendly professional way that could mean anything.

"This is Lark Reyes," Maya says, and I force myself to smile back as she does quick introductions. David is head of A&R, late forties with graying hair, and Sadie is the marketing director, probably mid-thirties with sharp dark eyes and perfectly styled blonde hair.

They're both welcoming, asking about the hotel and whether I've had a chance to explore the city. Standard small talk that should put me at ease but mostly just makes me hyperaware of how much is riding on this meeting.

We all sit around the conference table and someone offers me coffee, which I accept even though I'm already jittery with nerves. At least it gives my hands something to do.

"So Lark," David starts, leaning back in his chair. "We've been following your work for a while now. Your streaming numbers are really impressive for an independent artist."

"Thank you," I say, taking a sip of my coffee.

"But what really caught our attention is your songwriting," Sadie adds, leaning forward. "That emotional honesty, that vulnerability. The way you take really specific personal experiences and make them feel universal. That's what connects with people."

Okay. This is good. They're complimenting me. This is going well.

"Your demographic is perfect too," Sadie continues. "Young women primarily, but you're crossing over into the broader market. And your look is great. Authentic, relatable, not overly produced. That authenticity is really valuable."

There's something in the way she says it that makes me slightly uncomfortable, like I'm a product being assessed rather than an artist, rather than a person, but I push the feeling aside.

"We'd love to hear more about your creative process," David says. "How you approach songwriting, what influences you draw from."

I talk for a while about how I write, about processing emotions through music, about the artists who've influenced me. They're all nodding along, asking good questions, seeming interested.

"That's wonderful," David says once I finish. "Really. Your core talent is undeniable. We're definitely interested in moving forward."

My heart jumps. "Really?"

"Absolutely," David says, and then he exchanges a look with Sadie that I can't quite read. "Your talent is there, but we have a few thoughts about direction. Ways we could maximize your potential and really break you into the mainstream market."

And there it is. The *but*.

"Okay," I say slowly, trying to keep my voice open and receptive even though my stomach is already starting to sink. "I'm definitely open to feedback."

"So your current sound is great," Sadie says, leaning forward slightly with her hands clasped on the table. "Very authentic, very you. But we think there's room to make it *bigger*. More commercially viable."

"What does that mean exactly?" I ask, my fingers tightening slightly on my coffee cup.

"Production value, mainly," Maya jumps in, her tone matter-of-fact and businesslike. "We need to beef it up significantly. Bigger production, layered vocals, polish the sound, bring in some top producers and DJs for remixes. Create tracks that can cross over to pop radio and dance floors."

I'm nodding along, trying to process what they're saying. Bigger production. Commercial appeal. These are *good* things, right? These are the things that actually make careers happen, that turn artists into household names.

"And your lyrics are beautiful," Maya continues, and something in her tone makes me brace for impact. "Really poetic, layered with meaning. But sometimes they're a little too complex for mainstream audiences. We might want to simplify some of that imagery, make it more immediate and accessible. More people can connect with simple, direct emotions than intricate metaphors."

"Simplify my lyrics," I repeat, and the words feel strange in my mouth.

"You know, nothing big, just make them more universally accessible," Sadie says quickly, like she can sense my hesitation creeping in. "You're so talented at creating these intricate lyrical landscapes. But sometimes that complexity can alienate casual listeners who just want something simple they can sing along to in the car without having to think too hard about what it means."

"We're not trying to change who you are as an artist," David says, his voice warm and reassuring like he's telling me something for my own good. "We're just trying to help you reach your full commercial potential. This is how the industry works. You take the raw talent and you shape it, polish it, package it for mass consumption. That's what we do here. That's what we're good at."

I nod, taking a sip of my coffee. It tastes bitter on my tongue. Or maybe that's just how this conversation tastes now.

They keep talking. Words washing over me in waves that I'm struggling to process. Producers they want to bring in who have worked with major pop stars whose names I recognize from radio. Songwriters they could pair me with to "strengthen the commercial hooks" and "modernize the sound." Marketing strategies for a more mainstream image. Photo shoots and styling sessions and social media campaigns designed to maximize engagement.

And I'm nodding along, saying things like "that makes sense" and "I'm open to collaboration," because this is the opportunity, right? This is what I've been working toward for years. You don't say no to a major label, especially not when they're talking about investing real money in you, believing in your potential enough to fly you out here.

But it feels wrong. Off. Like they're describing someone else's music, not mine.

"We also think bringing in some co-writers would be beneficial," Sadie says, pulling up something on her tablet. "Plus we'd want to work with a stylist. Develop your visual brand. It's not just about the music anymore, it's about the whole package. The aesthetic, the story, the lifestyle."

The whole package. Like I'm a product on a shelf, not a person who writes songs because they mean something to me.

"One other thing worth mentioning," David continues, "is that we have partnerships with several major sports organizations. We handle a lot of the entertainment booking for events —NBA playoffs, NHL championships, major tennis tournaments, college football bowls. We're always looking for emerging artists to feature at these high-profile events. Huge exposure opportunities."

"One of our bigger partnerships is with Formula One," Sadie adds casually. "We supply the entertainment contracts for all the US races. Each event features a showcase of new artists we're developing—it's incredible exposure. The Las Vegas race in November, for example, has a massive pre-race concert. Hundreds of thousands of people, huge media coverage. That's the kind of platform we can offer our artists. Offer *you*."

She says it matter-of-factly, like it's just one of many opportunities they're listing, not specifically about Jack. Just part of their roster of partnerships.

"So those are our initial thoughts," David says, sitting back. "Obviously there's a lot more to discuss if we move forward. Contract terms, recording schedules, marketing budgets. But we wanted to give you a sense of our vision for how we'd develop your career."

"Thank you," I manage, my voice sounding strange to my own ears, like it's coming from somewhere far away. "I really appreciate the opportunity and your time. This is a lot to process."

"Of course it is," Sadie says warmly. "Take your time. We'll send over some materials for you to review—examples of the producers we'd want to work with, some reference tracks for the sound we're envisioning. No pressure to decide anything today."

We wrap up with handshakes and promises to be in touch soon. Maya walks me out, chatting about how excited the team is, asking if I need anything, reminding me that they see real potential and want to make this work.

And then I'm standing outside the conference room, trying to process what just happened. They want to change everything. My sound, my lyrics, my look. Everything that makes my music mine. Or maybe I'm being unreasonable. Maybe this is just how it works. Maybe every artist goes through this and comes out the other side better for it.

I don't know. I honestly don't know.

Jack's waiting in the lobby when I come down, exactly where he said he'd be. He's sitting in one of those uncomfortable modern chairs, scrolling through his phone, but he stands up the second he sees me emerge from the elevators.

"Hey," I say, and the relief that floods through me at seeing his familiar face is almost overwhelming.

His expression shifts immediately, reading me the way he always does now. "How did it go?"

"Good, I think? Maybe?" I glance back at the elevators, trying to organize my thoughts into something coherent. "They really liked my sound. Said the emotional honesty and vulnerability in my songwriting is exactly what they're looking for in new artists."

"That's great." He's watching my face carefully. "So why do you look like someone just told you your dog died?"

"I just..." I start, then trail off because I don't know how to explain the knot in my stomach.

He takes my hand, threading his fingers through mine. "Come on, let's get out of here. You can tell me outside."

We walk out into the LA sunshine, the heat hitting us immediately after the aggressive air conditioning inside. Jack steers us down the street toward a coffee shop with outdoor seating, and I'm grateful for his solid presence beside me, for the fact that he's not pushing me to talk before I'm ready.

"They're interested in signing me," I say once we're settled outside with overpriced iced lattes, and the words should feel celebratory but instead they feel complicated and heavy. "They want to move forward. Said my streaming numbers and social media growth show real potential, and they love my songwriting."

"That's incredible," Jack says, but he's still watching my face. "And?"

"And there's a but. A big but." I wrap both hands around my glass, trying to cool my sweaty palms. "Actually, several buts."

"Tell me," he says simply, his eyes locked on mine with complete focus.

So I do. I tell him everything. About how they want to change my sound, make it more pop, more commercial. Bringing in big-name producers and co-writers to "strengthen the hooks" and "modernize the production." Simplifying my lyrics because they're "too complex for mainstream audiences" and people want something they can sing along to without thinking.

"They kept saying they don't want to change who I am as an artist," I explain, hearing the doubt in my own voice. "But then in the next breath they're listing all these things they want me to change. My sound, my lyrics, my image. They want to bring in a stylist to develop my 'visual brand' and create a 'cohesive aesthetic' across all platforms."

Jack nods slowly, listening to everything without interrupting.

"I mean, this is how the industry works, right?" I continue, my coffee forgotten. "You don't just walk into a major label and have them accept you exactly as you are with no changes. There are always going to be notes, suggestions, ways to make things more commercial and radio-friendly. That's just reality."

"Is it?" He's watching me closely, his expression serious. "Or is that just what they told you to make you accept it?"

"Jack." I set down my coffee, feeling defensive for reasons I don't fully understand. "They're the experts. They know what sells, what gets played on radio, what breaks artists into the mainstream. They've launched actual careers. Multiple platinum-selling artists. They know what they're doing way better than I do."

"Maybe," he concedes carefully. "But you know your music.

You know what you're trying to say with your songs, why you write the way you do, what matters to you. Do their suggestions honor that or fundamentally change it?"

I open my mouth to respond, then close it again because I don't have a good answer.

"Listen," he continues gently. "I'm not trying to tell you what to do here, or whether you should or shouldn't sign with them. If this is right for you, and you feel good about it in your gut, then go for it."

My palms cling to the cold glass, the condensation the only thing that feels real right now.

"It's your decision," he continues. "But if they're asking you to compromise things that matter to you, to fundamentally change what makes your music yours, then believe me when I say you're talented enough that someone else will want to sign you. Someone who recognizes what you have and doesn't want to sand down all the edges that make you interesting."

I look down at my hands. "What if nobody else wants to sign me? What if this is my only shot and I blow it by being too precious about my 'artistic vision' or whatever?"

"Then you keep making music on your own terms until the right opportunity comes along," he says simply. "Your streaming numbers are growing, you're building a real following, people connect with your songs. You don't need them. *They* need *you*."

I want to believe that. I really do. "I don't know," I finally admit, shrugging helplessly. "Maybe I'm overthinking it. Maybe once I actually work with them it'll feel different, more collaborative. Maybe I'm just scared of success or change or something and that's why it feels wrong."

"Maybe," Jack says, but he doesn't sound convinced. "Or maybe your gut is telling you something important and you should listen to it."

The thought sits heavy in my chest like something solid and

immovable. The knowledge that I might be standing at a crossroads without really knowing which path leads where.

For better or worse, I still don't know.

CHAPTER 22

JACK

The hotel gym is empty when I get there at six-thirty in the morning, which is exactly how I like it. Just me, the weights, and the floor-to-ceiling windows overlooking West Hollywood as the city wakes up. Lark was still asleep when I left, curled up in the hotel sheets with her hair spread across the pillow, looking so peaceful I almost didn't want to leave. But my training schedule doesn't take days off, even when we're in LA celebrating good news.

And yesterday *was* good news. Really good. Tidal Records is interested, wants to move forward, sees real potential in her music. We'd spent hours talking about it over dinner last night —her excitement about the opportunity mixed with uncertainty about all the changes they want to make to her sound.

The lyric simplification, the pop production, the whole commercial package thing. I want this to work out for her so badly, but I also don't want her to lose what makes her music special in the first place.

I'm halfway through my second set when my phone buzzes

on the bench beside me. Thomas. I set down the dumbbells, my muscles burning pleasantly, and answer.

"Morning," I say, slightly out of breath.

"We have a situation," Thomas says without preamble, his voice tight in that way that means he's already had three coffees and been dealing with this for hours. "Have you seen social media this morning?"

"No, I've been at the gym. What's going on?" I grab my water bottle, taking a drink while I wait for him to explain.

"Multiple tabloids are running stories suggesting that you and Lark are a PR relationship. That it's all staged for your image rehabilitation and her music career." He pauses, and I can hear him clicking through something on his computer. "It's everywhere, Jack. Instagram, X, entertainment news sites. People are analyzing your photos, looking for 'proof' that it's fake."

I close my eyes, leaning back against the weight bench. Of course. Of course this is happening right when things are actually going well, right when we've figured out that this thing between us is real and not just for show. The universe has impeccable fucking timing.

"How bad is it?" I ask, already knowing the answer won't be good. "What started it?"

"A gossip account on X posted a thread last night breaking down the timeline. When you two started posting together, how it coincided perfectly with your Monaco incident and her label meetings. Someone did the math on her follower growth, pointed out the timing was 'too convenient.' It spiraled from there." Thomas sighs. "The fact that they're even questioning it means we need to address it. Put out a statement, shut this down before it affects either of your careers."

"Yeah, okay," I say, my mind already racing ahead. "What are you thinking?"

"Simple, direct statement confirming the relationship is

genuine. Maybe a quote from each of you about how you met, how it developed naturally, all the standard language we use for these things." His keyboard clicks rapidly in the background. "Keep it brief, honest, shut down the speculation without being defensive. I can have something drafted in an hour. You and Lark just need to approve it before we release anything."

"Send it over when you have it," I tell him, pushing myself up from the bench. My workout is done. I need to get back upstairs, tell Lark what's happening before she sees it herself and spirals. "We fly back tonight, but I'll make sure we both review it before you release anything."

"Perfect. You'll hear from me soon," Thomas says, already moving on to the next thing on his list.

"Thanks, I'll talk to you later," I say, and hang up.

I pull up X and immediately see what Thomas meant. #Jack-AndLark is trending. The top tweets are a mix of people defending us and people "exposing" us with badly analyzed photos and elaborate conspiracy theories.

Look at their body language in this pic, it's totally staged. She's not even looking at him naturally.

She gained 100k followers since they started dating. Convenient timing much? She's a clout chaser!

He needs good PR after Monaco. She needs exposure for her music. It's a textbook manufactured relationship.

Y'all are so naive. This is OBVIOUSLY for his sponsors. Wake up.

Thread after thread of people dissecting our relationship like it's a puzzle to solve, looking for signs it's fake, comparing it to other celebrity PR stunts. Screenshots of our Instagram posts with circles and arrows pointing out "evidence." Some of the theories are actually kind of close to what we originally planned, which would be funny if it wasn't so damn frustrating.

I grab my towel and water bottle and head back to the room, my earlier workout energy completely gone, replaced by a sick feeling in my stomach. This is my fault. I'm the one with the tabloid history, the one whose life gets picked apart on social media. Lark signed up to help me with my image and grow her social media, not to have her character attacked by strangers on the internet.

When I let myself into the room, she's awake, sitting up in bed with her phone in her hands, her knees pulled up to her chest. She looks up when I enter and her face is already wide-eyed with shock.

"Have you seen social media?" she asks.

"Yeah. Thomas just called." I drop my gym bag by the door and sit on the edge of the bed. "It's everywhere, huh?"

"Everywhere," she confirms, and then lets out this slightly hysterical laugh. "Jack, people think we're *fake*. They think this whole thing is staged. The irony is insane."

I can't help but grin despite everything. "Right? If they only knew."

She's scrolling on her phone, shaking her head. "This is *hilarious*." She looks up at me. "Some of the timeline stuff is kinda accurate. But they're saying I'm a clout chaser. That I'm not actually talented."

"That's complete bullshit," I say immediately, moving closer. "Your talent has nothing to do with me. Tidal was already interested before we even started this whole thing. Your streaming numbers were growing on their own. The fake dating just helped boost your social media numbers, but they reached out because of your music."

"Try telling them that," she says, gesturing at her phone. "Half the comments on my last post are people saying I'm a gold digger or a fame whore or that I'm just some random girl desperate for attention." Her voice wavers slightly. She's trying to sound light, like it's all a big joke, but I can tell it's hitting her hard.

Fuck. I want to take her phone and throw it out the window,

delete every social media app, protect her from all of this. But I can't. This is the reality of my life, and now it's hers too.

"It's not great," I admit, taking her hand. "But we can handle it. Thomas is drafting a statement. We'll put it out, confirm we're actually together, and it'll blow over eventually. This stuff always does."

"Everyone in Dark River is going to see this," she says. "Your brothers are going to have questions. Everyone we know is going to be talking about it and asking if it's true and wanting to know details and—"

I move closer, taking both her hands now. "I'll take care of my brothers. I should have come clean to them ages ago anyway, and believe me this is like number ten on the list of crazy things I've done over the years, so they won't really care. As for everyone else, they can think whatever they want. We know the truth. The people who matter know the truth. Everyone else is just noise."

She smiles a bit. "Okay. I guess that makes sense."

"Exactly," I say, squeezing her hands. "Plus this is a nice little trial run for when you're a big star and something wild happens. This one we get to handle together."

She laughs. "Okay, okay, you're right. Ugh, I'm gonna have to tell my parents too though. I can't keep lying to them about it anymore. That's going to be fun."

"Hey, I'll just charm them when I finally get to meet them," I say.

She rolls her eyes but she's smiling.

An idea forms in my mind, sudden and clear. "What if we don't go home?" I say.

She looks up, confused. "What?"

"What if we don't go back? What if we go somewhere else instead? Just us, no cameras, no pressure, no one dissecting our every move or asking if we're really together."

"That's crazy. Where would we even go?" she asks, but I can see interest sparking in her eyes.

"Somewhere away from everything. Somewhere we can just be together without worrying about who's watching or what people think." I'm already pulling up my phone, already searching. "I could book us a place in the mountains. Private cabin, middle of nowhere, just us."

"You want to go on a spontaneous mountain getaway?" She's smiling now. "You're insane."

"Maybe," I admit, grinning at her. "But we were going to fly home tonight anyway. What's a few more days? I'm thinking Banff. Canadian Rockies. I know someone who handles luxury cabin rentals up there. I can have us in a private place by tomorrow—fireplace, hot tub, mountain views, the whole thing. Completely away from everything."

"Banff," she repeats slowly, and I can see the appeal registering on her face. "Like actually Banff? The place with the turquoise lakes and the mountains that look like a postcard?"

"That's the one. Private cabin, just us. No one knows we're there. No tabloids, no social media shit, no one asking questions. Just a few days to be together and figure out what this is without all the noise."

She looks at her phone, then back at me. I can see her wavering, that practical side that plans everything warring with the spontaneous side.

"We'd have to book flights," she says, but it's not a no. It's the beginning of a yes.

"I can have that done in ten minutes."

"And a place to stay."

"*Five* minutes."

She considers this. "And we'd have to let people know we're not coming back as planned."

"That's what text messages are for. 'Hey, extending the trip, back in a few days, love you bye.'" I'm grinning at her now, at how much I want this.

She's biting her lip, trying not to smile, and I know I've almost got her. "This is crazy."

"Yeah," I agree, taking her hands. "But you were just in an incredible meeting yesterday. You've got a big decision to make. And we're actually dating now, not just pretending. And everyone back home thinks we're fake anyway, so we might as well go somewhere we can actually be ourselves without performing for anyone. Let's go be crazy together."

She studies my face for a long moment.

"Okay," she says, and her smile breaks wide and genuine. "Let's do it. Let's go be crazy together."

And just like that, we're going on an adventure.

CHAPTER 23

Lark

The cabin is tucked away down a private road that winds through towering pine trees, their branches heavy with snow even though it's late August. Jack navigates the rental SUV carefully around the final curve, and then the cabin comes into view. "Holy shit."

"Worth the spontaneous booking?" Jack asks, glancing over at me.

"Jack, this is bonkers." I lean forward to see better through the windshield. "You said cabin. This is not a cabin. This is like a luxury mountain estate situation."

He laughs. "My friend owns a few properties up here. I stayed at one years ago but never this specific one. Photos looked good though."

"Photos did *not* do it justice," I tell him, still staring. The place is a mix of warm wood and stone, with massive windows that seem to take up entire walls. Mountains rise up behind it, their peaks still white with snow against the evening sky, and the whole thing looks like something out of a magazine spread about how rich people vacation.

We'd grabbed lunch in the town of Banff after landing in Calgary, burgers at this place called Melissa's that Jack swore by, and the whole drive up into the alpine I kept checking my phone. People are still losing their minds about whether we're real or fake, dissecting every photo, building elaborate conspiracy theories.

Maren had texted a few times, checking in about LA and the tabloid explosion. Jack's phone kept buzzing too, his brothers wanting to know what the hell was going on with the rumors. He'd sent them a quick message saying he'd explain everything later, that it was complicated but we were fine. But being here, tucked away in the mountains with Jack, all of that already feels distant.

We grab our bags and crunch through the thin layer of snow to the front door. The air is cold and clean, completely different from the LA heat we left behind this morning. Jack punches in a code and pushes the door open, and I stop in the doorway because what the hell.

"Okay, now you're just showing off," I tell him.

Soaring ceilings with exposed wooden beams. A massive stone fireplace taking up an entire wall. Floor-to-ceiling windows showcasing that ridiculous mountain view. The furniture is a mix of buttery leather and plush fabrics, fur throws draped over chairs, and warm lighting that makes everything feel expensive and inviting at the same time.

"Is this too much?" Jack asks. "Cause you know, if you want to head back to Dark River tonight I can just—"

"Don't you dare." I set my bag down and walk straight to the massive windows. The mountains are going purple and gold as the sun sets behind them, stars just starting to appear. "This is perfect. Completely nuts and perfect."

He comes up behind me, wrapping his arms around my

waist and resting his chin on my shoulder. "Good. Because we're not leaving until we're ready to face the world again."

"Dangerous promise," I say, leaning back against him. "Might be a while."

"I'm counting on it," he murmurs against my neck, and I smile.

The rest of the place is just as ridiculous. The kitchen has marble countertops and fancy appliances. The main living area has leather couches arranged around the stone fireplace, a full bar setup in one corner, and a pool table with pristine green felt. It's the kind of space that belongs in a magazine spread about luxury mountain living.

Upstairs there's a loft area with built-in bookshelves and reading chairs that look perfect for curling up in. And the master suite has this enormous bed with bedding that looks criminally soft, yet another fireplace, and windows that frame the mountain view perfectly.

"I'm never leaving this room," I announce, flopping dramatically onto the bed. It's even softer than it looks.

"Works for me," Jack says, and pulls me up into a kiss that makes my toes curl and my brain forget how to function properly.

After unpacking, we both shower, the hot water washing away all the travel grime. Jack finishes first and heads downstairs while I blow-dry my hair. The last few weeks with Jack have been better than I ever could have imagined. We fit together in a way that still surprises me sometimes.

After Brandon, part of me didn't think something like this was even possible for me. If I'd ever be able to trust someone enough to let them all the way in, or if those walls I'd built would be permanent. But Jack has this way of slipping past every defense I've ever constructed. He's bright and warm and somehow he makes me feel safer than I've ever felt with anyone.

I change into leggings and an oversized sweater and head

back downstairs. Jack's already there, a fire crackling in that massive fireplace, two glasses of red wine poured and waiting.

"Look at you being all domestic," I tease, accepting the glass he offers.

He laughs. "Hidden talents." He nods toward the windows. "Come check out the view. It's even better now."

We walk over together and I stop when I see it. The mountains are just dark shapes against the evening sky, stars scattered everywhere like someone spilled glitter across black velvet.

Jack wraps his arm around my waist, pulling me close. The fire crackles behind us, and standing here with him, wine in my hand, mountains outside the window, I feel this overwhelming sense of rightness. Like this is exactly where I'm supposed to be.

"I can't believe we're actually here," I say, taking a sip of wine. It's good, smooth and rich. "That we just said fuck it and flew to Canada on a whim."

"Best spontaneous decision we've made since the supply closet in Miami," Jack agrees, two fingers tracing an idle circle on my hip.

I flush, remembering that night, then say, "The tabloid thing already feels far away, which is probably bad. I should be worried about damage control or managing the narrative or whatever."

"That's the point of being here." He sets his glass on the window ledge and turns me to face him. "Thomas is handling the statement. It'll blow over eventually. And we get to just be here without anyone watching or analyzing every photo we post or deciding what's real and what's fake."

"Just us," I say quietly.

"Just us," he confirms.

The silence stretches out, comfortable and easy, the kind you can only have with someone when you don't need to fill every second with words. The mountains fade completely into darkness, more stars appearing, and I can't believe how right this feels. How much I want days like this to stretch on forever. Adventures with him, quiet moments with him, all of it.

"You know," Jack says eventually, and I turn to look at him. There's this mischievous glint in his eyes that I'm starting to recognize as trouble. "I think you still owe me a game of pool."

The memory hits me immediately—that first night at the Black Lantern, when he'd tried to get me to play and I'd turned him down to be responsible and work. When this whole crazy fake dating thing started because I was trying to one-up Brandon and Jack swooped in like some rom-com hero.

"Oh, do I now?" I say, unable to keep the smile off my face.

"You do." He nods toward the game room. "I mean I've heard so much about your legendary pool skills, but I never actually got to see them in action."

"I was working!" I protest. "Someone had to serve drinks to your victims after you destroyed them at pool."

"Excuses, excuses." He offers up that full, dimpled grin that does dangerous things to my pulse. "But now we're here. No work, no responsibilities, no excuses. Just you, me, and a pool table."

"You're really going to regret this challenge," I warn him, and I'm already setting down my wine glass. That competitive spark is fully ignited now.

"We'll see about that," he says.

I head over to the pool table and select a cue, testing the weight and balance in my hands. Jack racks the balls and steps back. "You want to break?"

"Absolutely." I chalk my cue, line up my shot, and break with a crack that sends balls scattering across the table. The ten ball drops cleanly into a corner pocket. "Stripes it is," I announce, maybe a little smugly.

"Show off," Jack says.

I sink two more balls before finally missing, and then it's his turn. He moves around the table, studying angles, lining up each shot carefully. Ball after ball drops into pockets with satisfying thuds, and I'm remembering why he was so good at beating Mike and his friends that first night.

"Still as good as ever, I see," I say, watching him line up yet another shot.

"Can't let you win too easily," he says with zero shame.

"Please. You're just stalling the inevitable," I counter, laughing.

He finally misses and steps back. "Your turn."

The game gets seriously competitive after that. Trading shots, trading trash talk, both of us completely focused on winning. The fire crackles and pops beside us, casting warm flickering light across the table, and every time we pass each other there's this electricity in the air that has nothing to do with the game.

I'm down to my last two balls when I line up what should be a relatively easy shot. But before I can take it, Jack moves to stand directly in my line of sight. Arms crossed. Smirking like he knows exactly what he's doing.

"Excuse me," I say sweetly, not moving from my position bent over the table. "You're in my way."

"Am I?" He doesn't budge. "Didn't notice."

"That's cheating."

"Not cheating," he says, that smirk getting wider. "I always fight dirty when there's something I want."

His eyes have gone dark and they're focused entirely on me in a way that has absolutely nothing to do with pool and everything to do with the way I'm bent over this table. The intensity of his gaze makes heat flood through me.

"Well you're going to lose anyway," I tell him, my eyes not leaving his. "Might as well move and accept your fate with some dignity."

"Make me," he says.

I straighten up slowly, deliberately, letting the pool cue rest against the table. "Oh, is that what you want? For me to make you move?"

He closes the distance between us. His hands find my waist and he turns me, backing me up against the pool table. "That's exactly what I want."

And then we're kissing and everything else just disappears. His hands slide into my hair and mine tear at his shirt and the kiss is desperate, hungry, like we've been holding back all day and finally don't have to anymore. I make a sound against his mouth and he groans in response, pulling me closer, harder, until there's no space between us at all.

His hands move to my waist, gripping tight, and I grind into him, feeling him stiffen in his jeans. The pool table digs into my back, but I don't care. All I care about is the way he's kissing me like I'm the only thing in the world that matters, like he's been thinking about this as much as I have.

When we finally break apart because we actually need oxygen to survive, both of us breathing hard, his forehead drops to rest against mine. His hands are still on my waist, holding me close, and I can feel his heart racing.

"Lark," he says, and my name sounds different in his voice.

I look up at him, at the way the firelight catches in his eyes, at the expression on his face that makes my chest feel too full and too tight at the same time.

"I love you," he says quietly, and the words land like something physical in the space between us. "I know we haven't actually been together for long, and I know that's fast, but I don't care. I love you. I'm in love with you."

My heart is pounding so hard I can feel it everywhere—in my throat, in my fingertips, behind my eyes, in every single nerve ending.

"I love you too," I say, and the words come out steadier than I feel inside. "I love you so much. I think I have for a while now, I was just too scared to admit it to myself."

"Scared of what?"

"That this would end. That you'd go back to racing full-time and realize I don't fit into that world. That I'd be the girl who fell for Jack Midnight and got left behind when real life started again." I laugh but it sounds shaky even to my own ears. "Take your pick, really. I had a whole list of fears going."

He makes me look at him properly, his hands framing my face. "I'm not leaving you behind. Ever. We'll figure out the distance thing with racing. You'll come to races when you can, I'll come home when I can. We make it work because I'm not losing this. I'm not losing you."

"Promise?" It comes out smaller than I intended, more vulnerable.

"Promise," he says firmly, no hesitation. "You're stuck with me now, Reyes. Better get used to it."

He kisses me again and this time it's different, like he's sealing that promise into my skin. I kiss him back with everything I have, pouring all the feelings I've been too scared to name into it, all the hope and want and love that's been building for weeks. When we finally pull apart, both of us are smiling like complete idiots.

"So," I say eventually, trying to catch my breath. "I believe I was about to win that game before you so rudely interrupted with your distraction tactics."

He laughs. "Game's over. You win. You always win."

"Damn right I do," I say. "Don't you forget it."

"Never," he promises, and then he's kissing me again and I'm pretty sure we're done with pool for the night.

His hands slide down to grip under my thighs and he lifts me. I squeal and wrap my legs around his waist, my arms looping around his neck, and he carries me across the room. The fire crackles in the fireplace, and he lowers us both down onto the rug in front of it. The rug is plush and soft beneath my back, and he grabs pillows from the couch, tucking them under my head.

The weight of him pressing against me, all hard muscle and heat, makes me shudder with pleasure. I love him. I love him so much it's almost overwhelming. A month ago this was supposed to be fake and now he's everything.

One of his hands cradles my face while the other slides into my hair, and the kiss deepens fast, becomes urgent and demanding. My hands grip his shoulders, then slide up into his hair, pulling him closer. I press against him, wanting more, needing everything.

My sweater is already being pushed up, his hands sliding underneath the fabric. I sit up just enough for him to pull it over my head and toss it somewhere behind us. When he sees I'm not wearing anything underneath, his eyes darken in a way that sends heat straight through me.

"You're beautiful," he says. "Been thinking about this all night."

"Then stop thinking and do something about it," I challenge.

He laughs, and god I love his laugh. His smile. "Where's the fun in rushing?" He lowers his mouth to my breast, but doesn't give me what I want yet. Just breathing on my nipple, letting me feel the warmth of his breath but not actually touching. Teasing.

"You're a real bastard, you know that?" I point out breathlessly, and I can't even stop my body from trying to twist into his mouth. "I swear if you don't—"

He cuts off my complaint by closing his mouth around my nipple and sucking hard. My hands fly to his hair immediately, gripping tight, and he groans. Music to my fucking ears.

"Jack, please," I gasp, because I need more and he knows it.

"Please what?" he asks, kissing down my stomach, taking his time. Paying attention to every inch of skin, every dip and curve. "Tell me what you need."

"Put your mouth on me," I say without any hesitation. "Stop teasing and make me come."

"Fuck, I love when you talk like that," he says, and the heat in his voice makes me clench. "So fucking hot when you tell me exactly what you need."

He kisses along my inner thighs slowly, deliberately avoiding where I want him most. I make this frustrated sound and he drags his lips gently against my skin, clearly enjoying this too much.

"Jack, I swear to—"

"What?" he asks innocently, looking up at me. "You'll do what?"

"I'll finish myself if you don't hurry the fuck up," I threaten, and one of my hands starts sliding down my stomach.

He catches my wrist immediately, pinning it beside my hip. "The hell you will. That's mine."

"Then do something about it," I bark, and there's mischief and heat sparking between us.

"Oh, I'm going to do a lot of things about it," he says, his voice dropping lower. "And you're going to take every single one."

He spreads my legs wider with his shoulders, settling between them, and finally puts his mouth on me. The second his tongue flattens against my clit I gasp, my hips lifting sharply, trying to get more pressure, more contact, more everything.

The taste of me on his tongue must drive him crazy because he groans against me, and the vibration goes straight through my clit. I'm already wet, already soaked and ready for him, and he's taking his time like he has all night to do this.

"Oh fuck," I moan, my free hand flying to his hair, gripping tight. "Yes, just like that, please don't stop—"

He works me slowly at first, long strokes of his tongue. Taking his time learning what makes my hips lift higher, what makes me moan louder, what makes my thighs start to tremble.

When he focuses on my clit with steady pressure, I make this sound that's half moan, half whimper.

"Right there," I gasp, my hand tightening in his hair. "Stay right there, please—"

He keeps the rhythm steady, exactly what I need, while he slides two fingers inside me. The stretch makes me cry out, and when he curls his fingers upward to hit that spot deep inside me, I nearly come right then.

"Oh Jack, fuck..."

He doesn't let up. Keeps working that spot with his fingers while his mouth stays focused on my clit. I'm making these sounds I can't control—breathy moans and gasps that tell him exactly how close I'm getting.

"That's it," he groans against me. "Let me hear you. Love those sounds you make."

The pleasure builds impossibly fast. My thighs are trembling, I'm starting to clench rhythmically around his fingers, my breathing is getting faster and more erratic.

"I'm close," I gasp. "So close, I'm gonna—please don't stop—"

"I've got you," he says, increasing the pressure with his tongue, his fingers moving faster. "Come for me, baby."

I break. My back arches completely off the rug, my hands yanking his hair, and I come, screaming his name like a warcry. Loud and dangerous and completely uninhibited.

The pulsing, the waves rolling through me, are so intense I can barely process them. He works me through every single one, drawing it out, making it last, until I'm gasping.

"I can't," I pant, my chest heaving. The sensations are still rolling over me and it's too much and not enough all at once. "Too sensitive, I can't take anymore—"

He places one last kiss against me before crawling back up my body. When he reaches me he pulls me into a kiss that's desperate and hungry, and I taste myself on his lips.

"I need you," I say against his mouth between kisses, my

hands already shoving urgently at his jeans. I'm desperate for him, my body aching and empty and needing him inside me. "Inside me. Right fucking now."

"Bossy," he says, but he's already kicking off his jeans and boxer briefs.

"Someone's gotta keep you in line," I tease, biting my lip, letting my legs fall open wider in invitation.

His eyes darken. "Oh, I'm gonna make you pay for that."

I grin. "Thank god."

He positions himself between my thighs and pushes into me in one hard thrust. The stretch, the fullness, the way he fills me completely makes me nearly scream. My body welcomes him, clenches around him, like it was made for this.

"Fuck," he groans, his arms braced beside my head. "You feel incredible."

My legs wrap around his waist, pulling him deeper, and when he starts to move it's hard and fast and exactly what I need. The sound of our bodies moving together fills the cabin, skin against skin, and it's the hottest thing I've ever heard.

"Harder," I gasp, because I need more, need everything.

"You want it harder?" He shifts his angle and the next thrust hits that spot deep inside me that makes everything go white. "Like this?"

"Yes," I sob, my nails digging into his shoulders. "Just like that, yes—"

"I'm going to fuck you until you come all over my cock," he promises, and every thrust after that hits the same spot, over and over, building the pressure.

The dirty talk combined with what he's doing to my body is too much. The pleasure builds fast, winding tighter and tighter, that coil in my belly ready to snap.

"Touch yourself," he orders, his voice demanding. "I want to feel that pussy squeeze me when you fall apart."

My hand slides between us, fingers finding my clit and

rubbing in tight circles. The added stimulation combined with him pounding into me, hitting that perfect spot with every thrust, winds me impossibly tight.

"That's it," he groans, his eyes locked on where my hand is moving. "Touch yourself while I fuck you. Show me how close you are."

"Jack," I warn, my voice breaking. "I'm going to—I can't—"

"Come for me," he demands, his hand gripping my hip harder, his thrusts getting deeper, more brutal. "Come all over my cock. Let me feel it."

The orgasm slams into me and I scream his name again, my whole body seizing up in waves so intense my vision blurs. My pussy clenches around him rhythmically with every pulse.

"Fuck yes," he groans, and his rhythm falters. "That's it. Your pussy feels so good when you come on my cock."

He keeps moving, his thrusts getting more erratic. When I start to come down, he's still chasing his release, and watching him lose control is one of the hottest things I've ever seen.

"You want my cum?" His thrusts get harder, more desperate. "Want me to fill this pussy up?"

"Yes," I moan, tightening my legs around his waist, pulling him deeper. "I need it. I need to feel you come inside me."

"Tell me again," he demands. "Beg for it."

"Please," I say, the words tumbling out desperate and needy. "Please come inside me. Fill me up. I want your cum so bad. I need it. Please, Jack—"

That does it. His final thrusts are hard and deep and almost brutal, and then he's pulsing inside me, emptying himself with broken groans. The heat of him filling me up, the way his whole body goes rigid, the raw broken sound he makes are absolutely perfect. His cock throbs inside me and my pussy clenches around him, milking every last drop.

For a long moment we just lie there, both breathing hard, both trembling. He's still inside me, softening now, and his cum starts to leak out around where we're still joined. The wet heat of it makes me clench again, makes me want to keep him inside me forever.

He lifts his head slowly, his forehead coming to rest against mine. His eyes are soft and full of love and satisfaction and something almost reverent, like I'm the best thing that ever happened to him.

"I love you," I whisper.

"I love you too," he says, his eyes locked on mine. "So fucking much. More than anything."

A smile tugs at my lips. "Best crazy idea you ever had."

"We," he corrects immediately, brushing his nose against mine. "Best crazy idea *we* ever had."

"Yeah," I agree, and when he kisses me it's soft and slow and sweet. "We."

CHAPTER 24

Jack

Sunlight streams through the windows, warm on my face, and the first thing I'm aware of is Lark completely wrapped around me. One leg thrown over mine, her arm across my chest, her face buried against my neck where I can feel her breath, warm and even, against my skin. Her hair is everywhere—this wild tangle of dark silk spread across the pillow and my shoulder.

I just lie here soaking it in. Her body pressed against mine, solid and real. Her peaceful breathing. Even in sleep her fingers curl loosely against my ribs, like she needs to be touching me. Outside I can hear birds calling to each other and the faint sound of water from the stream nearby.

And I'm realizing something that should probably terrify me but doesn't: I could do this every morning for the rest of my life and never get tired of it. Never want anything different. This right here, waking up with Lark in my arms, is enough. More than enough.

When did I become this person? The guy who thinks about forever with one woman? Part of me wants to believe it's possible. That I can have this and racing. That I won't fuck it up like I fuck up everything else eventually.

Nobody ever made me want to try before. The idea of commitment always felt like something to run from. But Lark… Lark changes everything. She makes me want things I didn't know I was missing.

She stirs against me, making a soft sound. Her leg tightens around mine and her hand spreads flat against my chest. I'm already getting hard just from the warmth of her body pressed against mine, from knowing we're both still naked under these sheets.

I run my hand down her spine slowly, feeling every curve. My fingers trace lower, over her hip, squeezing slightly. I can't get enough of touching her.

She makes that sound again, this pleased little hum, and shifts closer. Pressing herself more firmly against me. Her eyes flutter open slowly, adjusting to the bright sunlight. She blinks a few times, confused for a second, and then she looks at me. A slow smile spreads across her face, sleepy and soft and so beautiful.

"Creeper," she mumbles, snuggling closer against my neck, her voice still thick with sleep. "Watching me sleep like some kind of stalker."

"I can't help it," I say, pushing hair out of her face. "You're too fucking pretty to look away from."

She lifts her head slightly to look at me, eyes still half-closed but clearly pleased.

"Flatterer," she says, stretching against me deliberately, pressing her whole body against mine. "Trying to get in my pants with your sweet talk?"

"You're not wearing any pants," I point out, my hand sliding down to grip her bare ass. "So I'd say I'm already there."

She laughs, low and a little husky. "Fair point."

"You know, last night you made me promise to make you

breakfast this morning," I say, even though getting out of this bed is the last thing I want to do right now.

"You did," she agrees, but her hand is sliding down my stomach now, lower, and her eyes have that look in them that makes my mouth go dry. "But that can wait."

"Yeah?" My hand tightens on her hip.

"Yeah." She shifts, pushing me onto my back and climbing on top of me in one smooth motion. The sheet falls away completely and she's naked and beautiful above me, her hair falling around her face, and I forget how to form words. She grins down at me, wicked. "I have a better idea."

Saying goodbye to Lark at the Banff cabin, knowing she was heading back to Dark River while I flew to São Paulo, Brazil, was harder than I expected. But this is the job. This is what I signed up for.

The Interlagos circuit is one of my favorites—challenging corners, unpredictable weather. I spent all day today in the garage and simulator, going over race strategy scenarios with the engineers, reviewing telemetry data from Friday's practice sessions. As a reserve driver, I need to know every detail of Davis's and Luca's setups in case I have to jump in the car. It's not likely, but it's my job to be ready.

These race weekends are always the same mixture of the best and the worst. Best because I'm here, in the paddock, surrounded by the sport I love. The smell of racing fuel, the sound of engines screaming down the straight, the energy of a Grand Prix weekend building, this is where I belong. This is home in a way nowhere else has ever been.

Worst because I'm so close to it and yet I can't race. I'm watching from the garage instead of being in the car. Watching Davis struggle to extract pace from a Ferrari that

I know I could put on the podium. Eighteen months of this. Eighteen months of being right there but not quite there.

But if Thomas is right about what he wants to discuss tonight, maybe that's about to change.

São Paulo at night is cool, the air almost pleasant after the dry heat of the day, nothing like the mountain cold I left behind in Canada. The restaurant Thomas picked is in Jardins, one of those places with white tablecloths and waiters who move like they're performing ballet, tucked into a quiet street away from the chaos of Avenida Paulista.

Thomas is already there when I arrive, sitting at a corner table by the window with a view of the tree-lined street outside. He looks relaxed in slacks and a button-down, and waves when he sees me.

"Flight okay?" he asks, already signaling the waiter.

"Long but fine. Slept most of it." I settle into the chair.

The waiter appears and Thomas orders a whiskey for himself, glances at me with a raised eyebrow. "Water for you?"

"Yeah, sparkling," I say. Race weekend means no alcohol, even if Thomas is off duty enough to indulge.

The waiter returns quickly with Thomas's whiskey in a heavy crystal glass and my sparkling water with lime, and takes our food order.

"So," Thomas says once we're alone again, taking a sip of his whiskey. "Your sponsors are very pleased. The image rehabilitation has exceeded expectations." He's more animated than usual, gesturing slightly with his glass. "The situation with Lark—Miami, the race appearances, the social media consistency—it's been exactly what they needed to see. Professional, stable, mature. Thankfully the rumors about fake dating have died out. Without any proof, people have already moved on to the next thing."

"Good," I say, taking my own drink. The water is cold and

crisp, not quite as satisfying as whiskey would be but that's the trade-off. "Those rumors were getting annoying."

"Agreed, the whole thing was ridiculous," Thomas laughs.

One of these days I'm gonna have to tell him the truth. Maybe once I've got my seat back and he can't have a heart attack over it. I take another sip to cover my amusement.

"Also, Robert called me personally last week." Thomas leans forward, his expression more serious now. "He said he's proud of how you've handled everything this year. Said you've shown real growth, that he's seeing the maturity he always knew you had. Coming from someone who's invested millions in you since you were twelve, I'd say that's significant."

Something warm spreads through my chest hearing that. "Yeah, he sent me a text too. Nice to hear, especially after how disappointed he was earlier this year."

"Agreed. He doesn't say things like that lightly." Thomas leans back slightly, studying me over his glass. "Your contract situation is looking very solid, Jack. Ferrari is impressed with your reserve work, your consistency, your focus this season. If things continue on this trajectory, you're looking at getting your full-time seat back next season. We might even see an announcement soon, based on what their lawyers have indicated."

Thank fucking god. I've been trying to get my full-time seat back for the last eighteen months. Fighting for it, working for it, sacrificing for it. It's all I've ever wanted—my seat in Formula One, Ferrari driver, eventually world champion. Everything I've built my entire life around since I was a kid.

"That's what we've been working toward," I say, keeping my voice steady even though relief is flooding through me.

"Which is why we need to discuss logistics." Thomas sets his glass down, his expression turning more serious. "Next season, if you get that seat, you're back to the full circuit schedule. It's going to be intense, especially when you're proving yourself after being out of a full-time seat. More pressure than you've ever had, more scrutiny. Everyone will be watching to see if you can still perform at that level."

"It's part of the job," I say with a shrug. "I was a full-time driver for years before the injury. I know what it takes."

"I know you do." Thomas nods. "I just want to make sure we maintain this momentum, keep everything on track. And honestly, it'll be good to have you back in Europe full-time. The small-town thing, visiting family, dating the local girl, it's been great for the image, really humanized you. But it makes conducting business harder when my client is half a world away in the Pacific Northwest."

Small-town girl. Local girl. Like Lark is just some temporary detour, some PR strategy that served its purpose.

"Yeah, well, I'll still be back home more than usual," I say, hearing the defensiveness creeping into my voice. "To see Lark. And I'll fly her out to races when I can."

Thomas blinks in surprise, like this wasn't the response he expected. "Jack, I didn't mean to imply anything negative about her. She's great, really. It's just..." He gestures vaguely. "With your track record, and then the travel, the pressure, the time apart—it's brutal on even the most solid couples. I just figured this one would run its course naturally, like they always do." He picks up his glass again. "But hey, if you two can make it work long-distance with that schedule, more power to you. I hope you do, honestly. I'm just being realistic based on what I've seen."

"Right," I say, my jaw tight.

"Anyway," he's already moving on, pulling up something on his phone. "Let's talk about the media schedule for next week. You've got that interview with Sky Sports, and then—"

I should correct him. Tell him he's wrong, that Lark isn't like the others, that this is different. That I'm different with her. But the words stick in my throat.

He keeps talking, scrolling through his calendar, completely unaware that he just detonated something in my head. My mind is stuck on what he said, playing it on repeat.

I just figured this one would run its course naturally, like they always do.

Two days ago, waking up with Lark in that cabin, I wasn't questioning anything. I was sure we could make this work. Sure the distance was manageable, sure what we have is strong enough.

And then Thomas makes one casual observation based on a decade of watching me bail on relationships, and suddenly there's this voice in my head I can't shut up.

The food arrives and I eat mechanically, the steak probably excellent but I barely taste it. Thomas is talking about tire strategies and weather forecasts for Sunday's race, comparing data from last year's São Paulo Grand Prix. I nod when I need to, make appropriate sounds.

But I can't stop thinking about *my track record.*

Because he's not wrong about the facts. I've never had a relationship last past a month, and even that's pushing it. The second things ever got serious, I ended it. Clean break, move on, don't look back. It's what I've always done.

And the schedule next season will be brutal. Twenty-four races means I'm gone most of the year. Flying between continents, living out of hotels, barely having time to sleep between obligations. When I'm stressed about performance and Lark needs me but I can't be there. When she has something important and I'm on the other side of the world. When we go weeks without seeing each other. What happens when the pressure gets to be too much? What happens if I fall back into old patterns because that's what I've always done?

What if I end up hurting her? Because guys like me always do eventually. I shove the thought down. That's not going to happen. We're good. I'm not going to fuck this up. But the doubt is there now, planted.

"Jack?" Thomas's voice cuts through. "You with me?"

"Yeah, sorry." I take a long drink of water. "Just tired. Long flight."

"Understandable. Get some rest tonight," he says, already signaling for the check. "Big weekend ahead. Eyes are on you, especially with the contract situation so close. Stay focused."

"Always am," I say.

We finish up and say our goodbyes outside the restaurant. Thomas heads back to his hotel and I walk back to mine, the cool night air doing nothing to clear my head. My phone is heavy in my pocket. I should text Lark. Check in, see how she's doing, let her know how things are going here.

But I don't. I just keep walking, Thomas's words echoing in my head with every step.

CHAPTER 25

Lark

It doesn't sound right at all.

My laptop sits balanced on my knees, headphones on, listening to the demos I recorded in Seattle this past week. Maya set the whole thing up—three days in a studio with a producer Tidal Records works with sometimes, recording new versions of my songs in the pop sound they're going for.

They sent me the final recordings this morning. The tracks are supposed to show the label what I can do with their production style, and prove I can adapt my music to fit what they're looking for.

Except they don't sound like *me*. At all.

I hit pause on the third track and just sit there staring at the audio waveform on my screen. This is "Wildfire," the song I wrote right after the divorce when I was so angry I could barely see straight. I recorded the original demo myself earlier this year in a small Seattle studio with just my guitar.

This new version sounds like it was designed by an algorithm. They've smoothed out every edge, added these electronic beats that don't mesh with the lyrics, and Auto-Tuned my voice until I sound like any other pop singer on Spotify's Top 50.

And then there's the lyrics. Maya sent over the changes early this week and we went back and forth, and I agreed to most of them even though I hated every single one. They took out anything too specific, anything too raw, anything that actually meant something to me. Polished to the point of being sterile.

I pull off my headphones and toss them onto the coffee table, then immediately wince because they're expensive and I can't afford to replace them if they break.

Jack's been in Brazil all week for the São Paulo Grand Prix. The race is tomorrow, then he flies home. We've been texting, but my apartment feels too quiet without him. I keep catching myself looking at the couch expecting to see him there. I wish he was here. He has this knack for cutting through my spiraling, for making things seem less overwhelming. Which I could use right about now.

I hit play again on the demo and immediately regret it. That's not my voice. That's not my song. What am I doing? What if I sign with them and hate every single thing I put out? What if I compromise everything that makes my music mine and it doesn't even work? What if—

A knock at the door startles me out of my spiral.

"It's me!" Maren calls from the other side.

I jump up from the couch and yank the door open. She's standing there with a white bakery box in one hand and a bottle of wine in the other.

"I brought cookies and wine, as requested."

"Thank the universe you're here." I pull her inside. "I need your opinion on these demos before I completely lose it."

"That bad?" she asks, heading toward the kitchen. I follow her and grab two wine glasses from the cabinet while she sets the bakery box on the counter.

"I think so. But I need you to tell me if I'm crazy," I say, setting the glasses down.

"Gladly. I've been curious all day about what you recorded." She opens the wine and starts pouring while I peek into the bakery box. Chocolate chip, oatmeal raisin, snickerdoodles, and what looks like some kind of fancy lemon thing with white chocolate.

"Perfect," I say. "If there was ever a time for a sugar and wine pairing, it's right now. Ugh, I love you."

"I know you do," she grins, handing me a glass. We head back to the couch and settle in with the cookies within easy reach. "Now let me hear what's got you spiraling."

I had texted her this morning right after listening to the tracks for the first time, just a rambling stream of consciousness about the demos and the label. She'd responded immediately with "Coming over after work with cookies and wine. Let's figure this out," which is exactly the kind of friend response I needed.

I grab my laptop from the coffee table, pulling up the tracks from the Seattle sessions. "Okay, so these are the demos from this week. They want to see what I sound like with their production style. But I need you to listen and tell me if I'm being crazy or if these are actually as bad as I think."

"Bad how?" Maren accepts the earbud I hold out.

"Just listen," I say, hitting play on "Wildfire."

I watch her face while the song plays. She nods along but I can't read anything from her expression, which is both comforting and terrifying.

"Well?" I ask when it ends.

"Hmmm. Play me the original."

I pull up my demo from earlier this year. We listen and the difference is stark. Mine has all this urgency and anger and pain coming through in every note. The new version sounds like it could be anyone singing about anything.

It ends and Maren taps her fingers on her knee, thinking.

"Give it to me straight. Be brutal. I need it," I say, taking a sip of wine.

Please tell me I'm wrong. Please tell me it sounds amazing and I'm just being difficult and precious about my art or whatever.

She grins. "Well I don't know about brutal. But I think the new one… okay, it kinda sounds like generic reality TV show music. Like those songs they play that always sound exactly the same. Your original always gave me goosebumps."

I groan, dropping my head back against the couch. "Ugh, that's what I was thinking too. Dammit. I was hoping you were going to say it was all in my head and I'm going to be the next big thing."

She laughs. "Well I still think you're going to be the next something amazing, but this isn't it. But then again what do I know about music?"

"Giving yourself an out?"

She nods, sipping her wine. "Yes. Very important that when you give people advice you state you don't really know what you're doing so if they follow it and it goes bad, you aren't responsible."

I laugh despite everything. "Smart strategy."

"I learned from the best." She grabs a chocolate chip cookie. "So what are you thinking?"

"Ugh, I don't know. I feel like maybe I'm being unrealistic about how the industry works. Like what if this is my only shot, you know? And even if it's not perfect I throw it away and then lose out on my chances. Maya keeps saying trust the process, that I need to prove I can adapt before they'll give me creative control. And maybe she's right? Maybe this is just how it works and I'm being difficult."

Maren's brow furrows. "It's a tough call. I'm not going to lie and say everything will work out perfectly if you follow your gut. Sometimes following your instincts means taking the harder road with no guarantees. But you also have to live with whatever decision you make. If you sign with Tidal and put out music that doesn't feel like yours, will you be okay with that? I guess that's the real question."

I don't have an answer. I take another bite of cookie to fill the void.

"What does Jack think?" Maren asks.

"I haven't really talked to him about it in detail. We've texted about it a little, but he's been so busy with the race weekend."

"Makes sense." Maren pauses. "I should have brought Calvin over. Get a third opinion."

"Yes, I'm so torn I need all the perspectives." I kick my feet up onto the coffee table. "Maybe I should pull up those articles about label deals again. Refresh my memory on what's actually standard versus what's a red flag."

We order pizza and spend the next few hours eating and dissecting every angle. I show Maren some of the industry articles I'd bookmarked months ago when this first started, the ones about contract clauses and creative control timelines. She asks good questions, plays devil's advocate when I need it. We debate back and forth so much that my brain feels like it might actually explode, so we veer to less stressful topics.

Maren tells me about how her second book is going, and then she gets into the latest project at their Victorian. They've been working on the house for the past year and it's pretty much done, but they both love house projects so they're always finding another room to improve.

After both of us start fighting yawns, Maren glances at her phone and groans. "Shit, it's almost eleven. Calvin's probably wondering if I got kidnapped."

I nod. "Thanks for spiraling with me tonight."

"Anytime. That's what I'm here for." She stands and stretches. "Call me tomorrow?"

"Absolutely. We'll see if I actually make a decision about any of this." I walk her to the door.

"You will when you're ready." She hugs me tight. "You'll figure this out. I know you will."

"Love you," I say into her shoulder.

"Love you too," she says, pulling back to look at me. "And seriously, text me. Even if it's just to freak out more."

"I will."

The door closes behind her and suddenly the apartment feels too quiet. I'm back to being alone with my thoughts and my laptop and the tracks that sound nothing like me.

I spend the rest of the evening trying to work on the songs, practicing them, seeing if maybe I can find some way to make them feel more authentic. But every time I sing along, every time I try to connect with the lyrics the way I used to, it feels off.

By the time I finally give up and close my laptop, it's after midnight and I'm no closer to feeling confident about this decision than I was this morning.

Ugh. I need to sleep. Stop thinking about this for five minutes.

I drag myself to the bathroom to brush my teeth. My phone buzzes on the counter and I glance down, hoping it's Jack since I've barely heard from him today. His texts have been weirdly short all week, just quick replies between whatever Grand Prix obligations he's got going on.

It's a local number I don't recognize, but my stomach drops when I see the name.

It's Brandon. New local cell. Saw this. Thought you should know what kind of guy you're dating now. Hope you're very happy!

There's a link to a video.

No. Absolutely not. Brandon texting me is never good news, which is why I've had him blocked for two years. Brandon texting me with a video about Jack? That's a nightmare I wasn't prepared for tonight.

I should delete it.

But my finger hovers over the link. And then I'm clicking it because apparently I'm a glutton for punishment and terrible at making decisions.

It's Jack at a party. I recognize the outfit immediately, the same one from that Monaco video that went viral months ago, the one that caused all his sponsor problems. But why would Brandon send me this? I've already seen the Monaco video. Everyone saw it. It was everywhere when it first came out. We talked all about it when Jack first explained what happened.

I'm about to close it when something catches my eye. The video length at the bottom of the screen. *Ten minutes and forty-three seconds.*

That can't be right. My finger hovers over the play button.

The original Monaco video was maybe thirty seconds long. Just a quick clip of Jack standing near a table with drugs visible in the background. Bad enough for his sponsors to completely freak out, but explainable. He told me the whole story. Five minutes max, in and out to grab Sofia for Luca, just terrible timing with someone's camera.

But this is ten minutes. Ten minutes I've never seen before. Ten minutes that Brandon somehow got his hands on and decided I needed to see. I can see the likes are already at over a hundred thousand. *Fuck.*

There's this pull in my chest, this horrible curiosity I can't shake. Like watching a car crash happen in slow motion. Why would this be going viral again? What's on this video that wasn't on the first one? Some part of me wants to just delete it, block Brandon's new number, go to bed and pretend this never happened...

I hit play.

Jack walks into the party and immediately starts greeting

people like he knows them. Handshakes and those half-hug things guys do, actually smiling and laughing at something someone says. He looks comfortable here. Relaxed. Like this is a party he wants to be at, not somewhere he reluctantly showed up to rescue his teammate's drunk little sister.

Someone hands him a beer and he takes it without hesitation, takes a drink, and keeps talking with people. My stomach twists. He's not rushing around looking for Sofia. Not scanning the crowd like someone on an urgent mission. He told me that he was in and out. But he's just standing there talking, laughing with people who clearly know him, looking completely at ease.

The camera pans and I can see that table. The one with cocaine on it, people bent over it doing lines like it's casual background noise at a house party. Jack's standing right there. Not doing lines but chatting with people who are.

This doesn't look like a rescue mission. This looks like Jack at a party doing exactly what Jack does at parties. This looks like the cautionary tale about the player who parties too hard and leaves broken hearts everywhere he goes.

The video keeps playing and I can't look away even though I want to. Even though some part of me is screaming to stop watching right now, that whatever comes next is going to hurt. A woman approaches him. Tall and gorgeous in that effortless model way that makes me feel instantly, viscerally inadequate. The kind of woman who probably doesn't even own sweatpants, who looks like she stepped out of a magazine spread even when she's stumbling drunk in heels that cost more than my rent.

She pulls him down and kisses him. The video cuts off right there.

I watch it again. My finger hits replay before I can stop myself, like maybe I saw it wrong the first time. Like maybe if I watch again it'll be different, it won't hurt as much, I'll see something that makes this okay.

But all I see is the easy way he moves through that crowd like he belongs there. The fact that he doesn't look surprised when that woman kisses him, doesn't look uncomfortable, just looks like Jack at a party where beautiful women throw themselves at him.

He lied to me. He *fucking* lied to me.

When he told me about Monaco, he made it sound like he was this reluctant hero doing an uncomfortable favor for his friend. But this video shows he's not even looking for Sofia in any of it.

And now I'm sitting here questioning if any of it was real. Was Sofia even at that party? He said Luca called him panicking, but what if that was all made up to make himself sound better to me, to his family?

I wish I had Luca's number. I could just text him right now and ask if Sofia was really there, if Jack really helped her. But that would be insane. Texting my boyfriend's teammate at midnight to verify whether my boyfriend lied to me about why he was at a party months ago before we were ever together? That's a whole new level of spiral I'm not sure I'm ready to sink to.

Though apparently I'm already watching a video on repeat that my ex-husband sent me specifically to hurt me, so maybe the ship has sailed on the sanity front.

The thing is, if he left this much out about Monaco, what else has he left out? What other convenient omissions have there been that I just accepted because I wanted to believe him? How many other times has he told me a version of events that was technically true but missing all the parts that would've made me think twice?

I slide down onto the bathroom floor, staring at the paused frame of that woman leaning into Jack, her arms around his neck.

I shouldn't even be pissed about the kiss. I know that logically. We weren't together then. He wasn't mine. I have absolutely zero right to be jealous about what he did or who he kissed before we were even a thing.

But watching it makes jealousy burn through me anyway. Hot and ugly and so humiliating I want to throw my phone across the room. Because that woman is exactly the type Jack dates. The type everyone expects him to date. Models and actresses and trust fund socialites who look perfect in photos and don't have anxiety spirals about record label contracts while eating cookies on their couch at midnight.

I open Instagram before I can stop myself, searching for the video like I'm actively trying to hurt myself more. It's everywhere. Absolutely everywhere. Posted and reposted with thousands of comments, millions of views. The comments make me feel physically sick.

Bet he's cheating on that girlfriend lol

Ugh he's so hot I wish that was me

Once a player always a player 💯

His PR team working OVERTIME trying to clean this up

That poor girlfriend she probably thinks she's special 😂😂😂

Literally the hottest guy I've ever seen

Why does he even have a girlfriend when he could have anyone

I'm that girlfriend in the comments section. The woman who fell for the fuckboy's lines and convinced herself she was different. That he'd changed for her. That she was special.

The tears start and I'm furious at myself for crying. I'm twenty-six years old. I survived Brandon. I spent two years in therapy rebuilding everything he systematically tore down, learning to trust my instincts again, learning to stand up for myself, learning that I'm enough exactly as I am.

And here I am sitting on my bathroom floor at midnight crying over a guy who makes women feel special until he gets bored and moves on to the next city, the next race, the next gorgeous woman who thinks she's the exception.

All the warning signs were there from the beginning. The reputation that spans continents. The lifestyle of constant travel and parties and beautiful women throwing themselves at him. The fact that commitment-phobic Formula One drivers don't suddenly transform into relationship material just because they met some bartender from a small town in Washington.

But I fell for him anyway. I believed him when he said I was different, when he said this was real, when he looked at me in that cabin in Banff and told me he loved me like it was the easiest truth in the world.

And now I'm on my bathroom floor at midnight, crying over a video my vindictive ex-husband sent me specifically to twist the knife.

I was such an idiot to think I was the exception to Jack Midnight's pattern.

CHAPTER 26

JACK

The first-class seat is comfortable enough, the kind of luxury I've gotten used to over the years but still appreciate. I'm waiting for the flight to take off, sipping the whiskey I ordered as soon as I sat down, scrolling through my phone while the flight attendants do their safety demonstration that nobody pays attention to.

I'm fucking exhausted from the race weekend. Simulator work, dozens of media obligations, sponsor meetings, and watching Davis drive my car into P18 while Luca grabbed P3 in the identical machinery. P18. Eighteenth place. Driving a Ferrari I could be winning championships with.

I feel for the guy, but he's in over his head. It took everything in me not to *whoop* when he crossed the finish line in that position, because at this rate I'll be back in the seat before next year even starts. Hell, maybe even by the next race if Davis keeps fucking up so spectacularly.

My phone buzzes. Thomas calling. He's on his way back to

Europe while I'm heading to Dark River, different flights since we're going opposite directions. We saw each other three hours ago at the track, said our goodbyes, so I can't imagine what's so urgent it can't wait until we're both on the ground.

"Hello?" I answer, taking another sip of whiskey.

"There's another video," Thomas says immediately. "From Monaco. From that party. Someone leaked it last night and it's spreading fast online. It shows a bit more than the first video did."

My stomach drops, that familiar dread crawling up my spine. "How much more?"

"Longer footage from the same party. About ten minutes total." His voice is clipped, professional, but I can hear the underlying concern. "Shows you arriving, talking to people, having a beer. Talking to everyone who was doing lines. Shows you with Elise." He pauses deliberately. "Shows you kissing her."

"Great. That's just fucking great." Of course there's more footage. Of course someone had their phone out recording the whole fucking time, just waiting for the perfect moment to release it for maximum damage. Because nothing in my life can ever just stay buried, can just be over and done with. I take a long drink, the burn doing nothing to calm the anxiety already building. "Have you heard anything from Ferrari yet? Is this messing up the contract?"

"I spoke with Matteo an hour ago," Thomas says, and I can hear him typing in the background, probably already drafting statements. "They're not thrilled obviously, but since this is from months ago and you've been on exemplary behavior since then, they're not as worried as they could be. You've done everything right: Miami, the social media presence with Lark, staying out of trouble. That goodwill is buying you some leeway right now. It helps that they miss your skill badly enough that I think they're willing to overlook this as old news."

Some of the tension in my shoulders eases slightly, but not much. "So we're okay? Contract's still looking good?"

"Should be. We'll put out a statement similar to the one from earlier this year. That this doesn't change anything, you've learned from past mistakes, you're focused on your career, the standard language. It'll blow over." He pauses. "But Jack, you need to stay squeaky clean from here on out. Any more incidents and all this goodwill evaporates. Understand?"

"Yeah, I understand," I say, taking another drink.

"Good. I'll send you the draft statement to approve before we release it. Keep your head down this week."

"Will do," I say, and hang up.

I pull up the video on my phone immediately, needing to see what we're dealing with. It's already trending on X, thousands of people weighing in with their opinions about my latest scandal.

The video starts and my stomach sinks lower with each passing second.

It's not technically wrong. It's not doctored footage. Everything shown actually happened: I was at that party, I did have a beer, I did talk to people. But it *looks* like I was just there having a good time instead of trying to discreetly extract an eighteen-year-old girl from a dangerous situation without causing a scene.

And there's the kiss.

Elise stumbling toward me, clearly drunk or high or both, throwing herself at me. And for maybe two seconds, two fucking seconds, I kiss her back before my brain catches up and I pull away. Of course the video cuts off right there, doesn't show me pushing her back gently, doesn't show me helping her sit down and find her friends.

We'd dated casually for maybe a month two years ago, hooked up at a few parties since when we were both single. She got engaged six months ago and despite *many* flaws, I'm not trying to break up someone's marriage. But the video doesn't show any of that context, doesn't show my reasoning. Just shows me at a party, looking comfortable and relaxed, kissing someone.

Fuck.

A PR nightmare that Thomas and I need to manage carefully. It's not personal, it's just damage control and image rehabilitation and all the other corporate bullshit that comes with being in the public eye.

My phone buzzes again. Robert this time.

Robert: *Just saw the video circulating. Is this going to affect the contract situation?*

I type back quickly, trying to project a confidence I don't entirely feel.

Me: *Thomas says Ferrari's handling it well. Since it's old footage and I've been on good behavior, they're not panicking. Should be fine.*

Robert: *Good. You're so close, Jack. That's a huge relief. Keep me updated if things shift.*

I stare at that message. *You're so close.*

The flight attendant announces we're about to take off and I need to put my phone in airplane mode. I down the rest of my whiskey and lean back in my seat, closing my eyes.

The only thing I want right now is to be back with Lark. To have her curled up next to me in that cabin in Banff, mountains outside the window, fireplace crackling, nothing else mattering except us. Like we could make this work no matter what. But that feels like it happened in a different lifetime now. Thomas's words from dinner keep circling back, mixing with my own doubts until I can't tell which thoughts are mine and which are his.

I tap out a quick text to Lark.

Me: *Flying back now. I'll head over to your apartment once I land.*

I stare at the message after I send it, waiting for the typing bubbles to appear. They don't.

The flight attendant tells me firmly to put my phone on airplane mode, so I do, and try to connect to the Wi-Fi. It won't load, and as the plane begins to roll away from the gate, the pilot comes across the PA system: *Ladies and gentlemen, we'll be taking off momentarily, but we wanted to let you know that we're working to correct a glitch in our in-flight Wi-Fi. We hope to have it working soon after take off. But, well, that may not be possible.*

"Fuck," I whisper. No Wi-Fi. The flight from São Paulo to Seattle is over twelve hours. With no fucking Wi-Fi.

I left Sunday evening after the race, exhausted from the weekend but wired from the crazy week and the ongoing PR issues that refuse to die. I doze off a few times but mostly just sit there thinking about the contract situation. How close I am to getting my seat back. How I can't fuck this up now.

And the Wi-Fi is still dead.

Thoughts of Lark keep breaking through. Looking forward to seeing her, to just being back with her after a week apart. But then Thomas's words creep back in. I push them down.

When I finally land in Seattle Monday morning, I check my phone immediately. Still nothing from Lark. No response to my text from yesterday.

I text her again while I'm waiting for my luggage.

Me: *Landed. Heading to your place.*

Still nothing by the time I grab my bag and head to the rental car. Lark's usually pretty good about responding, though she can be slow to text back when she's deep in music stuff. Probably working on those demos, lost track of time.

The drive from Seattle to Dark River takes a couple hours. I check my phone at red lights. Still nothing. Not even a read receipt.

By the time I'm getting close to her apartment, there's this gnawing feeling in my gut I can't shake. If something serious had happened, Maren would've texted. Or one of my brothers. So she's probably fine. Just busy. Stressed about the label stuff maybe. But still.

I pull up outside her building and spot her car in the lot. Okay, she's home. That's good. I take the stairs up to her floor and knock instead of using the code she gave me. I don't want to startle her by just walking in when she's clearly not expecting me.

She opens the door and I know immediately something's wrong. Her face is completely shut down, arms crossed over her chest. Her eyes are red like she's been crying.

Fuck.

"Hey," I say. "You didn't respond to my texts so I figured I'd just come by. Is everything okay?"

She steps back without a word, letting me in but not meeting my eyes. The silence feels wrong. Heavy.

I walk in and turn to face her. "Are you alright? Did something happen with the demos?"

"Did you see the video?" Her voice is flat. Emotionless.

"Yeah, I saw it." Relief floods through me that it's not something serious. I run a hand through my hair. "It sucks that it's out there, but Thomas doesn't think it's going to affect things too much. Ferrari's not happy but they're not panicking. Since I've been on good behavior for months now, they're willing to—"

"I don't give a fuck what Thomas thinks," she cuts me off sharply, and the fury in her voice catches me completely off guard. "Is that really what you think I'm worried about here? Your fucking contract? You *lied* to me, Jack."

My brain scrambles to catch up. I stare at her, trying to process what she just said. "*What?* I didn't lie—"

"*You* told me you were at that party to grab Sofia," she says, and she looks fucking pissed. "You made it sound like you barely had time to find her before someone started filming. Like you were in and out in five minutes, heroic rescue mission accomplished. The video doesn't show any of that. Maybe Sofia wasn't even *at* that party. You were drinking. Socializing. Standing right next to a table full of cocaine. Making out with someone."

"Are you serious? I had to be *discreet*." Frustration is already building. "There must have been three hundred people at that party, Lark. I couldn't just burst in and grab her without causing a massive scene. Do you know how fucking crazy that would look? Some older guy dragging a teenage girl out of a party? I had to blend in, make it look casual, like I belonged there. And it was a mansion. I didn't even know where she was when I got there."

"So you decided to drink and hang out?" Her voice is sharp, cutting.

I'm tired from the flight, from the weekend, from contract and PR bullshit, and now I'm being accused of lying about something I didn't fucking lie about.

"Half a beer, yeah. To blend in." I'm getting really defensive now, I can hear it in my own voice but I can't seem to stop it. "What was I supposed to do, announce to everyone that I was there on a rescue mission? Do you know what that crowd is like? If I'd said I was there for Sofia, people would have told me to fuck off, and would have tried to keep her there. And at the time she wasn't exactly jumping to leave the party, so I had to be careful about how I approached it."

"And the kiss?" Her voice could cut glass. "How did that help you blend in exactly?"

"That was Elise," I say, running both hands through my hair

now because I don't know what else to do with them. "An ex-hookup from a couple years ago. She threw herself at me and I pulled back. Yeah, maybe I could have done it quicker, but fuck, it was a party and I was single at the time. It took a second to register what was happening. It's not my fault the video—"

"I don't even care about the kiss!" She rubs her hands over her face. "Ugh, I swore I wasn't going to bring that up because it doesn't even fucking matter, but I just—" She drops her hands, and there are tears in her eyes now. "I can't believe you told me some heroic rescue story and you're still trying to stick to it. And I *believed* your version. That's what kills me!"

The tears break something in my chest but I'm too tired and too angry and too defensive to let it show.

"It wasn't a lie!" My voice is rising now. "Everything I did was to avoid making a scene so I could get Sofia out safely. Every single choice I made was to get her out of there without anyone noticing or making it harder."

"You lied by omission," she spits out. "You knew I had concerns about your reputation, Jack. We talked about it multiple times. And you still chose to tell me a sanitized version of what happened."

"Why should I have to give you a play-by-play of every single second?" I shoot back. "I told you the important part. I was there for Sofia. Everything else was just circumstantial details that didn't change the actual truth of why I was there. You wanted me to narrate every fucking moment?"

"Those details matter, Jack!" She's yelling now. "The context matters! And the fact that you didn't think I deserved to know the full story matters more than anything."

"You're taking a ten minute video and assuming the worst about me," I argue, desperation creeping in now. "You're not even listening to my explanation, you're just—"

"I *am* listening," she interrupts, her voice breaking. "You're just not saying anything that makes this better."

“So what do you want me to say?” My voice is rising again, frustration boiling over. “That I’m sorry I didn’t give you a breakdown of every second I was at that party? That I should have known you’d see some edited video and immediately assume I’m exactly who everyone warned you about?”

“Maybe you *are*!” she yells, and there are tears streaming down her face now. “Maybe everyone online is right. Maybe I’m just the summer girl who helped fix your image so you could get your contract back!”

The words hit me like a physical blow. “Is that really what you fucking think?” My voice is hard, cold. “That you’re just some image rehabilitation project? That I don’t actually care about you?”

“I don’t know what to think anymore,” she shoots back, wiping her eyes furiously. “How am I supposed to trust anything when you pick and choose what to tell me?”

The silence stretches between us, heavy. She’s looking at me like she’s waiting for me to say something that will fix this. But I don’t know what that is. Maybe there isn’t anything.

Maybe she’s right. Maybe I’m not cut out for this. I’ve never been good at relationships, never stayed in one long enough to actually learn how to do them right. And now I’m proving exactly why.

“Maybe we should have kept this fake,” I hear myself say. The words hang in the air between us like poison.

Lark goes completely still. When she speaks, her voice is a whisper. “What did you just say?”

I should take it back immediately. Tell her I didn't mean it, that I'm just tired and stressed and saying shit I don't mean, which is the truth. But that familiar wall is already sliding into place.

"Maybe this was easier when it was just an arrangement," I say, hearing how cold my voice sounds. "No expectations. No one getting hurt."

"You know what? Maybe you're right. Maybe this should have stayed fake." Her voice breaks. "I can't *believe* I thought you were different."

She's right. I'm still the same guy who fucks everything up, who runs when things get difficult, who hurts people without meaning to. So I just stand there. Silent. That wall getting higher with every second I don't apologize, don't take it back, don't tell her I love her, which I absolutely do. But something in me won't let me say it.

"So that's it then?" she says, and her voice is shaking with anger and hurt. "You're just going to shut down and leave? Run the second things get hard?"

"Lark..." I start, but I don't even know what I was going to say.

"I want you to stay and actually fight for this, and you can barely even look at me." The tears are streaming down her face. "Just tell me you want to stay. That this matters enough to work through it."

It does matter. She matters more than anything, but that wall is back up and the silence stretches too long.

"I need you to leave," she finally says. "I can't do this right now. Please just go."

I turn toward the door, each step feeling like I'm walking through concrete. Every part of me is screaming to turn around, to fix this, to tell her I'm sorry. That I love her, that I want to stay with her forever. That I'll figure out how to be better at this. But I can't make myself do it. I reach for the doorknob, pause for just a second with my hand on it, then pull the door open and walk out, letting it close behind me with a soft click that sounds like finality.

I don't go back to the cabin. Don't pack up my shit or say goodbye to my brothers. I just get in my rental car and drive straight to the airport, book the next flight to Monaco, and sit in the departures lounge staring at nothing.

This is who I am. Who I've always been. The guy who fucks things up and runs. Never stays in one place long enough for anything to matter. It was a mistake to think I could be different, that I could be the kind of guy who deserves someone like Lark. And now I've hurt both of us, exactly like I always knew I would.

She does deserve better. And now I've proved it.

CHAPTER 27

Lark

It's been three days since Jack walked out of my apartment and I can't stop replaying the fight in my mind. Every word. Every accusation. Every moment I wish I could take back.

I don't know which emotion is stronger. How pissed I am at him for lying by omission about Monaco. How mad I am at myself for attacking him when I'd told myself I'd approach it calmly. Or how I miss him so badly it physically hurts, like someone hollowed out my chest and forgot to put anything back.

I groan, rolling over in bed and burying my face in the pillow. I should get up and be productive. Instead I'm lying here like a tragic heroine in a Victorian novel, probably about to die of a broken heart.

I'd had a whole plan about how I'd talk to him. In my head I'd pictured this serene version of myself who would sit him down calmly and explain why I felt hurt, ask him why he didn't tell me everything, and have this mature adult conversation where we both communicated our feelings like emotionally healthy people.

The reality was me building up a fuming rage as the hours went by without sleep, refreshing social media obsessively and reading comment after comment about how I was probably just another one of his conquests. And then the second I saw his face, I exploded into accusations. Not my finest hour. But it definitely wasn't his either.

I'd fallen right back into an old fear of being lied to, of secrets, of being kept on the outside of someone's life. The terror that maybe my fears about him had been right all along, that I was just the summer girl helping fix his image, that everyone online was right.

I didn't tell him I was scared. I just attacked and went straight for the jugular. And then when he started shutting down, when I could see him building that wall brick by brick, I'd practically begged him to stay and fight for us. But he just stood there in silence, proving every fear that I wasn't worth staying for.

And he hasn't texted. Part of me wants to reach out. To apologize for some of the things I said, for jumping to conclusions so fast. But the other part is still so hurt and angry that he walked away and pissed that he said maybe we should have kept it fake.

Maren came over yesterday and we'd talked it all out over an entire bottle of wine. She thinks I should call him, that we both said things we didn't mean. But I can't bring myself to do it.

My phone rings and Maya's name flashes across the screen.

Shit. She's probably calling about the demos. She'd told me they *loved* them and would be in touch soon about next steps, which should be great news. At least if my personal life is actively burning to the ground in spectacular fashion, maybe something good is happening with my career. That's what I should be focusing on. Except for the fact that I *hate* the demos.

"Hey Maya," I answer, trying to inject some energy into my voice. Trying to sound like a functioning human instead of someone who's been living in emotional wreckage for three days straight.

"Lark! I have news!" Her voice is so bright and excited it's almost painful. Like she's operating on a completely different emotional frequency than I am. "Are you sitting down?"

"Uh, yeah, I am," I lie, still horizontal on my bed in the same pajamas I've been wearing since yesterday. Or maybe the day before. Time has lost all meaning.

"Well, as we talked about briefly at the meeting, we at Tidal handle entertainment contracts for various sports venues and events across the US. One of our biggest partnerships is with Formula One." She pauses, clearly for dramatic effect. *"And* we've had a last-minute dropout for the Las Vegas Grand Prix. We want you to fill the slot."

My brain stutters, trying to process the words. Formula One. Vegas. Las Vegas Grand Prix. My stomach flips and twists like it's auditioning for Cirque du Soleil. *Performing live.*

This is huge. This is massive. This is the kind of opportunity that could actually change everything. And then, approximately one second later, the second thought hits me like a truck: *Jack will definitely be there.*

"You still there?" Maya asks.

"Yes! Sorry, I'm just..." I sit up, my brain trying to catch up. "Wow. That's incredible. When is it?"

"Two weeks. I know it's incredibly short notice, which is why I need an answer right away. These opportunities get planned months in advance usually, but one of the new artists we booked had to drop out at the last minute and we immediately thought of you."

"I'm so honored, really, thank you," I say. My heart is racing. Two weeks to somehow fix stage fright I've been battling for years. Two weeks to become the performer I used to be, back when I loved being on stage instead of being terrified of it.

This is everything I've been working toward, everything I've dreamed about since I was a kid singing into a hairbrush in my bedroom and pretending I was performing at the Grammys.

"It's more than huge, Lark. This is the kind of platform that genuinely launches careers. You'd be performing Sunday morning, one of seven artists in our emerging talent showcase. Small morning stage, three songs, but the coverage is national. *International,* actually. Between live TV, streaming, replays, *millions* of people will see it."

I ignore the part about *millions of people,* choosing to focus on the small morning stage part. Only three songs. I can do three songs. I've done three songs before without completely falling apart. Sometimes. When the crowd was tiny and half-drunk and not really paying attention.

But those demos. Those smoothed-out, polished versions that sound like they could be anyone. That had everything unique about my music stripped away and replaced with something marketable.

And Jack. Jack somewhere in that same city, in that same world, existing in the same space as me while we're not speaking. While we might be broken up. While my heart is still shattered into approximately ten thousand pieces.

"The songs would be from the new demos, right?" I hear myself ask, pushing the Jack thought away. "The pop versions?"

"Exactly. 'Wildfire,' 'Burning Bridges,' and 'Late Night Calls.' The new arrangements, the updated production. We want to see you deliver *that* sound live, prove you can connect with this kind of audience." She pauses, and I can practically hear her smile through the phone. "And Lark, if this goes well, if you show us you can perform this material the way we envision it, we'll sign you. Official contract. This is your showcase. Your *moment.*"

My heart stops, then restarts at double speed. I've been working so hard the last two years to give this a real shot, the whole time wondering if I was delusional for thinking I could actually make it in this industry. And here it is. Being handed to me on a silver platter. My childhood dream wrapped up in a bow with a contract attached.

But those fucking demos. The lyrics they gutted and replaced with generic phrases that could mean anything to anyone. The production that smoothed away every edge, everything that made them mine. Maya had sent over "style guidance" for my social media last week with suggestions about my aesthetic.

"Lark?" Maya's voice pulls me back to the present. "I need an answer. I know it's fast, but this is extremely time-sensitive."

"Yes," I say, and the word feels heavy in my mouth. Final. Like I just agreed to something I can't take back. "I'm in. Let's do it."

"Wonderful!" Maya says. "I'm so thrilled, Lark. This is going to be incredible. You're going to absolutely kill it."

We spend the next ten minutes going over logistics. Flights, hotel, stage times, what to expect. My brain is only half-processing the details, the other half still stuck on that word. *Yes*. I'm committed. Like I just signed away something important without fully reading the contract.

When we finally hang up, I sit there staring at my phone.

Vegas. Two weeks. Formula One.

The hollow ache in my chest that's been there since Jack left expands, takes up more space. I should be excited. This is everything I wanted. So why does it feel like I just agreed to step off a cliff?

Then there's the stage fright that Maya doesn't even know about because I've been so careful. Only posting the tiny open mic clips where things went okay, where I managed to push through the panic for two minutes. Never posting the moments where I froze. Never posting the Blue Room disaster. *Definitely* never posting that.

She thinks I can handle this. She has no idea I might get up on that stage in Vegas and completely fall apart in front of thousands of people and every camera in the world.

And then, because I apparently can't help myself, the thought I've been trying to avoid crashes over me: Jack will be there. Jack, who I'm still so stupidly, painfully in love with that it makes me want to scream into a pillow.

I'll have to exist in his world without him. Perform in his universe while knowing he's somewhere nearby and we're not speaking. Perfect. Just fucking perfect.

I pull up my texts with him, scrolling back through our conversation history like I'm deliberately torturing myself. Photos from Banff with the mountains in the background, both of us grinning like idiots. Inside jokes that don't make sense to anyone but us. Heart emojis scattered throughout like confetti. "I love you" said so easily, so naturally, like it was the simplest truth in the world.

And now. Nothing. Three days of complete radio silence that somehow feels louder than any words we actually said to each other during our fight.

Are we broken up? In a fight? He left for Monaco without a word, without his stuff from the cabin, without anything. Which seems pretty definitive. You don't just fly to another continent if you're planning to work things out. You don't walk away from someone you love if you actually want to fix things.

I'm not going to let him ruin this opportunity, too. I'm not going to let heartbreak derail the one good thing that's happening in my life right now. At least I hope it's a good thing.

I need to move. Do something. The walls of my apartment are starting to close in. I push myself off the bed and pad into the kitchen, my body running on autopilot.

Don't think about Jack. Think about the opportunity. The

exposure. The career-launching platform that Maya just handed you on a silver platter.

I start making coffee because it's either that or day-drinking at ten in the morning, and I'm trying to be a functional adult here. The familiar routine is soothing—measuring grounds, pouring water, hitting the button and listening to the machine gurgle to life. I lean against the counter and let my head drop back, staring at the ceiling.

What if Jack brings someone else to the race? Some gorgeous model type who fits into his world way better than I ever did. What if I have to watch him with someone new while I'm trying to perform songs that don't even sound like me anymore.

The coffee maker beeps and I pour myself a massive mug. My phone sits on the counter where I left it, face down. I should probably text Maren. Or my mom. Someone who can talk me down.

But when my phone buzzes, I practically lunge for it like a desperate person, my heart doing that stupid leap thinking maybe it's Jack, maybe he finally—

Kelly's name flashes across the screen.

Kelly, who chose Brandon over our friendship and then started dating him like our entire friendship meant nothing. Kelly, who I've spent considerable therapy hours trying to stop being angry at because holding onto that hurt was only hurting me.

My hand hovers over the phone. I should just delete it. Pretend I never saw it. Go back to successfully ignoring her existence. But curiosity is a terrible, powerful thing.

I pick up the phone and open the message.

Kelly: *I know this is overdue, and I know it's shitty to do this in a text, but I don't know if I could face you in person. I'm back in Seattle now. I dumped Brandon. I'm so sorry about what happened at your open mic night. I had no idea he would insist we go, and I'm sorry I let* *him talk me into it. He's a horrible person and I guess I've finally realized that. I messed up, and then I kept trying to tell myself I was happy when I wasn't. I'm not asking you to forgive me, but I just wanted you to know I was wrong, and regret the hurt I caused. I'm sorry I didn't apologize sooner. For all of it.*

I read it three times. Kelly dumped Brandon. Kelly is apologizing. Kelly is admitting she was wrong. Two years. Two years of radio silence. Two years of seeing them together on social media, living their life while I picked up the pieces of everything they destroyed. And now this.

I set the phone down and press the heels of my hands against my eyes. I don't know what to feel. Angry? Relieved? Vindicated that she finally sees what I saw all along about Brandon?

Part of me wants to text back something cutting. Something that makes her feel even a fraction of the pain she caused when she chose him over me, when she showed up at my open mic night on his arm to twist the knife one more time.

But I'm so tired of being angry. So tired of carrying this hurt around like luggage I can't put down.

My fingers hover over the keyboard. What do I even say to this? "It's okay"? Because it's not okay. "I forgive you"? Because I'm not sure I do. Not yet. Maybe not ever.

I take a sip of coffee, letting the warmth ground me. Then I type slowly, carefully.

Me: *I need to think this over and I'm not sure that I can forgive you. But thank you for reaching out. I really do wish you the best.*

I hit send before I can second-guess myself. It's honest. It's not cruel. And it's all I can manage right now. The typing bubbles appear immediately.

Kelly: *I understand. I wish you the best too, Lark.*

I set the phone down and just stand there in my kitchen, mug clutched in both hands, trying to process the emotional whiplash of the last hour. Vegas. Jack. Kelly. My career. My heart. Everything feels like it's spinning too fast and I can't quite catch my breath.

I turn to George, my potted plant on the counter that's somehow thriving despite my complete negligence.

"George, buddy," I say to the plant. "It's like Wacky Wednesday or something. What other wild text or call is going to come through? Is Brandon going to apologize next? Is my high school ex going to propose? Are aliens going to land and ask for my demo?"

George, mercifully, doesn't respond. Just sits there looking unreasonably cheerful with his bright green leaves, like he's got all the answers and isn't sharing.

I take my coffee to the couch and curl up in the corner, my mind still racing. Two weeks until Vegas. Two weeks to prepare. Two weeks to figure out how to perform songs I don't connect with, how to exist in Jack's world without falling apart, how to prove to Maya and Tidal Records that I'm worth signing.

No pressure or anything.

Trivia night at the Black Lantern is always chaos in the best possible way. The place is packed but not slammed, that perfect level of busy where everyone's having a good time without the stress of being in the weeds. Teams are scattered around the bar, huddled over their answer sheets, arguing in loud whispers about state capitals and eighties movie trivia.

Sarah's running trivia for the first time tonight and absolutely killing it. She's got the mic, her voice projecting over the crowd with this confident energy that makes me ridiculously proud. I usually handle trivia, but with everything happening with my music I've been training her up, and she's a natural.

"Alright, question seven!" Sarah announces, and the bar quiets down. "In what year did—"

"She's so good at this," Maren says beside me, leaning against the bar. We're both watching from our post, taking advantage of the lull between questions when nobody's ordering drinks.

"Right?" I grin. "I told her she'd be great. She was so nervous about it too."

"You're a good teacher." Maren bumps my shoulder with hers. "So. Vegas. Formula One. Are we freaking out? Are we excited? What's the vibe we're going for here?"

I sigh, fiddling with a coaster. "I mean, it's insane. This could actually change everything for me."

"It *is* huge," Maren agrees, watching me carefully. "You don't sound as excited as I thought you'd be."

"No, I am! I'm excited. It's just..." I trail off, trying to find words for the tangled mess of emotions. "It's a lot. The timeline is crazy. Two weeks to prepare. And the songs they want me to do are the pop versions. The ones from the demos I recorded in Seattle."

"The ones you didn't love," Maren fills in gently.

"Yeah. Those," I say. "And I haven't been sleeping well, which doesn't help. Though on the plus side I've been really productive at three in the morning. I started working on a new song." Jack-inspired, but that's a conversation that requires wine and tissues I don't have right now.

"Silver lining," Maren says with a small smile.

"Exactly. Anyway, Maya says if this goes well, if I prove I can deliver this sound live, they'll sign me. Official contract. So it's worth it, right? It has to be."

"It has to be," Maren echoes, but she's still watching me with that careful expression. Like she's trying to read between my words.

"If I don't completely bomb it." I laugh, but there's no humor in it. "I mean, that's the real concern here. What if I get up there and freeze? What if the stage fright kicks in and I can't get through a single song? You know my track record with performing live."

Maren's expression softens. "Hey. You've been working on that."

"Working on it doesn't mean I've fixed it." The memory of every failed performance makes my chest tight. "And this is Formula One. Thousands of people. Cameras everywhere. International coverage. If I freeze up there, it's not just embarrassing, it's career-ending before my career even starts."

"You've had good performances too," Maren says firmly, squeezing my shoulder. "You can do this. The stage fright is real, but so is your talent. And you're going to get up there and prove it to yourself. I know you will."

I want to believe her.

Sarah's voice carries over the crowd again, reading out the next question, and we both turn to watch. Eddie's team in the corner is having a heated debate about something, Marcus gesturing wildly while his teammate tries to shush him.

"Have you heard from Jack?" Maren asks quietly.

My stomach drops. "No. Nothing yet."

"Lark—"

"I know what you're going to say," I interrupt, keeping my voice light. "That I should reach out. That we both said things we didn't mean."

"I mean, yeah." Maren gives my shoulder a gentle squeeze. "Listen, believe me, I'm going to give him a big old kick in the pants for leaving so suddenly without talking to you or his brothers. Calvin too. But maybe it's worth texting him. Just to clear the air."

I force a smile. "No way. I have too much pride for that." I pause. "Maybe that's the problem. Anyway, lighter subjects. Please. I can't spiral about Jack right now or I'll lose it completely."

Maren studies me for a long moment, then nods. "Okay.

Lighter topics." She drums her fingers on the bar, thinking. "Ooh! What are you going to wear on stage? Because this is Vegas, Formula One, international coverage. You need something that screams 'I'm about to be a star.'"

"Ooh, now we're talking." I feel myself relax slightly, grateful for the subject change. "Something that says *'I'm talented and professional but also cool and approachable.'* You know, casual. Easy."

"So basically impossible," Maren laughs.

"Exactly." I'm grinning. "I was thinking maybe something—"

"Wait!" Maren's eyes light up. "What about that beaded dress you have? The dark blue one with the silver details?"

I pause, picturing it. I do look pretty damn good in that. "You think? Not too much?"

"Are you kidding? It's perfect!" Maren's getting animated now, counting off on her fingers. "It's classy, shows off your legs, will look *amazing* under stage lights, and that dark blue is ridiculously flattering on you. Plus it has all those little silver stars beaded on it. You'll literally be wearing stars while becoming a star. It's a sign!"

"Okay, yes, I love me some signs from the universe." I laugh. "I'll take all the extra cosmic support I can get. The universe speaking through sparkly embellishments."

"Exactly!" Maren laughs. "The stars have aligned. On your dress." She's grinning so wide now. "Ooh, and maybe some cute boots? Knee-high maybe. Or heels. Tricky though."

"God, I love cute clothes," I say, and for a moment I actually feel lighter. Like maybe everything will be okay. Like maybe I can do this.

Maren reaches for her back pocket, then pats her other pockets, frowning. "Oh shoot, I left my phone at home again." She looks at me apologetically. "You okay if I run and get it? I'm expecting a call from my editor tonight and I don't want to miss it."

"Yeah, of course, go ahead." I wave her off. "It's not too busy. Sarah's got trivia handled. I'm good."

"You're the best." Maren squeezes my hand and heads for the door. Her house is only a few minutes' walk from here, so she'll be back before I know it.

I turn back to the bar, pulling out my phone to scroll through my Vegas performance outfit ideas on Pinterest, trying to stay in that lighter headspace we just created. Sarah's voice carries over the crowd, and there's laughter from one of the teams. It's a good night. Easy.

The door chimes. I glance up automatically, expecting to see a regular or maybe a young couple looking for a place to grab drinks.

Brandon stumbles in.

"What the fuck," I breathe.

He's drunk. Obviously, spectacularly drunk. He catches himself on the doorframe, then straightens up with exaggerated care and heads straight for the bar. A few people look up, conversations pausing. The easy energy in the room shifts immediately.

He reaches the bar and leans heavily on it, and the smell of cheap gin hits me from three feet away.

"What the hell are you doing here?" I keep my voice low but firm, very aware that we have an audience now.

"I hope you're happy." His words are slurred, his eyes unfocused. "Kelly left me. Just fucking left. Packed her shit and went back to Seattle." He points at me with one unsteady finger. "And your asshole boyfriend punched me. Did you know that? Jack Midnight punched me in the face a few weeks ago. And I was a *saint* and didn't report it, though I fucking should have. So are you happy now, Lark? Is this what you wanted?"

I'm not sure which part of that to process first. But mostly I'm just furious that Brandon is here, in my space, drunk and making a scene.

"Yeah, actually, I am pretty happy about that." I cross my arms. "Now get the hell out of here before I call the cops."

"You think you're so much better than me now," Brandon spits out, his voice rising. "With your fancy boyfriend and your little music career. But you're still just—"

"You need help, honey?" Eleanor appears at my elbow like a guardian angel in a cardigan. She's one of our regulars, part of the Romance Raiders book club that meets here every other week. Mid-seventies, always has a paperback with a shirtless cover model, and sweet as pie until you piss her off. Right now she's glaring at Brandon like she's planning exactly how to dispose of a body.

"No, I've got this," I say, but I'm grateful for her presence. I can see Eddie and Marcus standing up from their table in my peripheral vision, other regulars shifting in their seats. My people. Ready to back me up if I need it.

"You've got nothing," Brandon snarls. "You're a bartender playing dress-up as a musician. You always were too much. Too loud. Too ambitious. That's why—"

"Stop talking." My voice cuts through his, sharp and clear. The entire bar has gone quiet now, everyone watching. I'm vaguely aware that I'm giving everyone the best damn show they've seen at trivia night in years. Might as well make it count.

"You don't get to do this anymore," I continue. "You don't get to come into my workplace and try to make me feel small. I'm done shrinking myself for you. I'm done second-guessing everything because you spent years making me doubt myself." I lean forward, my hands flat on the bar. "So here's what's going to happen. You're going to walk out that door right now. And you're never going to come near me again. Not at this bar, not anywhere in Dark River. Are we clear?"

"You can't tell me—" He reaches across the bar like he's going to grab my arm.

"*Yes I can.* Get the hell out of here. I'm not going to ask you again." My voice is steel now, all the therapy sessions and self-work and rebuilt confidence pouring into every word.

The kitchen door swings open and Jayson appears, wiping his hands on his apron. He's a big guy, easily six foot, and right now he looks ready to commit violence. "Everything okay out here, Lark?"

"I've got this," I say, not taking my eyes off Brandon.

But Brandon's looking around wildly now, at Eleanor still planted at my elbow, at Eddie and Marcus on their feet, at Jayson, at all the regulars staring at him with varying expressions of disgust and anger.

"Oh, is everyone in this fucking place on this *bitch's* side?" he yells, stumbling around the bar and staggering toward me.

I don't think. Don't hesitate. Just react.

My knee comes up and connects solidly with his balls. *Hard.*

Brandon makes a sound like a deflating balloon and crumples, catching himself on the bar before sliding to the floor.

There are audible gasps from around the bar, followed immediately by a few shocked laughs. Someone near the back yells, "OH SHIT!"

"I said get out," I tell him, my heart pounding but my voice steady.

Jayson steps forward, Eleanor's already moving closer, and I can hear chairs scraping as more people stand. But something in Brandon's expression shifts—maybe a flicker of sobriety breaking through, or just self-preservation finally kicking in. He staggers to his feet, still bent over, looking around wildly at the circle of hostile faces.

He stumbles toward the door, moving like every step hurts, and crashes directly into Maren as she's walking back in.

"What the—" Maren stops, taking in the scene. She presses herself against the doorframe as Brandon lurches past her and out into the night. The door swings shut behind him.

You could hear a fucking pin drop in The Black Lantern.

"What just happened?" Maren asks, looking from me to Eleanor to the crowd of standing regulars.

"I just kneed Brandon in the balls," I say, and suddenly I'm smiling wide. Because holy shit, I just did that.

Maren's jaw drops. "Oh my god. OH MY GOD. I can't believe I missed that because I went to get my stupid phone!"

Sarah's voice comes over the mic, barely containing her laughter. "Okay folks, let's get back to trivia. Question nine: In what year was the first women's self-defense class officially recognized as—"

The whole bar cracks up. Someone whoops. Eddie starts a slow clap that turns into actual applause.

Maren is staring at me with this mix of shock and pride and absolute delight. "You actually kneed him in the balls."

"I *actually* kneed him in the balls," I confirm, and then I'm laughing too, this giddy relieved laughter that bubbles up from somewhere deep in my chest. "That felt amazing."

"You're my hero," Maren says solemnly.

"You know what? I'm feeling pretty damn good about myself too," I say, still grinning like an idiot.

Eleanor pats my hand where it's still pressed flat against the bar. "That's my girl. I'm adding that move to my repertoire." She heads back to her table, already pulling out her phone. Probably texting the entire Romance Raiders group chat.

Jayson gives me a thumbs up from the kitchen door before disappearing back to his domain.

And for the first time in three days, the weight in my chest feels just a little bit lighter.

CHAPTER 28

JACK

The Ferrari garage in Las Vegas hums with pre-race energy in the late afternoon. Through the open garage door, the sun has just begun sinking toward the horizon and the Strip is coming alive, neon signs flickering on as the sky fades from blue to orange. Every casino is lighting up and the buzz of the crowd is building, music and announcements echoing across the circuit. Hours before the race and Vegas is already electric.

Davis got food poisoning from a bad meal last night. Spent the early morning hours throwing up, and the team doctor pulled him from the race two hours ago. Which means I'm racing tonight. Starting P18 because of the mechanical issue Davis had in yesterday's qualifying. Seventeen cars ahead of me. Seventeen opportunities to prove I deserve to be here.

This is it. This is what I've been training for, waiting for, fighting to get back to for eighteen months. My shot at getting my full-time seat back.

My phone buzzes in my pocket for the third time in ten minutes. My brothers, mostly. They've been texting on and off for the last two weeks, ever since I left Dark River without saying goodbye.

Not the first time I've pulled a vanishing act when things got complicated, but apparently they're not letting it slide this time. Calvin and Theo both figured out something was wrong with Lark. They'd sent careful check-in texts, the kind of concerned older brother messages that made me feel like shit. All of them had given me endless shit once I'd finally admitted the truth, that Lark and I started as fake dating, then it became real, then I fucked it up spectacularly by walking out on her.

I ignore the buzzing and try to focus on the engineering briefing happening in front of me. Marco, the lead race engineer, is going over telemetry data from yesterday's qualifying session.

"The brake system was giving Davis trouble in the corners, but it should be good now," Marco says, pointing to data on his tablet. "We've adjusted some calibrations for your driving style. Should feel more responsive."

I nod, absorbing information. This is what I need to focus on. Not Lark. Not the fact that I haven't heard from her in two weeks. Not the hollow feeling in my chest that's been there since I walked out of her apartment.

My phone buzzes again. I pull it out, half hoping it's Lark even though I know it won't be.

Thomas. Of course.

Thomas: *Where are you? Need to talk about tonight. Media briefing in 30 minutes.*

I text back quickly.

Me: *Garage. Engineering briefing.*

Thomas: *Good. Find me after. This is happening, Jack. Don't fuck it up.*

No pressure or anything.

Marco continues the briefing. The track is unforgiving.

Narrow and high-speed with concrete barriers that don't give you any margin for error. One mistake and you're out.

"P18 is not ideal," Marco says to me, which might be the understatement of the century. "But the car is fast. Luca's been P3 and P4 in recent races with this package. You can move forward. It's just going to require patience and picking the right moments."

What he's not saying, what everyone in the paddock is thinking, is that getting into the points from P18 would be a minor miracle. Top ten means passing at least seven cars on a circuit with limited overtaking opportunities. The online betting odds I saw this morning had me finishing P14 at best. Even the most optimistic racing journalists are predicting P12 or P13. A points finish? P10 or better? That's wishful thinking.

Thomas had been blunt about it during our call this morning. "Look, no one expects you to win from P18. Hell, most people would be shocked if you crack the top ten. Just drive clean, show them you can race smart, don't bin it into the barriers. That's all Ferrari needs to see."

But that's the thing. I don't want to just drive clean and finish P12. I want to prove I'm better than that. That eighteen months on the sidelines didn't dull my edge. That I can still do things other drivers can't.

I nod at Marco, my mind already running through the race, calculating possibilities. It's going to take perfect execution and a bit of luck. But I've made impossible overtakes before.

Lark

The green room backstage at the Las Vegas Strip Circuit is smaller than I expected, which is saying something because my expectations were already pretty modest. It's really more of a glorified closet with a mirror, a chair, and a folding table.

The race doesn't start until later this evening, but the pre-race entertainment is already in full swing. I'm part of the "emerging talent showcase" on a smaller side stage, which is basically the opening act before the opening act. The thing people mostly ignore while getting settled.

But if Maya is right, the footage will be everywhere.

Through the thin walls I can hear the bass from the main stage, and my stomach does that familiar clench. Stage fright has been my constant companion for years now, and tonight it's brought all its friends.

My phone buzzes on the table and I grab it, desperate for distraction.

Maren: *YOU'RE GOING TO BE AMAZING. I'm manifesting success for you right now. Calvin says to tell you to break a leg!*

Maren: *YOU'VE GOT THIS. Can't wait to hear all about it!!!* 🩶

I smile despite the nerves churning in my stomach. Maren and I FaceTimed an hour ago, and before that I'd called my parents, who were so proud they both got teary, which made me teary. Thank goodness I chose to wear waterproof mascara tonight.

I'm wearing the dress Maren and I picked out weeks ago. Deep blue with silver stars beaded all over it. My hair falls in soft waves, my makeup looks good, and I feel confident about how I look. Now if only I felt half as confident about getting through three songs.

The door opens and Maya walks in, phone pressed to her ear.

"Mm-hmm, yes, I understand, but we need the sound levels adjusted before the next performer or—" She spots me and holds up one finger in the universal *give-me-a-second* gesture while finishing her call. "Right. Okay. Handle it. Thanks."

She hangs up and immediately types something on her phone with her thumbs moving at lightning speed.

"Lark! Thirty minutes," Maya says, still typing. Then she glances up and actually looks at me, and her expression does this thing where her professional smile falters for just a second. "Oh."

My stomach drops. "What? Is something wrong?"

"That's what you're wearing." It's not quite a question.

"Yeah, I thought... you said something elegant and stage-appropriate?" I'm suddenly very aware of every bead on this dress.

Maya sighs. "I sent you a list last week. The stylist picked out options that fit the rebranding aesthetic. This is..." She gestures at me. "Very pretty. Just not quite what we discussed."

"I didn't get that email," I lie, and I'm definitely going to hell for this because I absolutely got that email. The problem was that all the outfits looked atrocious and like something I would never be caught dead wearing. So I may have decided that email was more of a suggestion than a requirement.

Maya studies me for a moment like she's calculating whether this battle is worth fighting, then shakes her head. "Well. It's too late now anyway. You look great, honestly. Just not exactly the direction we discussed."

"I'm so sorry." I've worked in customer service long enough to make that sound genuine.

"It's fine." Maya picks up her phone again. "Okay, so you're third in the lineup. You'll do your three songs. I heard the sound check went well earlier, so I think you're all set."

She glances up from her phone, giving me her full attention. "The label executives are watching the livestream back in LA. This is your showcase, your chance to prove you can deliver this sound live and handle a real audience. You do well tonight and we move forward with an official contract."

"Right. No pressure or anything." I try to smile but it comes out more like a grimace.

"You're going to be great!" She squeezes my shoulder briefly before her phone buzzes again. "We're so excited about your potential. Just remember everything we talked about—big energy, connect with the crowd, really sell these songs."

Her phone rings and she's already answering it as she heads toward the door. "Yes, hi, I'm dealing with that right now—" The door closes behind her and she's gone, swept back into whatever crisis is happening.

The room feels smaller without her chaos filling it, which is probably better for my nerves. Just me and the bass thumping through the walls from the main stage.

I walk over to the corner and open my guitar case, reaching inside the pocket for my phone charger. My hand closes on crumpled paper instead. *Shit.* I pull it out and smooth it flat, my throat tightening.

It's the first draft of "Until You Say Stay." I wrote it about Jack the day after our huge fight, and I'd completely forgotten I'd shoved this in here. The finished version is better now, polished, refined. I've played it dozens of times at home, even recorded it a few times without posting anything.

But seeing this handwritten first draft brings every second of that fight flooding back. The way he looked at me and the things we said. How much I miss him crashes over me like a wave I wasn't prepared for. I trace my finger over the crossed-out lines and frantic rewrites.

Two in the morning, tears streaming down my face, but my fingers flying across the guitar strings like they knew exactly where to go. The words pouring out raw and honest and completely mine. That's what my music is supposed to feel like.

Not the versions I'm about to play. The ones that have had every piece of me stripped away and replaced with something generic. Something safe. Something that isn't even my style, that I don't even like.

I shove the paper back into the pocket, but the feeling won't go with it.

My hands are shaking.

I don't know if I can do this. Walk out there and perform songs that aren't mine, smile and sell something I don't believe in, prove I'm willing to erase everything that matters to me.

A knock on the door. "Twenty minutes, Ms. Reyes."

Twenty minutes to decide who I want to be. I look at the pop versions sitting in my case, then at the pocket where I shoved that first draft.

Maya's going to kill me.

JACK

The briefing wraps up and I have a bit of time before the last of the pre-race obligations start. The race isn't until 8 PM, prime time under the lights for television audiences around the world.

I can hear music filtering through the paddock from one of the stages they've set up for pre-race entertainment. Some emerging talent showcase. I find a quiet corner away from the garage chaos. My driver's room is small but functional, a bench, a mirror, hooks for my gear. My race suit hangs there waiting, red and black with my name embroidered on the chest. MIDNIGHT. Number 7.

In an hour or so I'll climb into that car and race for everything I've worked toward. My career, my seat, my future in Formula One.

But I can't stop Lark from filling every quiet moment in my head. She slips into my thoughts like smoke under a door, uninvited and impossible to keep out. And I don't *want* to keep her out.

I keep circling back to those words. *Maybe we should have kept this fake.* My biggest fuck-up in a life full of fuck-ups.

A knock on the door pulls me out of it.

"It's open," I call.

My teammate Luca walks in, still in his team polo, looking relaxed and confident the way he always does before a race. "There you are. I've been looking for you."

"Just trying to get my head straight before tonight," I say.

"Good. Because I need to talk to you about something." He leans against the doorframe. "Sofia wants to make a statement. About Monaco. About what really happened at that party. She has videos she was recording on her private Instagram. They back up everything."

I tense immediately. "We've been through this, Luca. The answer is still no."

"Just hear me out before you—"

"She'll get *destroyed* online," I interrupt. "You know what people are like. She's eighteen. She doesn't need that kind of attention, and your family doesn't need the headache. I can handle people thinking I'm an asshole. I've had plenty of practice."

"She's nineteen now, actually. An adult. And she can handle it." Luca crosses his arms. "My family supports this completely. My parents, my sisters, all of us. We've talked about it extensively. It's been months of watching you take shit for something you didn't do. Something you did to protect her. We're done watching it happen."

"Look, I appreciate the loyalty, but Monaco isn't even a problem anymore." I gesture vaguely. "Ferrari's putting me in the car tonight. Thomas says if I drive well, the seat is mine. Full-time. So clearly they've moved past it. We should too."

"It's not about Ferrari," Luca says firmly. "It's about the truth.

You're letting people believe you were doing cocaine at a party when you were actually helping someone who needed it. That's not the same thing."

"People believe lots of things about me. Most of them true." I shrug, going for casual even though he's clearly not going to let this go. "What's one more story?"

"This one's different and you know it." He's not backing down, that stubborn set to his jaw that I recognize from a hundred races where he refused to give up a position. "We're putting out a statement tonight. After the race. Sofia, me, and my family. The full story. What actually happened. Why you were there."

I look at his face and realize there's no point arguing. He's already made up his mind, and when Luca decides something, he's immovable. Probably where he gets his racecraft from.

"Fine," I finally say. "But if this blows back on her at all—"

"It won't. We've hired a PR team. Communications specialists. Sofia's statement will make everything clear—she's grateful, she's speaking out voluntarily, all of that." He grins suddenly. "Besides, the internet loves a redemption arc. You might even come out looking like a hero for once."

"Stranger things have happened," I say dryly. "Though I'm not holding my breath."

"That's what I'm here for. To believe in you when you're too busy being cynical." He checks his watch. "Not much longer now, so get your head straight. Focus on the race."

He leaves, and I'm alone again with my thoughts about Lark, my excitement about the race, and the weight of everything that's about to happen.

I sit down on the bench and pull out my phone. Lark's name stares back at me from my contacts. Two weeks of silence that I created. Two weeks of being too scared to reach out and admit I fucked up.

Luca's right. I've spent eighteen months fighting to get my

seat back. Training, simulator work, corporate appearances, playing nice with sponsors. Doing everything Thomas and Robert asked of me. All of it to get back in a race car.

But it wasn't just about wanting to race again. The video wasn't my first scandal—hell, it wasn't even my worst behavior, just the worst optics. I got into a fist fight while I was still healing from my crash, threw punches when my contract was already in question. Attended plenty more questionable parties without the excuse of rescuing anyone. I gave everything when I was on the track, but couldn't shake the recklessness off it. Not until these last few months.

Some of that shift started before Lark. But she crystallized it. Watching her pursuing her music with relentless devotion—it made my own half-assed efforts look pathetic.

And I never fought for her. Never showed her she was worth fighting for. I just let her think she was part of the image rehabilitation, another item on my PR checklist.

Maybe it's too late. Maybe I burned that bridge so completely there's no rebuilding it. Maybe she's done with me, moved on, decided I'm not worth the emotional energy.

Soon, I'll race. I'll prove to Ferrari and everyone else that I deserve my seat back. That I'm ready for this, that eighteen months on the sidelines taught me something about patience and control and fighting for what matters.

And then I'll figure out how to prove to Lark that I deserve her back too.

Tonight everything changes. One way or another.

I just hope I'm not too late to fix what really matters.

CHAPTER 29

Lark

The small side stage is exactly that. Small. Set up near one of the main entertainment areas but not the huge stage where the headliners perform. The "emerging talent" stage, which is industry speak for "people will probably ignore you but we're giving you a chance anyway."

Through the gap in the curtain I can see the crowd. A few hundred people maybe, scattered around drinking, talking, scrolling on their phones. The sun is mostly down and everything is lit up like Vegas does best—neon and excess and way too bright.

Maya walks up as I'm hovering in the wings. "Alright, so you're up in about two minutes. Remember what we talked about—big energy, really sell it. The executives are watching."

My stomach churns. "Maya, I need to talk to you."

"Can it wait? You're literally about to—"

"I can't do the pop versions."

She stops mid-sentence. "What?"

"The songs. The arrangements we recorded. I can't perform

them. They're not me, they're not even the genre I want to do." The words tumble out faster now. "And if I go out there and do them anyway, that's what I'll be known for. That's what people will think I am."

Maya blinks at me like I just told her I'm planning to juggle fire on stage. "Lark." Her voice is carefully controlled. "That's not what we discussed. That's not what the label is expecting to hear."

"I know. And I know this isn't professional, and I should have said something way earlier." I force myself to meet her eyes. "But I can't do it. I should have told you that a long time ago, but I think I only just realized it myself. I completely understand if you'd rather pull me from the lineup."

Maya looks at her phone, then at the stage, then back at me. Her jaw tightens. "We can't have the slot empty. You're already booked, your name's been announced." She crosses her arms. "Do what you need to do. But I can't guarantee you'll get the contract. They specifically wanted to hear this sound. So you might be losing everything here."

The weight of that settles in my chest, but I nod. "I understand. I'm really sorry."

"Are you sure about this?" She's searching my face. "Because once you walk out there, that's it. No do-overs."

"I'm sure."

She stares at me for another long moment, then sighs like I just made her entire evening exponentially harder. "Fine. It's your career. Go tell the sound guy about the change. You've got ninety seconds."

"Thank you."

"Don't thank me yet." She's already lifting her phone back to her ear. "You might have just completely tanked your future."

I catch the sound guy doing final checks near the stage entrance. "Hey, sorry, last minute change—I'm going acoustic. Just me and the guitar, no backing tracks."

He looks at me like I just asked him to rebuild the entire sound system. "Are you serious? We set up the whole—"

"I know, I'm so sorry. Can you make it work?"

He glances toward Maya, who's very deliberately not looking in our direction, then back at me with obvious reluctance. "Yeah. I guess. But you're on in like sixty seconds."

"Thank you so much."

I move back to the wings with my guitar. My heart is pounding so hard I can feel it in my throat. The stage fright that's been simmering all evening kicks into high gear now, mixing with adrenaline and terror and this weird sense of relief that I can't quite explain.

I just blew up my deal with Tidal Records. Probably. Almost definitely.

And I'm about to walk out on that stage anyway.

"Next up, all the way from Washington State, please welcome Lark Reyes!" The voice booms through the speakers.

Polite applause. Underwhelming but expected. Nobody knows who I am. I'm background music while people wait for the race.

I walk onto the stage, guitar in hand. The lights hit immediately, bright enough that the crowd becomes shapes and shadows.

"Hi," I say, somehow sounding steadier than I feel, which is a win considering I might throw up. "I'm Lark. Thanks for having me."

Some murmurs. A little clapping.

A guy yells, "THIS BETTER BE GOOD!"

"Couldn't agree more, pal," I say into the mic. "If this sucks, trust me, we're all gonna be disappointed."

The crowd laughs and a few people are putting their phones down. The panic in my chest loosens slightly. *Okay.* I can work with this.

I settle onto the stool and adjust the mic stand. My guitar

feels familiar and grounding, the one constant in this surreal situation. The stage fright is already bubbling up, that familiar panic that makes me want to run. But I'm here now. I made my choice. And I'm not backing down.

I start strumming the opening chords of "Wildfire." Not the pop version. My version. The original acoustic arrangement I wrote in the aftermath of my divorce when I was so angry I could barely see straight.

The first note comes out clear and strong. Someone near the back whoops.

The first verse flows. My voice finding its center, my fingers remembering where to go. A few people near the front turn to watch.

By the second verse, more eyes are on the stage. The fear is still there, but I'm pushing through it. Note by note, line by line. People are actually listening now. The song ends and there's real applause.

"Thank you," I say, steadier now. "This next one is called 'Burning Bridges.'"

My version again. The one with the lyrics I figured out at 3 AM, the bridge that builds instead of simplifies. The melody that captured what I felt when I was finally angry enough to leave. More people are watching now. Phones up, recording. A couple near the stage stops talking to listen. A woman is dancing, drink forgotten.

When the song ends, the applause is louder, enthusiastic, with some whistles.

"One more song," I say into the mic, and I'm smiling now despite the nerves still buzzing under my skin.

I was supposed to play "Late Night Calls" next. It's on the set list, it's what I practiced. Safe choice. Good energy to end on.

But my fingers move to a different chord progression entirely.

"This is a new one I wrote recently," I hear myself say, even though I didn't plan this, didn't even consider playing it tonight. "It's called *Until You Say Stay*."

JACK

The hospitality area is crowded with sponsors and team personnel when I cut through on my way back from my final media obligation. Guitar chords drift through the pre-race noise, a voice rising above the hum of the crowd. Clear and compelling enough to make me slow my pace and turn toward the sound.

"This is a new one I wrote recently," the voice says. "It's called *Until You Say Stay*."

The entertainment stage is set up across from the paddock, and there's a crowd gathered at the railing overlooking it. People swaying with their phones up, filming. The voice draws me toward it like gravity, recognition dawning over me as I push through the crowd.

Lark is on stage with her guitar.

For a second I'm convinced I've finally cracked, that two weeks of thinking about her constantly has manifested some kind of fever dream. That my brain has decided to torture me by conjuring her image in the one place I least expect it.

But she's here. The Vegas skyline glitters behind her under the floodlights and she looks ethereal on stage, like she stepped out of one of those dreams where everything feels too vivid to be real.

Every trace of the stage fright I've seen her battle has vanished. She commands that audience with the confidence of someone who was born to be on stage.

She owns them completely.

Lark

The second the words leave my mouth, I know there's no taking them back.

This song. The one I wrote about Jack at two in the morning while crying at my kitchen counter. The one I've never performed for anyone. And I'm about to sing it in front of hundreds of strangers. With Jack somewhere in this same venue.

My fingers find the opening chords and my chest tightens, but I don't stop. The first verse comes out raw, every word pulled from somewhere deep. The crowd has grown now, people drawn over by the music, and they're listening. *Really* listening.

The chorus builds and I'm pouring everything into it. Every ounce of hurt and hope and confusion from the last two weeks. The way he made me feel seen and terrified all at once. The way I pushed him away because I was too scared to believe any of it was real.

People are swaying. Some are filming. Near the stage, a woman wipes her eyes.

The final chorus swells and I let my voice soar, every bit of longing and regret bleeding into the words. When I hit the last note and let it fade, there's a beat of complete silence.

Then the applause erupts. People are cheering. Someone yells "YEAH!" from the back.

I did it.

I performed live without freezing up, without letting the fear win, with my own songs instead of the watered-down versions Maya wanted.

"Thank you so much," I say into the mic, grinning now, adrenaline flooding my entire system. "Thank you, Vegas!"

More cheers, more applause. Then I'm walking offstage with

my guitar and my heart pounding and this wild, electric energy coursing through me.

I feel powerful, like I just proved something to myself. That I could get on that stage and perform. That I could overcome the fear that's held me back for years. That I could choose my own vision over someone else's sanitized version of who they wanted me to be.

Brandon's voice, the one that's been living rent-free in my head for years telling me I'm too much, too loud, too ambitious? Finally quiet. Finally gone. And I know now that it's never coming back.

I'll find another way. Another label, another opportunity that doesn't require me to sand down every edge that makes me who I am. And if that doesn't happen, I'll keep working at the Black Lantern, keep making music on my own terms until something clicks.

Because I'm done compromising. Done shrinking myself to fit into someone else's box.

JACK

As the song built to the final chorus, I caught pieces of our relationship woven through the melody. Things I said to her in Banff. Moments we shared that I thought I'd ruined. It cuts through every wall I've built in the last two weeks.

And when she finished, the crowd erupted.

Now she's gone and I'm still clapping hard, whistling with two fingers in my mouth like I'm at a stadium.

She's gone from the stage, but she's *here*.

Lark is here. In Vegas.

She performed her own songs instead of the newer ones the label had been pushing. And it was the right fucking call because the crowd ate it up. She was incredible up there, fearless in a way that makes what I'm about to do in a race car look like nothing.

I'm so fucking proud of her. Underneath that is this desperate, clawing need to find her right now. To tell her I heard every word of that song. To tell her I'm sorry for walking away, for letting my fear win when I should have stayed and fought for us.

Lark

I can't access the paddock area where the drivers are, despite trying to sweet-talk the security guard into letting me past. When I mentioned I was one of the drivers' girlfriends, he actually laughed and said he hears that from like a hundred girls a day. Fair enough, I guess.

I should just be thankful Maya didn't rip my backstage pass away and kick me out of the venue entirely. Instead she just gave me this look of pure disappointment and told me my career with Tidal was over. She's probably right. But weirdly, I feel better than I have in years. Lighter, like I just put down something heavy I didn't realize I'd been carrying. The only thing missing is Jack.

I'd tried calling him, but it went straight to voicemail. Then I vaguely remembered him mentioning once that he leaves his phone in his driver's room for a few hours before races because he hates distractions.

So here I am, leaning against the railing with a vodka soda, watching the pre-race chaos unfold. The high from performing is still buzzing through me, this electric feeling I can't quite shake. I just performed my own songs in front of hundreds of people and didn't completely fall apart. The contract might be gone, but I proved something to myself tonight that feels bigger than any record deal.

The sun has fully set and Vegas is doing what it does best. Every surface is lit up in neon, the track glowing under massive floodlights that turn night into day. The crowd noise swells and falls in waves. Music pumps from speakers. Announcers' voices boom overhead. The whole circuit feels alive, pulsing with energy.

My phone buzzes and I pull it out to see the continued flood of messages. My parents both sent tearful voice memos about how proud they are after watching the livestream. Maren sent approximately fifteen texts in all caps with heart emojis and exclamation points. I'm grinning at my phone, feeling so loved and supported it makes my chest ache in the best way.

I wonder if Jack saw my performance. If he heard the song I wrote for him. What possessed me to sing it instead of one of my other songs, I don't know. It wasn't even on the original set list. But in that moment every part of me was reaching out to him, trying to tell him something I couldn't say to his face. That I know we're right for each other. That he's it for me, and I know I am for him. I can feel it like an invisible thread, connecting us even when we're apart.

I sigh and take another sip of my drink. The huge screens flash above me, cycling through the starting grid. Driver photos appear stories high, giant faces that loom over the crowd with their team colors and starting positions. Luca Rossi in P4 for Ferrari, looking confident in his race suit.

Then I choke on my drink.

Jack's name is on the screen. Jack Midnight. Ferrari. Starting position P18.

My mind is spinning. Jack's the reserve driver. He shouldn't be racing tonight unless something happened to Davis. It doesn't matter what. What matters *is* Jack is driving. *Tonight.* Starting from the back of the grid.

My chest tightens in a way that has nothing to do with stage fright or performance nerves. I know how much this means to him. This is everything he's been working toward for eighteen months.

And more than anything, I want to be there right now. By his side. But I'm out here behind barriers with thousands of other people, and he's in there preparing for the most important race of his life.

"Lark Reyes?"

I turn to find a nice-looking older man standing beside me at the railing. He's maybe mid-fifties, wearing an expensive blazer and the kind of warm smile that usually means someone wants something from me.

I suppress a sigh. I don't want to be rude, but I've officially hit my limit for human interaction tonight. My brain is already operating at maximum capacity between Jack and the race and everything that just happened on that stage.

"Yes?" I manage. He does look vaguely familiar though. "Sorry, do I know you?"

"Walter Becker," he says, extending his hand. "Horizon Records."

Holy shit.

Horizon Records. That's where I know him from. I've seen his photo on their website. They're one of those labels that artists actually want to sign with. They represent some of my favorite indie artists.

"Oh my God," I manage, shaking his hand. "Hi. I mean, it's nice to meet you. I know who you are." *Great. Real smooth Lark.*

He laughs, looking genuinely pleased. "Well, this feels quite serendipitous. I had tickets to this race tonight because my niece is a Formula One fan, and I almost didn't bother checking out the musical acts. But you? I caught your performance. You're really something special." He pauses. "Are you represented by anyone? I assume you're here with Tidal Records based on the showcase."

My brain is short-circuiting. Horizon Records. Walter Becker. This cannot be happening right now.

"Um... No, I'm not with them," I say. And I probably need to rip this Band-Aid off before he finds out from someone else. "I should be honest with you about why. Tidal wanted me to perform these really polished, commercial versions of my songs. They had me re-record everything with their producers, changed the arrangements, simplified the lyrics. I said yes initially, but tonight I performed my original versions instead. The ones I actually wrote. Without their approval."

He raises his eyebrows, but doesn't look horrified, which is something.

I meet his eyes. "So that bridge is pretty much burned. I just thought you should know before this conversation goes any further." Like he wouldn't find out anyway. There's zero chance Tidal isn't already bad-mouthing me to everyone in the industry.

Walter nods, looking more intrigued than concerned. "And why did you make that choice?"

Because apparently I'm incapable of playing it safe even when my entire career depends on it.

"Because those versions weren't my songs anymore," I say. "They wanted something safe and marketable, and I get that's the business. I really do. But I'd rather fail with my own music than succeed with something that doesn't sound like me."

He smiles like the Cheshire Cat. "Good. That tells me everything I need to know. Artists with conviction who fight for their vision? Those are exactly the people I want to work with." He pulls out a business card. "Call me this week. You have something genuinely special, and I'd love to talk about what Horizon could do for you."

I take the card with slightly shaking hands. "You're serious? Even knowing I just walked away from another label?"

"*Especially* knowing that. I like working with people who have a backbone." He gestures toward the stage. "Most artists play it safe. You didn't. I know a star when I see one. You commanded that audience, and your sound is fresh. I hope you and I can have a further conversation."

"Thank you," I say, and I can hear the relief in my own voice. "I'll call. I promise."

"Good," he says with a warm smile. "I'd better get back. I'm not supposed to be doing business tonight as it is. Enjoy the race."

He disappears back into the crowd, leaving me standing there holding his card and my vodka soda like some kind of bewildered lottery winner who can't quite believe the numbers on the ticket.

What are the actual odds? I blow up one record deal and get offered another in the same hour. Jack gets called up to race from P18 on the same night I'm performing in Vegas. We're both here, both fighting for what we want, both risking everything.

The universe is either laughing at us or rooting for us.

The announcers are getting louder, the energy ramping up. I can barely think over the roar of the crowd and music blasting from every speaker. I look back up at the giant screen showing Jack's photo. About to race for everything he's been working toward.

And I'm going to be right here watching. Cheering for him even if he doesn't know I'm here. Even if I don't know what we are anymore.

Tonight feels like the kind of night where impossible things happen. Where you get the career you've always wanted and maybe, just maybe, you get the person too.

CHAPTER 30

JACK

"Midnight!" Thomas's voice cuts through. He's standing a few feet away, phone in hand, looking impatient. "We need to move."

I force myself to turn away from the railing and follow him toward the garage even though every instinct is screaming at me to go find her instead. I need to compartmentalize. Push Lark and that song and everything I'm feeling into a box and lock it down. Focus on what's directly in front of me. Seventeen cars sit between me and the front of the grid. Seventeen obstacles between me and proving I deserve to be back in this seat, that eighteen months on the sidelines didn't dull my edge.

As I walk toward the garage, I can't stop hearing her voice. Can't stop thinking about those lyrics she wrote, about the fact that she's here at a Formula One race in Vegas when I had no idea she'd be anywhere near this circuit. Maybe the universe is giving me another shot at this. Maybe I haven't fucked it up beyond all repair.

First I have to win this race and reclaim my seat at Ferrari.

Then I'm getting my girl back.

I climb into the car and everything else fades away—the roar of the crowd, the blare of the announcers, every thought except the one right in front of me. The mechanics strap me in and the steering wheel clicks into place. This is where I belong. This is where everything makes sense.

The Strip Circuit is a spectacle under the lights. Every casino, every building lit up like they're competing for attention. The track snakes through it all, barriers close on both sides, unforgiving. Every overtake on this track is a high-risk gamble. Seventeen cars ahead of me. Seventeen obstacles between me and proving I deserve to be here.

I can see Luca up in P4, his scarlet car vibrant under the lights. He's been on podiums lately, proving this car is capable of winning. Now I need to prove I'm capable of driving it there from the back of the field.

The formation lap begins and we all file out, warming tires and brakes, testing temperatures. The car feels good underneath me. Responsive. Alive. We form back up on the grid. The countdown begins on the overhead lights.

Five red lights appear one by one.

My hands tighten on the wheel. Every muscle coiled. Every sense is razor-focused.

The lights go out.

Go.

The g-force slams me back into my seat as twenty engines roar to life around me. I nail the start, the car launching forward like it's been shot from a cannon. Two cars ahead hesitate and I'm already threading the needle between them, claiming the inside line into Turn 1.

This is what I needed. This clarity. This absolute focus where nothing exists except me and the machine and the track ahead. The hum of the engine behind my head is a physical thing, vibrating through my chest, through my bones. The tachometer climbs and climbs as I push through the gears, the speed building until everything else becomes a blur of light and sound.

I'm one with the car. Every input translates perfectly—steering, braking, throttle. It responds like an extension of my body, doing exactly what I ask before I even finish the thought.

P17 already. Then P16 as I out-brake someone into Turn 3.

Lap after lap, I pick them off. The Haas on lap 3 with DRS down the main straight. An Alpine that makes a mistake in Turn 7 on lap 5, running wide and giving me the inside line. A Williams that I out-brake into the hairpin on lap 8, taking the position before they even know I'm there.

P14. P13. P12. P11.

"Brilliant driving, Jack," Marco says through the radio. "One more for points. This is wild, mate. Keep it up."

One more car between me and the points. But I don't want P10. I want more. Fuck finishing in the points. I want the podium. I want to win.

I push. Every corner on the absolute edge. Every straight with the throttle pinned. The car is responding perfectly, every adjustment I've made clicking into place.

Lap after lap, I keep climbing. Everything I've learned in all my years in Formula One, in eighteen months of watching from the sidelines, all the simulator work, all the training—it's all clicking right now. Every instinct sharp. Every decision instant.

On lap 28, I catch up to Luca. He's fighting his brakes, I can see it in the way he's braking early into corners. I get a run on him out of Turn 9 and pull alongside down the straight.

"Sorry, amico," I mutter as I take the inside line and pass him cleanly.

P6.

I keep pushing. On lap 35, the car in P5 makes a mistake in

Turn 14, runs wide over the curb. I'm there immediately, diving to the inside, taking the position before he can recover.

P5. Then P4 as someone ahead pits for tires.

"Jack, you're P4," Marco says, disbelief clear in his voice. "The Mercedes is leading. Two cars between you. Be careful with your tires."

Careful isn't in my vocabulary right now.

The cars ahead pit and suddenly I'm P2. The Mercedes is right there in front of me, close enough I can see every twitch of his rear wing.

Five laps to go. Four laps. Three.

I'm faster. I can see him struggling with grip in the high-speed corners, the rear of his car sliding slightly. My tires are newer. I have the advantage.

Two laps to go.

The long straight approaches and I get a perfect exit out of Turn 10. DRS opens up and I pull alongside him, the engines screaming as we hurtle toward Turn 11 side by side. The braking zone approaches fast. Too fast.

I brake later than I should, later than is smart, riding the absolute edge of what's physically possible. The Mercedes has to back out or we both crash into the barriers.

He backs out.

I'm ahead.

P1.

"FUCK YES!" Marco shouts over the radio. "P1, Jack! One lap to go! Bring it home!"

The final lap is the longest of my life. Every corner precise. Every input perfect. No mistakes. No giving the Mercedes a chance to come back at me. I can hear the roar of the crowd even over my engine, this wall of sound that rises as I pass each grandstand. It burns through me, this electric energy that makes every nerve ending feel alive.

I cross the finish line and the emotion hits me like a physical force, crashing over me in waves.

I won. From P18 to P1. I fucking won.

"THAT'S P1!" Marco's screaming. "THAT'S A WIN! INCREDIBLE DRIVE, JACK! INCREDIBLE!"

The team principal comes on the radio, his voice breaking. "Jack! Magnificent! Absolutely magnificent! Welcome back!"

I'm shouting into my helmet, adrenaline and relief and pure fucking joy coursing through every cell in my body. I pump my fist as I do the cool-down lap, the crowd in the grandstands on their feet, fireworks exploding over the Strip in bursts of red and gold. The cheers are deafening even through my helmet, thousands of people losing their minds.

I pull into parc fermé and kill the engine. The sounds of celebration hit immediately. Mechanics running toward me, cameras flashing everywhere, the crowd roaring so loud it's like standing inside thunder.

I pull myself out of the car and stand on it, raising my fists to the crowd. The team swarms me, everyone screaming and hugging and clapping me on the back.

Thomas appears through the crowd, grinning so wide his face might split. "You just fucking landed your seat!" he yells over the noise. "That was incredible! Ferrari can't say no to that drive! Jack, that was the drive of a lifetime!"

I'm grinning back, still trying to process what just happened. "I told you I could do it."

"Yeah you did!" Thomas pulls me into a hug, then pushes me toward the podium.

Luca appears, pulling me into a back-slapping hug. *"Bravo, amico! Fantastico!* That was incredible!"

The crowd is screaming, fireworks bursting overhead in cascade after cascade of light and color.

This is everything I've worked for. Everything I've sacrificed for. The vindication, the proof that I'm still one of the best drivers in the world, that eighteen months on the sidelines didn't dull my edge.

But as I stand there soaked in champagne with a trophy in my hands and the crowd cheering, there's one face that won't leave my mind.

Lark's.

She's somewhere in this circuit. She performed tonight. She sang that song.

And I need to find her.

CHAPTER 31

LARK

People around me are jumping, waving Ferrari flags, losing their absolute minds. The massive screens throughout the paddock area are showing replays of his final defensive moves, that last corner where he held off the other driver by pure will and racecraft. The Ferrari team behind the barriers is going ballistic, engineers and mechanics hugging each other and shouting.

P18 to P1. *He did it.*

And I'm standing here among strangers trying not to cry because I'm so proud of him I could burst. This is what he looks like when he fights for something. When he lets himself care enough to risk everything.

When he finally parks and kills the engine, there's this long moment where he just sits there in the car, hands still on the wheel like he can't quite believe what just happened.

Then he's climbing out, yanking off his helmet, and even from where I'm standing I can see that grin. My heart does something painful and wonderful in my chest and the tears

I've been holding back start streaming down my face. I don't think I've ever been this happy for someone else in my entire life.

The Ferrari team swarms him immediately. Everyone wants to hug him, congratulate him, be part of this moment. Someone throws him a Ferrari cap and he's laughing, pure unbridled joy. Luca jumps on him, nearly taking them both down, and Jack's just laughing and smiling like he can't stop.

The crowd is deafening now, thousands of people chanting his name. People around me are shouting about the drive of a lifetime. I wipe my eyes with the back of my hand but more tears keep coming. Happy tears. Proud tears. They usher him toward the podium and I push through the crowd, getting as close as I can to the barriers.

When he climbs the steps and holds up that trophy, the entire circuit explodes in noise and color. Fireworks burst overhead in reds and golds, and the roar is so loud it vibrates through my entire body. His eyes scan the crowd below. And then they lock onto mine.

He sees me. He knows I'm here.

Jack

Her eyes lock onto mine and everything else falls away.

The roar of the crowd, the announcers blaring, Luca saying something beside me about the drive being fucking magic. None of it registers. All I can see is Lark pressed against the barriers below, tears streaming down her face, hands covering her mouth. She's laughing and crying at the same time, looking up at me and the whole world narrows to just her.

I grab the champagne bottle and spray it, the foam exploding everywhere. Luca's soaked and laughing, spraying me right back, and the team is going wild below us. The crowd is losing their minds, chanting and cheering.

My eyes find Lark again in the crowd. She's still crying, still smiling up at me, and everything else is just noise. I hold up the trophy and the circuit explodes with cheers, but I'm looking at her when I do it.

The second we're dismissed, I'm moving. Down the steps, pushing through Ferrari team personnel trying to congratulate me, engineers wanting to talk about the drive, photographers shouting for one more photo.

Thomas appears at my elbow looking like he just won the lottery. "Jack," he says, and he's more excited than I've ever seen him, "holy shit, that was incredible. The media wants you, Ferrari executives are waiting, we need to—"

"Give me ten minutes," I say, not stopping.

"Jack—"

But I'm already gone, weaving through the crowd. My heart is hammering harder than it did during the entire race, harder than it did on that final corner when I was defending position with everything I had. I'm still in my champagne-soaked race suit, scanning desperately for that blue dress I saw her wearing.

Where is she?

I push past security trying to redirect me toward the media pen. People are reaching out, trying to congratulate me, slap my back, get selfies. I barely register any of them.

Then I see her pushing through the crowd toward me with the same desperate energy, and our eyes meet across the chaos.

She breaks into this huge smile and I'm grinning like an idiot. I whistle sharp and loud to get security's attention, pointing at her. "Let her through!"

The guard looks skeptical, but I don't wait. I'm already running.

She's running too.

We collide and I'm cupping her face in both hands, kissing

her before either of us can say a word. She tastes like salt from tears and something sweet, and her hands fist in my race suit as she kisses me back just as fiercely. Camera flashes explode around us, people shouting and cheering, but none of it matters. Nothing matters except her mouth on mine and the fact that she's here and we're together.

When we finally break apart, we're both breathing hard. I keep my hands on her face, my thumbs wiping away tears. She's laughing, her eyes bright.

"You came," I say. "You're here."

"Of course I'm here." She's grinning through the tears, her hands gripping my shoulders. "You were incredible, Jack. That was… I've never seen anything like that. I think I was screaming the whole time!"

"I heard your song." I brush her hair back from her face, and I can't stop touching her, can't stop looking at her. "Earlier tonight. I watched you perform."

Watching her up on that stage, completely owning it, performing her songs her way even though it probably cost her everything. That took more guts than anything I did in that race car. She was fucking fearless.

Her breath catches. "You did?"

"Every word." I lean my forehead against hers. "You were incredible. I'm so proud of you." My voice drops. "I love you. I'm so fucking sorry for leaving, for walking away, for what I said. I was an idiot."

"Stop," she cuts me off, her hand pressing flat against my chest right over my heart. "I'm sorry too. I attacked you instead of listening. I said things I didn't mean. I was hurt and I lashed out when I should have just talked to you, and deep down I knew you weren't lying but I let everything bubble up and then had too much pride to take it back."

She pulls back slightly, talking with her hands now, and I've missed her so much it physically hurts. She's talking faster, the words tumbling out. "Which is completely insane when you think about it, and honestly if I'd just stopped for two seconds to actually think instead of spiraling I probably could have—"

I pull her in hard and kiss her, cutting off the rest of whatever she was going to say. She makes this small surprised sound and then she's kissing me back, her hands sliding up to grip my shoulders, then my neck, pulling me closer. Her mouth opens under mine and I deepen the kiss, tasting salt from her tears and that strawberry chapstick she always wears. One of her hands moves into my hair and she's pressing against me like she's trying to eliminate any space between us.

When we finally break apart, we're both breathing hard.

"I love you," she says against my mouth. "So much."

"I know, and I love you more than you can know." I kiss her forehead, her nose, her lips. "You're it for me, Lark. I'm done running."

"You're it for me too."

I kiss her again because now that I have her back, I never want to stop. She melts into me completely, her body pressed against mine, her fingers threading through my hair, and everything else disappears. There's just her. Just us. Just the absolute certainty that she's mine and I'm hers, and this time I'm staying.

EPILOGUE

One year later

Lark

The Vegas suite has floor-to-ceiling windows that overlook the entire Strip, neon lights stretching out in every direction like some kind of electric rainbow. Even at eleven at night, the city is alive and glowing, casinos showing off with their elaborate light shows and massive digital billboards.

I'm curled up on the oversized sectional with my guitar, barefoot and wearing one of Jack's Ferrari hoodies that's gotten soft and worn from so many washes. There's a half-empty glass of wine on the coffee table next to my notebook, which is completely covered in lyrics and crossed-out lines and little doodles I drew in the margins when I got stuck on the bridge earlier. Song snippets, random phrases, a terrible sketch of what might be a palm tree or possibly just a very unfortunate blob.

I stretch my legs out on the couch, rolling my ankles to work out the stiffness from sitting in the same position for the last hour. The melody I've been working on is finally flowing tonight after fighting with it for days. It's happy and bright and upbeat, something completely different from the heartbreak songs that made up most of my first album. Something about being in Vegas with everyone I love is making everything feel lighter, like the creativity is just pouring out of me without the usual struggle.

I literally just left my parents' room about twenty minutes ago. I'd gone down there to play them some of the new songs I've been working on, and my mom cried within the first thirty seconds like she always does, which still makes me cry every single time.

Everyone's been here for three days now and it's been nonstop chaos in the best possible way. All of Jack's brothers flew out for the race this weekend. Maren too, obviously. And I surprised my parents with plane tickets a month ago since they'd been wanting to come to one of Jack's races. I suspect they love him more than me at this point but I'm not complaining. He's pretty damn easy to love.

We rented out a bunch of rooms on the same floor and it's turned into this wonderful situation where people are constantly bursting into each other's rooms unannounced. My mom showed up at seven this morning with coffee she'd gotten from the lobby, already dressed and ready to explore the city. Calvin wandered in yesterday afternoon looking for his sunglasses that he'd apparently left here two days ago and had zero memory of losing. It's wonderful chaos and I'm loving every second. Having everyone in one place is rare so I'm soaking up every single moment, storing away memories like I'm trying to preserve them in amber.

My phone buzzes on the cushion beside me and I set down the guitar to grab it, grinning when I see Maren's name light up the screen.

Maren: *DINNER CONFIRMED tomorrow 8pm!! That fancy*

steakhouse. Though I was torn because I'm still having vivid dreams about last night's carbonara.

I laugh out loud. We've gotten everyone together for dinner the last few nights and it's been absolute madness in the best possible way. My parents, all of Jack's brothers, little Chloe, Maren and Calvin. Last night I think I legitimately pulled a stomach muscle from laughing so hard at one of Theo's stories about teenage Jack.

Me: *Perfect! Can't wait. Worth abandoning the carbonara?*

Maren: *BARELY. But yes. Also I'm gonna pop down in the morning for coffee but about to pass out I'm so tired*

Lark: *I'll have the coffee ready. Love you!*

Maren: *Love you too*

I'm smiling as I set my phone back down and pick up the guitar again, strumming through the verse and humming along quietly. The bridge is finally starting to work. I just needed to slow down the tempo, let it breathe for a few measures before building back up to the chorus. Sometimes the simplest fixes are the ones that take forever to figure out.

The album dropped two months ago and completely exploded on social media in ways I still can't quite process. It's been climbing the charts steadily, getting radio play I never dreamed of. Walter and my agent call almost daily with festival offers and bigger venue options and opportunities I never imagined when I was bartending at the Black Lantern and posting videos from my tiny apartment with terrible lighting. The tour starts in six weeks. Fifteen cities to start, all carefully coordinated around Jack's race schedule so we actually get to see each other instead of living on FaceTime at three in the morning.

The suite door opens and Jack walks in, still wearing his Ferrari team polo from the track today. His hair is slightly messed up like he's been running his hands through it, and he looks tired but happy.

"Hey," he says, and his whole face lights up when he sees me curled up on the couch. "You are a sight for sore eyes."

He crosses the room and pulls me up into a kiss before I can even set down the guitar. It's warm and soft and unhurried, and my entire body still lights up at his touch like it's the first time. Every single time. I don't think that's ever going to fade.

"How was the track?" I ask when we break apart, still wrapped in his arms.

"Really good. Like, really good." He guides us back down onto the couch, pulling me against his side. "Media stuff was the usual circus, but it was fun having all the brothers there. It's been years since they've been able to visit me on track. They were asking about everything, wanting tours of the garage, meeting the team."

"I'm so jealous I couldn't stay longer." I pout slightly, settling against him. I'd managed to be there for the first half of the day, but had to leave for back-to-back Zoom meetings with the label about tour logistics. "Stupid responsibilities ruining my fun."

"Yeah, it's tough being a superstar," he laughs, pinching my side gently. I squirm and swat at him.

He shifts, getting comfortable, his hand resting on my hip. "But the best part was Chloe. Theo got there maybe an hour after you had to leave and she absolutely lost her mind over everything. She wanted to touch every single thing, asked about a million questions in approximately ten minutes. I let her sit in the car and she just about combusted with excitement."

"Oh no." I'm grinning because I can picture this perfectly. Little Chloe with her blonde pigtails and endless energy, bouncing around the Ferrari garage and charming everyone with her enthusiasm. "You've created a monster."

"That's completely the plan." He looks way too pleased with himself. "I warned Theo ages ago that she's going to be a racing menace by the time she's sixteen."

"Theo is going to kill you for encouraging this."

"Theo knew exactly what he was getting into when he decided to let me be her favorite uncle." He pulls me in closer. "Come here. It's been seven hours since I've seen you, which is seven hours too long."

I curl up against his side automatically, fitting perfectly into that space between his arm and his chest like I was designed for it. My head rests right over his heart and I can hear it beating, steady and strong. This is my favorite part of any day, regardless of where we are or what we're doing. When everything slows down and gets quiet and it's just us. No cameras, no schedules, no obligations. Just this.

"Maren confirmed dinner for tomorrow night," I say, playing with the hem of his polo, running the fabric between my fingers. "Eight o'clock. That steakhouse she and Calvin were going on and on about last night."

"Perfect. Calvin brought it up again today at the track, said it was supposed to be an experience." His hand finds mine, fingers lacing together automatically in that way they always do now. "So we're really doing it? Telling everyone?"

I look down at the ring on my finger. The engagement ring that's been living there for two months now, hidden from everyone except Maren and Calvin. Maren sniffed it out immediately even over FaceTime, which thank goodness because keeping it from her would have been completely impossible. She knows me too well. Tomorrow we're telling everyone else. We wanted to do it in person, all together, with both of our families around us.

"Yeah," I say, twisting the ring slightly. "I'm ready. Are you?"

"Definitely." He squeezes my hand. "I could barely hold it in today with everyone at the track. Almost slipped up like three times."

"Me too, it's been killing me. I almost told my parents this afternoon when I was playing them the new songs, but I held strong so we could do it with the whole family tomorrow." I laugh, thinking about how my mom's going to react. She's going to completely lose it. "It's going to be so chaotic."

Jack laughs. "Your mom's going to cry before we even finish the sentence."

"Immediately. Like the second she realizes what we're saying, the waterworks start." I grin. "And Maren's going to scream loud enough to get us kicked out of the restaurant."

"Absolutely," he agrees. "Security will be involved."

We sit there quietly for a moment, comfortable and easy in that way we've gotten after a year of being together. The kind of quiet that doesn't need to be filled with words because we're both just content to exist in the same space.

"I saw a wedding chapel today," I say, not entirely sure why I'm bringing this up except it's been bouncing around in the back of my mind for hours now. "When I was walking back from that coffee place with my mom this afternoon. One of those classic Vegas ones with the neon sign and everything."

"Yeah?" Jack sounds amused. "Did it have an Elvis impersonator? Please tell me it had an Elvis impersonator."

"Almost certainly. I think they all do at this point, right? It's like a legal requirement for Vegas wedding chapels." I laugh. "But it got me thinking about how everyone's going to ask us tomorrow about actual wedding plans and we literally have none. Like, not even vague ideas or a general timeline. We're just going to have to shrug and say we haven't figured any of it out yet."

"We've both been busy." He's playing with my hair now, completely unbothered by this lack of planning.

And to be honest, I'm not worried either. Planning the tour has been its own full-time job.

"You've been finishing the album," he continues, "and

working with the team on tour logistics. I've been racing all over the world basically nonstop. We'll figure it out eventually when things calm down."

"I know we will," I say, "but *'eventually'* might legitimately be like two years from now at the rate we're going." I'm thinking out loud now, the idea that's been bouncing around my head all day starting to solidify. "When are we actually going to have time to sit down and plan some big traditional wedding? You're going to be traveling constantly for the racing season, I'm about to be on tour for months, and trying to coordinate everyone's schedules is essentially impossible. I mean, this weekend is the first time all of these specific people have ever been in the same place at the exact same time."

"That's actually a really valid point," he says, and he's smiling now like he already knows where this is going. "What exactly are you saying?"

"What if we didn't wait?" I say it before I can second-guess myself. "What if we just got married this weekend while everyone's already here?"

"You want to get married *this* weekend," he says, his hand stroking my arm.

"Yes, I really do." I'm getting more and more excited as I work through it out loud. "I mean, really think about it for a second. Everyone we love is already here in Vegas. Your brothers, my parents, Maren and Calvin, even Chloe. When is that ever going to happen again?"

He cocks his head, gives me a wry smile. "I'm liking where this is going."

"Right? We're already engaged. We already know we want to get married. And we specifically told each other we didn't want some huge traditional wedding with like three hundred people, remember? We said we wanted something small and intimate and us." I'm talking faster now, getting more excited as the idea gains momentum. "And this is *Vegas*. The city where everything changed for us. Where you won that insane race. Where we figured everything out. And now everyone's here... it feels kind of meant to be!"

He laughs. "You know what's funny? I was thinking the exact same thing today at the track. Looking around at everyone together and thinking how perfect it would be if we could just do it now."

"See, that's a sign!" I'm bouncing slightly now, unable to contain the excitement building in my chest. "We could find a venue tomorrow while you're doing all your final prep stuff with the team. Somewhere actually nice and beautiful, not some tacky chapel with plastic flowers and questionable carpeting. We tell everyone to get dressed up for a fancy celebration dinner after the race. And then surprise, plot twist, you're actually at our wedding instead."

His smile is wicked. "They're going to completely and utterly lose their minds."

"Absolutely, and in the best possible way."

"But your parents though..." He pauses. "They're going to want the whole big traditional thing, aren't they?"

"Oh my mom is definitely going to have opinions about this decision." I laugh, tapping my fingers against his chest. "But we can totally do something else later if we want to. Something bigger with all the extended family and all your racing world friends and everyone else."

His smile gets even wider. "Maybe in Mexico with the rest of your extended family?"

I light up. "Oh yes! We do this intimate one with just our immediate family, then a bigger celebration after the tour, in Mexico with all my aunts and uncles and cousins." My brain is already spinning with possibilities. My family would love that. A whole weekend celebration with everyone. "What do you think?" I ask, searching his face.

He looks at me and pulls me tightly into his arms. "I think I can't fucking stand not being married to you for one more second."

Then he's kissing me and I'm kissing him back just as fiercely. His hands slide into my hair and I pull him closer, both of us pouring everything into this kiss. Every *yes*, every *this is right*, every *I choose you*.

When we finally break apart, we're both breathing hard. We look into each other's eyes and then, suddenly, I'm laughing out loud, the reality of what we just decided hitting me. "We're going to plan an entire secret wedding in three days."

"We better get started then." He's grinning, completely unfazed by the insanity of what we're about to pull off. "I'll handle the venue tomorrow between track sessions. You figure out what you want to wear."

"Deal." I'm already buzzing with excitement. "We tell everyone it's just a fancy celebration dinner after your race. They're going to completely lose it when they figure out what's happening."

"That's the best part," he says.

I look up at him and my heart does that thing it always does when I realize this is my life now. Him. Us. This love that's bigger than anything I ever imagined. "Vegas wedding with everyone we love." I say it one last time, knowing now that it's real, that this is actually going to happen. "Then Mexico later for the huge celebration with all the extended family."

He nods and kisses me again, and I sink into it completely.

We sit there wrapped up in each other, Vegas glittering outside the windows, our families sleeping nearby with no idea what we're about to pull off.

A year ago we came back to each other in this city. And now we're getting married here, surrounded by everyone who matters most.

And as I fall asleep, safe in his arms, I'm almost sure he's humming the melody to the song I wrote just for him, *Until You Say Stay*.

—The End—

Thanks for reading! If you enjoyed Jack and Lark's story, check out the whole Midnight Men series.

A NOTE FROM NATE

Thank you for reading. 🩶

Before you go, I want to say something plainly: I'm a man writing steamy romance. That's who I am as a writer, and part of what makes my books different. It's also a responsibility I take seriously. This genre has been built and shaped by women whose work I admire deeply. I write with consent at the center, my perspective informed by that work and sharpened through careful listening and honest feedback.

I bring my voice to the page, and I bring it with respect, care, and the belief that intimacy should feel powerful, chosen, and emotionally true. If you trusted me with this story—with these characters' bodies and hearts and futures—thank you. That trust matters to me more than you can know.

If you enjoyed the book, I hope you'll check out the rest of *The Midnight Men* series. Each book follows a different couple and works as a standalone, but the town, the family, and the connections carry through.

I also have a new project brewing: a small-town, steamy contemporary romance series set in the Napa Valley. It's full of romance, beautiful settings, good wine and, of course, quite a bit of steam. The series is called *Solstice Hearts,* and if you love the Midnight Men, I think you'll enjoy it.

Book one of this series, *Until the Storm Breaks* is also available as an audiobook, read by the incredible Stephen Dexter and Callie Dalton. They exceeded my highest hopes with their performances, and I encourage you to check it out if you'd like to experience this story in a new way. And soon, *all* the *Midnight Men* books will be available in audio as well.

I also have a website, where you can sign up to hear about new releases, special projects, bonus content, and other fun stuff.

If you're enjoying my work, I'd be grateful if you left a review or shared it with a friend, a book club, or anyone you think might love it. In a crowded online world, personal recommendations still mean everything.

Writing contemporary romance has been one of the most rewarding turns in my life. I'm drawn to stories about connection—about people who carry history, who hesitate, who want something real and aren't yet sure they deserve it.

I don't take it lightly that you chose to spend your time with these characters. Every book exists because readers keep showing up and trusting me with stories about love, healing, and second chances.

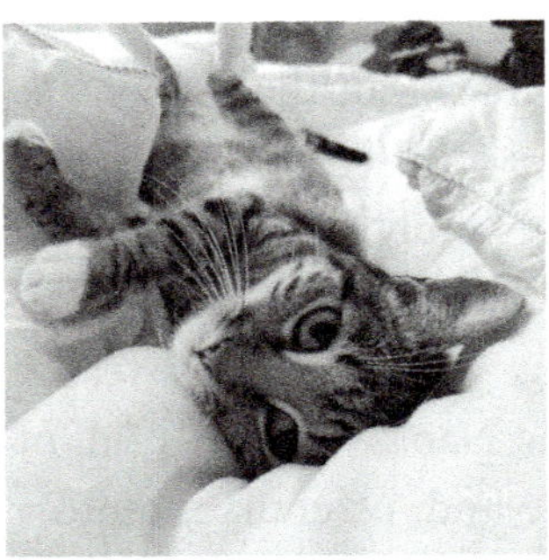

I write from Washington state, usually with my cat Nala nearby. I'm grateful you're here, and I hope this story stays with you.

-Nate Wilder 🩶

NATE WILDER BOOKS IN ORDER

The Midnight Men Series

Book 1: Until the Storm Breaks

Book 2: Until You Say Stay

Book 3: Until the Stars Fall

Book 4: Until the Sparks Fly

ABOUT NATE WILDER

Nate Wilder writes small-town romance. Steamy, emotional, and full of the kind of chemistry that keeps you reading past midnight.

A former journalist and chef, he's a devoted romance reader who believes the world needs more love, more steam, and more happily-ever-afters.

He writes from Washington state, where he is supervised in all matters by his opinionated cat, Nala.

- instagram.com/natewilderauthor
- tiktok.com/@author_natewilder
- amazon.com/stores/Nate-Wilder/author/B0FJZW722L
- bookbub.com/authors/nate-wilder

Printed in Dunstable, United Kingdom

81602483R00234